VOLUME IV

SHOCKWAVES

NEW STORIES OF THE VAMPIRE WARS

Edited and co-authored by
JONATHAN MABERRY

With

JOE MCKINNEY

DANA FREDSTI

JADE SHAMES

JAMES R. TUCK

LUCAS MANGUM

JEFFREY J. MARIOTTE & MARSHEILA ROCKWELL

NANCY HOLDER

JENNIFER BROZEK

LOIS H. GRESH

JOHN SKIPP & CODY GOODFELLOW

MIKE WATT

JOHN DIXON

WESTON OCHSE

YVONNE NAVARRO

Become our fan on Facebook **facebook.com/idwpublishing**
Follow us on Twitter **@idwpublishing**
Subscribe to us on YouTube **youtube.com/idwpublishing**
See what's new on Tumblr **tumblr.idwpublishing.com**
Check us out on Instagram **instagram.com/idwpublishing**

ISBN: 978-1-63140-640-9   19 18 17 16   1 2 3 4

COVER ART BY
TREVOR HUTCHISON

COLLECTION EDITS BY
JUSTIN EISINGER

PUBLISHED BY
TED ADAMS

COLLECTION DESIGN BY
RICHARD SHEINAUS
FOR **GOTHAM DESIGN**

EDITORIAL ASSISTANCE BY
SARAH DUFFY

Ted Adams, CEO & Publisher
Greg Goldstein, President & COO
Robbie Robbins, EVP/Sr. Graphic Artist
Chris Ryall, Chief Creative Officer/Editor-in-Chief
Matthew Ruzicka, CPA, Chief Financial Officer
Dirk Wood, VP of Marketing
Lorelei Bunjes, VP of Digital Services
Jeff Weber, VP of Licensing, Digital and Subsidiary Rights
Jerry Bennington, VP of New Product Development

For international rights, please contact licensing@idwpublishing.com

V-WARS created by Jonathan Maberry.

CONTENTS

"Wet Works" Pt. 1 • *Jonathan Maberry* 1

"Our Man in Mali" • *Joe McKinney* 4

"Wet Works" Pt. 2 • *Jonathan Maberry* 31

"Expat" • *Dana Fredsti* 35

"Wet Works" Pt. 3 • *Jonathan Maberry* 60

"Weird Blood" • *Jade Shames* 68

"Wet Works" Pt. 4 • *Jonathan Maberry* 87

"Other Men's Blood" • *James R. Tuck* 90

"Wet Works" Pt. 5 • *Jonathan Maberry* 112

"Necessary Monster" • *Lucas Mangum* 115

"Wet Works" Pt. 6 • *Jonathan Maberry* 138

"The Real HousewiVes of Scottsdale"
Marsheila Rockwell and Jeffrey J. Mariotte 141

"Wet Works" Pt. 7 • *Jonathan Maberry* 170

"The Things They Murdered" • *Nancy Holder* 174

"Wet Works" Pt. 8 • *Jonathan Maberry* 193

"The Unfortunate Case of Sister Ruth" • *Jennifer Brozek* 195

"Red Empire" Pt. 1 • *Jonathan Maberry* 212

"Bloodline" • *Lois H. Gresh* 222

"Silver or Lead" • *John Skipp and Cody Goodfellow* 240

"Red Empire" Pt. 2 • *Jonathan Maberry* 267

"Young Bloods" • *Mike Watt* 270

"Chop Shop" • *John Dixon* 294

"Red Empire" Pt. 3 • *Jonathan Maberry* 323

"From Germany With Love" • *Weston Ochse* 326

"Legacy" • *Yvonne Navarro* 345

"Red Empire" Pt. 4 • *Jonathan Maberry* 370

ACKNOWLEDGMENTS

Thanks a million times to my creative partners at IDW Publishing: Justin Eisinger, David Hedgecock, Jeff Webber, Ted Adams, and the whole team! Special thanks to Rob Daviau, the madman game designer who created the rules for the V-WARS: A GAME OF BLOOD AND BETRAYAL board game.

DEDICATION

V-Wars: Shockwaves is dedicated to the members of
the Horror Writers Association.
www.horror.org
And, as always, for Sara Jo.

WET WORKS PART 1

By Jonathan Maberry

Global Acquisitions LLC
Pittsburgh, Pennsylvania
Day 17 of the Red Storm

"Are we going to die down here?" demanded Luther Swann.

"First off," said the big man with the knife, "stop yelling."

"I'm not yelling," yelled Swann.

They stood facing each other in a red room that had been white ten minutes earlier. The floors, the walls, even the ceiling was splash-painted in red. It dripped and ran and pooled. It glistened in the light from the few unbroken bulbs. In the corners where the light did not reach, it gleamed like thick, black oil. Everywhere else it was a bright red. Not the red of clown noses or party balloons. Not a happy red. Not a candy red or a Christmas red. This was darker, more viscous, so much less appealing. And it stank of copper and mingled urine, of gun smoke and pain.

"You *are* yelling," said the big man quietly, "and you really need to stop."

"I am not yelling, goddamn it."

"Shut up," said the big man. "Right. Fucking. Now."

"Don't tell me what to—"

The big man's hands had been down at his side. The left holding a knife, the right covered in blood. Now the right hand had closed around Swann's throat. The professor had not seen that hand move. There was barely even a blur and suddenly hard fingers circled his throat. Not hard. It was not an attack. Not yet, anyway. The threat, however, was eloquent.

Luther Swann stopped yelling, but in a low, ice-cold voice he said, "Take your hand off me."

"You going to behave?"

Swann tried to swat the hand away. He failed. He tried to pull it away. And failed there, too. He tried to step back out of reach and the big man followed him step by step until Swann's back thumped into the red-smeared wall, at which point the man tightened his grip. Just a little. Enough.

"Listen to me, Doc," said the man slowly, precisely; making sure his words were clear. "This isn't over. You hear me? We're in deep shit and I don't know how we're going to get out of this. I need to figure this out or we are both dog meat, *capiche*? Now I'm going to let you go, and you get stupid, I'm going to knock you the fuck out and maybe I'll even leave you here so the fang gang out there have a little breakfast buffet. If you shut up and behave, then maybe—just *maybe*—I'll take you with me. Now, can I let go without you going all drama queen on me?"

Swann stared up into hard, blue eyes for a long moment, then he nodded.

The man smiled a charming smile. As if this was just another day and they were two completely different people. As if the world was different. He dropped his hand and looked around.

The room was a charnel house. Six bodies lay sprawled in a lake of blood. None of them whole. None of them human.

The door was closed and locked, but Swann knew as well as the man with the knife that the lock would not hold. Not against the monsters that were hunting them.

No... it would not hold at all if the monsters really wanted to get in.

"Ledger," said Swann, his voice quiet now, though even he could hear the latent shrillness of a panic barely controlled, "are we going to get out of here?"

Captain Joe Ledger walked across the bloody floor. His gun was soaked, the slide locked back, the magazine empty, and it lay in a quarter inch of gore. The small-blade knife was all he had left, although Ledger had done terrible things with it.

Terrible things.

Even so, there was worse on the other side of that door.

Much worse.

OUR MAN IN MALI

By Joe McKinney

Timbuktu, Mali
September 19th

For five days, Walter Laurens, who worked as the West African Regional Control Officer for the U.S. Department of Military Sciences, had been unable to make contact with his top agent.

A week of silence.

Not unusual, by itself.

Dr. Miriam Bloch worked in some remote areas of the Sahara Desert. Communication wasn't easy, even with advanced DMS technology.

She'd been given the cover story of a doctor working on Ebola for Doctors Without Borders, but her real job was to learn everything she could about the *bayi* species of vampires that had recently surfaced among the Tuareg people of Northern Mali, and as the Tuareg were semi-nomadic, she was constantly on the move.

A few missed calls were understandable.

Except that, over the last four months or so, the quality of her work had become erratic. Her progress reports were often incomplete, failing to answer even some of the more obvious questions, and more than once Laurens had been forced to ask the same question several times, over several emails, before she finally addressed it satisfactorily. She was still the best doctor in West Africa—she'd delivered his own son, Roger, after all—but he was worried about her. So he got in his Land Cruiser and headed north on one of the few roads that led out of Timbuktu.

He traveled most of the afternoon on bad roads, arriving in the Tuareg village with less than two hours of usable sunlight. The village was a typical one for the Tuareg nomads, consisting of twenty large, domed huts with patchwork roofs and low grass walls. Their openings were barely tall enough for a child to walk through without stooping, but Laurens knew from past experience that once inside the hut was large enough for a family of ten or more. A village this size could easily hold three hundred men, women, and children. Big for a Tuareg community.

Only there was no one around.

He turned off his vehicle and squinted through the windshield, looking for any signs of movement.

Nothing.

He climbed out of the vehicle and stared about at the quiet huts, the vacant doorways. A breeze carried a cloud of dust through the village, but that was all that moved. He couldn't help but feel that something was very wrong here. During his last three years in Africa, Laurens had been in countless villages like this one. There were always chickens and dogs running around, always children chasing each other through the grass, laughing and shouting the way kids do.

But there was nothing here.

No old women shelling beans, no old men watching him through the slits in thick black veils. The Tuareg were nomads. They could uproot a village at a moment's notice and take their lives on the road, but that didn't look like what had happened here. They'd left too many valuable things lying around, washtubs and portable stoves, things they'd never leave behind.

So where was everybody?

"Hello?" he called out.

Nothing.

He turned around in a slow circle, studying every doorway. "Hello?"

Not even a dog barking.

Laurens walked over to one of the huts and stuck his head inside—and immediately recoiled from the stench of death. He backed away from the opening and took several deep breaths, face pinched in surprise and disgust.

He pulled his pistol, steeled himself, and ducked back inside. It took several moments for his eyes to adjust to the darkness, but once they did, he could see the hut was empty. The smell was bad, but there were no bodies, no blood, just round, woven rugs on the floor and empty nests of blankets where the former occupants had spent their nights. There was no sign of a struggle.

And yet, death was here.

He explored the other huts and found the same sickly sweet stench of rotting flesh in each one. No bodies, though. Confused, he went on searching, and had just cleared his eighth hut when he saw Miriam Bloch's Land Cruiser crashed in a ditch and covered over with dusty grasses and twigs.

He rushed into the ditch, throwing the vegetation aside. Inside, he saw blood on the driver's seat and on the steering wheel.

And that was when it hit him.

He was staring at a full-blown crisis.

Miriam was a friend. There weren't many Americans in northern Mali, and everybody knew each other, even if they weren't connected to the Agency. But he wasn't concerned about a missing friend right now.

Miriam was a DMS agent, privy to classified information. She carried the sum total of the DMS's knowledge of the Ice Virus in her head, everything from how to slow its progression in an infected person to how to weaponize it. Part of the reason he'd been deployed here was because of the volatile political climate in the region. Here in Mali they had local tribal warfare, and French colonial influence, and Islamic extremists like al-Qaeda, Ansar Dine, and even ISIL, all competing for a slice of the pie. If any one of those groups had seen through her cover story and taken her hostage, the DMS was going to have to bring in the big guns.

He was about to renew his search when his phone rang.

It scared him so badly he nearly cracked off a shot.

He fished the iPhone from his pocket and read the caller ID. Kathy, his wife. He took a deep breath, collected himself, and answered.

"Hey, babe," he said, forcing his heartbeat to stop racing.

"Hey," she said. She sounded tired. "You okay? You sound stressed."

"No," he said. "I'm good here. Just cleaning up a few things at work."

Though Kathy had been with him since he transferred from the State Department to the Department of Military Services ten years before, she'd never been told what he really did for a living. She knew he maintained a cover story as a geologist for a local salt company, but that was all she knew.

Laurens could hear their son crying in the background, and he could almost picture her in their kitchen back at the American compound, Roger on her hip, both hands on the fussing baby, phone sandwiched between her cheek and shoulder as she tried to do everything at once. He'd dragged her all over the globe on DMS business, and she'd never complained. Even here in Mali, where they had Sharia law, and women were treated like garbage, she kept her chin up. She was a trooper.

Better, he suspected, than he deserved.

But she hadn't slept well since Roger came along. She'd had blackouts and memory lapses. He'd woken up several times in the middle of the night to find her missing from the bed. More often than not he'd found her near the front door, eyes open and walking around, but still asleep.

"Sounds like I'm doing better than you," he said. "He sounds fussy."

"It's the colic again."

"And you? How'd you sleep?"

"Not too good. It was a rough night."

He stepped into another hut and gagged a little. He put his free hand under his nose.

"Walter?"

"I'm here," he said. The stench was overpowering. "I'm sorry you can't sleep."

"Maybe tonight'll be better. When are you coming home?"

Something caught his eye over at a back corner of the hut. Laurens crossed the hut and knelt down next to the nest of blankets where Dr. Miriam Bloch had, until recently, made her bed. There was no pillow, no pictures of home. The only concession to her foreign status, besides her medical journals and her tablet, was a pile of laundry. Mixed among the t-shirts and khaki shorts he saw black, lace-trimmed panties and sports bras, things no Tuareg woman would ever wear.

"Hard to say," he said, lifting a pair of the black panties on the tip of his finger. There was no blood on her clothes. "I'm thinking I might be a while."

"So, we're on our own for dinner?"

He let the panties fall to the ground. "Yeah, sorry, babe."

"Just come home to me," she said.

"Fast as I can."

"Love you."

"In love with you, babe."

Laurens hung up the phone and went back to examining Miriam's tablet. It was password protected, which was standard DMS security protocol. He'd have to wait until he got home to jailbreak it.

He rose from her bedding and was about to go on searching when he spotted the Blue Woman at the far end of the room.

Laurens froze.

One of the *bayi* vampires.

Only this one was dead, a bib of clotted blood streaking her chest. It looked like a giant chunk of flesh had been ripped out of her neck.

He stared at the corpse, fascinated, despite his fear.

He'd seen pictures, of course, mainly in Miriam's emails, but this was the first time he'd seen a *bayi* face to face.

My God, he thought, *they really are blue.*

The change in skin color was actually just a stain from the blue dye in the ceremonial robes they wore. They were real vampires, of course, as real as the Crimson Queen herself. But unlike their counterparts in Tuareg folklore, they weren't witches that fed off the blood of children.

They actually ate the same foods as everybody else in their village.

They did take nourishment from the communal emotional energy of their village, but exactly how that worked was not very well understood. What made them really unique, and justified the DMS presence in West Africa, was how accommodating they were. They'd allowed Miriam access to every ceremony, every private council. Even their late-night potion making parties.

Whereas other vampire races around the world had declared war on humanity, the Blue Women had made themselves an open book.

They'd even provided her with blood samples for her studies.

And it was from those samples that Miriam had done her best work. She'd managed to trace the antigenic shift in the Ice Virus from its patient zero source in Michael Fayne to the three women in this village who had become *bayi*.

Work, Laurens was told, that might one day stop the transition of future vampires.

Unfortunately, their spirit of cooperation did little good now that they were dead.

So sad, he thought. This could set the DMS back months.

He turned away from the corpse and, as he was walking back to the opening, his foot caught on the large rug in the center of the room. He tripped and nearly fell. Looking back, he realized that he had kicked enough of the rug away to reveal a hastily placed trapdoor in the floor.

He put Miriam's tablet down and pulled the rug out of the way.

Laurens couldn't tell how many bodies were inside the pit. The spaghetti bowl mess of severed arms and legs and bloodstained faces might have been ten people, maybe twenty. He couldn't really tell. They'd all been hacked to pieces. Arms and legs were broken in half. Juts of bare bone extended from a few of the broken limbs. Though his stomach was turning in knots, he knelt down and studied the remains. He saw odd gouges on a few of them, and looking closer, he confirmed his worst fears.

They were teeth marks.

He turned away from the pit and careened into a wall. It gave a little, but held his weight. Laurens stood there for a minute, his head a soupy mess, his gut twisting in knots.

He just couldn't process it.

The bodies, the broken bones, the teeth marks… it was all too much.

He managed to climb through the low opening that led outside and staggered into the fading sunlight.

The ground still felt like it was pitching beneath his feet.

He couldn't quite catch his breath.

He looked around at the other huts, and remembered the stench he'd encountered in each of them.

So many innocent people dead.

He bent over and vomited.

He pulled into the driveway at the American compound long after dark and realized he barely remembered the drive home. His mind was still back in the village.

He hadn't even noticed night had fallen.

Laurens climbed out of the Land Cruiser and started across the courtyard to his flat. Floodlights lit his way down gardened paths. The landscapers had been busy planting new flowers along the walkway and around the main fountain, but he barely noticed the splash of color.

All those bodies. All that blood.

A baby cried from the stairs off to his right, shaking him out of his thoughts.

Turning, he saw Sarah Galloway, one of Kathy's friends, trying to squeeze her way through the door. In her hands she juggled her writhing daughter (it was Jessica, or Jesse, something like that) born just two weeks before Roger, and a box that was way too big for her. It looked like she was about to drop everything.

"Hold on," he said. He trotted over, took the box. "Here, I got it."

"Oh, thank the Lord, that's so much better." She readjusted her grip on her daughter and straightened her veil. "I was losing my grip there."

"Where's this going?" he asked.

"Oh, you don't have to go to any trouble, Walter. Frank'll be right back. He told me I was trying to do much, but you know us girls. Always so impatient."

He offered her a bland smile. He didn't much care for the Galloways. From what he could tell they were Bible thumpers. Her husband Frank was a chemist. He worked for the same salt company as Laurens, though he didn't have any Agency connections at all.

Still, they were all Americans. They were all strangers in a strange land and all that crap. He had to be polite to stay in character.

"It's no bother," he said. He motioned with the box. "Where do you want it?"

But before he could start moving, Frank appeared around the corner. He ran forward, took the box, and gave his wife a look so lovingly and playfully reproachful that Laurens had to stop himself from rolling his eyes.

"Thanks, buddy," Frank said, nudging him with an elbow. "Women, am I right?"

Laurens nodded.

"I was so lucky he was there," Sarah said. "I thought I was going drop everything."

Frank leaned forward and rubbed noses with his daughter. "Don't you listen, sweetie pie. Momma wouldn't drop you."

The little girl cooed happily. Ordinarily, Laurens would have had little patience for public affection like that, but it made him think of Kathy. He'd left her alone with the baby, again. She was doing all the work, and doing it in a land controlled by Sharia law. They treated women like garbage here, and for a girl whose temperament was better suited to the bright lights of Dallas than the hot African sun, it had to be hard on her here. No wonder she wasn't getting any sleep.

But before he could think too deeply on it, his attention was pulled toward his Land Cruiser.

The back door was hanging open.

He hadn't left it like that.

"You know, it sure would be nice if you and Kathy would join us for dinner some night. When are you guys free?"

Laurens barely heard him. "Huh?"

"I think it'd be just swell to get the kids together for a play date," Sarah said. "Little Roger is getting so big."

"Yeah," Laurens said distractedly. "Yeah, he's pretty huge. Excuse me, would you?" He motioned toward his vehicle. "I need to check something over here."

"So, maybe dinner this weekend?" Frank called after him.

"Yeah, sure."

Laurens walked around the back of the Land Cruiser and looked inside, and felt his heart rise into his throat. Amid the tarps and ropes and tools and all the rest of it in the truck's backend was a thick pool of blood.

Blood everywhere.

His mind raced, even as his lip curled in disgust.

A baby cried from an open window and Laurens half turned toward the sound. Kathy and Roger were still waiting for him.

"Hey, Walter," Frank called from his vehicle. "You okay, buddy?"

Laurens gave him a wave, but he wasn't okay. Not even a little bit.

Whatever had hunted and killed the people in that Tuareg village was here now, in the American compound.

He had brought it back with him.

———✦———

Laurens opened the door to his flat and found Kathy sitting on the couch in their cramped little common room. Even after all this time in country, he couldn't make himself call such a place a living room. Roger was on the floor in front of her, on his back, sleeping with his tiny fist in his mouth.

She looked up at him and smiled. Her eyes were rimmed red from exhaustion.

"How long's it been since you got any sleep?" he asked.

"I took a nap earlier."

"I mean real sleep."

She shrugged. "It's okay. He's beautiful, isn't he?"

"Yes," Laurens said. "He's gonna like growing up in Texas."

She smiled. It was that same patient, yet pained smile he'd been seeing for months now.

"It won't be long, I think. Another few months."

"I promised I'd follow you to the ends of the Earth," she said.

"Yeah, but I didn't mean to take you literally. I'm hoping we'll be cycled back home soon."

He put a hand on her shoulder and she bent toward him, her cheek resting on his arm. "I'd like that," she said. "But it's okay, Walter. As long as we're together."

"I don't know what I did to deserve you," he said.

"I don't either. Just lucky, I guess."

His phone rang. He took it out and checked the caller ID. The Home Office. A message flashed on the screen. PROGRESS REPORT ASAP.

"Damn. I gotta take this."

She nodded. "Try not to be up too late, okay?"

He took Miriam Bloch's tablet and went to the spare bedroom the DMS had converted to his study. The jailbreaking software on his laptop cut through her tablet's security lock in seconds. He scrolled through the home pages, exploring her apps at random. She had several social media pages, but it had been almost two weeks since she'd visited any of them. There were over a hundred unanswered emails in her three different accounts, including several from him. Her medical apps were stale too. It was like she'd essentially dropped off the grid.

He did find something curious when he went through the history on her Safari browser, though.

Lilith.

She'd done hundreds of searches on "Lilith" and "estrie" and "Jewish vampires."

Curious.

He'd heard the name Lilith, of course, back in college, but he didn't really know anything about her. His time in the DMS had made him a quick study of folklore, though, and it only took him a few minutes reading through some of the websites Miriam had visited to come up to speed.

According to Jewish tradition, she was supposed to be the first wife of Adam, though apparently she refused to be subservient to him, which may or may not have had something to do with her refusing to have sex with him in the missionary position—the folklore sources weren't clear on that point—and that got her kicked out of the Garden of Eden. She then retreated to a cave and became some type of demon. The folklore wasn't entirely clear on exactly what type of demon, though, and in the various artist renderings he found she was sometimes a beautiful and highly seductive girl, usually nude, like a porn star with a devil's tail, while in others she was a weathered hag with wild hair and a baby's severed arm in her teeth. New mothers and their newborn babes were apparently her favorite meal, though she would also eat men from time to time.

At least when she wasn't seducing them in their sleep.

Going back to the home screen, something caught his eye.

13

There was an app there called Story Journal. He called it up, but found only two videos. The first was a short one dated four days earlier and the second was a longer one dated the next day. The first had a run time of thirty-eight seconds, while the longer of the two had a run time of nearly nine minutes.

He called up the shorter one first.

Dr. Miriam Bloch appeared in close-up. She was sitting on her sleeping mat inside the hut where Laurens had found the dead Blue Woman and the half-eaten corpses. The tablet was resting on her knees, and she was holding it with both hands, like the steering wheel of an out-of-control car.

She looked crazy. Wild hair, trembling lips, eyeballs that bounced around like bees inside a box.

"Holy shit," Laurens muttered.

Now, he was beginning to see why her work was suffering.

Several times she tried to speak, but failed. She couldn't seem to focus, couldn't remember the words to say what needed to be said. Laurens's grandfather had died of Alzheimer's years earlier, and he remembered the man struggling in frustration and bootless rage to remember who he was and who the people around him were. It was the same haunted look Miriam Bloch was giving the camera now.

"I can't fucking think!" she screamed, and it came so unexpectedly, Laurens flinched away from the tablet.

By the time he'd recovered his composure, the video was over.

Rattled, he had to force himself to watch the second video.

And immediately wished he hadn't.

Same pose as before. Same wild hair, same crazy, leering gaze. Only this time, she was covered in blood. It ran from the corners of her mouth and turned her hair into a sticky, matted mess.

Except now she was smiling.

Gone was the tortured self-doubt, the painful struggle to grasp for words. She was breathing hard, like a woman aroused.

The first thing she did was turn the camera down on her bare legs. She'd taken off her khaki shorts, and the camera caught a glimpse of small black panties, but it didn't even register with Laurens.

His gaze was focused on her legs.

Her hairy legs.

She ran the palm of her hand from her knee up to the top of her thigh, then turned her bloody hand to the tablet's camera. "See that," she said. "Stuff is sharp as shark skin. That's new."

Then she turned the camera back to her face.

And smiled.

And sat there.

The smile gradually fading.

For about a minute and a half.

"I think I did a pretty good job covering up the mess. They'll need a cleaner team out here, but I think I made it easy on them. Walter Laurens... God, you're an officious little prick, you know that? I never fucking liked you. Still, I made it easy for you. Fucking dickless son of a bitch."

Her head swung on her neck like a drunk about to pass out. She didn't appear to be lucid. She seemed, to Laurens, to be in a world all her own.

Lost.

And then she rallied. She shook her head, stared at the camera with renewed intensity, and said, "Anisha, the lead *bayi*. The Blue Woman. You know what she tried to do? Stupid bitch came at me with an amulet. Can you believe that? Like her religion means shit to me. My people were writing the fucking Bible while hers were still trying to figure out how to make a hut stand up on its own. I ate her throat. Ripped her a new one."

She held up what could only have been the lower leg and foot of a very small child, like she was saying the toast at a wedding.

"I feel good now."

She dropped the leg and ran a hand through her wild, blood-matted hair. She looked like some horrible caricature of a woman aroused.

Then her wild stare turned to something keenly intelligent, yet wantonly needful. Laurens had seen that look before, or at least thought he'd seen that look, on other women, in other rooms.

It was the throw me on the bed and fuck me look of a hundred wet dreams.

It was the desperate, reckless, shameless look of a drunken one-night stand.

And though he hated himself for it, he felt a stirring in his crotch that made him grab his cock and readjust himself.

He was so hard it hurt.

"Walter," Miriam said. "Walter, baby. I know you're watching me. I've seen you watching me. You could have me, if you want me."

On the video, she began to open her blouse, one button at a time.

She let the camera follow her hand as she undid the buttons, inch by inch revealing the blood-soaked tatters of a sports bra.

Then the tablet must have fallen from her hand, for there was a sudden blur of movement, and the next moment the camera was staring, out of focus, at the ceiling of the hut.

Off camera, he heard grunting and snarling, and the sounds of meat getting wrenched from the bone.

That view held for four minutes and twenty-nine seconds.

And then, with only seconds left on the video, Miriam leaned over the tablet, blood dripping from her mouth, and smiled once more.

"Hey, Walter, I made this for you. It's all for you, baby. I know you want some. Come and get it. I'll give it all up for you."

With that, the video ended.

Laurens stared at the screen for a long time, trying to process it all.

Finally, he swiveled his chair around and powered up his desktop. The device was a secure link-up to the DMS servers back at Quantico, and his only direct link with the eggheads at the Crisis Intervention Labs.

The technician on the other side of the link was holding a cup of coffee, and looked utterly unconcerned. "Hawthorne here."

"I've got a problem," Laurens said, doing away with the preamble. "I need help."

"Specifics."

"One of my agents has transitioned," he said. "I need one of your V-8 teams."

———— ◆ ————

Laurens was up the next morning before sunrise. He left Kathy turning restlessly, but mercifully asleep, in their bed, Roger in the cradle next to her side of the bed, and went to the kitchen to make himself some scrambled eggs.

He cracked them into a pan and was running a fork through the yolks when he heard a lot of yelling down in the courtyard.

Laurens turned off the burner and listened.

More yelling.

A man's voice.

He ran downstairs to the courtyard. Dawn was breaking over the city, and first light was filling the narrow gaps between the apartments. Off to his left, his neighbor Frank was staggering around like he'd just taken a hard hit to the head. He was completely nude and yelling nonsense at the top of his lungs.

He saw Laurens and raised his hands like he was offering up a gift and dropped to his knees.

Laurens ran over to him.

Only then did he notice that the man's groin and hips were soaked with blood. "What... what is this?"

"They're dead."

Laurens didn't need to ask any questions. He took in the blood on Frank's crotch and knew instantly what had happened.

Miriam.

She was here.

Laurens glanced up the stairs, toward Frank's apartment, and drew the pistol from his waistband. "Wait here," he said, and headed up the stairs.

There was blood on the door. It was standing open. Laurens kicked the door out of the way and charged inside. He made it just a few steps inside before he stopped, turned his head, and covered his mouth with the back of his hand.

Sarah and her child were in pieces.

A trail of blood and scattered body parts led into one of the bedrooms. Laurens raised his weapon and called out to Miriam. "I know you're in there. Miriam, come out. I want to talk to you."

No answer.

"Miriam, I can help you."

Again, nothing.

He pushed forward, trying not to step in the gore.

He searched the apartment, but the bedroom was empty. So too were all the others. He took one last look around, grabbed a pair of jeans and a t-shirt from atop one of the dressers, and went back downstairs.

Frank was still on his knees, sobbing, too blind with pain to notice the others who had gathered in their doorways to stare. He handed Frank the clothes he'd found upstairs. "Put that on. The police will be here in just a minute."

"They're dead," Frank said. He kept looking at Laurens like he hoped someone would tell him it wasn't true.

"Put your clothes on, Frank."

Then Laurens turned to face the gathered onlookers. They all looked stricken, all of them but Kathy. She was holding Roger on her hip, and the look on her face was completely inscrutable.

"Somebody call for the police," he said.

———•———

A twelve-man Vampire Counterinsurgency and Counterterrorism Field Team flew in from Stuttgart, Germany, later that afternoon. They were dressed as house painters, but with their chiseled physiques and direct, no-nonsense bearing and the numerous black Pelican boxes they brought with them, they weren't fooling anyone.

No sooner had they entered the compound than their leader, a tall, severe-looking Army captain named John Stevens, led Laurens upstairs, ordered him to sit down, and demanded a full briefing. He wanted to know everything. Not just Miriam Bloch's physical description and the nature of her work with the Ice Virus, but the personal stuff too. Did Laurens have a sexual relationship with her? Had she ever expressed feelings for him in the past? The questions went on and on.

While the young captain debriefed him, the rest of his team busied themselves around the office and the apartment and down in the courtyard, running wires and installing laser beam trip wires and a whole host of cameras.

"Looks like your people already know their way around," Laurens said.

"We started reviewing the on-scene surveillance when we got notice we were being mobilized here," Stevens said.

"Oh." One of the soldiers was watching a video on a laptop. It showed Kathy walking around their bedroom in the middle of the night. Frowning, he turned back to Stevens. "What about relocating my family to a safe house? I was told you'd take care of that."

"Already working on it. Your wife and son should be on the way there in about twenty minutes."

Laurens nodded. "So, what's the plan after that?"

Stevens motioned toward the doorway.

Standing in the doorway was a young woman wearing some of Kathy's clothes. She definitely didn't look like Kathy, though. She was every bit as hard looking as Stevens was, and Kathy's baggy t-shirt couldn't hide the bulge of a weapon on her hip.

"This is Lt. Deguara. She'll be assisting with the trap."

"Trap?" Laurens said.

"The estrie prefer newborns and their mothers as their prey. We're hoping that'll lure our target to us."

"And then what?"

"What do you mean?"

"Well, once you lure Miriam here, what will you do?"

Stevens frowned. "Mr. Laurens, make no mistake about it. We did not get called out here to take prisoners. We are here to exterminate your problem. We will lure the target here, we will engage the target, and we will kill it. You understand that, don't you? When you called for us, that was the course you chose."

Laurens swallowed the lump in his throat, then nodded.

Stevens nodded. "Now, if you don't mind." He hooked his thumb toward the door. "My team has a lot of work to do."

"Oh. Oh, okay. Sure."

Laurens stood up uncertainly. He waited for Stevens to say something more, but the man's attention was already directed toward a laptop with a lot of complicated, shifting graphics on it.

The message was clear.

He'd been dismissed.

Kathy was waiting in the hallway, just outside the door.

Their eyes met, and in an instant he knew that she'd overheard everything. "That woman took my clothes," she said.

"Just for tonight. These people, they're professionals."

"Professional killers, you mean?"

"Yeah."

Kathy wrapped her arms around her chest and hugged herself. She swallowed hard, looked at him, and then just as quickly looked away.

"Babe, this is what I do. I'm a spy."

"I know that," she snapped. And then, more softly, "I heard."

"I've talked to the team leader. They're taking you and Roger to a safe house. You'll be out of harm's way."

"Harm's way?" For a moment, he thought she might cry. But she got hold of herself the next instant and choked the tears back. "I can't believe this. Miriam... is she really one of those things now?"

"It looks that way."

"And you think she'd come here? You think she'd try to hurt me and Roger?"

"She killed Sarah," he said.

"And Jessica?"

"Yes, the baby too."

"But she delivered Roger. Why would she want to hurt us?"

"She delivered Jessica too." He glanced down the hall, where one of Stevens's soldiers was waiting to drive Kathy and Roger to the safe house. He motioned to the man and leaned in close to whisper to his wife. "Kathy, this change Miriam went through, that all the infected go through. It changes them. It changed her. Not just her appearance, but her mind too. She probably doesn't even know what she's doing."

That got her attention. She frowned at him, and for the first time since their long trip to the world's farthest corners began, he thought he saw disapproval on her face.

"Can you really get her?" she asked.

"These guys are the best in the world at fighting vampires," Laurens said. "They'll get her."

The soldier approached. "Sir," he said, and turned to Kathy. "Ma'am, we're ready for you now."

Kathy nodded. She was about to follow the soldier back down the hallway, when she suddenly stopped and turned a desperate gaze on Laurens.

"What is it?"

"I just need to, Walter. I have to know. Do you love me? Are you mine?"

"What kind of question is that? Of course I do."

"Say it, please. Say the words."

"Okay," he said. He took her shoulders in his hands and said, "Kathy, I love you. We're gonna make it through this. I promise."

Later that evening, Laurens and Captain Stevens were sitting in an apartment above a restaurant a few blocks from the American compound, watching a bank of video monitors. The team had set up cameras and listening devices all through the compound, and Stevens assured him that nothing could move in there without them seeing it.

Laurens was impressed.

The woman pretending to be Kathy was sitting in the nursery with a window open. The recordings of Roger crying played from the cradle, and every few minutes the woman would get up, lean over the cradle, and rock it gently. It even looked like she was talking to it.

She wasn't, though. Laurens had joked with Stevens about how much she got into her part, but the young Army captain didn't even crack a smile.

"She's not pretending to talk to a baby," he'd said. "She has proximity detectors in there. She gets information from these computers here and then relays that information to the rest of the team hidden throughout your apartment."

"Oh."

"When the target shows, she'll be ready."

"She can take a vampire all by herself?"

"She won't have to," Stevens said. "As soon as we get visual confirmation, the entire team will move in and engage. The target doesn't stand a chance."

"Miriam doesn't, you mean."

Stevens turned his chair toward Laurens and regarded him. Laurens felt like he was being summed up. "I want to show you something," he said. He fished through one of his Pelican boxes, and came up with a photo.

He put it on the counter between them.

It was a picture of Miriam, a still lifted from the video chat where she'd gathered her hair up in both hands and told Laurens she'd do anything he had a mind for, even as the blood ran from the corners of her mouth.

Sitting there, staring at the picture, he felt the same confluence of disgust and sexual hunger that had so disturbed him the first time he watched the video.

"What is that supposed to be?" Laurens said.

"An object lesson." Stevens put the picture down on the counter. "Dr. Bloch is an estrie, Mr. Laurens. She's one of only six the DMS knows about. We do know a little about them, though. We know, for instance, that they are capable of producing powerful pheromones."

"Pheromones?" Laurens scoffed at him. "That's absurd. Pheromones require some form of direct contact. A smell or something. The only contact I've had with her in over a month is through the videos on her tablet."

"Not true. You were in the village. You found her blood in the wrecked Land Cruiser. And, you handled her blood again when you removed the tarp from the back of your vehicle."

"And again when I went into Frank and Sarah's apartment."

"Probably."

"My God," Laurens said. He looked at his hands. "Could I... be infected?"

"Anything is possible. We still don't understand exactly how and why the virus strikes some people and not others. But I think we have more immediate problems."

"Like what?" Laurens asked.

"I think it's possible, based on what we've seen from other estries, that Dr. Bloch may have fixated on you. The pheromones are only released during sexual arousal, and I think it's possible—I think it's highly likely, in fact—that's she's fixated on you. This image certainly seems to suggest that she was aroused while thinking of you."

"No," he scoffed. "I told you, she's never looked twice at me."

Stevens shrugged.

Laurens leaned back and thought about that. He watched Lt. Deguara on the computer monitors, at the way she moved in his wife's clothes, and a thought occurred to him. The first thing Kathy had said when Stevens's team started tearing up their home was that another woman had taken her clothes.

Another woman had taken what was hers.

And Miriam had fixated on him.

People got nasty when they were jealous.

That was when it clicked inside his head.

"Oh my God," Laurens said. He jumped from his chair, grabbed his phone, and called Kathy's phone.

"What are you doing?" Stevens demanded. "This location is on lock-down."

"Calling my wife," Laurens said. He turned his back to the young captain, listening as two rings turned into five, and then to seven, eight. "Come on, damn it. Answer."

He hung up.

Ran his hands through his hair. He felt laser focused, totally in the moment. And scared out of his mind.

"She's probably sleeping," Stevens said.

"She's been a light sleeper lately," Laurens said. "Can you call your people? Check on her please."

"She's at a secure location."

"Call them," he said. "Please."

"I would have heard from my people if there was a problem."

"Call them, damn it!"

Stevens's expression turned hard, but he slipped on a headset and dialed the safe house just the same. He waited, listening, growing more and more upset with each passing second. Finally, he ripped the headset off his head and set it on the counter. "Damn."

"Oh God," Laurens said. "Captain, I need you to get me there right now."

"Yeah," Stevens said. "Yeah, I think you're right."

⁎

The safe house, like every other building in Timbuktu, was made of dried mud and wood that turned gray from the sun almost instantly. It was a two-story home, a mansion by local standards, surrounded by high mud walls with shards of broken glass sticking up from mortar on the top. There was only one gate and the lead Suburban rammed that without even slowing down.

Laurens crept forward and watched the commando team disembark from their vehicles through the windshield. His driver exited the vehicle, carrying a huge machine gun. He hadn't said two words to Laurens on the car ride over, but now he turned to Laurens and said, "You stay here. Captain's orders."

"That's my wife and son in there."

The man just nodded, then ran after the rest of the team.

Laurens slumped back into his chair and turned to the small bank of video monitors set up along one wall of the van. It wasn't anything like the elaborate command center Stevens had shown him back at the American compound, but it had everything he needed.

Every member of the team wore a body camera, and their devices relayed the video feed back to the monitors in front of him. Even if he couldn't go in with them, at least he could watch the whole affair play out by switching back and forth between the various monitors.

Laurens slipped on a headset and listened to the clipped dialogue of the team as they cleared walkways and colonnades and foyers.

They found the first body just inside the front door.

One of the local Tuareg men hired as security.

Laurens was watching Captain Stevens's video feed at the time. It was dark inside the house and the team's night vision body cameras turned everything a watery shade of green, but there was enough visibility for him to see that the man's neck was ripped open.

Stevens knelt down beside the body and touched the corpse's face.

"Still warm," he said.

Using hand gestures, Stevens directed his team to split into three groups of two. The soldiers then moved out to explore the rest of the house. Laurens was still watching Stevens's video feed when one of the other soldiers cried out in pain and was just as suddenly silenced.

Stevens and his teammates ran for the sound.

Laurens toggled through the various video feeds until he found the soldier who had let out the scream. The soldier, a man named Franklin, was on the ground, facing a corner, not moving. A few feet from him, his partner, a man named Gonzales, was also on the ground, his throat ripped out, a widening pool of blood spreading beneath his head. Moving across the frame was a pair of bare, hairy legs.

"Oh God," he said.

Laurens toggled the monitor controls again until he found Stevens's link. The man was leading what was left of his team down a hallway, their gear clattering softly as they raced toward a darkened doorway at the far end.

They hit the door at a run and burst into the room.

And saw their teammates dead on the floor.

Off to the left was Miriam Bloch. She was wearing nothing but a pair of black panties. She held a small, curved blade in her right hand. The night vision goggles made blood look black, and she was covered with it from head to toe.

"Move, damn it!" Laurens said at the screen. Stevens and his team were just standing there. "Come on, somebody move!"

But the men seemed transfixed, like their feet were rooted to the floor. None of them moved an inch, not even when Miriam advanced on the man standing to Stevens's right. Stevens watched her, his helmet cam tracking with his gaze. Miriam approached the soldier standing next to Stevens and calmly, effortlessly, mercilessly, slashed the knife across his throat.

He fell to the ground, and still none of the other soldiers moved.

A deer in headlights.

They just stood there and got slaughtered.

Stevens was the last to fall.

Then Miriam rose from her bloody work and let the knife clatter to the floor. Whether it was Stevens's rank or some other instinct that turned her attention to the young captain's helmet cam, Laurens neither knew nor cared.

Laurens saw only her.

She captivated him, and even as a voice inside his head screamed that she was an obscenity, he wanted her. He felt utterly emasculated by her, even as his cock stiffened.

Then she knelt on the floor, on her hands and knees, and crawled toward the camera. It never even occurred to him that she was nose to nose with a man she'd just murdered. He saw only her. She was speaking only to him.

"Walter. Walter, baby. Where are you?"

She went down on her elbows, her ass rising.

"I know you can hear me."

She gave her ass a shake.

"Just you wait 'till I find you, Walter. It's gonna be delicious."

The smile slid from her face. She stood up, the video feed catching only her blood-streaked, hairy legs as she walked out of sight.

Christ, what was he going to do? Kathy and Roger were in there, somewhere. The compound was equipped with a panic room. It was fireproof, assault proof. After Benghazi, the State Department had learned its lesson. But could it hold off a vampire?

He was going to have to go in there.

Something scratched at the side of the van.

"Walter."

He froze. That was Miriam's voice, teasing him.

The scratching got louder. It went around the back. Up the other side. He followed the sound, unable to breath, too scared to cry out.

And yet, strangely, fearfully, he wanted to be close to her.

The scratching sound reached the passenger door and stopped there. Laurens was on his knees behind the front passenger seat, holding onto the headrest for dear life, and he still hadn't taken a breath.

Her face appeared in the window, shiny with the blood of other men. "Walter," she said, and scratched at the window. "Let me in, baby."

He shrank into the dark, crippled with fear. "Leave me alone," he said.

"You don't mean that, Walter. You want me. I want you too. I can smell you. I want to taste you. Your skin… your tongue in my mouth. You would taste so good."

Laurens crept toward the window, unable to stop himself. Her voice was a hook in his nose, pulling him closer. He climbed around the seat, and pressed his face against the glass. She was only centimeters away from him, her eyes glistening like wet obsidian.

"Come on, Walter. Let me in, baby. I want you."

She suddenly snarled and punched the glass, sending a spider web of cracks out from her fist.

"And you know I don't have to ask permission, don't you?"

"Go away," he said weakly.

"You are—"

She was cut off mid-stream. There was a flash of movement behind her. Something dark hit her hard in the back of the head, knocking her through the window. Glass erupted from the impact and clattered all over the dashboard as Miriam's head and shoulders came through the window.

Laurens fell back, heart thudding against his ribs.

But Miriam wasn't coming after him. Blood, her own blood, was spreading from cuts all over her face. Her eyes had turned glassy and she looked shocked and confused. He thought, maybe, he saw terror there too.

Then something pulled her from the window.

He heard the sounds of women yelling and fighting. A body hit the side of the van, rocking it on its springs. There was a scream, Miriam crying out in terrible pain.

Laurens heard a familiar voice. "That's my man, you bitch. You can't have him."

Miriam's next scream was cut short.

Silence settled over the yard. He heard nothing but the night wind blowing sand against the windshield, and after a long moment, he worked up the courage to step out the back of the van.

Miriam was dead in a heap, her neck sliced so deeply the back of her head was almost touching her spine. Staring at her, Laurens felt a hole in his gut, like the tether that had connected him to the young doctor had suddenly been cut.

It left him feeling empty.

He turned away.

Standing a dozen feet off was Kathy, mouth bloody, chest heaving. There was blood all over her blouse, but he hardly saw that. She was leveling a stare at him he'd never seen before. She looked utterly mad with rage, or lust, or something that was more than both of those emotions.

And then he saw her claws.

"No," he said. "No, no, no."

She watched him for a long moment without speaking, then turned and walked into the tall grass that had grown up around a nearby palm tree. She reached down and picked up their son. Then she headed back to the driveway, shaking first one hand and then the other. By the time she stepped back on the packed dirt of the driveway, her claws were gone.

She was Kathy again.

Covered in Miriam's blood, but Kathy.

Reeling, he staggered around in a circle. A thousand questions raced in his mind. How did it happen? When? Miriam Bloch had delivered their baby. Maybe then. She was working with the blood samples from the *bayi* around that time.

Or maybe Kathy had infected Miriam. Miriam's troubles started after Roger was born.

Once he made that mental jump—God, his wife, one of them!—the rest of the pieces fell in line. Her blackouts. Never being able to sleep. Her complaints of terrible headaches in the morning. Waking in the middle of the night and her not there in the bed.

Four months at least she must have hid it from him.

Finally, his legs couldn't hold him any longer and he dropped onto his butt in the dirt and put his face in his hands.

When he looked up again, Kathy was sitting beside him, bouncing Roger on her knee, but watching him closely.

Somewhere in the back of his mind, his training took over.

The DMS had bugged his home. Had set up surveillance throughout the entire compound. And they'd done that even before Stevens and his team arrived.

Months before.

They had recordings of his son crying.

What else did they have? Did they know about his wife? He thought back to the video feed he'd seen earlier, about the security team that had been sent over to the safe house to protect his wife and son. He'd assumed Miriam had killed them.

He glanced over at his wife and wondered if that were true.

Her maiden name was Barry. Barry was an Anglicized version of O Baire, a name common all over Ireland. Celtic, he thought. What did he know about Celtic folklore? What kind of monster lived in her recessive genes?

He thought about how many times she'd asked him if he loved her over the last few months. So out of character for her to be so needy. And he watched her holding their child, still as loving as the first time she'd held the baby to her breast.

More so, even.

What kind of vampire was she?

"*Leannan sith*?" he finally asked.

She stopped moving her leg. Roger settled, cooing quietly. "That's what I think," she said.

Laurens looked at his son and smiled, but it was the smile of an exhausted man.

"Walter, are we… are we okay? Do you love me? Can you love me, after knowing this?"

He met her gaze. She looked like Kathy again, even though her hands were bloody. She'd gotten it all over Roger's chubby little legs.

"How long has… have you…?"

"Since Roger was born, I think."

"She infected you?"

"I think so."

"Were you going to tell me?"

"I was so scared. I know the work you do. I've known for a while."

He nodded, but said nothing.

"Walter, please. Do you love me?"

"You asked me that before," he said.

"Please, Walter, I need to know."

He knew what it would mean to say yes. He was a DMS agent, sworn to eradicate her kind. And she was a vampire, forced to feed upon his. She'd promised once to follow him to the ends of the earth. It looked like they'd finally gotten there.

To say yes would change everything.

So he took her hands in his, and gave his answer.

WET WORKS PART 2

By Jonathan Maberry

Renaissance Hotel
Pittsburgh, Pennsylvania
Morning of the Red Storm

There are days, Swann knew, when the world seemed to shudder as if in erotic anticipation of all the ways it was going to hurt him. Since the outbreak of the Vampire Wars he'd had too many days like that. At first they were rare enough to catch him unawares. Back then he was trusting enough to think the battle won, the worst over. When the world proved otherwise, he often felt hurt. Not physically hurt, though there was some of that, but emotionally hurt. Betrayed. The world was not supposed to be *like* this. He knew that some of his own inability to process the pain came from who and what he was. A professor of folklore, a respected lecturer and author, a white male in the academic world. His vanity was the first thing the world took from him. His feelings of comfort, even of privilege went next, stripped away by exposure to a greater variety of people and circumstances than he had ever previously considered. Swann, a liberal and humanist, had thought he understood the world; he believed he was in touch with the range of human evil and human goodness, of sacrifice and pain and greed and intolerance and misery and hope.

The learning curve had cut him like a sickle.

Day after day. Event after event. Battle after battle.

When the Ice Virus triggered the dormant genes for vampirism, Swann became part of the national conversation. He was the world's foremost expert on the folkloric versions of vampires. There were hundreds of kinds of vampires in world culture. They were all so different from one another and none of them resembled the pale, tragic romantic figures of Hollywood and popular fiction. When a barista named Michael Fayne was arrested for the savage murder of several women and claimed to be a vampire, police brought Swann in as a consultant. Not that anyone actually believed that Fayne was a supernatural monster, but the detectives hoped Swann's knowledge of the subject matter could help decode Fayne's delusion.

That worked and it didn't.

Because Michael Fayne was an actual vampire. The first human to manifest what appeared to be supernatural powers. Enhanced strength, heightened senses, an insatiable bloodlust. The reality of what Fayne had become shocked Swann perhaps even more than it did the police. Or, if not harder, then it shook his core beliefs.

Then the medical test results came back. Fayne was a vampire, yes, but he was not a supernatural creature. Vampirism was genetic. The gene was an old one, but it had become dormant because all through history people with an active V-gene had been viewed as monsters and hunted to extinction.

Now that had changed.

Even with the horrific nature of Fayne's crimes, Swann had been reluctant to view all vampires as monsters, as enemies. And he was right. As more and more cases emerged it quickly became apparent that there were as many vampire personality types as there were other human personalities. Evil and good, predatory and not, violent or passive. None of those belonged to either species. Sadly, both sides seemed to produce true monsters and enthusiastic killers.

And that was how the war began.

Well, *wars*.

Large and small, there had been a lot of battles since the Ice Virus took hold. The media reported everything. Every drop of blood, every life taken, every burning city. Every life lost. It was great for ratings. Some reporters seized the outbreak to make careers for themselves.

Even Swann's friend, Yuki Nitobe, had done that. She was the first to break the story and had ridden the wave all the way to international celebrity. Though, to be fair, the closer Yuki got to the story behind the story, the more it hurt her, too.

And now there was today.

On the TV the news cameras were showing pictures of Hell itself. Raging fires rising from a cluster of medical buildings. The news anchor cut in, looking both appalled and excited.

"I'm told we have received a video from the persons responsible for the attack on the Texas Medical Center," he said. "I need to caution you that we have not had the chance to review this tape. Viewers are strongly cautioned. Here we go. This is from a group claiming responsibility for this attack."

The screen split into three images. The burning medical center, the news anchor, and then a box that was at first just a square of dark red. Swann realized at once that it was a backdrop. A figure came into shot and sat as the cameraman tightened focus so that the person's head and shoulders filled the screen. He was male, Swann could tell that much, from the breadth of shoulders. However, he wore a red cloth mask that hid his features, and there were small wire mesh screens covering his eyes. His voice was mechanical, clearly filtered through a device that made it sound coarse and inhuman.

"I speak to you now at the dawn of a new era," said the man. "I do not speak for the vampire nation. I do not speak for the world of cattle. We are not bloods, we are not beats." His voice was loaded with contempt as he spoke those common nicknames. Bloods and beats. Vampires and humans. "I speak in the name of He who was and He who is to come. I speak for the true faith, for the red faith, for the blood of the Eternal. I speak to the world that was and will be no more, and I speak for the world that has come to replace the old, the decayed, the corrupt, the impure, the diseased, and the blasphemous. I speak for the glory of the one, true god. The red god. The god of blood. The god of purity. The god of this world. *Our* world. Listen and understand, the world you knew is over. It is gone and it will never come back. The old world has died. And you have lost your right to be alive in the world that will come. You have

one chance. Vampire or human, you have a hope yet and that is in repentance and acceptance. Recant your old sinful ways. Fall to your
knees and take responsibility for what you have done to their world. *Beg
for the mercy of god, and god will answer.* Be warned, though, god is
harsh and god is jealous and god will know if your repentance is genuine." He paused. "If you are watching this message, then you have already seen the hand of god. You have already witnessed punishment.
You have already seen his power." Another pause, longer this time and
then he leaned a little closer to the camera. "You think you have seen
war, but you have not. You think you have seen the rise of vampiric
power, but you have not. You think that your armies and your police are
strong enough to protect you, but they are not. Not now. Not any longer.
The Red Empire rises. *All hail the Red Emperor!*"

He screamed those last five words, and then the screen went dark and
was immediately replaced by the anchor, looking shaken.

Luther sat on the edge of his bed, half-dressed in socks, boxers, and
a dress shirt, staring at the TV screen.

"Oh my god," he said.

And he slid slowly off the bed and onto the floor.

EXPAT

By Dana Fredsti

I know something's wrong the minute the newcomers walk into the Buccaneer because Aztec hisses and runs into the kitchen, tail puffed out the size of a small Christmas tree.

See, Aztec is the kind of cat that should have been a dog. He pretty much loves everyone as long as they have fingers to scratch his chin or rub his belly. I'd found him on the streets of West Hollywood after a particularly shitty wrap party, an orange runt covered in oil and fleas. He'd started purring as soon as I picked him up, and has pretty much kept it up ever since. Even when Maria first manifested the I1V1 virus, Aztec still slept curled up against her. In fact, I've only seen him freak out like this once before, when a couple of asshole poachers stopped by the Buccaneer for drinks and made the mistake of bragging about their latest haul.

When Aztec doesn't like someone, I pay attention.

First glance they're nothing but your typical poser Eurotrash types, a dime a dozen back in Hollywood. Two guys, one in his fifties or thereabouts, the other a cocky-looking twenty-something, and one gal aiming to look thirty, but most likely topping forty. She reminds me of my ex, which backs up Aztec's first reaction even more.

Second look takes in their unnatural—and totally self-conscious—grace, and the hint of red behind their eyes. They all look like they'd be more at home in an *Underworld* movie than, well, just about any place else. Bloods. They aren't even trying to be subtle.

I mean, who wears black leather dusters in Costa Rica, right?

They walk up to the bar, the woman taking the lead. Thin as a whip, honey blonde hair pulled back from her angular face in a tight bun, like a ballet dancer. Given her build and the way she holds herself, I wouldn't be surprised if that had been her day job before she decided to join the Too Cool for School Vamp Club.

"Your cat doesn't like us," she says, an amused smile on her face.

I don't like them either, but refrain from saying so.

"He's not partial to strangers," I say, polishing the inside of a pint glass with more concentration than necessary to hide the fact I'm lying.

The older man curls his lip. "I don't like cats."

Kind of like coming into someone's house, looking at a crying baby, and saying, "I don't like kids." Just rude, y'know? But… I keep that thought to myself as well, and consider the best way to handle the situation. I do a quick scan of the current clientele.

A honeymooning couple from Michigan, a group of college kids from Texas, a few of my regulars, mostly expat Americans. And they're all too busy drinking and talking to pay much attention to the newcomers. No 'ticos—the local term for native Costa Ricans—except Liza and Diego, cook and busboy/sous chef, respectively, and they're back in the kitchen. My wait-staff—Ana, a sweet eighteen-year-old tica—is running unusually late.

That makes things easier. The locals in this area aren't partial to vampires or foreigners.

I look across the patio into the dirt and gravel parking lot. A big honking black Escalade, windows tinted and opaque, straddles two parking spaces. The Buccaneer is perched halfway up the mountain above Dominical and the beach, so without a four-wheel-drive you wouldn't make it up most of the mountain roads, especially during rainy season, but even so the Escalade is the kind of vehicle assholes use to bully people driving smaller cars.

"That yours?" I ask mildly, nodding toward the Escalade.

The younger guy—a real "I'm too sexy for my leather duster" asshole—nods smugly.

Of course it is, I think. I know the type. I used to be one. Big car, little penis, or, in this case, big car, little canines.

Although in my case… I'd just been an asshole.

I glance back at the Escalade. For just an instant, I think I see someone in the back seat behind the heavily tinted window. It must be a trick of the light, though, because by the time I blink, whatever I think I've seen is gone.

I turn back to my unwelcome customers, opting to play the genial host for the time being. "Can I get you folks a drink?"

A rumble of thunder punctuates my deliberately innocuous question as the skies open up in one of Dominical's frequent late afternoon downpours. The sound of rain spattering on the roof, ground, and lush foliage surrounds the bar, drops of water splashing onto the balcony rail that runs the length of the covered, open-air dining area.

The kid grins, exposing his abnormally sharp teeth as he gives the diners a once-over. His gaze settles on one of the Texas college kids, a pretty young thing in a pink halter-top and shorts, already several margaritas into the late afternoon. His grin widens even more. "I think I'll have that."

"A margarita? Good choice."

"That's not what I meant," he says, smile turning dangerous. I want to tell him it'd be more effective if he wasn't such a fucking poser, but I don't.

I give a smile of my own, the one that used to send my assistant out of my office in tears.

"That's all you're gonna get in my bar."

Mister Too Sexy puffs up, ready to go all agro on me. I slip my hand under the bar, finding the grip of my Desert Eagle just as the blonde puts a hand on his shoulder and says, "Jared." Her voice is quiet, but it's clear who's the boss of this trio. And it's not Mister Compensation Issues here.

Blondie gives me a nonthreatening smile. My fingers unclench, leaving the Desert Eagle in its hiding spot for the time being.

"I'll have a skinny margarita."

I give an inward chuckle at her "skinny margarita" order. Like my ex, this gal was already thin enough to be a poster child for heroin chic, and now for sure she doesn't need to worry about excess calories. Guess old habits die hard.

"What about you, gentlemen?" I pause just enough before "gentlemen" to infer the opposite. I can't help it. They glower at me.

"They'll have beers," Blondie orders for them.

I nod, take two cold Imperial Silvers out of the fridge and set them on the counter with wedges of lime. Then I get to making her skinny margarita, which is basically lime juice, tequila and a little simple syrup. Truth be told, I like 'em better than the sugar bombs made with the mixer, so maybe Ms. Hollywood just has good taste in drinks, if not in traveling companions.

"You staying near here?" I ask.

"Villa de Cielo."

"Nice place."

It isn't. Despite its lofty name, Villa de Cielo's only a few hundred feet off the highway, making it an easy target for opportunistic thieves. The upkeep of both grounds and lodging is half-assed at best. It's also one of the only places in the area that'll rent to bloods.

"It's not exactly what we're looking for."

I give a noncommittal grunt and set her drink down on the bar. She nods her thanks.

"We looked into a few other places… and found one that looks perfect. It's farther up the mountain, much more privacy. Just up the road from here, actually. Casa de Amigos, to be precise. Have you heard of it?"

My shoulders stiffen. I know where this is heading.

"We were told the owner would be here," she continues. "At least I think that's what the groundskeeper said." Her nose wrinkles, a delicate move that manages to convey a world of contempt. "He should learn to speak English."

She's talking about Hector, who's been doing maintenance and groundskeeping for Amigos Villa Rentals since the dawn of time. When I first moved here, I'd felt the same way. Now I love listening to the locals speaking Spanish, the sound as soft and soothing as a gentle rainfall.

My own vocal style has softened as well, as I'd slowly morphed from hard-assed film studio mogul to laid-back barkeep and owner of what's currently the most popular expat bar in the area. I'm not sure if the popularity is due to the quality of the food or my smiling face, but it sure as hell isn't the accessibility of the location.

The Buccaneer is the only actual business among the residences and vacation villas tucked away off the steep and winding roads. Most of the houses on the mountain are owned by moderately well off to stinking rich foreigners, most come to enjoy a tropical retirement. I admit I'm one of the stinking rich ones, but I'm not ready to retire just yet.

Blondie takes a sip of her drink and licks her lips appreciatively. "This is good." She looks me in the eyes and licks her lips again, suggestively this time. "Very good." Her blue eyes glint with a red glow not caused by the reflection from the setting sun. "Are you the owner—" she pauses oh so briefly. "—Mr. Logan?"

She knows my name. That ain't good.

I'm saved from having to respond by the male half of the cute newly-weds stepping up to the bar, empty glasses in hand. "Could we get a couple more of these and an order of the sweet and sour chicken wings?"

He glances uneasily at the bloods, but has the sense not to say anything.

"Sure thing." I take the glasses and set them on the counter behind me, then call the order into the kitchen as the guy hurries back to his bride. We don't have any sort of fancy electronic system—I just stick my head through the door to the side of the bar and holler, "One sweet and sour," and then get back to work making the drinks.

"You're very good at what you do," Blondie purrs, watching my every move. "Very agile hands." She runs a finger along the rim of her glass, doing her best to vamp me—in the old-fashioned sense of the word— and not doing a very good job of it. To paraphrase a quote from one of Gene Kelly's more underrated films, she should try underplaying the part. Very effective.

I don't respond and a frown works hard to wrinkle Blondie's previously Botoxed brow. The Vampsy Twins glower, ready to Hulk Smash at her command, downing their beers as if trying out for the synchronized chugging event at the Olympics, slamming their empty bottles down on the bar.

"Another round?" I sweep the dead soldiers off the counter into a recycle bin below and pull out two more Silvers and pop the tops off without waiting for a reply. The two vamps don't argue when I plunk the bottles in front of them.

"You still haven't answered my question, Mr. Logan," Blondie says, still going for the sexy pout. "Are you the owner of Casa de Amigos?"

"Let me tell you something about this area." I pick up a glass at random and start polishing it with one of the bar rags. "The first person to manifest the V-virus in our little town was a tourist from New Jersey. She and her family were staying at one of the swanky beachfront resort hotels a few miles north. Turns out she had a lot of Middle Eastern ancestry so we ended up with an *ekimmu* on the rampage." I lift up the glass, check it for spots, then glance at Blondie and her backup vamps. "I'm assuming you three know your vamps, right?" They look totally blank so I don't bother waiting for an answer.

"*Ekimmus* are pretty nasty, and hard to stop. At any rate, this woman slaughtered the rest of the guests, including her family. She also wiped out the hotel staff, most of whom were ticos, and all of them local. Guess it was a real horror show. As a result, the locals aren't nearly as fond of foreigners as they used to be, but the economy here depends on tourism, and a lot of us expats have money to pump into the system, so they deal with us."

"What's your point?" Jared growls.

I give a small laugh. "My point, kid, is that the owner of Casa de Amigos wouldn't be doing himself any favors if he rented to a bunch of foreign bloods."

"What if we could offer a great deal of money... and more?" The purr is back in her voice as she reaches across the bar to run a finger down the front of my T-shirt, tracing the words "Pura Vida" over my chest. Pura Vida, Costa Rica's official tourist motto. The pure life.

Having this bitch touch those words sullies them.

"Nothing you've got would tempt me."

Eyes flashing, Blondie drops her hand and gives a small nod, as if reaching a conclusion. Her two sidekicks grin in a way that raises the hair on the back of my neck.

"I'd think you'd be sympathetic to our cause." Blondie pauses almost delicately, then continues. "After all, your wife is one of us."

Her words hit like a punch to the gut, but I manage to hide it. I don't bother asking how she knows.

"Doubtful. If anything my ex-wife and you have more in common." My tone makes it clear this is not a compliment.

The hint of red in her eyes flares more deeply. "You know what I mean."

"Yeah, I do." I drop my voice to an undertone. "And now you know why we keep it quiet and why I'm not gonna do anything that might bring trouble to our door."

"You think we're trouble?" This is Jared.

I don't bother answering. I don't have to. We both know the score.

She leans forward, close enough that I can smell the faint carrion stench under the smell of tequila on her breath. "You will eventually have to choose sides. If you're smart, you'll do it sooner rather than later."

The saloon-style doors to the kitchen swing outward and Diego appears, a plate of fragrant chicken wings in hand.

"Excuse me." I meet Diego halfway, taking the wings from him and shooing him back into the kitchen. Then I take the wings and fresh drinks to the newlyweds, enjoying the sight of their hands entwined as they lean their heads together, watching the rain fall below the veranda, maybe hoping to catch sight of a sloth or howler monkey, or maybe even some bats. They thank me when I set their food and drink down on the table, then go back to cuddling as dusk brings on the nightly chorus of frogs and other nightlife.

May your lives always be so peaceful, I think by way of a silent blessing.

Better than "May you live in interesting times."

Back at the bar, Blondie finishes up her skinny margarita while her companions suck down their second round.

"You want another?" I ask, more out of habit than anything else. All I really want is for them to leave.

She shakes her head and gracefully dismounts from the barstool. "We're done here for the moment."

I manage to say "That'll be twenty-five bucks" instead of "Fuck you." I don't bother asking for *colones*. Some tourists don't like to bother with the local currency and I'd bet Blondie was one of them. Sure enough, she nods to the older vamp, who pulls out a twenty and a five, slaps the bills down on the bar stop, and stalks out to the parking lot, Jared close on his heels. Blondie turns to leave.

"What, no tip?" I can't resist waving the red flag.

Blondie stops, turns back, and regards me thoughtfully, all traces of Theda Bara mannerisms gone. "Why, yes," she says. "Reconsider our offer."

"Or what? You got a horse head with my name on it?"

She grins widely, not bothering to hide the sharpness of her teeth anymore. "Something like that."

She leaves. I hear the slamming of car doors, and seconds later the Escalade peels out of the parking lot, spraying gravel as the driver, most likely Jared, pretends he's a stuntman. I watch the car vanish down the hill, my previous good mood replaced by worry.

HashtagVampBuzzkill.

The rain slows down and then stops. More people, mostly local expats, wander in to the bar. The parking lot fills up, but still no Ana so Diego does double duty in the kitchen and on the floor. I should call her, but soon I'm too busy to worry as I fall into the rhythm of the evening making drinks, calling orders into the kitchen, and chatting up the customers. It's a good night, but I'm more than ready to go home by the time last call rolls around at quarter to midnight.

The last customers trickle out. Diego and I clean up the tables and bar area, and then help Liza finish up in the kitchen. Waving off their offers to help with that, I divvy up the very generous tips between Diego and Liza and send them on their way.

I take the bags of trash and recycling out to the bins around the side of the Buccaneer, pausing for a minute to listen to the sounds of the jungle as the wind picks up, rustling through the lush foliage. The chirps and croaks of frogs and toads. Chattering and howls from capuchins and howler monkeys. The infrequent guttural bellows and coughs of crocodiles lurking in the estuaries. A far cry from honking horns, racing motors, and the never-ending party of Hollywood.

Tossing both trash and recycling into their respective bins, I turn to go back inside. I kick something that skitters across the gravel, coming to a stop a few feet away. There's not a lot of illumination here, only one small motion-activated light below the roof, but enough that I can see that I've tripped on a shoe. I pick it up, holding it up to the light to get a better look.

Dark red, high-heeled woman's pump. It's faux leather and cheaply made, the toe scuffed and the wide heel worn down. When Ana wears them to work, I tease her, call her Dorothy and ask her if there's no place like home.

My heart suddenly hammering inside my chest, I go back inside and grab a mini-Maglite from behind the bar. I also retrieve my Desert Eagle. Going back to the bins, I hold the Maglite with the butt end clenched between my lips, flipping open both lids with my left hand while clutching the Eagle in my right. I shine the Mag into first one bin, then the other. Nothing but dark green trash bags, bottles, and cans. The bins were emptied yesterday, not a lot in there.

No bodies.

No Ana.

The adrenaline rushes out of my body, leaving me as limp as one of my wrung-out bar rags. I try to tell myself the shoe belongs to one of the Girls Gone Wild types from Texas who had too many margaritas, lost it, and didn't notice. But I know better. This is a warning.

I grab the metal cash box, then stick my head into the kitchen.

"Aztec, time to go home!"

When he doesn't come trotting into view, I go all the way into the kitchen and check the cupboards, corners, nooks, and crannies. No Aztec. He must have gone on walkabout, so I leave food and water on the floor near the cat bed we keep there for him and crack open the window over the sink wide enough for him to wriggle back in. The window is high off the ground and blocked off by a thriving malinche tree. Perfect for a cat to get in and out, but inaccessible to most people. I hate leaving without him, but I'm tired and stressed and want nothing more than to get home.

My house, Villa de Estrella, is about a mile up the mountain from the Buccaneer. Not far at all as the crow flies, but the drive takes five to ten minutes, depending on the weather and visibility. The road curves as much as Lombard Street, and potholes, mudslides, and crumbling edges make it slow going, even with high beams on.

I drive home as carefully as I can, seeing things in the shadows off the sides of the road that aren't really there. The closer I get, the tauter my nerves stretch. Blondie and crew no doubt know I live in the villa above Casa de Amigos, and who's to say they haven't decided to pay a visit to my wife?

I'm as close as I've ever been to a nervous wreck by the time I pull up to the sturdy iron gates at the top of my drive. I can see the lights illuminating the front of the villa, the bronze front doors closed. Hector's SUV is tucked away at the far end of the drive, leaving room for my car. Everything looks normal, but the churning in my stomach doesn't stop until I'm inside, shouting Maria's name before I've got the front door open and dash into the entryway, feet nearly skidding on the tiled floor.

"Maria!" My voice echoes off the stucco walls and high wood-beamed ceiling. A gecko scurries along the wall, startled by my voice.

"Gary?"

I hear Maria's voice and turn, relief so strong it almost makes me collapse as my wife comes into view. She's all curves and laugh lines, her mouth full and real, unlike the collagen trout pout of my ex. Maybe it was the contrast between Maria's natural beauty and the plastic surgeon-dependent artifice of so many women in Hollywood, but I fell for her like a bungee jumper, throwing myself off the edge, the snap back leaving me dangling like an idiot in the hopes she'd see something more in me than the Hollywood asshole I'd become.

And she did.

She glides toward me from the living room. When I first met her, Maria walked slowly, with a slight hitch in her gait. I found out later her left leg was partially paralyzed from a case of botulism that had nearly killed her in her teens. Now she moves with a preternatural grace that makes the earlier overly deliberate movements of the bloods seem cartoonish by comparison, even Ms. Bolshoi Ballet. Maria's a *patasola*, moving through the jungle with the stealth and grace of a jaguar or a snake, sinuous and strong, her vision adjusting to the blackness and shadows. *Patasolas* are flesh eaters and drinkers of blood, but they're also protective of nature and the forest animals, and unforgiving of humans who enter their domain and harm them. Maria has never been a fan of loggers, hunters, miners, and especially not of poachers, so she hasn't really changed all that much.

I wrap my arms around her, needing to feel every inch of her against my body, feel her heart beating against mine. She snakes her arms around my waist, hands running up and down my back, fingers pressing and massaging just the right places.

"There was trouble tonight at the bar," she says. It's not a question.

"How did you know?" We're both speaking in English. We switch back and forth, giving both of us practice in our second language.

She points to the living room. I follow the direction of her finger and see Aztec curled up in one corner of the chocolate brown leather couch, nose buried in his tail, which is almost back to its normal size. My anxiety level drops another notch or three. I'm glad to see the little bugger.

"He came running in with his tail like this." Maria holds her hands up to indicate just how big Aztec's tail was when he got home.

"Yeah, we had visitors tonight." I drop a kiss on Maria's forehead. She looks up at me solemnly, gazing at me with those amazing green eyes, the color of olives, set against smooth bronzed skin.

"So you know we've got bloods looking to move in," I say as she leads me into the living room, where two glasses and a pitcher of mojitos sit on the coffee table.

She nods. "I heard them talking to Father."

Hector is her father, which is why I'd initially kept him on as groundskeeper instead of hiring someone younger and cheaper.

Don't get me wrong. Hector works hard and keeps the grounds and the buildings immaculate, but he expected to be paid accordingly and the former owners had given him a generous salary. At the time I figured I'd hire someone younger, eager for work that'd take half the salary and that spoke English. Most ticos I'd met spoke some English, at least a smattering. If Hector spoke any, he kept it a secret. The former owners told me I'd get used to it; they'd always managed to get their needs across.

Sure, I'd thought, *but who wants to play charades every day?*

So I was about to have The Talk with Hector the day after I'd taken possession of the villas. I'd called him into the main house, gearing up to do my best mime impression of Donald Trump "you're fired." Hector arrived a few minutes later, accompanied by the most beautiful woman I'd ever seen. The rest is history and there's no way in hell I'm gonna fire my father-in-law.

"Did they see you?" I still want to know how Blondie found out Maria's a blood.

"No." She fills the glasses and hands one to me.

"Huh." I take a hefty swallow of a perfect mojito, better than the ones I make. "They'd heard about you."

"I also had a visitor today." She hesitates briefly. "Luis."

I growl. I can't help it.

Luis is Maria's sort-of-kind-of ex, in that she dated him a few times before I moved here, and he wouldn't take no for an answer when she broke it off. Even though it's been three years since Maria and I got married, he still comes sniffing around now and again. Pretty much the poster child for Sting's song Every Breath You Take. He does freelance maintenance and gardening for some of the local vacation rentals, including Villa de Cielo.

"He must have told them about you."

Maria doesn't disagree. "He says these vampiros want to rent Casa de Amigos. That they will pay lots of money. And that maybe I should talk to you about it."

Why am I not surprised? Maybe because Luis has a history of buddying up with assholes. Maria doesn't want to believe this and I've never been able to prove it, but if he's not hooked into the poaching scene, then Uwe Boll is actually a cinematic genius and we were all wrong about House of the Dead.

She pours more mojito into my nearly empty glass and I notice a ring of bruises around her forearm. The type of bruises left by fingers.

"Did that asswipe hurt you?"

Maria shakes her head. "It didn't hurt. And Father made him leave after that."

Okay, it's not like Maria couldn't mop the floor with him if she wanted, but she refuses to give into anger for fear of it turning into bloodlust. As a result Luis has no idea what kind of raw power he's messing with, so he pushes the envelope.

"Before he left, though, he said they have more friends arriving soon, including someone very *importante*."

I take another slug of mojito. This isn't good. Why would a bunch of bloods, especially someone very *importante*, want to hole up in Dominical, where their kind is barely tolerated? If the locals turned hostile, the *Fuerza Publica*—the local police—are gonna look the other way, and there's no standing military force to step in if things go to shit on either side.

"Think you can ask around, see if the local bloods know anything?"

Maria nods, albeit reluctantly. I don't blame her. The small population of local bloods tend to stick together, but Maria stays on the periphery, not wanting to be seen as taking sides against bloods or beats. The locals on both sides already looked on her with suspicion, what with her marrying a rich American. There's always resentment when someone in a small community gets a windfall, even when the recipient is as generous as Maria.

We've kept Maria's condition fairly quiet, and she's never fed on a local or anyone who didn't deserve it. I mean, for instance… no one had missed the poachers. They were bad news, and probably responsible for the death of a young college student activist for endangered species. His body had been found washed up on a nearby beach, tangled in the roots of a mangrove, a bullet wound in his forehead. The poachers' bodies had been found in the same cluster of mangroves west of Puente Cascada. At least, what was left of them after the crocodiles had finished snacking.

So like Maria to make sure her leftovers don't go to waste.

But if these newcomers start treating the ticos like the main course at their own Hometown Buffet, who's to say people won't forget?

Oh well, I can't figure anything out tonight. The stress and the rum in the mojitos have taken their toll and I'm ready to sleep. Maria takes me by the hand and leads me to our bedroom where eventually, we sleep.

Hey, I'm tired, but not dead.

———•———

When I arrive at the Buccaneer the next afternoon, there's a white car with POLICIA on the side in big blue letters, a grim-faced police officer leaning against the driver's side door. I recognize him. Miguel Sanchez, a local boy and a decent cop. He's had more than one drink at the Buc-caneer over the last two years, but there's no trace of his usual friendly—and inebriated—smile.

I raise my hand in greeting. "*Hola*, Miguel. We don't open for another hour," I say, even though my gut tells me he's not there for a drink.

Sure enough…

"I'm not here for a drink." I hear a hint of regret in his voice. "We got a call from Carmen Garza." Carmen is Ana's mother. "Ana didn't come home last night. You seen her?" His English is good. If I remember cor-rectly, Miguel spent a few years in the States doing the kind of things that normally has a person in the back seat of a police car. "What time did she leave work?"

I get that gut-punched sensation again. "She didn't show up for work last night."

Miguel's eyes narrow. "Carmen said she left for work at three yester-day. Same time she always does."

"She never got here."

I flash back on the red shoe I found. Miguel is sharp. He sees some-thing in my expression and says, "*Hablame*, Gary."

Talk to me.

I consider my options. Miguel has always been a straight shooter with me, and never been anything less than courteous to Maria, ac-cepting her for who and what she is now. Ana's life is on the line. I need to trust him.

We walk into the patio area and I unlock the kitchen, where I retrieve the shoe from my office and pull a couple of Silver Reserves from the fridge unit. Going back out to the patio, I deposit the shoe on the bar. "Found this outside when I was taking out the trash last night."

I open the beers and plonk one of them in front of Miguel. He looks at the shoe, takes a quaff of beer, and says, "What do you think?"

"I think someone is making a point. Trying to intimidate me."

"Why?"

I take my own pull of beer, but before I can reply the black Escalade careens into the parking lot. I turn to Miguel. "You might want to make yourself inconspicuous about now."

Miguel gives a small nod, picks up his beer, and slips into the kitchen.

The Escalade's doors open to disgorge its passengers. There are four more of them. One female and three males. All Americans, all apparently the same vampire genus as Blondie and her original two backup vamps. At least the other female dresses appropriately for the climate, looking all innocent waif in a gauze sundress and flat sandals. She looks at me with big red-tinged green eyes as they saunter in, smiling enough to expose her sharp canines. I can see the carnal glint in her eyes, though. Madonna and whore all in one cutesy bloodsucking package.

"Have you thought about our offer?" Blondie asks.

"Yup. Still no."

"Hmm. Too bad." She turns back, as if something has just occurred to her. "By the way," she adds, "you seem to be short a waitress."

I lean in close. "You hurt Ana, you'll regret it. Now get the hell out of my bar."

Blondie pouts. "And here I was looking forward to another skinny margarita. Oh well…" She stands and signals to the others. "Just remember… we tried to play nicely."

"Not very friendly, is he?" Waif says in a thick-as-molasses drawl.

Blondie smiles at me and gives a little wave. "We'll be seeing you."

Miguel comes back out to the bar. "You gonna tell me what this is about?"

I hesitate, only because I'm aware if I tell the truth, or at least the truth as I see it, I could be putting his life in danger if he goes poking into things.

On the other hand, ignorance can be just as dangerous as knowledge, so I tell Miguel what I know so far, including Luis's involvement and the fact that some *muy importante* blood is supposed to show up.

"Dominical is a strange place for *vampiros* to go on a holiday," Miguel observes.

"I think these bloods are looking for more than a vacation spot."

Miguel looks thoughtful. "You think maybe they're *terroristas*?"

I think about it for a minute. It makes a certain amount of sense. Costa Rica has no standing military, which means no big guns. We're far away from any major city, so any reprisals from the government would be slow in coming. And they'd probably have no trouble recruiting bloods from surrounding areas, especially those who've been pushed out of their homes by the locals.

I share my thoughts with Miguel. We both agree that terrorists or just assholes, this crew is bad news and something is going to have to be done about them. He finishes his beer and digs out his car keys. Before he leaves, he says, "You should know Carmen is saying some shit about Maria."

I grimace. Carmen wasn't a fan of Maria before she caught the virus because Carmen is the sort of person who sees someone else's good fortune as a personal slight. She knows about Maria's condition, but the fact that I've given her daughter a good job, and that Ana and Maria are friends, helps mitigate the situation. Now it sounds like all bets are off.

I sigh. "I'll call her tomorrow and see what I can do."

———◆———

When I get in my car to drive home, the smell hits me first, a sickly sweet stench of decay. The red shoe's mate is sitting on the passenger seat. Only this one isn't empty. A cheap beaded anklet circles what's left of the slender ankle still attached to the foot inside, the flesh at the top ragged as if cut with a serrated blade or ripped at by sharp teeth. Insects buzz around it.

Son of a bitch.

It's fresh, which means this happened shortly after they left the bar. I'd misjudged them, so concerned with protecting Maria that I'd underestimated just how real the threat was underneath the leather dusters and posing.

The first shoe had been the warning shot across the bow.

Now?

War had been declared.

But maybe, just maybe Ana is still alive.

My cell rings. It's Miguel. My heart sinks.

"They found Ana."

"Where?"

"Rio Cascada. Below the bridge."

I shut my eyes for a minute. Any hopes of Ana still being alive vanish. Much like the Rio Tarcoles a few hours north, Rio Cascada has a substantial population of saltwater crocodiles. But while Tarcoles is a heavily trafficked tourist attraction, Rio Cascada is off the main roads and people know to stay away or be careful.

I tell him about the shoe. He says not to touch it and he'll meet me at the bar.

"Can you come to the house instead?" I ask.

He agrees. "A good idea. With the crazy shit Carmen is saying, it's better for Maria not to be alone."

As soon as we disconnect, I call Hector and ask him to stay with Maria until I get home. Then I drive home as fast as possible to find Maria on the couch, red-eyed and grief-stricken. She's heard the news about Ana.

My question is, who will they go after next?

I find out the answer to my question the next morning when Liza calls in hysterics. Her three-year-old daughter is missing; the bedroom window is wide open and smudges of dirt and blood mark the sheets.

It's not hard to break into a house around here. Most of them are practically open air anyway, with netting to keep out the mosquitos and other pests, but no real locks. Not a lot to steal. So whoever snatched Esme basically walked up to the bedroom window, climbed in, grabbed the kid, and vamoosed. I calm her down as best I can and call Miguel.

My waitress and now my cook. The message is clear.

"We have to give them what they want." Maria looks at me pleadingly. She's a big softie when it comes to kids and animals.

If I gave into these creeps, I'd be enabling what could to be a terrorist cell or, best-case scenario, a group of sociopathic bloods that want to play their own version of The Most Dangerous Game. If I didn't, they'd continue to pick off my employees and friends, and do their best to implicate Maria.

Either way, me and mine lose.

So… what to do?

I'm a former film producer, not a mercenary. If this were one of my films, I'd be stripping out of my civvies, oiling up, and strapping on a shit-load of weaponry—all in a montage of close-up, slow-motion shots, of course—followed by a lot of improbable carnage, lens flares, and explosions, all backed by overly dramatic music to artificially up the tension.

In reality, however, while I can intimidate the hell out of most people in the industry and am handy with firearms, I've got no Van Helsing mad-ninja vampire-killing skills. All I have is my willingness to do anything to protect what is mine... and one hell of an imagination.

There's a little-known real-life incident that happened during WWII on a place called Ramree Island. A platoon of Japanese soldiers tried to hike through the swamps and join up with another platoon rather than face the invading Allied forces. They should have chosen surrender because most of the men who went in to the swamps didn't come out. Ramree was a nesting ground for saltwater crocodiles, hundreds of them, and they'd fed well that night. The story always reminded me of Quint's infamous monologue in Jaws, about the sinking of the Indianapolis. The stuff nightmares are made of and, boy, I wanted to make a movie based on the story. I'd never managed to get the pitch off the ground. Now, however, it's given me an idea. Of course, I'm banking on the fact these assholes have no idea what a *patasola* is. Hell, they hadn't heard of *ekimmus* and it seemed like a blood has to be *this* Anglo-Saxon to be a member of their little club.

I convey my idea to Maria as quickly as possible. I know she's not going to like it, but I know my wife. Hurt her, and she'll turn the other cheek. Hurt anyone or anything she cares about? The rules have just been changed. She's not bloodthirsty by nature, but if ever there was a Mama Lion in human form, it's Maria. And these bloods have just declared open season on her family.

"Can you do it?"

She nods. "I... I think so."

I take her hands. "*Will* you do it?"

Her expression shifts to one of determination and cold vengeance. "*Si.*"

———◆———

I call Miguel and get his voicemail. I leave a message asking him to meet me at the Buccaneer before it opens, and I'll fill him in on everything then. Hector promises to stay with Maria until I get home, and I head off to my bar. Four o'clock rolls around and no Miguel. I turn away a few of my regulars, explaining that the plumbing is out. They grumble, but not too loudly, and head off to one of the other local watering holes.

Then I wait to hear from Blondie and crew. Sure enough, the Escalade pulls up around five. The doors open and disgorge Blondie, Jared, and Waif Gal.

"Where's the girl?" I ask, waiving any formalities.

"She's safe, for the time being. Aren't you going to offer us drinks?"

I point to the "closed" sign.

"No can do."

"A pity."

"How about you get to the point?" I glance pointedly at my watch.

"It's simple," Blondie says. "You bring us the keys and a signed and legal rental agreement for Casa de Amigos and you'll get what you want. If not, you'll have more trash to take out… and we'll make sure your wife gets plenty of attention from the local authorities. Too bad your friend Miguel won't be one of them."

I'm quiet, trying to hide the bouquet of emotions coursing through me as I take in her meaning. I'd be lying if I said fear wasn't one of them. But mostly what I feel is anger. Pure homicidal rage that these fuckers have invaded my world and hurt innocent people to get what they want.

Aztec had called it right from the start.

It takes me a few minutes, but I get myself under control. "Where do you want to do the exchange?"

Blondie smiles widely. "Oh, you choose."

"Fine," I say. "Puento Cascada."

Waif Girl giggles. "Oh, he means that lovely scenic bridge where they keep finding the bodies in the mangroves."

Blondie nods. "Two hours."

I hold still when she walks over to me and runs a finger down my jaw. "If you're lucky, we'll keep you around to make our drinks."

The others laugh. I just stare up at her expressionless, not bothering with any of the dozens of pithy one-liners that spring to mind. I was never that good at writing dialogue anyway, and I'm too busy concentrating on hiding my elation that they agreed to my location.

— • —

When I get home, the iron gates to my home are standing open. The place has been torn apart just enough to let me know it could have been worse—a leather couch cushion ripped in half, ceramic dishes shattered on the tiled floor. Hector is sprawled out on the living room floor, sporting a black eye and a split lip, blood trickling down his chin. He's just coming to as I kneel next to him and help him sit up.

"Where's Maria?" I ask.

"That bastard Luis," he snarls back. "What are you going to do to bring my daughter back alive?"

"I knew it," I say. I'm not talking about Maria's kidnapping. I'm talking about Hector's sudden use of English.

The phone rings before I can call him on it. I pick up the receiver.

"Maria's with me," he says without preamble. "Bring the keys and the agreement."

"This your idea, Luis?" I ask in deceptively mild tones even as the rage starts building inside.

He gives an ugly laugh. "I told them you wouldn't care about some little tica brat so they'd better have something you did care about."

"Well, okay then," I say. "I'd say you've just made a really bad mistake, Luis, but you've already made so many it would be redundant."

I hang up as Luis tries to figure out how badly I've just insulted him.

— • —

The clouds open up as I drive down the mountain, another one of those sudden downpours that sends water sluicing over my windshield and turns the road into a mini-river. Once I hit the highway, I turn the lights and wipers on high, slowing down and pissing off drivers behind me so I can find the shitty little road leading to Puente Cascada.

The bridge in question is right below a small waterfall that dumps into a deep pool, then continues toward the sea, widening into the estuary, clear trickling water giving way to still brown shallows, the mud thick on the banks and mangroves stretching their roots along the sides. The trees and foliage are thick, making it a great place for all sorts of illegal activities if a person doesn't mind the possibility of getting attacked by a croc.

I use a Maglite to find the best footing as I walk along the path, the light picking up the reflection of reptilian eyes half-submerged in the water. A basilisk lizard dashes across the trail, and the sounds of the jungle rise around me. Sweat drips down my forehead and back as the humidity and heat seem to build up around me the closer I get to Puente Cascada. Fat raindrops start plopping down around and on top of me, and my foot slips in mud. I feel like the stupid hero in one of my lower budget flicks, the guy you want to root for, but he's just so stupid that you really can't.

By the time I reach the bridge, the rainfall tapers off to a light but steady drizzle. Luis stands on the other side, one arm wrapped around the waist of my wife, the barrel of a pistol pressed against her right temple. He grins at me. I ignore him, looking straight into Maria's eyes, which glow an almost phosphorescent green in the rapidly fading light.

I shine my light into the still brown waters and see maybe one pair of reptilian eyes reflected back at me. I also see the gnawed-on remains of a body in a now-shredded *policía* uniform. Miguel.

The bloods are lined up along the length of the bridge. I hear a soft whimper and look over at Jared, who holds a burlap bag with something wiggling inside. Esme, Liza's daughter. Blondie stands dead center on the bridge as if posing for a photo shoot. Guess she's ready for her close-up. My Maglite beam catches the reflection of five pairs of red eyes lining the bridge, looking like a photo in dire need of the remove redeye tool in Photoshop.

"Did you bring the keys and the agreement?" She's completely dropped the vamp tramp routine and is all business.

I take a plastic bag out of my jacket pocket. Inside is the rental agreement. I put my hand in one pocket, jingling the keys inside without removing them. Blondie motions to the older male. He obeys with a sneer, his black duster swirling out around him as he stalks toward me, wooden slats shaking beneath his heavy footsteps. I pull out my Desert

Eagle and toss the plastic bag on the wooden slats of the bridge. He picks it up before the rain washes it off the side.

"Here ya go."

"Keys."

I shake my head. "Let the kid and Maria go first."

Blondie laughs, the sound as jarring as breaking glass. "You just don't get it, Mr. Logan. This isn't a film studio. You're not in charge here. I call the shots. *We* call the shots from now on. And if you want to stay alive, you'll remember that and act accordingly."

"You mean like old Renfield here?" I gesture at Luis. Blondie looks blank.

"Jesus." I shake my head in disgust. "You really don't know a damn thing, do you? This is just one big ego trip to you, isn't it?"

"Give me the keys," she snarls, all wounded ego.

I fling the keys toward Blondie with as much force as I can muster. They hit her square in the chest and fall to the wooden slats below. "Catch."

Narrowing her eyes, Blondie gestures toward the burlap bag. "Jared."

Before I can blink, Jared tosses it over the railing into the murky water below. I hear the kid's muffled shriek of fear as the bag hits the water. Movement immediately boils around her as the bag sinks into water and mud.

Luis starts laughing. "Eh, guess the crocs will get a meal tonight."

I look over at Maria, who is staring at Luis with sorrow and anger combined. With no warning, she seizes the hand holding the gun and rips a chunk out of Luis's arm with four very sharp reptilian fangs before shoving him aside with great force. He shrieks in pain, staring at Maria in shock. Payback time.

Maria's eyes glow and suddenly the jungle goes quiet, the chirping, humming, howling, and rustling cut off as if someone turned the volume to zero. Power builds in the air like electricity.

Then Maria lifts her arms to the sky and opens her mouth. The sound that emerges is almost too high for human ears to detect. The jungle comes alive with sound and movement, startling the bloods. I use the moment to fire two shots into the vampire nearest me, my old pal the cat hater. He collapses onto the wooden slats, one arm dangling between railings off the bridge.

Then hell really breaks loose. All around me, the mud and water boils and explodes into a frenzy of movement as crocodiles start swarming toward the bridge, swimming and slithering through the thick, pungent-smelling ooze. The bloods on the bridge are frozen in place for a moment, too shocked at what they're seeing to react. Luis screams and skitters away from the river's edge, holding his mangled wrist.

Before anyone can stop me, I leap into the water, all the while praying to every deity I don't believe in as I wade toward the bag, feet sticking in the mud on the river bottom as I do my best to avoid the crocodiles. They're not trying to attack me, but they're not exactly stepping politely out of my way. I avoid being trampled and reach the bag just as it sinks beneath the surface, hauling it out with one hand and dragging it to shore. I open the bag to find Esme, sodden and in shock, but otherwise unharmed. I hold her close to me as things play out.

The crocs aren't the only residents of the jungle joining the party. Capuchins and howler monkeys swarm out of the trees toward the bloods. Hell, even the sloths have their lazy asses in gear. They show no fear of the crocs, which in turn ignore them for more cold-blooded prey. Spiders, geckos, basilisk lizards swarm toward the bloods, the basilisk bobbing their heads but ignoring the spiders and other insects that would be their normal prey. The moving carpet of bugs surges with single-minded focus toward the bridge and the bloods. The expressions on Blondie and crew's faces are kind of priceless.

"It's not nice to fool with Mother Nature," I whisper to no one in particular.

Waif Girl is the first to move, sprinting off the bridge with a cat-like agility... only to be brought down a few yards later by a jaguar, its canines puncturing her skull with ease. Damn. I didn't realize we had any jaguars in the area. It had to be close to answer Maria's call so quickly.

Jared looks panicked and sprints toward the side of the bridge where his fallen compatriot lies. A squadron of toucans, parrots, and owls soar down to intercept him with beaks and talons scoring his flesh. He strikes out with his fists, knocking a few of the birds senseless to the ground. But there's no way for him to fight off all of them, and they're taking pieces of flesh out of his face, hands, and arms as he stumbles against the bridge railing. An especially vicious pair of parrots slashes at his eyes, bats burrowing into his hair and coat collar, claws raking his neck. The railing, worn after several years of weathering, gives way, and Jared topples into the estuary, where he's quickly drawn and quartered by opportunistic crocs.

The vamps on the river's edge don't stand a chance as the crocodiles attack. Crocs can move fast, hauling croc ass faster than you'd expect. Teeth sink into flesh as the crocs fight with one another to drag the bloods into the river, where they perform their death rolls. The sound of screams blends with the primordial bellows of the crocs.

One enterprising croc grasps the vamp I'd shot by his dangling arm, doing its best to pull him through the railing into the river. The arm separates from the shoulder with a tearing noise.

A soft whirring sound fills the air, filling in the auditory gaps between the howls, hoots, grunts, and bellows of the jungle's residents and screams of their prey. The clouds part and the full moon illuminates the clearing. Blue Morpheus butterflies swarm the bridge, along with moths, mosquitoes, dragonflies, and other winged insects. They whirl around Blondie, who at first bats at them with her hands as if they're just an annoyance... until they coat her head, covering eyes, ears, mouth, and nasal passages.

Vampire or not, she still needs to breathe, and that's not happening here. She rips at the insects coating her, her screams muffled then replaced by choking sounds as colorful butterflies crawl inside her mouth and down her throat. More flutter down to take their place. Soon her entire body is coated with layers upon layers of wings, as she staggers off the far side of the bridge and stumbles to her knees before falling face down in the mud. One of the smaller crocodiles slithers toward her body, waiting until the butterflies have flown away before grasping one of her legs in its jaws and dragging her back into the river for dinner.

I think she's dead when it starts chewing on her. But I don't really care one way or the other.

Luis lies on the other side of the river, holding his injured wrist and staring with bug-eyed terror at Maria as butterflies, birds, owls, frogs, lizards, monkeys, crocodiles, and jungle cats fly, flitter, slither, and swarm around her. She's like some sort of vampire Snow White, but her songbirds are lethal instead of cute. She's a primal force of nature, sexy and powerful as hell.

"*Madre de dios.*" Hector's voice comes from the path. I look over to see him staring at his daughter in awe. He's accompanied by many other familiar faces. Ticos who work in the local stores and live in the small towns around us. I recognize Ana's mother Carmen, Liza, and Diego among them. All of them hold some sort of weapon, anything from crowbars to switchblades, to makeshift spears and even a few handguns. My heart sinks. Some of these people are related to Maria as well, but their expressions are pitiless as they stare down at us from the path.

Maria stares back at them impassively, her expression as serene as ever.

"It's her fault!'" Luis mewls in Spanish, holding his injured wrist aloft like a banner. "She did this! She made me do these things!"

They all look at him, then look at Maria.

I can see it in their faces as judgment is passed.

They file down the path slowly, one by one. The crocs ignore them, content with their current meals. Carmen, Ana's mother, is the first in line. She walks up to Maria, genuflects and makes the sign of the cross. Maria takes Carmen by one hand and lifts her to her feet, embracing her with all the compassion and love in her heart. Meanwhile, Liza is sobbing with hysterical joy as she lifts Esme in her arms.

Maria is one of them. She's there to protect them. And I may be an expat from Los Angeles, but I'm in it for the long haul too.

Luis shrieks as a pair of crocs converge on him, taking him in two different directions at once. I smile. If and when Blondie's friends arrive tomorrow, they'll still have a welcoming committee. Just not the one they expect.

La Pura Vida. The good life.

And we're going to keep it that way.

WET WORKS PART 3

By Jonathan Maberry

Global Acquisitions LLC
Pittsburgh, Pennsylvania
Day 17 of the Red Storm

Captain Joe Ledger held up a finger for silence then leaned to press his ear to the door. Swann tried to read his expression and saw concern, anger, and something else. Humor? No, that had to be wrong. It was a look he'd seen before on this man's face. A poet might call it battle joy, or something like that. It wasn't a sane look. Swann could imagine the Viking *berserkers* having that look, and maybe the Spartans on that last morning in the Hot Gates.

"What do you hear?" asked Swann.

Ledger closed his eyes for a moment. "I hear an idiot asking questions when he should be keeping his goddamn mouth shut."

"Oh. Sorry."

"Other than that… it's quiet." Ledger straightened. "Not crazy about it being that quiet."

"Isn't that a good thing?"

"No."

"Why not?" insisted Swann. "Maybe they went away."

"Sure," said Ledger, "and maybe bright blue pigs will fly out of my ass and sing a Travis Tritt song."

Ledger slowly folded his rapid-release combat knife and slid it into the spring-loaded holster clipped to the inside of his right front pants pocket. The bodies were like islands in a sea of red. Then he tapped a small mechanical bud in his left ear.

"Cowboy to Bug," he said and stood with his head cocked in an attitude of listening. "Cowboy to Bug. Come on, man, don't leave me hanging out here in the wind."

After a long moment Ledger sighed and then cursed under his breath.

"What is it?" asked Swann. "Are we going to be okay?"

"Okay? Seriously, Doc? We are way up shit creek," he said. "Like miles up. We're resource-poor and there are more of those bastards out there. Red Empire thugs and worse."

"Worse? What could be worse?"

"You don't want to know."

"I think I do, actually," insisted Swann. "Ever since you came into this thing you've been treating me like an outsider. I hate to break it to you, friend, but I've been in this since the beginning."

"Oh, don't get your panties in a bunch, Doc," said Ledger. "I know how long you've been doing this dance. Since the jump. Since Michael Fayne. Must have been fun."

"Which means I have a right to know everything."

Ledger began moving from body to body, patting them down, searching their pockets. "The truth is, I've mostly been on the fringes of this V-War bullshit. Except for that time in Farmville, Virginia, with that bunch of jackasses trying to turn *nelapsi* vampires into super soldiers. That was a cluster fuck of epic proportions. Got most of that V-8 team chopped to sushi. But aside from that I've been what you might call 'otherwise engaged.'"

"Doing what, for God's sake? Polishing your bullets?"

"Cute, but no." Ledger duck-walked over to another corpse and repeated the search. "It may surprise you but when people started popping fangs and everyone lost their damn mind, it did not mean that all other forms of terrorism dried up and blew away. You think ISIL, al-Qaeda, the Taliban, and all those other ass-pirates decided to come to their senses and not try to burn down the whole world? Nope. Would have been nice. Maybe I'd have had the chance to go catch a movie or get a massage. But that's not the way the world works. There are other things going bump in the night."

"Like what?" demanded Swann. He pointed to the nearest corpse. "These men aren't militant religious extremists. They're vampires."

"Sure," said Ledger as he took a knife from a concealed sheath on one of the corpses, "but they're also middle men. They were working as brokers for a group of ISIL dickheads in Syria."

"Middle men? For what?"

"Selling technology. Look, very, very short version of a history lesson. When the Cold War ended and all those countries broke off from Russia there was a lot of tech lying around. Everything from computer hard drives to stockpiles of weapons. Russia was too broke at the time to do anything about it, so a lot of stuff found its way onto the black market. There's a non-Muslim Turk named Ohan who's gotten very rich selling this shit to anyone with a bank routing number and a grudge. He acquired a bunch of nasty Soviet stuff from Kazakhstan and has been selling it to fucktards in ISIL and Boko Haram. Some of the stuff he's selling is very, very nasty."

"What? Like nuclear weapons?"

"Like bioweapons," said Ledger. "Stuff that would kill more people in a day than have died in every battle since the V-Wars began. I'm talking designer pathogens and the research notes that would allow any good team of corrupt asshole scientists to tweak it even further. You want to kill only black male children? Done. Want to kill Ashkenazi Jews? Easy as pie. You want to kill left-handed redheads with big tits? Sure. Ever since the human genome was mapped it's upped the game for total fucking madmen to create designer bioweapons."

"That's impossible…"

"Grow up. This is the 21st century, professor, we left the 'fiction' out of science fiction a long time ago," said Ledger. "We have self-drive cars, combat robots, nanotech, holoportation conference calls, the God particles, reusable rocket ships, and—Oh! Cool." He removed a small automatic in an ankle holster on a dead man's leg. He ejected and inspected the magazine, checked the action, and slapped the magazine back into place. "Twelve shots and only one mag. Not a lot but better than waving our dicks at them."

"What does all that have to do with the Red Empire?"

Ledger rose and crossed to the door again and listened. "Still quiet." He leaned his back against it and spoke, his voice low and quiet. "One of the things about global politics and terrorism is that different investigative agencies can be working on two ends of the same case and not know it. That's what happened here. I tracked a shipment of weaponized bacteria from Kazakhstan to Syria and then here to the States. The courier was definitely on Ohan's payroll and was supposed to make a handoff to a black market technologies broker here. Guy named Sprull."

Swann frowned. "Wait... *Jonas* Sprull?"

"Yup."

"He's a vampire."

"I know that now. Didn't know it this morning. Wish I did. I also wish I knew who Sprull was planning on selling the stuff to. Had I known that I'd have brought a full team with me and done that whole 'scorched earth' thing. Would have made me a lot happier to have a whole team of first-chair shooters instead of me running a solo gig."

"Wait," said Swann, "you were going to try and take down Jonas Sprull alone? He always has people with him."

Ledger smiled. It was a ghastly sight because his face was spattered with other men's blood. He nodded to the corpses. "*Those* people? Yeah, we've met."

"They were vampires."

"So I found out."

"But..."

"This isn't the movies, Doc. I don't need stakes and crosses. I've found that a nine-millimeter bullet in the brainpan works quite well. So does a cut windpipe. After that it's rinse and repeat. No, don't look at me like that. You're the one who went on the news and told everyone that vampires didn't have any supernatural powers, right? They're meat and muscle, blood and breath just like us ordinary mortals. That means they can die. Fuck, Doc, I've met some really scary and deeply weird stuff in my job and I can tell you without fear of contradiction that everything and everybody can die."

Swann pointed to the door. "Then why are you afraid of what's out there?"

"Because, some things in this world are a lot harder to kill."

"Like what? What's out there that you're so afraid of?"

Ledger wasn't smiling anymore. "They call themselves the Red Knights. The species is *upierczy*. If there's an apex predator among the collective vampire community, then they have my vote."

"You're saying they're as formidable as the *nelapsi*?"

"No," said Ledger. "I'm saying the *upierczy* are ten times more dangerous.

Swann felt the blood drain from his face. "God. But... but... I thought..."

"Listen to me, Doc, we met some assholes down in Virginia who called themselves Red Knights, but that wasn't what they were. They took that name the way Xerxes' personal guard took the name 'Immortals.' The label carries with it a certain degree of raw fear. Anyone who knows that name gets a gut punch reaction. And going to war carrying a name like that makes a soldier feel like they're something more than muscle and bone. Like a sports team. The Spartans, the Eagles, the Tigers, the Warriors. You get the picture? We fought *nelapsi* who were using the Red Knight name in order to borrow power from the real Knights."

"But... who *are* the Red Knights? The real ones, I mean?"

"*Le Rouge Chevaliers*," said Ledger, "are members of a brotherhood of assassins that emerged during the later Crusades. Over the centuries they've been tied to acts of murder, sabotage, and destruction that by today's standards would be classified as terrorism. They were created and trained by a secret cabal within the Catholic Church called the Red Order as part of a dirty little deal with a splinter group within the armies of Islam, called the *Tariqa*. The Tariqa had their own team of killers called the *Hashashin*—"

"The Hashashin, sure," said Swann, "they were expert killers, and it's where the word 'assassin' comes from, but they weren't vampires."

"No. They were like ninjas, I guess. Real kickass motherfuckers, too. There was nothing comparable within the Crusaders, so the Red Order created its own elite special ops team, you might say. They sent monks out to find vampires."

"But..."

"And they found them. This was before those people with active V-genes were hunted down by the Inquisition and whoever else was rocking the Van Helsing shtick. The *upierczy* were collected, taken out of normal circulation. They were given protection while they trained, and for centuries they served as unofficial, off-the-radar hit men for the Church. Yeah, I know, somewhere Dan Brown is getting a wicked stiffy, but let's face it, Doc, some conspiracies are a lot more than theories."

"So, you're saying the *church* is behind all of this? The bombings, the killings…?"

"No. That part of it's past tense. The Red Knights broke off from the Order a few years ago. I, ah, may have had something to do with that. It's need to know, and you don't. Point is, the Red Knights are real, they're active, they're scary as fuck, and they are hunting us."

"But you just killed six vampires…"

"Sure, so yay me. You're not listening to what I'm saying. The real Red Knights are much more powerful, much better trained, much more *evolved* than any vampire you've ever met. They are to the *nelapsi* what SEAL Team Six is to the Cub Scouts. That, sadly, is not a joke. People who scare me are scared of them." Ledger looked at the closed door. "That's what's coming for us, Dr. Swann. I can handle one, maybe two. But from what I saw on the way down here I think there's a whole strike team of them. A dozen at least. That's why we are in deep, deep shit."

"Oh god…"

"What I don't get," said Ledger, "is why they're here. What's their plan? Do the vampires of their new Red Empire want to create a pathogen to wipe out humans? That wouldn't make sense. They're blood drinkers, right? That means we're all juice boxes to them. Killing us all wouldn't be a smart move and they are not dumb."

"It's because of Sprull," said Swann. "They're not here for the bioweapons."

"Bullshit. This place is a dummy corporation that Sprull uses as his little hidey-hole. This is his showroom for the nasty shit he pedals to buyers from every fringe group with a grudge and a checkbook. Why else would the Knights be here?"

"For the same reason I'm here," said Swann.

"Which is? Talk quick, Doc, because I'm starting to hear noises out there that I do not like."

"Jonas Sprull isn't just a vampire," said Swann, "and he isn't just a black market technology broker."

"Then what is he?"

"Sprull is a true believer. His entire operation has been a front for a radical group within the militant vampire community. He's the fundraiser and he's an enabler. He puts the weapons in their hands and his connections with black marketers selling technology is what has been giving them the edge. He's a fanatic."

Ledger frowned. "A believer in what?"

There was a sound outside. Footsteps. Many of them. Then something hit the metal door hard enough to shake it in its frame. Ledger spun and backed away, bringing the gun up into a two-handed grip, barrel pointed at the door. For all of the big man's bravado he was sweating badly.

"Jonas Sprull is a key officer in the Red Empire," said Swann. "I used to think the Empire was a myth, but sources I trust tell me it's real."

"Pretty sure I know who that source is," said Ledger. "People I know have been checking into the Crimson Queen for a while now. She's scary but she seems to have her head screwed on straight. Been neutral but not passive, if my intel is right."

"That's a good way to put it."

"If she says this Red Empire thing is real, then I guess I have to accept that, much as I really don't want to. World has enough problems."

"It's real and it's powerful and they will do absolutely anything to bring him back."

"Him? Him who?"

"Why... Michael Fayne, of course."

"Fayne? Last I heard he was dead."

"The Red Empire wants to resurrect him."

"Bullshit."

"No. They think he's not really dead. They think he went into some kind of deep hibernation and they want to wake him up."

"*Why*, for Christ's sake?"

There was another powerful blow on the door. And another. Cracks began snaking out on the walls around the frame.

"Because," said Swann, "they think he's the chosen one. The Messiah. They believe that if they can bring him back from death, so he can lead them all in a holy war to conquer the entire planet."

WEİRD BLOOD

By Jade Shames

—1—

I t was after a long night. I had stepped in a puddle and my shoes were soggy. Another night with friends at the bar—trying to mingle. Trying not to think about Grace, even though I was wearing a shirt she had bought for me.

I dragged myself down Bedford Avenue fighting to forget every dumb little joke I made. Every time I boasted about when I'd worked for Christian Slater's dog, or made a farting sound with my lips whenever there was an awkward moment in the conversation.

Full disclosure: I'm the guy a lot of people dislike. The asshole at the bar telling your girlfriend she has viridian flecks in her eyes. I read in a book that you can appear ten times smarter just by using obscure colors. For instance, don't say, "I love your nail color—it's orange." Say "atomic tangerine." Say "what an interesting shade—like a bourbon brown." Don't qualify whether you like it or not. Just say "interesting." I'm a freelance graphic designer and when I can't find work, which is often, I mooch off friends or donate plasma or other bodily fluids. I'm not really a "proud guy."

But there are two things you should know about me:

People may think I'm a douchebag, but I *know* I'm a douchebag. I have to live with it every day. I have to go to bed and wake up thinking, "What kind of douchebag shit am I gonna say today?" It's not easy.

The moment I have any hope that my interaction with someone might be more than just social ephemera, I turn into a complete wreck.

I'm like the hulk if Bruce Banner were played by Ryan Reynolds and the hulk were played by Woody Allen.

Case in point: tonight. I really liked this girl named Jennifer, and it felt like she could see right through to my inner Woody. She had a really nice ear-to-ear smile and this shiny, hennaed-black hair that curled around her slightly too-large cheeks. She laughed at nearly the exact same jokes I did. It was a relief because Grace hated my sense of humor.

I once joked, admittedly too soon, that the one good thing about the attacks on New York was that the rent was finally manageable. Grace had been a survivor of the attacks and she didn't speak to me for hours—despite that fact that I was kinda right. I moved to Brooklyn during what the hipsters call *The Renaissance*. All the money went into rebuilding, and the police department was broke. So the few cops who bothered to come to our neighborhoods didn't care that we were having parties in partially dilapidated apartment buildings.

That's where I was—in an unlicensed bar called Geronimo. The ceiling was made of found shards of colored glass—each a different size and shape, and they all fit together to form an angular dome. The heavy streetlamp light filtered through the glass ceiling and dyed everyone in tawny and rose. I sipped an old fashioned and talked to Jennifer.

At one point, she asked me if I'd come outside with her for a smoke. I agreed even though I didn't smoke. Then, as we stood together outside the bar and watched the first snowfall of the season, I noticed she wasn't smoking either.

Then we went back inside and I completely blew it by ordering two more shots for everyone—all on me. I was telling some anecdote and I slipped and knocked over a stranger's beer. I wasn't even that drunk, but I really looked it. The stranger happened to be a bumpy-faced, green-skinned blood, and the room got tense. My friend James slapped my shoulder and told me I had a few too many. His girlfriend, Aubrey, told me I should take a cab home. I stepped into the bathroom to pee, and when I came out I saw Jennifer talking to some other guy.

Drunk... creep... liar...

Halfway home, I threw up my last drink into someone's garden.

...shithead... loser.

And just when I couldn't take any more torment, I reached for the keys and realized that I hadn't brought them. They were probably still on my dresser.

I felt tears coming. And then there was a voice.

"Something wrong?" she asked. I turned and saw a beautiful woman at the foot of my front steps. She wore a long black coat. Her hair was wild and thick. Her body was almost cartoonishly feminine, but her race was unidentifiable. It was as if she was a blend of all races. The result was a kind of exoticism you would see in a high-fashion magazine from another planet.

At first I didn't even say words; I just released air from my mouth. But then I said, "I locked myself out."

She inhaled deeply and I smiled. I was sick of feeling humiliated and for some reason that gave me strength.

"Do you wanna help me break in?" I asked.

It turned out to be easier than I thought. A short boost onto the fire escape and a little jimmying of the window got us inside in minutes. She immediately took off her coat and threw it on a chair.

"Would you like a hot toddy or something?" I asked.

"Yeah," she said. "You can use some of this."

She tossed a bag of fresh mint on my kitchen table.

"You were carrying around a bag of mint this whole time?"

"Yeah, it's why I was out. I wanted to make a mojito, but I realized on the walk home that I hate mojitos. I was thinking of a mint julep—but I usually make that with peppermint schnapps."

"I don't think I have peppermint schnapps."

"That's OK. A toddy sounds even better."

She smiled. I put the kettle on.

"What's your name?" I asked.

"Mira. What's yours?"

"Henry."

The conversation went dead and we were quiet for a moment. Then, Mira blew a raspberry. I laughed lightly as the kettle whistled.

My next moment of clarity was the following morning. I woke with the sun in my eyes and Mira was gone.

I grabbed my head and staggered through my apartment in my underwear with one red eye. Each empty mug on the coffee table and indent in my sofa accessed another memory of the night before. The out-of-control pawing we did. Her nails across my skin. I checked my forearm for evidence and found long, raised, red lines.

There was still a very faint sweat stain from when her back was pressed against my wall.

"Oh damn."

Her underwear poked out from behind my sofa. I remembered removing them.

"Don't worry," she'd told me. I knelt in front of her—frozen in shock. Her cucumber dick bobbed in front of me. She grabbed my hand and told me to trust her. Then she guided my fingers up her thighs and into a place I never thought could co-exist with male genitalia.

Maybe *confusion* is an integral part of arousal—because I remembered having the best sex of my life.

———•———

That afternoon, I had lunch with James. He had picked up my debit card from the bar and tossed it over to me with a smile when we sat down in our booth. I was experiencing an intolerable hangover.

"Right across the street is the cafe Michael Fayne worked," James told me as he pointed out the window. "A friend of a friend used to know him—as a barista, not a blood."

"Holy shit… I think I had sex with one last night," I said right as the young waitress approached us. We were all quiet for a moment. Then we ordered coffee. James and I leaned in to make the conversation more private.

"Was she weird looking?" he asked—I could tell he was jealous.

"No, she was beautiful. Incredibly beautiful. She was exotic for sure, but she was still very much a woman." I felt shame.

"Did she *say* she was a blood?" he asked.

"No."

"Then what was it? If she was a blood… how did you know?"

I was caught and I didn't handle it well. James knew something was wrong.

"Well," I said, wiping my lips. "I've never seen anyone that looked like her."

"Long teeth? Red eyes?"

"No no no. She was just different… like, you know how bloods come in all kinds of species and some of them have things that humans don't…" I looked down. He knew I was hiding something. I knew he knew. It was over. "She had both male and female body parts," I said, looking up to see that the waitress had arrived with our coffees.

For the rest of our meal, it was tense and I didn't blame him for feeling awkward. But the tension was broken when, right after we asked for the check, an elderly man caused a scene as he refused to be seated next to a guy with long, sharp teeth. I was embarrassed by him. As a human living in New York, you can sometimes forget about this kind of discrimination for periods at a time. But *they* never forget. I felt a sudden sense of pride for hooking up with a blood and James nodded to me, which seemed to mean, "Hey, whatever you're into is OK."

Before we left, James said that he had almost forgotten something. He pulled a piece of paper from his pocket and handed it to me. He told me it was Jennifer's number.

"That is…" he said with a condescending smile, "…if you're still dating women."

———•———

As soon as I got home, I put Jennifer's number into my phone and called her. I got her outgoing voicemail message: "Hi, this is Jennifer Harper, please leave a message."

Very professional. Commanding, even. She doesn't even say she'll call you back as soon as possible like most people do. Most people apologize on their outgoing message. *I'm so sorry I missed your call! Please please please leave me a message! I promise I'll get back to you! I promise!* Jennifer doesn't need to apologize. She's a busy woman. Deal with it!

I realized I was lost in my head and had inadvertently recorded several seconds of my breathing.

"Hi!" I said quickly and a bit too loud. "I'm… this is Henry. Um. From the bar the other night. James gave me the piece of paper that you gave to him which he then gave to me which I then called and now I'm leaving you a message. Anyway, give me a call back, or not. It's not a requirement. It's entirely your choice."

I ended the call.

The next several hours were spent in crippling humiliation. I was surprised at how long and heavy my hangover was continuing to be. I felt like I had chipped teeth in my brain. I took another handful of aspirin and binge-watched *Cheers* until I couldn't keep my eyes open. When I threw myself into bed, I checked my phone and realized it had lost power. I plugged it in and began to doze when I heard a computerized ping. I checked my phone and saw that I had a missed text from *Jennifer Bar*:

Funny voicemail. How about Friday at Code Blue?

I sighed a "holy shit" of relief, and responded with a: *yeah, cool. See you @ 8.*

I suddenly felt my pain subside.

Tap. Tap. Tap.

I sat up in bed and listened for the door.

Tap. Tap.

There was someone outside. I quickly put on some white canvas pajama pants and a Perfect Strangers band shirt, and I walked to my door. To get into the foyer of my complex, you need to unlock a large steel door. Then there's stairs that lead to the three other apartments. If someone was tapping on my *apartment* door, it must be another tenant in the building.

I opened my door and Mira was leaning against the frame. She smiled at me.

"Hi, Henry."

"Hey," I said. Wanting to seem cool, I leaned against my end of the doorframe in the same way she was. "What's happening?"

"Are you free?"

She kissed me very softly on the lips. She slowly withdrew and wet just my bottom lip with her tongue and teeth. She kissed me again, and again it was so soft it reminded me of my first kiss when I was thirteen. It was this juxtaposition—the extreme sexual aggression mixed with childlike sweetness—that ultimately silenced any and all desire to ask how she got past my thick steel foyer door.

We stumbled into my bedroom. It was even better than the last time. I completely lost myself in her body—not even minding the extra bit. When she asked me to finish, I remembered that I hadn't last time. I was too drunk. This time, I was in a perpetual state of almost finishing. I grabbed the condoms from my dresser drawer and fumbled with the wrapper.

"No," she pleaded. "Finish in me." There was something desperate in her voice.

"You're on the pill?" I asked.

"Just do it," she said. I felt a rush of hot, nauseating paranoia.

"Just please tell me you're on birth control."

"Yes, yes, I'm on the pill. Just cum in me."

No. No. No. No. No. Something was wrong with this. My self-loathing took over:

You really think a blood sex goddess could possibly be into you? Loser. She feeds on idiots like you!

I crawled away.

"What are you doing?" she asked, frustrated. Her neck craned around to see me.

"I... I just don't want to do it that way."

She stood and faced me. Her eyes were penetrative. She spoke with a robotic kind of certainty, "But that's the way *I* wanna do it."

Mira crept over to me and gave me little kisses from my lips to my navel. She threw me on top of her. I felt her... *member*... against my belly as we had sex. Then, at the penultimate moment, I pulled out and finished on my duvet.

"Shit!" she cried. "Why the fuck did you do that?"

"I don't know. I just wanted to," I said, feeling slightly vindicated.

"I told you to do it in me."

"What's the big deal?" I asked, sensing it was a very big deal.

Mira sniffed my bed sheets and then tossed them away.

"It's ruined," she muttered.

I rested propped up on my elbows and watched her dress. Trying not to let my nervousness show, I asked her if she was a blood and if this was some kind of *feeding* situation.

"How's your head?" she asked.

"Better."

"The moment I leave it'll get a lot worse."

Mira smacked the sole of her foot against my chest and pressed me against my mattress—her strength surprised me.

"I'm going to let you experience it one more time so that you know what it's like to be without me. And when I come back, you're going to do what I say. OK?"

I couldn't speak and she left with a door-slam.

— 2 —

On Thursday night, one day before my date with Jennifer, I met James and Aubrey at Geronimo. We had a few drinks and I loosened up enough to mention Mira. The alcohol did nothing to sooth my throbbing temples.

"She's a succubus," said Aubrey.

"A what-u-bus?"

"A succubus. A creature of the night that preys on men's lust." Aubrey went on to explain that she learned about these creatures from her mythology class in grad school—a topic she never seems to leave out of any conversation.

James asked how my head was. I told him it was bad but didn't say how bad it was. I asked them if they thought I should go to a hospital or the police.

"Jesus Christ, yes!" said Aubrey. "She's clearly done something to you."

"Maybe we shouldn't jump to the conclusion that this was some sort of vampiric sex magic," said James.

I chimed in, "It's true. Maybe this is completely unrelated."

"You're defending her and it's weird," said Aubrey. "She sounds like a psycho."

James said, "Just because she's a blood doesn't—"

"It's not because she's a blood, it's because she has clearly done something to Henry!" Aubrey interjected. Then they bickered for a while. It reminded me of the last few months with Grace. After three years in a relationship, it's easy for "being right" to replace the orgasm. I actually kinda missed it.

I told them I needed air and stood up and put on my jacket. The pain in my head was starting to make me dizzy.

Outside, I could almost see my breath in the air. I thought about how recently Grace and I were planning a cross-country road trip. Maybe she sensed me pulling away. I panicked whenever I thought about her as the potential mother of my child—she would have definitely been a soccer mom. I used to sit across from her at brunch and admire the angles of her face and her artisan-soap washed skin—but then my inner hater would spin things around:

Sure, her jowls are fine now, but look at that sag potential! By the time she's forty-five it'll be all jowls, all the way to the floor—along with those breasts. Being the piece of shit you are, you'll probably leave her for some hot younger woman.

One morning, about six weeks ago, I was in my bathrobe making a turkey sandwich and Grace walked in, fully dressed, and told me she had something important to say. She had met someone else. She was moving out. After that I wasn't hungry. Over the next week, she cleaned out her stuff and left me with the spaces those things once occupied.

———— • ————

When I got to my apartment, I went to the refrigerator. I moved the milk and saw a very moldy turkey sandwich. I grabbed it and threw it in a plastic bag and walked outside.

After I tossed the bag in the garbage, I saw a woman inspecting my fire escape. She had red hair tied back into a ponytail. She wore cowboy boots and smoked a hand-rolled cigarette. The air reeked of marijuana.

I nodded at her and walked up the steps to my foyer.

"You live in the building with that fire escape?" she asked and pointed to my fire escape.

"Yeah?"

"I'm special agent Sophia Kobe of the FBI," she said and flashed me a badge.

"Oh, hi, um, what's this about?" I asked, electrically panicked. Had I violated some law breaking into my own apartment?

You're such a fuck-up.

"May I come up to your apartment?"

I walked her up the stairs and led her inside. I was extra sensitive to law enforcement overstepping their bounds, and a part of me wanted to ask her for a warrant—but that side of me was silenced by another, more cowardly, side.

"Have you seen this person?" Sophia asked as she flashed me a picture. Like a punch in the solar plexus. The woman in grainy black and white was Mira.

"I don't know what she may have told you..." said Sophia. "But she's a very dangerous person."

"Dangerous how?" I asked.

"In 1995, a team of European research scientists got lost in a snowstorm in Tibet. There in a valley, they saw a Riwoche—a breed of horse thought to be extinct for thousands of years."

Sophia began shaking as she spoke. A small trail of blood dripped from one nostril. "There are things living in this world—hiding and evolving all on their own."

It sounded like the mutterings of a blood-hater. I doubted this woman's connection to any form of law enforcement and felt unsafe with her in my home. I took a deep breath and asked her if I could have her badge number. Sophia looked me over again and twisted her lips in disgust. She threw a piece of paper at me and slammed the door as she left. The paper had her number on it.

———◦———

On Friday, the pain in my head was ever-present and I rushed to the West Village, where I was meeting Jennifer in an illegal restaurant called Code Blue. The restaurant was built on the fifth floor of an apartment complex still in construction. Two walls were completely exposed, and steel beams poked out like bone from a very serious gash. Bullet holes riddled one wall, and someone had stuffed paper flowers in them. I was dressed up in a way that looked like I didn't have the time to dress up.

I got into the manual elevator and pulled myself to the fifth floor. I saw Jennifer sitting by herself at a table. A waiter wearing a hardhat delivered her a glass of red wine.

And then I left.

I couldn't believe I was doing it. I didn't even text her an excuse. I just hopped back on the subway.

I felt my head swim a little less when I got back to Brooklyn.

You just stood her up. Why the fuck did you do that?

"I don't know," I said out loud.

You did it for Mira, asshole.

I ended up at Geronimo. The crowd was heavy and the music was a bit too loud but I felt soothed by it. A girl's bare breasts were poking out from scissor-cut holes in her tee shirt. A blood massaged them while the girl balanced her knees on a barstool, and only a couple creepy guys and girls watched out of the corners of their eyes.

The bass line of a Syphone song shook the room. I went to get a drink and suddenly I felt no pain. I spun around and Mira was standing behind me.

I breathed heavy. It was too loud to hear each other speak so neither one of us did. The power surged and the lights strobed for several seconds. Mira mouthed the words "I love you."

Then she was pulled into the crowd by someone. I pushed through to see. Grace was speaking with Mira. I couldn't believe it. I didn't believe until I noticed Grace's arm tattoo: a lion devouring Saint Ignatius. I couldn't make out what either woman was saying, but Grace seemed to be pleading with Mira. A small red line fell from Grace's nose. Mira grabbed my arm and pulled me through the crowd and out into the smoker's backyard.

Outside, the air was thick. She led me to the gate that separated the bar's property from a community garden. It was away from the patrons and the artificial light. Squinting into the darkness, I saw Mira place her fingers in the chain links.

"How do you know my ex-girlfriend?" I asked. Mira climbed over the gate and plopped down.

"Let's do it in the garden."

"Tell me what happened back there!"

"There's something different about you," she said. "It took me a while to find it and I made mistakes along the way, but all that matters is that we're together now."

"Mistakes?"

"Your scent was all over her clothes. I got confused."

"Were you the one she left me for?" I asked. I waited for a response. I asked her again.

Mira let her jacket fall to the grass and she slipped out of her dress. She pressed her naked body against the gate and I ran my fingers over the hexagons of skin that poked through.

"Darwin did more than give us evolution," she said. "He gave us pride. For the first time in history, we weren't the orphaned children of God—we were survivors."

A mosquito hovered across my line of vision. I gathered my remaining willpower and took off running away from her—through the smoky backyard and into an alley. I heard her cry, "I'm getting sick of this! You're not the only one who's different!"

———◆———

As soon as I got back to my apartment, I rummaged through the miscellaneous junk on the top of my dresser until I found Sophia Kobe's number. When I went to input the number in my phone, I saw that I had three unread text messages from Jennifer asking where I was.

Asshole.

The phone vibrated. Grace was calling me. I answered.

"Henry, I saw you go outside with Claira," she said. "Do you know where she is?"

Claira?

"Wait. Let me explain. I owe you that," she said. "Claira came into my life at an inopportune moment…"

"While we were together?" I asked.

She breathed into the receiver for a few seconds and then asked me, again, if I knew where she was.

Grace begged me, "I need her. Please…"

Disgusted and horrified, I ended the call and BANG! Something hit the outside of my window. I jumped and crouched into my bedroom door's frame.

I tried to see through the glare of my lamp and into the darkness outside the window. Something moved.

I darted down my stairs and out into the drizzling rain—each drop released a bit of mist from the asphalt. I slid into an intersection and threw my arms at a cab coming my way. He pulled over.

Inside the car, I told the driver to go straight, and I called Sophia.

"Hello?"

"Sophia?"

"Yeah…"

"You were at my place the other day asking about someone. I *know* Mira. I think she might be at my apartment right now."

"Listen to me very carefully. Her name is not Mira. She is very dangerous. Is she with you?"

I looked out the back window of the cab. Through the blurry ovals made by the rain, I made out a small figure—it appeared to be following me.

"OK, just stay where you are," said Sophia.

"No! I'm coming to you."

"Keep her there!"

"You JUST told me she was dangerous!"

"…right. Well, she's not *that* dangerous." I heard a hacking cough on the other end of the receiver that was unmistakably weed-related.

"Any amount of danger is not OK with me right now!"

Sophia reluctantly told me her address and the driver sped up to the on-ramp of the BQE.

— 3 —

It was not the apartment of an FBI agent. Half-eaten take-out food rested next to hundreds of marijuana roaches and one actual roach. There was a couch and a cot and a coffee table—that was it.

"OK," I said. "You're not from the FBI."

Sophia dropped to the couch and sat with her forearms resting on her knees. She rubbed her temples.

"I'm a fertility specialist."

"Who or what is Mira?"

"She introduced herself to me as Sadie. A while back, she came to my office and wanted to know why she couldn't get pregnant. I had recently published a series of papers on interspecies breeding and the benefits of using vampiric DNA. Sadie is… as you probably know… not human. The truth is I still don't know what she is. She's I1V1-positive but… I found other irregularities in her DNA—ones I had never seen before."

"What kinds of irregularities?" I asked.

"Her *species* doesn't have genders. Theoretically, they can reproduce with each other. She could also smell blood types, and she believed someone in New York City had a slight mutation in their blood allowing breeding compatibility with hers—she could smell it in the air."

"Holy shit. She said my scent was all over my ex-girlfriend's clothes and that she 'got confused.'"

"You may be the lucky guy with the weird blood." Sophia rubbed her temples and a small red drop fell from her nose. She picked up a joint, lit it, and took a puff.

"You've been with her, too." I said. I pointed to her nose. Sophia grabbed a used napkin and patted her blood. She released a little cloud from her lips and blinked several times.

"She produces a very powerful series of pheromones," she said. "Your body goes into withdrawal."

My head was throbbing. I sniffed and tasted copper.

Sophia handed me her joint. "It helps," she said. "Trust me."

I took a small puff and handed it back.

"Sadie and I were working together—or rather I was working with samples of her blood. One of her evolutionary advantages is that she can control the appearance of her age. I thought I could use that function of her DNA to create a kind of anti-aging vaccine. But so far all attempts have been failures. My brilliant vaccine ironically increases the aging process. I sunk a lot of time into this project and, as you can see, nothing else." She gestured to her crummy living situation.

"So your vaccine makes you age faster?" I asked.

"Five hundred times faster." Sophia said and coughed. She put out the joint and rubbed her eyes. "I still think it's possible, but I need more of her DNA. She was cooperating with me regularly until about six weeks ago—she just stopped showing up. I made a fake badge and asked around until I found a neighbor of yours who said he saw her on your fire escape. Sorry for the deception, by the way. It's just easier to ask questions when you're FBI."

A flash lit the living room and then everything went dark. I ran to the light switch and flicked it on and off. Sophia turned on her flashlight app and told me it happens all the time. Her phone made one tiny stream of light—our shadows, like silhouette monsters, grew and shrank along the walls.

"Henry, if she bears your child, I believe it could be very bad. She used to talk about her species being superior to all others. She said she wanted to breed in order to bring an end to the wars. Her species can mature faster than ours. They're stronger, and they'd be much more fertile."

"Jesus! Fine, well, I'm the last of my bloodline so all I have to do is *not* impregnate Mrs. Dick-Chick Uber Alles."

"It doesn't make sense," Sophia said, suddenly standing and pacing. "If I were her... I'd be breaking down my door right now to get to you..."

Both of us turned to face the door and braced ourselves. Nothing happened.

A noise made us jump. It came from both of our phones. Sophia glanced at hers and told me not to worry about it. She said it was just an Amber Alert.

I remembered the last thing that Mira said to me—I wasn't the only one who's different. "Oh god no," I said. My jaw went slack.

Asshole... asshole... asshole.

"Two years ago," I told her. "I needed rent money and… I… donated sperm."

Sophia grabbed her car keys and said, "I know where she is."

The raindrops were fat and Sophia drove like a maniac. We hydroplaned onto the sidewalk and knocked over a newspaper kiosk as we turned. The little bit of THC in my bloodstream intensified every sound and only marginally aided my migraine.

"Vials of my failed aging vaccine are kept in a storage facility up here. My guess is that she smelled your DNA coming from somewhere else in the city. She followed the scent to the child made of your donated sperm. Now all she needs to do is bring it to maturity."

"What?!"

"She's going to rapidly age the baby using my vaccine until it reaches maturity and then she's going to inseminate herself with your child's seed."

"Oh my god!" I gagged on my own stomach acid. "That is… that's sick! Sophia, we need to call the authorities. We can't just go barging in like superheroes!"

The car screamed to a halt. Sophia pulled a gun from the glove box.

"This is what's going to happen. You will enter the storage facility and make love to her. Once she's pregnant she'll have no need for the child. It's the safest way."

The storm made the inside of the car a mess of white noise. My eyebrows were soaked with sweat and rainwater. It was difficult to feel anything that wasn't fear and discomfort.

I asked her what she was planning on doing with the gun.

There was a busted lock dangling from the gate. I scampered through the rain holding my jacket over my head. Everything was wet and freezing cold. I walked straight through the back door that was also broken. I noticed a security camera dangling from frayed wires.

Into the maze of lockers. A few fluorescent lights blinked overhead, but mostly it was dark. The only time I saw clearly was when lightning flashed.

There was one odd light source. It was green and coming from a unit farther down. I hugged the walls and followed the light. A rummaging sound grew as I got closer to the source.

Mira was tearing up a storage unit. Clothes, books, an old PC laptop— all in pieces pouring from the steel box. She drew a strange black liquid into a syringe. A baby was squirming in blankets on the floor. She knelt to it.

"Hey, girl!" I said just as lightning lit the facility so brightly that I could see her irises narrowing. She was in tattered, wet clothes, and her nails were black with grit. She didn't speak. She only stood, slowly, still holding the syringe.

It was time to do what I do best—lie to a woman in order to have sex with her.

"I had no idea that you wanted a baby," I said. "I would LOVE to have a baby with you."

"It's not just a baby. It's a new world order. I'm the next step in mankind's legacy," she said with cold certainty.

"And I love it! Let's do it—right now."

She walked toward me with cat-like reservations—still holding the syringe.

"You sure you can handle that?" she asked. "It's quite a commitment."

"I wanna make babies with you," I said.

"Lots and lots of babies," she whispered with her lips grazing mine. "A better world."

Mira dropped the syringe and threw herself at me. We pawed at each other and my clothes came off very quickly. She pushed my back to the floor and I winced as my skin made contact with the icy concrete.

The sex was insane. She was a rabid animal. Crazed and desperate, I pulled her to me and sucked her neck and shoulder and licked her hot, tangy sweat beads. The storage lockers and the baby and the rain and the eugenics all evaporated. My nerves surged with electrochemical reactions—mirroring the current night sky. I let go.

After I finished, she fell off of me and hugged her knees. She rocked gently from side to side and cried.

"I did it," she said in quiet elation. "I can feel it. It's real."

"Now!" I screamed as I grabbed the syringe and leapt away from her. Sophia ran in with her pistol drawn and shot *me* in the shoulder—this was not the plan we had discussed in the car. I howled as I fell to the floor, clutching my wound. The baby screamed.

"We did it," said Sophia.

Henry, you dumb fuck. Never trust an ex.

Mira said, "Are you nuts? People will hear that."

"Don't worry. I have a full tank of gas and a box of Depends. You relax in the backseat and I'll have us in Canada by tomorrow afternoon."

"I am so sick of this, Sophie! You come barging in trying to save me—messing with my whole plan. It wasn't easy stealing this baby!"

"It doesn't matter now. We have the child. We can continue our legacy," said Sophia.

"*My* child. *My* legacy. You didn't do shit. You've never done shit for me. You were a stepping stone—an easy lay to hold me over."

Sophia pleaded with her. She knelt at Mira's feet and kissed her legs.

"And I hate it when you're like this! Spineless!" said Mira. "Your whole godforsaken species is weak and stupid and spineless. Just move on!"

Mira pinched Sophia's cheeks with the fingers and thumb of one hand and lifted the woman off the ground. Sophia dropped her pistol and screamed as she scratched Mira's forearm.

"Please!" said Sophia. Her scream and the baby's scream harmonized.

Then, Mira tore out Sophia's throat and tossed her to the floor.

Sophia's body twitched. Another lightning flash revealed the amount of blood and bits of cartilage spewed over the polished concrete floor. I could make out some red specks on Mira's face. The baby's voice went hoarse.

I was still bleeding out on the ground—my hand pressed against my shoulder. My whole body turned to pins and needles. My vision was tunneling.

Mira straddled me. "I want to take you both with me," she said. "We could make this world better—together…" She leaned in close and whispered, "You're the one, Henry. You're everything I've been waiting—"

I jerked my wounded arm forward. She gasped and jumped off me. The syringe was stuck in her leg. She removed it and examined the glass tube. Empty.

At first, she tried to fight it. Gasping and writhing on the floor, I saw her revert to the body of a sixteen-year-old, but then her hands withered like a grandmother's. Her eyes grew big and round like an infant's, but her hair turned white and brittle. With a weak brattle she seemed to let go of the fight and in the next thirty seconds I saw her age a hundred years. As I watched, I regretted ever worrying that a woman I loved could ever grow out of her beauty.

When she turned to dust, you were curled up in the middle—a baby replica of the both of us.

I never found out anything more about your mother, and I still don't know how you survived. I've written about her to that vampiric taxonomy expert, Doctor Swann, but he never wrote back.

So all I can say is there may be a time when you feel the urge to procreate. And I'll be honest; I'm freaked out about it. But I'll do my best to keep you safe. You may have come from a monster, but you don't have to become one.

All right, kid. The sitter will be here any minute, and I have to get ready for a date.

WET WORKS PART 4

By Jonathan Maberry

Texas Medical Center
McGovern Commons
Houston, Texas
Morning of the Red Storm

Yuki Nitobe stood with a phone pressed to one ear and her hand covering the other. There was so much noise around her. Sirens, people yelling, other reporters doing nearly hysterical standups for their networks, and all of that against the constant, dull roar of the massive fire that was consuming half of the buildings at the nation's largest research facility. Walls of flame reached into the morning air and above those were towering columns of dense black smoke. It was looking at the furnaces of Hell itself. Even a quarter mile from the inferno the heat was oppressive, and strong winds were blowing flaming cinders into the trees and onto the roofs of other buildings. Dozens of streams of high-pressure water arched into the blaze but with no noticeable effect.

"Luther," yelled Yuki, "are you watching TV? Are you seeing this?"

"Yes," said Swann weakly.

"What?"

"Yes," he said louder. "I can see it. It's… God, it's awful."

"Did you watch my recap?"

"Yes. Is it true?"

"It's true," she said, then she flinched as something exploded deep within the conflagration. A ball of burning gas curled upward, veined with black and lit from within by intense heat.

"Are you all right?" demanded Swann.

Yuki wanted to tell the truth, to say that she wasn't all right. Not even a little. But she said, "I'm fine. It's just that this is insane. Why would they *do* this? This is a medical facility. It's neutral ground. Everyone knows that."

It was one of the very few areas where both sides of the war found common ground. There would be no attacks on a very short list of facilities. Hospitals were at the top of the list, along with water purification plants, working farms, nuclear power plants and the power grid. Attacks on those would hurt everyone, blood or beat. That same accord also forbade either side from using such places as refuges or bases. Sadly, most schools were not included as safe zones. Not enough of the more aggressive power players on either side respected schools, and the more radical elements distrusted the content of what might be taught.

The Texas Medical Center was the closest thing to hallowed ground as there was in the world. Humans and vampires could both get cancer, and that university was doing important advanced work in cancer screening and treatment.

"Who are they, Yuki?" asked Swann. "The news said that someone took credit for it. Some group called the Red Empire, but I've never heard of them. Do you know anything about them? What do they want? Why target the hospital?"

Yuki looked around to make sure no one was paying attention to her and then she moved into the relative shelter of the side of a parked ambulance. "Listen, Luther," she said quickly, "do you understand why they picked this place?"

"No... I..."

"Christ, Luther, get your head out of your ass. Don't you know what they've been doing here?"

"Um... yes, research. Vampire genetics and—"

"No," she snapped. "Not that. Everyone's doing that. Luther, the fire started in the Rykerson Lab."

She heard him gasp and Yuki knew that now Luther Swann understood.

After New York, after the first outbreak, after the patient zero of the Ice Virus plague began to kill, and after that vampire was finally brought down in a hail of gunfire, his body was brought here for study. Since then there had been wild rumors and conspiracy theories in which different groups—human and vampire—claimed that the patient zero had not, in fact, died in New York. The rumors claimed that he could not die, that he was some unknown breed of vampire with extraordinary healing powers. They said that he was being kept alive so that the human military scientists could use him to create some kind of biological weapon that could be used against all vampires. It was wild speculation and a lot of it was straight out of comic books. But there was always some truth in these urban myths. Yuki and Luther both knew that all too well.

The patient zero of the vampire plague had been brought there to the Texas Medical Center.

Michael Fayne had been brought there.

And now the entire medical center was burning.

Burning.

Burning.

"Luther," she said into the phone, "remember what the man said in that video? He said, 'You think you have seen war, but you have not. The Red Empire rises. All hail the Red Emperor.' God, Luther, I think maybe those crazy rumors have been true all along. I think Michael Fayne—or whatever he's turned into—is still alive."

"No," said Swann, but it was clear that he wasn't disagreeing with her. He didn't want this to be true. The horror was there in his voice, though. The realization. The understanding.

"Michael Fayne is the one they're talking about, Luther," said Yuki. "He's the Red Emperor."

She watched the building burn and turned to look at the faces of the people in the crowd. Some of them were probably vampires, she knew. They had probably seen the video on their phones or tablets, or listened to it on their car radios as they drove to see the blaze. All of them looked afraid.

No, they looked terrified.

This was more than an act of terrorism. This was more than the entrance of a new player to the tortured game of war and bloodshed. This was much bigger than that. The world had somehow just changed.

And everyone—consciously or subconsciously—knew it.

OTHER MEN'S BLOOD

By James R. Tuck

He stank of other men's blood.

It coated his arms and hands, soaking into his undershirt and gluing it to his body. It rode his skin in a grimy wetness pooled along the ridge of his belt, not soaking into the polyester weave. His boots sloshed with it as he crept along, short crab steps hugging the tunnel wall.

A shape moved up ahead, pushing through the darkness that hung between bare bulbs strung with wire along the ceiling. He crouched in a pool of similar darkness, pressing himself against the smooth concrete wall that held back crushing tons of dirt and rock. His breath came in long soft sweeps of inhalation and exhalation, silent and nearly still. No movement to betray his presence.

A sentry broke through the pool of light just past him. He had only three steps to measure the man, to assess him. Average height for the population and on the lower edge of the average weight, his face sank in around the eye sockets, cheekbones hanging like cliffs over a long fall of dark beard. He moved with an undisciplined amble, knees bowed, toes swinging left then right as he walked. His hands cradled a battered AK-47 slung across his chest on an old guitar strap, a flaming skull grinned from the embroidery.

Probably taken from a captured civilian.

The sentry's stride didn't break, didn't falter, he marched face first into the shadow, eyes hooded by the keffiyeh that wrapped his head. One step the sentry was in the darkness. Two steps the sentry was beside him.

He rose, pushing with his knees and pivoting, swinging his long arms up and around. Between his hands looped a stretch of stainless steel wire barely thicker than a strand of hair. It passed over the sentry's head, a whisper unheard in the dark, and descended in front of the man's face. It stopped when it landed on the collarbone. He kept pivoting, turning and dropping back into a crouch. The wire cinched, biting deep. The sentry jolted to a stop and fell back, dragged down by the line of cutting pressure across his Adam's apple. The sentry's weight fell across his back. He pulled hard on the garrote as the sentry thrashed, trying to stand up, to get away from the lacerating pain that held him pinned to his killer's back. Each jerk and spasm sawed the thin wire deeper and deeper still. His hands dropped a quarter inch as the wire cut through whiskers and then skin then meat then vein.

It snagged, stopping against cartilage. In his ear came the hush and gurgle of air rushing out, the sentry trying desperately to scream. Hot wet ran under his collar as the carotid severed, wicking into the cotton fibers of his shirt. The sentry's keffiyeh unfurled, draping over his face. The black-and-white cloth swayed gently as the convulsions slowed.

When the man on his back stilled, he counted to thirty, then leaned toward the wall, letting the dead weight slide sideways off his shoulder. The AK-47 clattered against concrete, muffled by the corpse it was strapped to.

He froze, eyes darting left and right.

No movement came from either end of the tunnel.

He slowly released the breath he'd been holding.

He unwound the garrote. It stuck in the fibrous cartilage and he had to yank to free it. A micro-spray of fluid came out with it, spattering his chin and across his upper lip. He swiped his sleeve across it but the warm penny stink of blood became the only thing he could smell. Deep in his brain his conscience kicked and revulsion rolled over him. It clotted his lungs, smothering him.

He hated this. Hated the smell of blood. Hated the feel of a life snuffing out at his hands. Hated killing. Hated how easy it was for him.

Hated himself.

He stripped the dead man of ammunition and moved on down the tunnel.

He could live with the iron tang of someone else's hemoglobin shoved into his nostrils but he couldn't die before he saved her.

———————

"I hate these tunnels."

He didn't say anything, just kept working, carefully placing the gray putty in the proper crevices, gently pressing it into the proper shape.

"They piss me off, the audacity of them. To dig into our country, using materials designated to build homes, just to kill our people." She sighed, adjusting the rifle in her hands. "It's inhuman." She stood just past him, but behind the floodlight, facing down the tunnel it painted nearly white with illumination. She didn't watch him work. That wasn't what she was there for.

She was there to provide a safe working environment.

"They should let you blow this whole system." She glanced back at him. "Just bring the whole thing crashing down."

He stepped away from the charge before speaking. "I'd need an escort the whole way. Might as well sweep them clean on foot."

"Hush. There have been rumblings from above."

He tried to keep his voice as steady as his hands but it jerked up on the last word like a fish on a hook. "Not your squad!"

She sauntered over, hips swaying a bit, just enough to distract him. "When they comb these rat tunnels, it'll be all boots on the ground, no exceptions." She leaned and kissed him on the cheek.

His mouth stayed in a hard line, jaw clenched. Even as a contractor he'd heard the noise about a mission to raid the entirety of the tunnel system and flush out the terrorists who used it to spread fear and chaos in their mad hatred of his people.

She's almost done. Just a few more months. Her hand slapped his jaw, harder than lightly, sharp enough to get his attention.

"Don't look like that, Neshama. I see your worry." Her voice was as firm as her hand.

"I only worry about *you*." He pointed into the darkness. "These are a deathtrap. Too many twists. Too many places for enemies to hide."

"Saul…"

The sound of boots on concrete came down the tunnel behind them. She stepped away, turning to face the depth of the tunnel. He moved to his satchel and began placing his tools into it.

Even married, fraternizing while on duty was a serious offense.

With that thought he regretted not grabbing her, pulling her tight, and kissing the hell out of her.

An IDF soldier stepped into the light. His uniform fit his body but still looked loose, as if he just didn't quite fill it. Saul knew him. Yakov. He lived below them in an apartment with two other soldiers who began their service the same time he had. All three of them had turned eighteen within a week of each other.

One month ago.

Yakov watched the two of them for a moment. Saul stood, closing his satchel.

Yakov's eyes trailed over the work area, picking out the brownish-red lumps of Semtex stuck to the smooth concrete walls like clots of old blood. He swallowed, his Adam's apple dropping into his collar and bobbing back up under his sharp chin. "Are you almost done?"

"I am done."

Yakov nodded and moved to the floodlight. "Let's go then." His hand closed on the handle of the floodlight. Saul moved to grab the other one. They lifted at the same time, tilting the floodlight over its axle. The tunnel grew dim as the light shone mostly on the floor. "Watch our backs, Eliora. These tunnels creep me out."

Eliora nodded, lifting her rifle. "These tunnels creep us all out."

As a team they began moving back to the entrance.

———— • ————

He pulled back his sleeve, checking the display. The yellow dot had not moved. His mouth went sour with fear at what that could mean.

She's still alive, still alive, still alive. I will it, so must it be done. God of my fathers, You keep her alive.

He turned his wrist and checked the compass strapped there. He had to wipe blood off the glass. The pointer wobbled over the E. He was still going in the right direction.

Earlier he'd used a small, shaped charge to push aside rubble he'd created months ago, directing the concussive force like a surgeon to open up enough room for him to crawl into the hell tunnels. It was the closest place he'd known of to where Eliora's GPS tag transmitted its signal. He'd run nine kilometers of pitch dark tunnels, using only a red-lensed flashlight to see by, before he'd found lights, and three more before he'd killed his first terrorist of the night.

Nine corpses later and he was close. The GPS indicated, and the last four sentries he'd killed had been patrolling instead of stationary. More action taken, the more likely he was on the right track. The tunnel he moved through struck deep in the heart of Israel, dozens of kilometers from the Gaza border. It remained fairly straight, he'd been consistently moving east since meeting the occupied tunnel, and also had few side tunnels.

He eased toward a juncture, watching the area ahead. His own blood stuttered through his veins, pushed by his hammering heart as each step he waited for the *click* of a mine trigger. An open area lay ahead, the end of his tunnel covered in a grid of rebar. Light spilled out onto the tunnel walls, long oblongs of color sliding between the iron bars in a pattern over and over and over. He forced his eyes past it. Looking at it for more than a few seconds made his stomach clench and his vision get slippery.

He dropped to his hands and fast-crawled to the edge of the wall. He didn't feel any sentries nearby, relying on the combination of his senses to report to him and the instant assessment hard-learned in training and combat.

Noise thrummed the air around him. Voices speaking Arabic over the ebb and flow of some white noise he couldn't identify.

He looked past the rebar that sealed the tunnel.

The room lay in darkness broken by patches of light.

In one circle, a dozen men hovered around an area that lay in a concrete box nearly the size of a large house. Most of them looked the same from where he crouched, the same loose-fitting clothes, the same keffiyehs, all bearded, all armed. Textbook terrorists. Like brothers in the same family.

Two stood out. One in an olive drab uniform so unremarkable it could have come from a dozen nationalities and one in a plain black t-shirt over the same olive-drab pants. They were on the far left of the room, surrounded by most of the terrorists who watched as they did something to a man strapped on the table in front of them. He was an IDF soldier, still in uniform but his shirt opened and hanging loose off the sides of the table. He screamed and jerked, cursing as the man in the black t-shirt plunged a syringe into his arm.

Saul looked away, dragging his eyes from the fascination of the scene, needing to assess the rest of the situation.

At the far end of the room was a large tunnel also bathed in light, a heavy-duty diesel truck with a long shallow bed parked at the entrance. He'd seen one like it before, hauling American soldiers in Afghanistan. On the back of the truck sat a wooden crate strapped in place between the bench seats that ran along each side of the back. A bar had been affixed down each side, about head level when seated. Short chains hung from it. The tunnel pointed east.

Toward Jerusalem.

In the center of the room was a long cage made of iron bars and plywood. The end of it hung out over a deeper pit.

Lights flashed and swirled in colors from inside the pit, the source of the dancing shapes on the wall behind him. His mind flung back to the third night of his honeymoon, when Eliora had drug him into a Paris nightclub. He'd hated the noise of it, unable to hear anything but a wall of sonic noise, hated the epileptic strobes that ruined his vision, hated the press of people that made it impossible to see any danger that might lurk in such an environment. He ignored the klaxon of panic in his chest as long as he could, though it grew with each passing minute. He tried to distract himself with his new bride's smile and her moving body. He held his control as long as he could before dragging her out and into a cab with the pretense that he couldn't wait to have her in the hotel again.

He'd never told her the truth.

Never confessed the depth of his involvement with S-13 and how those years affected him.

White light flooded into the cage from floodlights strapped across the top, making it easy to see that most of its occupants were soldiers, their uniforms marking them. A handful of civilians huddled in the cage, limbs thin and clothes tattered. They were not taken with the soldiers, their state of deterioration indicated they'd been down here a long time.

He looked for Eliora, straining his eyes to see her, to pick her out. There were five women in the cage. He ruled two out immediately. One was shorter and heavier than Eliora, her body built from exaggerated curves instead of Eliora's athletic sleekness. The other sat against the bars, long blonde hair hanging over her face.

Eyes roving, he dismissed two others being held by male counterparts. Eliora would never seek shelter in anyone's arms in a situation like this. Warmth infused his heart at the thought of her stubborn pride, a streak of it a mile wide in her. His woman was a valkyrie, an amazon, she'd be more likely to hold someone than to ever be held.

He found her.

Standing in a corner with a group of men, head bowed as they whispered, mouths closing shut when one of their captors would pass close to the cage.

She was planning an escape.

In the middle of a well-lit cage surrounded by armed guards.

It was suicide.

It was his Eliora.

He turned and examined the grate in front of him. It was made of rebar, the finger-thick steel bars welded into a grid and bolted to the concrete. The bars were painted black, the overspray patterning the walls and floor. He felt the hexagonal heads of the bolts, testing them. They were all tight. He dug in his tool satchel by feel, fingers searching the sides of it, skimming over enough Semtex to drop a full kilometer of tunnels to touch the tools strapped there with elastic loops. His S-13 training in demolitions taught him to know exactly where his tools were at all times. In seconds he pulled out a ratchet with an adjustable socket. Checking to make sure no one had looked his way, he settled the tool over a bolt head and began to work.

"Hello?"

The light scrape of breath came through the phone. He waited.

Seconds passed.

A minute.

He wanted to speak, to ask "Who is this?" but he held his tongue behind a clenched jaw.

Finally.

"Saul?" The connection was clear but the voice echoing and thin, the phone not held close to the mouth.

He still recognized it as Yakov. "What's wrong?"

"It started."

"What's wrong?"

"We hit the tunnels…" Noise came over the phone, a jumble of voices and the syncopated rhythm of booted feet. He held the phone tight, pressing it against his cheek. His heartbeat pulsed in his temples. A scream of frustration clawed at the back of his throat, scrabbling to get out, to rip into the phone and demand to know what was going on.

"Saul?"

"Talk, Yakov."

"They knew we were coming. We lost a lot of people."

He couldn't breathe.

"Eliora… she didn't make it out."

His eyes squeezed shut. His stomach lurched. His chest felt like it was folding in on itself.

Yakov's voice rose, words flying across the phone line. "She's not dead. They took her, dragged her off. They were trying to capture as many of us as they were trying to kill. Command pulled us out and are considering the losses as KIA but she wasn't dead when I saw her. They aren't letting us go back into the tunnels."

He swallowed, forcing his mouth to work. "They're leaving her to die?" He shut his mind to the images of what happened to prisoners of terrorists. He couldn't think those thoughts.

"Eliora told me about you, about S-13… I have her GPS code."

Soldiers were given jelly bean–sized ceramic GPS transmitters to swallow before infiltration missions. They stayed in the system for up to four days before passing through, allowing them to be recovered or rescued. He'd swallowed dozens of them before he walked away from S-13. Before he found peace with Eliora.

Hope blossomed in his chest, his heart lurching back into action.

With the code, he could locate her. With the code, he could find her. "Give it to me."

⸺⸺◆⸺⸺

He moved to the edge of the shadow by the cage, crouching by a table covered in a bloody white sheet and a handful of tools. The man on the far side of the room had stopped screaming, his noise replaced by the voices of the terrorists questioning the two men and their answers in butchered Arabic. The sound of their consonants made him think they were Russian, a country with deep ties to terrorists.

The two cage guards were on the other side talking, as far away from his position as they were going to get.

Eliora stood with her back to him, watching them.

"Neshama." He hissed, keeping his voice as low as possible.

Eliora stiffened. Casually, she turned and leaned against the bars of the cage. He watched her eye cut toward him and widen. A bruise darkened her jaw, spilling up toward her cheekbone, and the skin across the bridge of her nose had split from some impact. He swallowed a lump of cold rage at the sight.

She spoke, matching his volume, moving her mouth as little as possible. "You have to go. They will capture you."

"I'm going to get you out. Be ready."

"This is more than you think."

"Be ready."

She nodded, the barest increment, knowing him well enough to stop arguing. A black collar had been clamped around her throat. It had a square battery pack and radio receiver surrounded by silver spots he recognized as shock points.

These animals.

Eliora spoke. "Don't get killed over me."

"Neshama."

"Oh, Neshama," her lip trembled, the tiniest hint of her worry "Be careful. Love."

"Love."

He eased back, working carefully around into the shadow. He waited, watching the room as best he could but his eyes kept going back to Eliora.

He would get her out of that cage.

His hand slipped under the AK-47 strapped across his back. He'd taken it from the last sentry he'd killed. It stuck to his shirt, the blood on it and on the rifle itself dried to a crust. He broke it free with a shrug and moved it back to reach the small object tucked in his belt beside his kidney.

He drew out the tiny .22 loaded with subsonic ammunition and held it by his leg.

One of the cage guards began walking around the cage toward him. He didn't move, didn't adjust his position. Motion drew the eye quicker than anything else. He trusted his cover and waited.

The guard drew close enough that Saul could see his face. His skin was dark, someone who'd spent a long time in the sun, and his beard touched by grey. The left side of his face pulled down with a palsy, probably from childhood malnutrition. Saul recognized the carved look of someone raised on too little to eat.

He felt no compassion at the recognition.

The man walked past him. He rose and in two steps closed the distance, sliding his arm under the guard's armpit. His fingers snarled in the matted beard and yanked down as he pressed the barrel of the .22 into the folds of the guard's keffiyeh. Two quick squeezes on the short trigger spat two bullets into the man's skull. The cloth ate the POP! POP! of the projectiles and only he heard the wet melon thump of them rattling around the inside of the guard's skull, turning his brain into so much mush.

He looked around.

None of the terrorists reacted, all of them occupied elsewhere.

Using the beard and arm, he dragged the dead man back into the shadow and shoved him under a table. He pulled off the man's keffiyeh. Only two spots of blood stained the cloth where it pressed tight to the dead man's skull, the rest of it trapped inside the skull. One eye bulged, pushed forward by one of the bullets in its ricochet. The first time he'd used a .22 he hadn't pulled the man's head down and one of the bullets had gone out the eyesocket, making a mess.

He'd adjusted his technique since then.

He wrapped his head with the dead man's headdress, ignoring the burnt scent of scalp oil, and stood, walking through the gloom as if he were the guard. Eliora watched him, her face set in hard lines. Three IDF soldiers had joined her, leaning beside her, helping to block him from the other guard's sight. They were all in similar shape as her, roughed up, one of them cradled his arm in a sling made from his uniform shirt. Stepping quickly, he passed the dead man's rifle through the bars and kept walking, trusting his wife to keep it from sight until it was time to use it.

He walked around the cage at the same amble the guard he killed had been moving. His eyes moved around, taking stock of the situation, formulating a plan. The other guard wouldn't be fooled by him for more than a moment. He needed to put the man down quickly but odds were it wouldn't be quietly. He would have only seconds to spring the cage before having to deal with the terrorists on the far side of the room.

He passed by the truck. If he could free Eliora and the IDF soldiers, they could use the truck to get clear of the terrorists. He didn't know what lay down that tunnel or how they would get out of the other end but it was better than staying. Here was only death and torture at the hands of his country's enemies.

One of the civilians in the cage turned as he passed by. The man's eyes grew big at the sight of Saul's black fatigues and the weapons strapped to him. His mouth opened.

Saul tensed.

Before the man could make a sound one of the IDF soldiers was beside him, grabbing his arm and barking something in a harsh whisper. The civilian nodded and turned his back on Saul.

He could rely on the soldiers to help.

It might be enough.

If he could just drop the guard.

He rounded the corner, walking swiftly. He still had the .22 in his hand, held by his side.

The other guard was twenty feet away, looking down at the lights in the pit. His mouth hung open.

Saul picked up his pace, moving quicker, watching the other terrorists gathered around the table across the pit. They were silhouettes and shapes through the haze of the light noise bouncing out of the hole.

He offered up a quick prayer, the words foreign in his mind, any real sense of religion long dead from his days in S-13. He prayed that the guard stayed mesmerized. Prayed that he would be able to pull this off.

I can die, just let me get her out.

Five feet away he lifted the gun and lengthened his stride.

The barrel touched the guard's back and he pulled the trigger three times, shoving forward to muffle the shots against the man's body. The little gun emptied with three quick snaps, no louder than biting into fresh celery. The guard jerked forward, spine bowing as the tiny bullets punched into his lungs, pulping their way through. One of them hit a rib, ricocheting back and nicking the pericardium sac. He took two steps and tumbled headfirst onto the edge of the pit.

Noise exploded, hissing and howling, filling the air.

Saul stepped over and looked down.

Inside the hole were people but they weren't human.

Twenty faces stared up at him with mouths open. Men, women, and children. Their skin had drained its color to a bright, shiny jaundice and constricted to their bones. They clawed the air, straining for the dead soldier that lay out of their reach. Tears of frustration painted gaunt faces, running from eyes so bloodshot they looked like eggs boiled in paint. He'd never seen such animal fury contained in one place, a berserker rage that roiled and rushed out in their screams, driven in pace with the lights flashing along the edge of the pit.

Eliora's voice cut through his mesmerization.

"They're vampires!"

———•———

"This is my cell, son, not a secure line."

"I know, sir. I don't have time."

The sigh cut across the phone like paper rubbed over the mouthpiece. "One minute then, all hell's breaking loose."

He read off the GPS coordinates. "I need to know what cells might be working there."

"What for?"

"You said one minute." He pushed every bit of need into the next word. "Please."

"Hamas, Al Ghurabaa, possibly the White Flame."

He let the information sink in, mind turning.

The voice spoke. "We just had something go pear-shaped near there, son."

"I know."

"Best stay out of the way of the clean-up."

He swiped the button, ending the call.

———•———

Bullets ripped across the room.

"Move back!" Saul yelled. "Get away from this door!"

He dug in his satchel as his mind rolled through what he'd just seen. Vampires. He'd heard of vampires, the whole world had heard of vampires, but Israel had managed to curtail any major outbreak with stringent control.

Shit. Vampires.

His fingers pinched off small chunks of Semtex, pressing it against the hinges of the cage door. It was sloppy, most of the force would blow back, but he had no time for precision. Eliora shouldered the others back, using her elbows to move soldiers and civilians alike. One woman, the soldier with curves, spun around as a bullet punched her in the shoulder. Blood arced into the air, spattering the people beside her as she slammed into the ground and screamed. Eliora raised the gun Saul had given her and fired at the terrorists through the bars in quick three-round bursts, keeping her cool, picking her targets.

Plastic explosive in place, Saul pushed a pop-up timer into the middle lump, trusting that the force of it going off would be enough to detonate the other two patches of explosive on the other two hinges. He pressed the red button until it clicked, and moved quickly to get away, covering his ears.

Five seconds of bullets flying and screaming passed until the room went white and all noise was sucked into one THADOOM! of concussion.

Saul stumbled as the blast tackled him, ramming his shoulder into the bars of the cage. Turning back, he found the door had torn completely off the cage and flipped into the pit, dragging the dead terrorist down with it. The end of it stuck up, bouncing against the rim of the hole. He swung his AK-47 up as the first vampire crawled free.

Soldiers and civilians poured from the cage. The vampire leapt on the back of one man, riding him to the ground with thin arms clutched around the man's chest and long teeth buried into his neck. Blood shot out around the vampire's mouth, spraying wide in a fan across the floor.

A soldier grabbed the vampire's shoulders, trying to pull him off the man. Her feet slipped in the blood and she crashed to one knee.

The second vampire over the edge took her down faster than Saul's eyes could track.

He ran forward, looking for Eliora, shoving people out of his way. More vampires clambered over the edge of the pit, red eyes tracking targets before launching after their prey. The civilians dropped like lambs taken down by lions. The soldiers tried to fight but even the child vampires were too strong and fast for them. He watched as one little girl, not even four feet tall and dainty as a princess, perched on the shoulders of a soldier three times her weight, dug her fingers into his jawline, and ripped his head off in a shower of gore. She bathed in it, giggling as the decapitated body fell to his knees and she tumbled to the floor.

A vampire vaulted at him, sailing through the air. The thing's fingers and toes curled like claws and its chin rubbed its skeletal chest as pointed white teeth gnashed. He barely got the barrel of his rifle up and squeezed the trigger before it was on him. The bullets ripped into the vampire, shredding its back like pulled pork. Its scream stabbed into his head and he pulled the trigger again. Another three-round burst hacked into the thing's chest and out the other side in a torrent of vertebrae and blood. He shrugged the vampire's corpse off and it fell to the floor like a sack of disjointed bones.

Inside him a switch flipped.

He whipped his gun around, looking for more.

His brain fractured, the pieces crashing into one another. Everything shifted, becoming a sensation, a sight, a sound, a touch, a taste, a smell. All of it falling into the blank void his world had become. Everything was stimuli to be reacted to. Kill or ignore. The raw red state of mind that let him work.

A squeeze of the trigger pumped bullets into the vampire that climbed out first. It had drunk the man under it dry and now rose, its face a slick mask of gore. A fat tongue darted around its lips, scraping thick, filmy blood back into its mouth.

The rounds took it in the temple as it crouched, bursting through skull and tumbling, rolling, rumbling, becoming a swarm of lead that tore the top of his head off like a rotten beehive.

Saul turned and found his next target.

The AK-47 chattered in his hand again. The bullets stitched across the child vampire's tiny frame, making her jitter like an epileptic as she drank a double handful of blood scooped from the stump of her victim's neck. She fell back and kicked once, twice, and then was still. The severed head stared at her from inches away as she died.

He tracked the gun again, aiming it at the terrorists on the other side of the pit and the vampires attacking them.

Something grabbed his sleeve.

He looked.

On his sleeve was a hand.

It belonged to a woman.

His mind contracted, squeezing down at the sight of her face.

He knew her face.

Eliora.

"Saul."

He blinked, disoriented as his mind stuttered, synapses firing to compre-hend, to pull him out of the white noise of murder he'd slipped into.

"Saul."

His brain juttered, clickitey, clickitey, click.

"Saul!"

He shivered, cold running down the inside of his spine.

Inside his body.

"I'm here." he said "I'm back."

"We have to stop these things."

A glance showed him that most of the vampires had jumped the pit and were making short work of the terrorists over there. Gunfire popped off, sending flashes out, and screams rose and fell. Most of the terrorists were being eaten by the vampires. The two men who were not Arabs had flipped the exam table on its side and were using it as a shield to fire behind.

He turned and found the concrete around him to be a wash of red sludge, a soup of bodily fluids and viscera. Dozens of civilians and soldiers lay, their bodies too still, their skin too pale to be anything but dead. Mixed in with them were haggard piles of skin and bones, the corpses of the vampires.

A handful of soldiers still stood. They all bled, but were all alive. Three of them had a vampire pinned and were pounding its skull against the wet concrete. Saul heard when the melon split.

The blonde soldier had found a length of rebar and had driven it through the neck of a vampire. The thing jerked and flopped at the end of the steel bar, pulling the soldier forward and back as blood sprayed up her arms and over her face. She sputtered, eyes scrunched closed, but she held onto the rebar until the vampire stopped moving, its legs folding under it.

Two more soldiers held each other, one man pressing his face against the other's chest while sobs wracked him violently.

Saul looked at his wife. "We need to get out of here." He pushed the magazine release, letting it fall to his feet while fishing out one of the full ones he'd taken from the men he killed. Pressing it home he pulled another from his waist and handed it to his wife.

She reloaded and settled her rifle into her hands. "The truck?"

"It's all we have."

"Let's go then."

Their boots sloshed through an inch of blood as they moved, the floor built in a depression. As they moved they signaled the soldiers to follow. One by one they did, all of them moving quickly toward the truck.

As they drew near, the floor began to vibrate under their feet, sending tiny ripples through the puddle.

Saul held out his arm. Everybody stopped.

The vibrations grew worse.

"What is that?" One of the soldiers asked.

Saul didn't answer, his eyes scanning.

The truck was moving.

Not forward, it was shaking, rocking on its suspension.

"Look at the box." Eliora said.

He looked. The wooden crate had been riddled with bullets, the wood chewed into near pulp. It rocked back and forth, the straps holding it twanging with the stress. One of them popped, snapping in two, the ends flying in separate ways.

Saul and Eliora raised their guns as the crate exploded into a million splinters.

Tiny wooden shrapnel flew at them, peppering his arms and face. He felt the bite of it along his cheek, thankful it missed his eye.

"What the hell is that?" one of the soldiers whispered.

Something that looked like a mound of hay shambled across the bed of the truck, heading toward them. Saul realized it was hair, mounds and mounds of it draping for a dozen meters, all the color of dead wheat, milky and nearly translucent. It caught on the bench seats, pulling back to reveal a woman underneath it all. She hunched over herself, hands clutched around a distended stomach. Her skin had the blue tone of asphyxia, her lips near white. She hissed, lips jerking wide around rotten teeth set in black gums. She lurched along, each footstep bouncing the truck over its shocks even though she stood only five feet tall. She stopped on the edge of the truck bed, perched there and staring at them with sweeping eyes that looked like empty sockets under the shadow of her bangs.

"This one's not like the others." Saul said.

The vampire took a step forward and dropped to the ground in a flurry of dead wheat hair.

Saul and Eliora fired at the same time.

The AK-47s chattered, spitting bullets that folded the vampire in half. She hit the back of the truck and bounced forward onto her hands and knees.

She crouched, covered by her hair, completely still.

Eliora's voice broke the silence. "Did we…?"

The hair moved, lifting and swaying as if caught in a breeze.

Saul's finger tightened, squeezing the trigger.

A voice shouted behind him, harsh and guttural. He glanced back. The man in the black t-shirt ran toward them, holding a black box in his hand and punching it with the other. Eliora spasmed, hands jerking up, body twisting. Her rifle clattered to the floor. He caught her as she swayed sideways, falling with her to the ground. A soft crackling bzzzzzzzz sounded and she twitched, eyes rolling back in her head. The other soldiers also convulsed on their feet before twisting and crumpling to the ground.

The collar.

Swinging the rifle around he let loose a burst bullets in the direction of the man with the black t-shirt. He was off-balance, holding Eliora's weight as she twitched in his arm, and firing one handed. Most of the bullets missed the man completely but one hit him in the thigh. The wound opened like a flower and the man went down hard, his face smashing into the blood-soaked concrete and bouncing up once before falling flat. The black box skidded away, rolling and tumbling. The man didn't move, didn't rise at all.

Eliora went limp. Her eyelids fluttered before opening. He pulled her as close as possible. She stared up at him, pupils dilated and covering the iris. They flicked like camera shutters and contracted as she came around. Her voice was hoarse. "Neshama?"

"Are you okay?"

She licked her lips, her face scrunching up. "Face is numb. What happened?"

He stood, pulling her up with him. "Later."

A scream ripped through the room.

The vampire was back on her feet. Her hair swirled out around her, whipping to and fro. Strands of it shot out, toward the soldiers that lay around it. The hairs plunged into them, stabbing through cloth and skin like hypodermic needles. The soldiers writhed in agony. Blood began to seep into the shaft of the hairs lodged inside the soldiers, climbing up each strand and turning it from cellulose white to a sanguine scarlet. The color crept all the way to the vampire's scalp, blushing down her forehead as the blood began to fill her.

Saul spoke out the side of his mouth. "You have to stand. Run to the truck and go."

"No."

He looked at Eliora, his eyes dead ashes in their sockets. "Do not argue." He picked up her rifle in his left hand, pointed them both at the vampire, and began firing as he walked away.

He didn't look back, trusting his wife to make her way to the truck. He fired a stream of bullets at the vampire until the guns locked back. The vampire danced under the hailstorm, anchored upright by the hair that pierced the soldiers who had all gone limp and still. He dropped the rifle in his left hand and hit the magazine release on the one in his right. He felt for another full magazine and came up empty. He shifted the rifle around, spinning it until he held the barrel, still warm in his hands. He swung it back as he drew near the vampire. She hissed at him, tongue flailing the air between slick-wet teeth. Her face was fully flushed from the blood soaked up by her hair when he drove the wooden stock of his weapon into it.

The butt of the rifle cracked across the vampire's skull. The vibration of it jolted up Saul's forearms, clacking his teeth together. The vampire swayed on her feet but didn't fall. He swung again and she raised her arm, catching the rifle and jerking it away. The strap drug down Saul's arm, friction burning the skin in a wide swath. He let it go, swinging the garrote in his left hand. The thin wire snaked around the vampire's throat and he lunged to grab it with his other hand. Yanking it tight, he twisted it together like a bread tie around a loaf. Long strands of hair hissed to the floor, severed by the razor wire. The vampire pulled back, tearing the garrote from his grip. She looked at him with eyes of hate.

His hand was in his satchel when the first hair struck him.

It burrowed deep and true, piercing into the muscle of his shoulder. The pain was sharp and cold, singing through his body like a blade on a whetstone. He watched as the hollow hair filled with his own blood and it wicked away.

The second hair slid under the skin of his hip, caressing across the bone to bite deep into the hollow of his thigh. That one burned.

He pulled his hand out as a full lock of that hypodermic hair peppered his midsection. His eyes went blind as they burrowed, contracting and pulling their way into his abdomen. His ears filled with a roaring. Ice spread across his midsection as the hairs went to work pumping out his blood.

His fingertips were numb and cold, could barely keep their grip.

Red filled his vision.

He was jerked forward as the hair ripped out of his skin.

The pain of that slapped him, white hot and complete from head to toe.

"Saul!"

He looked up at his name and shook his head, trying to see. The world swam and then locked into focus.

The side of the truck was inches from his face.

"Come on, get in!"

Eliora stood out the driver door, yelling at him over the truck bed. He looked down. The vampire lay under the back tire. It sat on her legs, pinning her down. Her hair flailed as she tried to push herself up. The truck lifted an inch, then two, before dropping back down.

His wife had run over a vampire with an American truck in a terror tunnel under Israel.

Insanity.

109

"Get it together, Neshama!"

He shook himself and took a step. Something snagged his foot. Hair, a lock of hair, still tinged with blood that could be his, had entwined itself around his ankle. He bent, bracing against the side of the truck as his head swam, and picked it up. It dragged along the ground as he walked to the cab and climbed in. His wife watched him from the driver's seat as he wrapped the hair around the long brown stick of Semtex, making sure the strands were deeply embedded. Satisfied, he reached into his satchel and pulled out a simple mechanical timer. Two twists gave them two minutes. It would be enough or it wouldn't.

He tossed the lump of explosive and bloodsucking hair out the window.

"Drive." he said.

Eliora flicked on the lights and pushed the accelerator.

———•———

"Mizrahi."

It wasn't a question but it was his last name. Saul looked up from where he sat outside the medical tent, waiting to hear about his wife's condition. A man stood in front of him who seemed to stretch to the stars. Carved of muscle and distinctly American, he towered over Saul.

The man didn't crouch or move to make it where Saul didn't have to stare up at him. "You left a mess down there for us."

"I don't know who 'us' is."

"And that's fine. Wilcox."

It took Saul a moment to realize the man had just given him a name. "Call me Saul."

"Want to tell me what happened down there tonight?"

"No."

"Excuse me?" The man's voice made it clear he was not used to being told no.

Saul sighed. "You are not my boss, not IDF, and not my wife. I'll be debriefed and I'd rather just do it once."

The man looked into Saul's eyes. "I can make this the only time you tell the story."

Saul believed him. "My wife was captured in the tunnel raid. I went after her. There were terrorists and vampires. We made it out but all the other soldiers captured with her were lost."

Wilcox grunted. "Terrorists and vampires. Doesn't seem fair to have both." He dropped to the ground, squatting in front of Saul. "We went down in the tunnel and looked around. Not much to see after you dropped all that concrete."

Saul shrugged. "I'm demolitions."

"Is that how you took out the *astiyiah*?"

"The what?"

"Vampire drinks blood with her hair. Tough as shit, damn near unstoppable."

"My wife ran her over with a truck."

Wilcox grunted again. "Good woman."

"The best I ever knew."

"You went in alone to save her from terrorists and vampires, I'd say she must be."

"I didn't know about the vampires when I went in."

"Would it have stopped you?"

"No."

"Thought so." Wilcox stood. Saul pushed himself up to stand with the man. The bandage wrapped around his waist pulled distantly, any other sensation held at bay by the anesthetic the medical team had applied. Wilcox looked at him sideways. "Well, Saul, this is the part where I offer you a job. Want to try and keep the world safe from vampires?"

"All due respect, to hell with vampires. I just want to take my wife home."

Wilcox smiled and gave a small salute. "Fair enough."

The man turned and walked away.

WET WORKS PART 5

By Jonathan Maberry

Global Acquisitions LLC
Pittsburgh, Pennsylvania
Day 17 of the Red Storm

"It's giving out!" yelled Ledger. "Swann, get behind me."

With a shriek like some great beast in agony, the metal hinges twisted and then tore loose from the frame, shooting pieces of broken steel flying as the door flew inward. The door landed on one bottom corner, pirouetted, and then fell with a ringing clang as shapes crowded through.

Joe Ledger opened fire point blank, catching the first of the Red Knights in the face. The small automatic spat again and again, and the rounds punched through faces and skulls and throats and chests. The knights hissed and screamed as they tried to evade but were trapped by their own numbers. If there had only been four of them Ledger would have killed them all and it would have been over.

There were so many more.

They packed the hall beyond the cellar door, and Swann thought he saw at least a dozen snarling faces. Red eyes blazed and mouths snarled to reveal savage and uneven white fangs. Powerful hands reached and black nails as thick as talons tore at the dead and the dying to claw their way into the room.

Ledger backpedaled and threw one despairing, calculating look at Swann, and in a moment of stinging clarity Swann knew that the soldier was debating how best to use his last bullets. One for Swann and then bury the barrel up under his own chin? Would suicide be the only mercy the two of them could hope for?

But then Ledger's eyes hardened and he aimed and fired his last rounds. A fifth Red Knight died, one scarlet eye blown black, and a sixth staggered and collapsed against the wall with most of his jaw shot away. Then the slide locked back and there was a single moment of almost unbearable silence as everyone—the Red Knights, Luther Swann, and Joe Ledger—all realized that the gun was empty and that the next act of this drama would be painted in the same red colors but by other hands. The savage snarls of the Red Knights transformed, becoming hungry leers of delight and anticipation.

Ledger switched the empty gun to his left hand and once again drew the rapid-release knife, flicking the blade into place. He did not yell a challenge; he did not pose or posture. Instead he rushed his attackers as if the advantage was all his, as if this fight was on his terms. It was like nothing Swann had ever seen. Even Big Dog, the head of the V-8 Special Ops team, had needed to psych himself up before a fight, shouting trash talk and doing everything short of thumping his chest like a mountain gorilla. Not Ledger. The man's face became blank, unemotional. There was none of that mix of fear and desperation and blood cruelty that marked so many soldiers Swann had known. This was the face of a man going to work. It was the face of a master of the craft, like the dispassionate jeweler as he cuts a diamond.

As one of the Red Knights lunged at him, Ledger used the empty pistol to smash aside the vampire's hands at the same time he brought the knife up and whipped it across the creature's throat. Ledger shifted subtly to the left as hydrostatic pressure shot a geyser of blood over his shoulder, and he used that shift to unlimber one leg so he could deliver a short, chopping kick to the next *upierczy's* knee, splintering bone and knocking the leg into a horrible and unnatural sideways bend. Ledger hit the dying first vampire again to knock him hard against the one with the crippled leg, and they both fell backward against the others who were still trying to crowd through the door. The tight confines of the doorway and the boneless sprawl of the dead monster corked the entrance for a moment, and Ledger used that fragment of time to chop and slash at the pale hands that tried to grab him. Swann saw fingers fly into the air, seemingly chased by drops of rubies.

Swann looked around for something, *anything* that he could use to help the soldier. But there was nothing except dead meat and blood. The room had one door and it was full of death.

Swann felt his heart sinking. This was how the world was going to end for him. The Red Knights would win. Even with the damage Ledger was doing, there were simply too many of them. Too many.

"God," murmured Swann in a voice too faint even for his own ears to hear.

NECESSARY MONSTER

By Lucas Mangum

From where she and Matthew stood, Nessa couldn't tell who attacked first. She clutched Matthew's hand. She hoped it wasn't someone from their side. This was supposed to be a peaceful demonstration. No heckling the police. No throwing things. No violence of any kind. She and the others had gathered to protest the escalating violence of the war between the so-called normal humans and those who had changed as a result of the Ice Virus. She hated the slurs "beats" and "bloods." She hoped her movement would remind the rest of the world that those affected by the virus were still human.

Now, something had gone horribly wrong.

Through the verses of Lennon's "Imagine," someone screamed. The pain in the cry was unmistakable. Angry curses filled the air in Greek and English. Nessa turned just in time to see a stream of pepper spray splash into a young woman's eyes. A man wearing fatigues tackled the offending policeman, throwing punches that cracked the officer's face guard.

"No," Nessa shouted. "Stop it."

Police and protesters collided. Nessa smelled pepper spray and blood. She didn't crave blood the way some of the others did. The violence associated with the iron smell nauseated her. Whenever she had to feed, it was on the blood of animals. Now, eating was the furthest thing from her mind. A protester stumbled backward as an officer struck him. He crashed into Nessa and Matthew, separating them.

The offending officer faced Nessa and pointed, "You see her tongue? She's a blood!"

Another officer rushed her and tackled her to the ground, spittle flying from his teeth as he cursed her in Greek.

"Matthew," Nessa cried. "Matthew, help."

The officer cracked his club across her face and blood filled her mouth. He tore at her blouse, tearing open the front and exposing her small breasts. She tried to squirm out from under him, but his weight kept her pinned. She scanned her surroundings for Matthew or anyone who could help her. More weight pressed against her now bare shoulders as another officer helped hold her down. The first officer leaned back and started to unbuckle his belt. She couldn't believe this was happening, how fast things had gotten out of control. She kicked at the officer undoing his pants and clawed at the one holding her shoulders. The first officer pulled his penis out and she screamed again, feeling her throat shred.

Where was Matthew? Was he restrained? Why couldn't anyone help her?

Her fingernails scraped against the face of the officer holding her shoulders, just beneath the riot mask. He cried out and cursed. Her vision went white as another blow from a nightstick connected with her skull. The commotion now sounded muffled, as if it was coming from a television with the sound turned down low. Blackness closed upon her from all sides and she welcomed it.

———◆———

Nessa sat with her shoulders slumped as she stared at her pale, bruised hands. Her head and torso throbbed from where the so-called Peace Officers had beaten her with their clubs and boots. Her tongue pressed against a loose molar, again filling her mouth with blood. She swallowed. Hunger pains stabbed at the lining of her stomach.

Above, a dirty halogen bulb cast dim illumination upon her surroundings. She sat at a long gray table. The room around her was a featureless steel cube, except for the wall to her right, which was equipped with a two-way mirror. In the upper corner, a red dot shined, indicating that the closed circuit camera fixed on her was indeed recording.

Though unsure what her captors had planned for her, she knew she would never be heard from again. Gone were the days of due process.

If the Greek government (or any government, for that matter) deemed you a threat to national security, you disappeared forever. That was the new way of the world.

Especially if you were a vampire.

She tried to imagine dying. A scary thought, but far scarier when she considered the cruelty of her captors thus far. If they were capable of beating her and her fellow protesters within inches of their lives and leaving her in this room to rot, they would likely ensure her final moments would be filled with agony. She'd heard stories about mobs of untrained gunmen stringing up her kind by the wrists or ankles and shooting them in places that guaranteed a slow death.

Maybe she'd signed on for this when she'd organized the protests in Syntagma Square, but her strong belief in the immorality of the V-Wars did nothing to quell her anxiety. She feared the pain, and the mystery of what awaited a creature like her. Even more than fear she felt sadness. Her protest movement had given her many friends and admirers who she would never see again. Worse, she hadn't been given the opportunity to say goodbye to them.

She longed, above all, to see Matthew. To know he had escaped. To touch his face. To kiss his lips. To revel in the way he looked at her like she was some kind of heroine for this new, dark age. She loved him and hoped he knew it, even if she'd never told him. She'd never let him all the way in because of who she was. Yes, a vampire, a *lamia* more specifically, but also a crusader who loved trying to make the world a better place far more than she could ever love a romantic partner.

God, she was hungry. Did they intend to starve her? That was cruel, even for her government.

A grinding sound reverberated through the room as a section of steel wall opened toward her. She stared into the black shadow of the entryway and waited to see who would step through. She narrowed her eyes and concentrated her strength into her hands, balling them into fists. A desire to fight whoever came through that door surged through her. She could feed and maybe the rush from the blood could provide her with enough strength to escape.

A fantasy, she thought. She had never been violent. She had never fed upon a human either. Her apartment in Athens had plenty of rats to sustain her. Still, she had felt a violent urge when the door opened, a hunger for blood and violence that had both surprised her and reminded her of what a frightened animal must feel like when it knows a threat is near. Perhaps the rats she feeds upon feel the same way in those final moments before her barbed tongue pierces their flesh.

The first man to walk through the door wore a black coat and tie. His hair was slicked tight against his skull and his eyes reminded her of stone. He crossed his arms over his slender chest and stared at her, his expression emotionless.

More footsteps proceeded from the darkness. A man wearing military fatigues and carrying an assault rifle entered the room. Behind him, a man in handcuffs with a black hood over his head staggered forward, pushed ahead by another soldier.

"What is this?" Nessa said.

The soldier herding the prisoner into the room shut the door behind him and kicked out the prisoner's leg. The prisoner gave a muffled grunt of pain and fell to one knee.

Nessa looked from the prisoner to the soldiers to the man wearing the tie. No one said a word. They only watched her.

"What the hell is going on?" Nessa said.

The soldier standing behind the prisoner raised his rifle and rammed the butt of it into the back of the prisoner's head. Nessa jolted as the prisoner fell to the floor. All thoughts of hunger vanished. She only felt confusion and fear.

The soldier who had knocked out the prisoner smirked at her. He was young, good-looking, with boyish skin and light blue eyes. It made his cruelty all the more worse to observe. She wondered if he'd been one of the men who had beaten her on the street.

The well-dressed man turned to exit the room and the soldiers followed, leaving the prisoner unconscious on the floor.

Nessa tried not to think about how hungry she was.

Or how easy it would be to feed.

The seconds crawled by as Nessa sat on the cold chair staring down at the crumpled, unconscious form before her. If not for his ragged breathing, she would have believed him dead.

Nessa's pulse throbbed in time with the hunger. The pains came more frequently and with increased intensity.

She wondered how much longer she could hold out.

She could sense the prisoner's blood as it pumped through his veins.

She licked her lips, tried to ignore the craving. The idea of taking a human life revolted her, but she thought that in a life or death situation, it might be necessary. She didn't think such a scenario would make feeding on a person morally correct. It would still make her a monster.

Why had they provided her with a human food source? Did they want her to feed? Why? What the hell did they want from her?

She shut her eyes and pressed her fingers to her temples. She tried to focus on breathing. When her eyes opened again, she examined the unconscious prisoner. She wondered again if she could feed in an increasingly dire situation.

She doubted it. Though three years had passed since she had started manifesting the *lamia* characteristics, she still considered herself human. That was why she was able to empathize with people so well, why she worked so hard to restore peace.

But she had never been in a situation where her survival depended on drinking the blood of a person. Maybe if it came down to her or some anonymous prisoner, she could bring herself to feed on human blood. Again, she became aware of her throbbing pulse and aching hunger.

She shut her eyes. No, she thought. I won't do it.

Nessa opened her eyes and got up from her chair. She knelt beside the unconscious man. The beat of his heart pounded between her ears, drowning out all other sound. His sweet heart, pumping the vibrant source of his life. Probably much more satisfying than rat's blood.

She reached down and took hold of the black hood. She yanked it off and gasped. The face beneath the hood was angular and covered with a thick beard. A straight white scar split the skin above the prisoner's right eyebrow. His dirty blond hair was splayed across the floor.

Nessa backed away and breathed his name.

"Matthew."

Nessa had met Matthew Crowder after he had seen one of her flyers hanging outside the University Club Building. Before organizing had been banned from their campuses. He'd arrived almost half an hour early to the meeting held at her flat near the University of Economics and Business. He'd held a coffee cup in both hands and shivered from the cold outside.

She had first greeted him in Greek and he blushed.

"Hi," she'd said, switching to English. "What's your name?"

"Matthew Crowder."

"Nice to meet you, Matthew Crowder. Why do you want to protest the V-Wars?" She asked every newcomer that.

Matthew blushed and dropped his eyes. "I don't know. I mean, I don't like the way things are going in the world, but really, I'm kind of hoping to make some friends."

She smiled. "I have to admire your honesty. I'm Nessa. I can be your friend. Your accent, are you American?"

"Guilty."

"You were on the front lines. Michael Fayne, Luther Swann, Hell Night."

"You say it like that's something to be excited about."

"You can't affect change by crying on Tumblr about the bad shit happening halfway across the world. You can only do that by getting out and demanding change, and you can only do that in the trenches."

"Seems like every country has trenches these days."

"A sad truth, for sure. I hope to change that."

"You really think we can make a difference?"

"Not with that attitude." She gave him a gentle nudge. "The idea is to be so big, they can no longer ignore us. They'll have no choice but to stop fighting and listen."

Matthew shifted from foot to foot, an uncomfortable expression on his face.

"What is it?"

"You're a…"

"A vampire. Yes. Specifically, a *lamia*. A Greek version of the vampire, but don't let that scare you. The legends about eating children are just that. Legends. Probably made up to make people fear us."

"But you do drink blood, right?"

"Never human. I don't think I could."

A mischievous look crossed his face. "What if someone was willing?"

She laughed. "Are you hitting on me?"

He shrugged. His face went red again. "I didn't mean…"

"Relax," she said. "And to answer your question, I don't even think I could eat a willing victim. The idea of taking another life really upsets me."

I have a hard enough time killing the rats, she almost said, but didn't want to reveal that unpleasant part of herself so early in a friendship, especially if later it would turn into more than a friendship. He was kind of cute, after all, even if he was reserved and not as passionate about ending the violence as she was.

More people filed in, mostly people she recognized, but some she didn't. She expected more people would come as the weeks went by, partly because of word of mouth, but also because there was a lot to be angry about. All around the world, people were being thrown into prison, harassed, and even killed just because they were considered different. There were even some cases of normal humans running into trouble with the law for simply associating with vampires. For the longest time, this was strictly America's problem. Now, it was everywhere. The governments of the world finally had something to agree on: to wipe her kind from existence.

She said all of this as she stood before the crowd.

"We have to come together," she said. "Beat, blood. This affects us all, and if we don't stand up for ourselves, it's only going to get worse. We'll assemble, peacefully, and we won't back down until the violence comes to an end."

As she spoke, Matthew looked at her with admiration in his eyes. She could tell by how he zoned in on her every word that he believed in her and knew she was special. Because of this, she'd fallen in love with him so easily.

Matthew stirred at the sound of Nessa's voice. She stepped back to give him some room. He coughed and brought his face up to meet hers. Even in the low light, his blue eyes were bright.

"Nessa. Where are we?"

"They took us and locked us up, but I'm not sure where."

"Why'd they put us together?"

"I think they want me to eat you."

He grimaced and for a second she thought he would throw up. "Why?"

"I don't know," she said. She slumped to the ground and balled her hands into fists. She tried to ignore the hunger pains.

"Are you all right?" he asked.

She shook her head. "Of course not."

"Think they'll kill us?"

"Eventually. Probably."

He put his head down and a tremor shuddered through him. "I don't want to die."

Her gut reaction surprised her. In spite of her love for him, she thought maybe he was weak. She had always thought that she would die like this, imprisoned and silenced for standing up for something. He had simply protested out of love for her, to impress her, and now that they had arrived at an obstacle, he was scared. But the more she thought about it, she couldn't blame him. The more she thought about the likelihood of her death, fear, like a sentient black hole, spread through her, devouring every bit of courage she had left.

"I don't either," she said and put her arms around him. She wanted to say more, but couldn't find the words. Telling him not to be afraid would do little to ease him. Several beats passed between them. "We're together now. Let's just be grateful for that."

He tightened his arms around her. His heart throbbed. She licked her lips.

Their first date had been a hike up Lykavittos Hill. Early on their journey up the wooded path, he took her hand. Maybe his advance had been premature and a bit presumptuous, but she found it endearing and smiled at him. Part of her thought that maybe he touched her so early to prove to himself that he wasn't afraid of her, even though she knew he was.

"I've never actually met a blood," he explained to her as they ascended. "There were some in my hometown, but I never… well, I never spoke to them. You're nothing like what I expected. You're so…"

"Normal?"

"Well, no. I actually think you're kind of extraordinary."

She smiled at that.

"I couldn't get up there and talk like that. Public speaking makes me nervous."

"It's easy when you believe in something."

"I have beliefs," he said. "Doesn't mean I'm comfortable announcing them to the world."

"What do you believe, Matthew?"

"I believe—I don't know. Moments like this are important. People getting to know people."

"And?"

"I don't know. I feel like there's a lot I haven't figured out."

"Like what?"

"Like why is this all even happening?"

"People are afraid. They feel threatened."

"Don't you feel like they should be? Not all vampires are peace-loving hippies like you." He laughed, but there was no humor in it. She got the impression this was something he thought a lot about. The fact that there were multiple sides to everything played a lot into his worldview.

"Just because people should be afraid doesn't give them the right to be violent. Violence only breeds more violence. It's up to us to demand meaningful dialogue between world leaders, blood and beat alike. It's not going to be easy, but eventually if enough people on both sides refuse to act violently, then we'll put an end to this nonsense."

"You honestly believe that? I mean, police beat the shit out of protesters on a daily basis, no matter how peaceful the assembly is."

"Like I said, it's not going to be easy. It certainly isn't going to happen overnight."

"Think you'll live to see it?"

A light breeze whispered through the leaves. She shrugged. "Not sure if that matters."

Matthew shook his head. "I couldn't imagine not living to see how I impact the world."

"I can only hope that I'm working for something meaningful. I think that's enough for me."

He smiled at her. "You sure are fascinating."

"I bet you think you're smooth."

"Not at all, actually." He looked away.

They reached the peak and sat down in front of the church of Saint George. The buildings of the city sprawled below them before giving way to the blue ocean.

"It's humbling, isn't it?" she said. "I used to come up here as a kid with my family, but I don't remember much of that. I came up here again, after the change. I wanted to get as far away from the world I knew as possible and be alone. I was scared. I didn't know what to expect. I only knew about vampires from the movies. I thought I was going to be a monster."

He gulped and looked over the horizon. For the first time since meeting him, he seemed to be somewhere else.

"What are you thinking about?" she asked.

He blinked as if coming to after being sedated and shook his head. "Nothing. I just… I'm trying to imagine what it was like."

Nessa stared across the horizon, remembering how her vegan diet had stopped satisfying her, how she had felt a constant thirst, how she had read all the legends and worried that she would turn into the type of creature that would prey on children, and the first time she stuck her pronged tongue into a live rat. It had squirmed and shrieked as she drained its life. As someone who had spent six years of her life not eating meat, it had horrified her. She had vomited and cried afterward.

The more she fed, she noticed an increase in her vitality. Her dark hair grew even thicker and started to shine. Her skin and eye color deepened. She had grown powerful. While she hated killing the rats, she had quickly learned that she couldn't live without live prey. It was either the rodents or people.

Matthew put an arm around her. "You don't have to tell me everything yet. I'm just curious."

She offered him a smile and returned her gaze to the city below. She imagined it engulfed in flames.

———————

The man in black who had eyes like stone reentered the room, accompanied by another soldier wearing dark fatigues and carrying an assault rifle. Nessa narrowed her eyes at him. Matthew turned around. When he saw the two men step inside, he got to his feet.

"What the fuck is this? You can't keep us here. I'm a fucking American. You know what kind of shit you'll get into for holding me."

The man in black smiled, baring polished teeth, and turned to the soldier. The soldier smirked. A laugh escaped his lips.

"What? This is funny to you? I want a goddamn phone call."

Nessa felt something like a lead ball in the pit of her stomach. Of course Matthew's threats were funny to them. Whatever would happen in this room would happen off the books. Matthew had yet to understand that.

The man in black looked at Nessa and mumbled something in Greek.

"What did he say?" Matthew asked.

"He said you're not getting any phone call."

"Well, you tell him…"

The man cut him off with more words in Greek. Matthew looked to Nessa for translation.

"And he said if you don't shut up, he's going to have you shot."

Matthew's bottom lip trembled. A whirlwind of mixed emotions blew across his face: fear, panic, rage, despair.

Don't say anything else. Please, don't say anything else.

Though he couldn't hear her thoughts, he heeded their warnings.

The man in black set his stone eyes upon Nessa. "When was the last time you fed?"

She said nothing.

The man in black nodded at the soldier who walked over and smacked her across the face. Matthew opened his mouth to protest, but the soldier flashed him a look that said *don't even think about it*.

"I asked you a question," he said.

"I don't know. I lost track of time. It's been a while."

"You're hungry, aren't you?"

She nodded.

"So why don't you feed?" He gestured to Matthew.

She shook her head, too distraught to form words.

"Your name is Nessa Sgouros. You think of yourself as some kind of peace activist. You used to cut school to take part in the protests organized by the Direct Democracy Now! movement back in 2011. You've been a problem for our government for a while and that was only made worse when you became a blood. Now you think you're, what, going to stop the escalation of this conflict?"

She didn't answer the rhetorical question and braced for a blow from the soldier. No strike came and the man in black continued.

"Between the four of us, I'll admit that I admire you, Nessa. You have strong beliefs and you stand up for them with little to no regard to your physical well-being."

"If you admire me, if you respect me, why don't you stand with me? Why can't you see this is all wrong? I've never harmed anyone. A lot of us have never harmed anyone."

The soldier raised his hand to strike, but the man in black shook his head.

"I said I admire you. I didn't say I agree with you." He bent close to her. "I despise your kind. You're an aberration. All of you. And I have just as little respect for people who stand with creatures like you."

For his last sentence, he glared at Matthew. He narrowed his eyes and tightened his jaw. Nessa thought he would order the soldier to shoot Matthew where he stood, just out of the pure hatred for a beat who had dared stand side by side with a blood. He returned his eyes to Nessa.

"What I admire is your tenacity. Your dedication. Because of that, I'm willing to let you live."

"I don't care about dying," she said. "You can silence me, but you can't silence what I've started."

"I'll even let you go," he said. "But first, you have to feed."

"I won't."

"You will. You can only go so long without human blood."

"I've never fed from another human."

"If you drink from Matthew, I'll let you go and you can go back to demonstrating against this worldwide conflict. Maybe you'll change some minds out there. It's doubtful, but you'll have a much better chance doing it out there than in here."

The man in black turned toward the door and left with the soldier in tow. Nessa and Matthew exchanged glances. Matthew's eyes were wide with fear. Nessa reached for him and he flinched.

"It's okay," she said. "I'm not going to eat you."

The tip of her tongue throbbed as the barb tried to force its way through. She shut her eyes and tried not to think about anything.

———•———

The night before the protest in Syntagma Square, Nessa and Matthew returned to Lykavittos. The city below was illuminated, looking like thousands of candles burning in the dark. They sat beside each other on the ledge, the lit-up church behind them. She put an arm around him.

"You ready for this?" she asked.

"Yeah, I'm excited. Well, maybe that's the wrong word."

"It's a huge commitment. We could be out there for days. Maybe even weeks."

"I know. I'm with you." He kissed her. It wasn't the first time he had, but this time it felt bigger, like it sealed some kind of deal, and she knew she had a real partner in this. He pulled away slightly and whispered, "I promise."

She returned the kiss, running her hands through his hair, plunging her tongue into his mouth. He pulled away.

"The barb. Will it stay inside?"

She giggled. "Of course."

"I read that the *lamia* sometimes seduce men so that they're easier to feed off of."

"I would never do anything to hurt you," she said and he nodded.

They resumed the kiss and fell into each other, shaking off their clothes and caressing each other's exposed skin. Waves of pleasure tingled across Nessa's body as Matthew kissed and touched. He was gentle, almost vulnerable, as they made love.

When it was over, he rolled off of her, sat up, and wept. She placed a hand on his back.

"What is it?"

He shook his head.

"You can tell me," she said. "Are you afraid about tomorrow?"

"That's not it. I just… I don't deserve this. I don't deserve *you*."

"I don't know what you're talking about, Matthew."

"In the States, I got into a lot of trouble. I did a lot of dumb things."

She cocked her head and waited for him to continue.

"I'm not the nice guy you think I am."

She brushed the hair out of his eyes. "Matthew, I don't care about your past. We all have one. I'm sure whatever it is can't be that bad."

Nessa saw his face go a shade paler. She took his hands. "You don't have to tell me now, but just know this: I know you love me. I know you believe in me. You have no idea how much that means, having someone to stand by me during all of this. It means the world to me."

He smiled and nodded, but the color didn't return to his face. Below them, the lights in the city continued to burn.

———•———

Nessa thought of that night now, as she sat in the cold metal chamber. Weak. Starving. Her body a throbbing canvas of pain. She cast a glare up at the security camera above and hoped whoever was watching could see she still had the strength to hate them.

Half an hour ago, Matthew had started to cry. He'd talked about how much he missed his mother. How he wished he and his father could reconcile after years of estrangement. How he wished he was back home with friends. Worst of all, he kept apologizing. It was as if he believed these feelings to be a betrayal of sorts. For a while, Nessa had cooed at him and told him it was okay, but gave up when it stopped working.

She thought of his words that night they made love. *I don't deserve this. I don't deserve* you. *I'm not the nice guy you think I am.*

By standing with her and going to prison with her, he had proven to her otherwise. He did deserve her. He deserved her love. He was more wonderful than he believed himself to be.

Nessa stared at the door willing it to magically open, so she and Matthew could escape together. She hated to give in to flights of fancy, but she was running out of hope. She even thought about praying, but why would a God that had let the whole world become a heap of shit move mountains to help her. She had never really believed in God. Her parents had raised her religiously, but she had never really bought it, and didn't think they really did either. Later her father had told her that the only reason they had raised her that way was so that she knew the option was there if she wanted it, not because they were religious. Any possibility of her changing her mind died the day she became a vampire. Not because she felt like she had been dealt a bad hand, but because she knew that her evolution and that of many others would only cause more conflict in an already deeply divided world. No God worth worshipping would allow such chaos.

Nessa drifted out of her thoughts and focused on Matthew. He was still crying.

"I'm sorry," she said. "I'm sorry I got you into this."

He shook his head. "No, you don't understand. Doing this was the only thing worth doing. The only thing that could make it right."

His choice of words struck her.

"Make what right?"

He averted his eyes and said nothing.

"Matthew…"

He took a breath, leaned against the wall, and cursed. She stared at him, waited for him to talk. The anticipation made her want to scream.

"Back in the States, I lived in a town called Flint just outside of Tyler, Texas."

Nessa tried to recall if she had heard of the town before. She couldn't place it. Matthew continued.

"There was this group of guys I used to hang out with. I'd known them since high school, and when I came home between semesters at UT Austin, it was always a big event. You know, lots of drinking, getting into fights, talking about old times. I wasn't much for starting fights, but I stuck up for my friends if they needed help. Just what friends do." Matthew took a breath that strained his features. "The last time I came home, before I left to study here, was at the height of the violence in America. Things were starting to look like they weren't going to get any better, like the world was getting ready to tear itself apart. Kind of still feels that way."

As he spoke, a sinking feeling that overpowered every other sensation overtook Nessa. Even the hunger paled in comparison.

"You hurt someone," she said.

Matthew's lips drooped and Nessa thought he was going to cry again.

"One of my neighbors in Flint, Marshall Pratt, was a school teacher, a husband, and a father. A real nice guy. Always around to lend a hand. Active in his church, which didn't impress me any, but in my town something like that mattered to people. I don't know exactly what kind of vampire he turned into, but he sent his wife and kids away as soon as the change took place. He believed himself to be turning into something spawned straight out of Hell. He stopped going to church. Apparently going scared him really bad. I know crosses and holy water don't really have an effect on vampires, but I think his religious background made him feel incredible guilt whenever he was near a place of worship.

"So this night I'm home, my friends are telling me all of this and we're getting drunk. The whole time, all I'm thinking is that whenever you turn on the TV, you're hearing about bloods killing beats. I asked if Marshall has killed anyone. My friend, Wallace, he says he can't prove anything, but he thinks so. There was a little girl who disappeared and the rumor around town was that she had last been seen around his yard. One of us suggests we do something to stop him, and… Christ, it was really bad."

"Stop," Nessa said. "I don't think I want to hear any more."

"I'm so fucking sorry."

"Just tell me this: did you actually participate in whatever your friends did?"

Matthew took another strained breath. He shook his head.

"No, I didn't do anything. I guess that's what feels worst of all."

Nessa tried to get her composure. She was so hungry she felt sick. The barb poked from the tip of her tongue and prodded the back of her teeth. She trembled with anxiety and anger. The image of Matthew looking on with his hands in his pockets as his friends beat an innocent man to death haunted her mind's eye like a ghostly impression on an old photograph.

"Nessa," Matthew said and reached for her.

She backed away. "Just don't."

Matthew's thoughts drifted to the night Marshall Pratt was murdered. He rode in the back of Wallace's F-150. A shotgun was laid across the floor. All four boys held forty-ounce bottles of Old English in various stages of consumption.

As the truck pulled up to Pratt's home, Matthew's skin grew hot. The reality of what he and the others planned to do now felt unavoidable, as if two strong hands had him in their clutches and were forcing him forward to his violent destiny.

Wallace had barely brought his truck to a stop when he pushed his door open and jumped out. He was a shorter guy, but what he lacked in height, he made up for in muscle. He was the kind of guy who spent hours at the gym every day and supplemented his meals with protein shakes. He was also the leader, an aggressive alpha male who liked having people fight alongside him.

Nathan, who they called Nudge, stepped out next, already huffing and puffing from the effort. Since graduating high school and not having football or track to keep him in shape, he had really let himself go. Only thing he was good for in a fight was holding someone down while the others threw punches.

Bradford rounded out the group. He had all the muscle of Wallace and half the brains. He shouted Pratt's name and Wallace silenced him with a slap across the back of the head. He responded with a giggle.

☠

Matthew was last to leave the truck, dreading every step closer to Pratt's house, but feeling powerless to stop it. Something about being around these guys made him give up his autonomy. Maybe that was why he'd opted to go away to college and then go abroad to get his graduate degree. He had wanted to change and grow. His better angels screamed at him to turn and run, to forget this whole thing, but he could feel those hands, pushing him forward.

What happened next Matthew would later recall in every nightmare. Every time he witnessed violence after that night, whether in film or in person, he would seize up, feel nauseous, and have difficulty breathing. It happened during the protest as the police turned on him and the other demonstrators. Ironic that during a day he stood up for justice, he would recall a time that he took part in such cruelty.

Nudge flung his considerable bulk against Pratt's front door. It fell in against his weight with a crash. There was a scream from inside and the rest of the boys scrambled through the door. Pratt was sitting in an easy chair, with a leather-bound book resting in his hands. Matthew thought it may have been a Bible. Before Pratt could make another sound, Nudge rushed him, tackling him to the floor. Pratt's skull connected to the hardwood with a wet crack.

Bradford started to laugh. He stood over Pratt, who was pinned to the ground, blood soaking his hair, fear swimming in his eyes. Bradford punched him in the nose over and over, laughing the whole time.

Wallace started in with the punches as well while Nudge continued to keep Pratt vulnerable. At no point did Pratt's eyes flare red. At no point did he display superior strength or speed. At no point did he come off as a monster.

Matthew's three friends hoisted the broken man to his feet and held him against the wall in cruciform. Wallace turned to Matthew.

"Come on, man," he said. "You're missing all the fun."

Matthew examined Pratt for any sign that he was something other than human, that he was a creature that deserved some kind of punishment. Pratt's eyes pleaded. His mouth hung open, leaking drool and blood. Matthew could see something like fangs between Pratt's lips, but even those made the man look more pathetic than scary.

"Hey, Matt," Bradford said between laughs, "don't be such a pussy."

Nudge had let go and was starting to break the legs off the coffee table. He held up the sharp end of one and grinned like a mad dog.

"Matthew," Wallace said. "What are you waiting for, man? Get your shots in before we stake him."

Something broke inside Matthew. *He's a monster*, he told himself. *He probably killed Alice Crane.*

Matthew laid into Pratt with everything he had, driving his fists into the man's face and body. The blows bloodied his knuckles and stung his hands. He screamed as he attacked, letting hate take hold. Not hate for Pratt. He didn't even think of Pratt. Matthew only thought of how much he hated his fucking town and everyone in it. Wallace, Nudge, and Bradford, his parents, himself. This was the end. He was never going home again. In the rush of violence, the beer wore off and he was forced to feel the full brunt of his self-loathing. Beating the shit out of someone else had only worsened it.

He ran out into the truck and closed himself inside. As more commotion came from inside Pratt's house, he examined the shotgun at his feet and contemplated using it on himself.

———— • ————

Nessa raised her head as the door to the cell opened. The well-dressed man entered, accompanied by a soldier. She couldn't tell if it was the same one from before. She was too exhausted. Too hungry.

"You're salivating," the well-dressed man said. She wiped at her chin. "Why won't you feed? Do you want to starve to death?"

He got close to her and the soldier raised his weapon, no doubt to make sure she didn't try anything funny.

"Do you know what happens to a body when it starves to death? Do you know how painful it is? How long it takes for your body to cannibalize itself?"

"You won't let me starve. There's a reason you're keeping me alive. There's a reason you want me to feed on him. Isn't there?"

The well-dressed man said nothing.

"I'm not stupid. I know you won't kill me, and I know you won't let me starve. So, why not? Why do you want me to feed?"

Nessa looked from the man in the suit to the soldier. Their expressions betrayed nothing. She looked to Matthew for guidance, but he looked shriveled and weak as he knelt in the middle of the room. He hadn't eaten in as long as she had. Maybe longer. Her eyes found the camera, staring down at her from the corner of the room.

"You need to record it, don't you?" The soldier tightened his jaw. "You want to get me on film eating someone I love so you can— what? Show the rest of the world what a monster I am? That my movement isn't worth supporting? Well, you can just forget it. I won't do it."

The well-dressed man looked at Matthew. "We heard what you told her. You didn't tell her that your friends staked that blood. Impaled him like he was a Hollywood vampire."

"I didn't do it," Matthew said.

"But you could've gone to the police. You could've done a lot more."

"Are you kidding?" Nessa said. "The police probably would've given his friends medals for doing it. They're fascists over there just like you over here. No one cares if you haven't hurt anyone or won't hurt anyone. They only care that you're different, and because you're different you're a threat."

"We didn't know that Pratt never hurt anyone. That's why I went along."

Nessa glared at him. She crossed the room and got in his face. "Matthew, you said you didn't actually hurt him. That it was just them. Was that true?"

He opened his mouth to answer, but his words caught in his throat. He dropped his eyes and gave a grim sigh.

"Matthew."

"It doesn't matter anymore. Whether I hurt him or didn't do anything to stop them from hurting him, I'm just as guilty."

"It makes a huge difference. It's one thing to stand and watch, but another entirely to participate."

He raised his eyes. Tears streamed from them. He didn't have to answer for her to put together that he had actively taken part in Pratt's death. The urge to kill him came suddenly and strongly. He had known her nature and knew what kind of person she was, and yet had led her on. He'd made her believe he was good when he wasn't. She looked down to see she had him by the throat.

"Kill me," he said. "Otherwise you'll die down here."

Gone from his eyes was the childlike fear that had been there when he'd first joined her in the cell. Instead, she saw a strange peace, as if now that this ugly secret had been revealed, he no longer carried its burden. Or maybe he wanted to die by her hand, out of some strange final act of love. Her tongue snaked out between her lips. The barb stabbed at the air. She almost forgot about the well-dressed man and the soldier. She almost forgot the camera.

She retracted the barb and let Matthew go. She backed away from him and faced the well-dressed man.

"No. I won't do it. I won't let you make me a monster." Even as she said it, a fury burned in her veins. The beast they wanted her to be itched for release. "I won't do it."

The well-dressed man nodded at her. He nodded at the soldier who raised his rifle and fired.

Nessa watched as Matthew's face exploded in a cloud of red. The screams tore their way out of Nessa and they didn't stop.

The well-dressed man's face hardened as his eyes stabbed into Nessa. "You'll never get out of here now, and without you, your movement will die."

Nessa dwelt on his icy words. The image of her lover's face blown off played in her head on repeat. He had sinned, but she had loved him and believed that he was truly remorseful for what he had done. The men who had killed him would never feel remorse. They were faceless drones of a system that had plunged the world into chaos. She thought about the camera. It had recorded them killing a beat in cold blood. She needed that tape.

As the well-dressed man turned to exit, Nessa leapt onto his back. Her tongue shot out of her mouth, its barbed tip plunging into the well-dressed man's throat. She drank. She drank and savored it. Too determined and psychically wounded to think of the moral implications of what she was doing. That all paled in comparison to her need to get that tape, to make the horrors of the day count for something. She drank in the man's life, felt it surge through her, sending hot tremors through her veins.

The soldier turned, seeming to just realize what had happened, and aimed his rifle at her. She pulled her face away from the suit's throat and howled. She used him as a shield and pushed him into the soldier. The gunfire went wild. She jumped over the suit and pinned the soldier to the wall. Rage unlike any she had ever felt boiled inside her. She felt alive, more alive than anytime she had given an impassioned speech, or made love, or the time she ran a marathon when she was seventeen.

"Where's the camera room?"

The soldier sputtered, and it came out gibberish. She reached down and, with strength she didn't know she had, snapped his forearm. A high-pitched shriek burst from his lungs.

"Shut up and tell me."

"Up the st-stairs. To the left."

She wanted to drink him, to make him pay for Matthew's death. No time. She broke his arm in another place and sprinted toward the stairs. Two more soldiers were waiting. She ducked and drove her shoulders at their knees. Newfound strength propelled her forward, knocking the human barriers aside. She heard screaming and realized it was her own.

She kicked open a door at the end of the hall and found the camera equipment. She found the drive and ejected it. With the drive in her hand, she made for the hallway. She wondered where she was. Some abandoned building. This had been a small operation, isolated in case something went wrong. It wouldn't stay small, though. More would come now that she had broken out. She could hear one of the soldiers calling into his radio for backup.

Nessa ran down the hallway, opening doors, trying to find the exit. She turned down another hallway, heard guns firing behind her. The fuel given her by the well-dressed man's blood pushed her until she found the right door.

A monster, she thought as she ran into the night clutching the drive to her chest, a necessary monster.

137

WET WORKS PART 6

By Jonathan Maberry

Global Acquisitions LLC
Pittsburgh, Pennsylvania
Day 17 of the Red Storm

One of the Red Knights, a real bull of a man, placed his hands against the press in the doorway and with a howl of black fury shoved with all of his might. The bones of the dead and the wounded splintered and the whole obstructive mass of bodies bulged through the doorway and then exploded into the room. A body struck Ledger and drove him backward all the way to the opposite wall as the rest of the Red Knights came streaming in.

The Knights fanned out, forming a half circle around the soldier. Swann, who cowered back a few feet from Ledger, was trapped in the same ring of death. The Red Knights smiled.

Those smiles were the most frightening thing Swann had ever seen. They made him cringe, they chilled, they promised awful things. There was no slow and easy death in those grins. The big Red Knight strode in, pushing roughly into the press, and the other vampires yielded to him. He stopped and stared at Ledger. Tears of blood broke from the vampire's eyes, and Swann had no idea what that might mean. It was not something he'd ever witnessed. He did not think it was a good sign.

The vampire pointed a black fingernail at the Special Ops soldier.

"Ledger…," he said, and there was so much passion, so much hatred in his voice that it made the name almost a curse.

Ledger stood ready to fight, weight shifted onto the balls of his feet, the empty gun in one hand, dripping knife in the other. He studied the face of the big monster.

"Nice to be recognized," he said. "Who in the wide blue fuck are you?"

"I am Anatoly of the House of Thorns. My name would mean nothing to you," said the vampire. "But I know you."

"House of Thorns, huh? Let me guess… you're one of his sons, right? You're one of his bastards."

"Say his name," demanded Anatoly. "Have that much respect before you die."

"His name? Sure. Why not? You're one of the sons of Grigor, the King of Thorns."

The other vampires hissed at the sounds of that name. They made complex signs in the air that reminded Swann of the way Catholics crossed themselves.

"I am the *last* son of my father," said Anatoly. Bloody spittle foamed on his lips. "I was not there when you killed my father, but I have prayed for a moment like this. Oh, how I have prayed. And I have made a hundred blood sacrifices so that this moment would happen. The stars and all the spirits of the dead have answered my prayers. Now the circle is complete and the House of Thorns is avenged."

"Let me stop you right there, Sparky," said Ledger. "First, fuck you and your house and your father. You want to know how he died? I stomped him to death. I stomped him so hard his eyeballs popped out. Sick, sure, but there it is. He died screaming and mewling like a pussy. He died begging for his life, but I'm not in the mercy business so fuck him and while we're at it, fuck you, too."

Swann did not think it was possible for a vampire to go pale, but what little color was in Anatoly's face drained away to leave him white as alabaster. The other vampires actually recoiled from Ledger. Swann had no idea what the House of Thorns was or who this Grigor was, but it was clearly a massive event in the history of these *upierczy*.

"You… dare…," began Anatoly, sputtering in his outrage, but Ledger interrupted him.

"I'm not finished, asshole. If you know me then you know how many of you sons of bitches I've killed. Alone, with my team, and with the women of Arklight."

All of the vampires hissed as if scalded. Swann flinched, too. He had heard stories about a group called Arklight. The same rumor mills that spoke of the Red Empire had whispered about a group of killers made up of women from different cultures, different countries, different religions, who were united in a longstanding war against men. Even before the V-Wars there were stories of ISIS camps being raided in order to free groups of women held as sex slaves. Those stories told of the appalling things done to the men. A few had even been left alive, though with no hands, no feet, no eyes, and no genitals. There were no pictures of anyone in Arklight, no names, nothing but the leavings of their attacks. And now Ledger spoke of them as if he knew them, and the Red Knights—these terrible monsters—recoiled from the mere mention of them.

"Witches," hissed one of the vampires, and the others took up the cry until Anatoly silenced them with a fierce growl.

"Arklight is nothing," he sneered. "Do you know how many of them I had? Do you know how many of them I used? They were to be fucked, to be our brood mares. They were nothing."

"Yeah, well, I hate to break it to you, Sparky," said Ledger, and now he did smile, "but one of them is standing right behind you."

Anatoly snorted and then laughed.

But there was something about Ledger's smile that must have made him doubt the man was joking. As one the Red Knights turned, Swann leaned to one side to look past them.

A woman stood there.

She was tall, slim, with the long legs and lean muscles of a dancer. Her face was lovely, her hair dark and long. She wore black clothes and shoes, and in each of her hands was a long, curved knife. Blood dripped from the tips of both knives.

"Hello, Joseph," she said.

Ledger grinned. "Hello, Violin."

THE REAL HOUSEWiVES OF SCOTTSDALE

By Marsheila Rockwell and Jeffrey J. Mariotte

Every time Ross followed the flagstone walkway leading toward Drake Pryor's massive front door, he felt like an anxious third-grader summoned to the principal's office. Saguaro cactuses were stationed at prominent points along the path like many-armed sentinels, and a spindly ocotillo blocked his view of the door until he rounded the last curve. Then, there it loomed, a construction of thick wooden planks held in place by rusted iron slats. The first time he'd seen it, Ross wondered if it would swing open or be lowered on chains. Only the dark, ornamental hinge straps and handle revealed its real nature.

He climbed the four steps that made the thing's twelve-foot height seem even taller, and wondered why anybody needed such an enormous entryway. Of course, Drake and Tiffany didn't *need* it. They wanted it—*Drake* wanted it, most likely—to impress and intimidate visitors.

Ross Williamson was not intimidated. He was a successful businessman in his own right, though not in Drake's league. They worked for the same company—or, more accurately, Ross worked for the company; Drake ran it. Echo Canyon International was as nonspecific as a business name could be, but that was the idea. They didn't want the universities and research labs buying information systems from them to know that they also paid professional warriors to provide security for those who installed and maintained electronic battle command systems in war zones. Drake had risen through the ranks on the defense contracting side to become CEO, while Ross's expertise in transportation and shipping only merited VP status. And that had only been for the last six months, since Drake had brought him from the Herndon, Virginia, office to corporate headquarters in Scottsdale.

He was reaching for the doorbell when the door swung open. Tiffany Pryor stood there, a smile etched onto a face that could have belonged to a slender nineteen-year-old, though Ross knew she was in her forties. Her lounging-around clothes, an assortment of silks and leathers that shouldn't have worked but somehow did, might have come off a Paris runway. A light floral fragrance wafted from her. "Come in, Ross. He's almost ready."

"How are you, Tiffany?" he asked as he stepped into the cavernous foyer. Two sets of marble stairs spiraled up from the far end, bound for the same second floor. Conspicuous consumption elevated to an art.

"Just fabulous!" She led him into a living room more spacious than some airport terminals. The smile never left her face. He wasn't sure it could. "How's Sharla?"

"She's fine. Looking forward to tomorrow night's bash."

"Fabulous!" Tiffany said again. "It's good to dress up once in a while, isn't it?"

"I suppose," Ross said. Echo Canyon supported various charitable and cultural organizations, including the Scottsdale Classical Arts Council, and the Black and White Ball was their biggest annual fundraiser. From what he'd heard, it involved people dressed in penguin colors making small talk, drinking too much, dancing badly, and writing checks big enough to hurt. And Sharla was looking forward to it, though he couldn't begin to fathom why.

"Ready to stand for inspection?" Drake's voice boomed from behind Ross. Spinning, Ross saw his boss crossing toward him, tactical boots loud on the tile floor. He was outfitted in desert camo, devoid of markings except a stylized badger emblem of his own design—the flames licking from its nostrils were a creative touch—and a colonel's eagle insignia centered on his cap. Drake belonged to no real army, but that was the last rank he'd held, so Ross supposed it was okay to claim it now.

"Looking sharp," Ross observed.

"You're a little sloppy, soldier. Suck in that gut."

His tone was commanding, and Ross complied without hesitation. His uniform matched Drake's, only without the eagle. He had never served, but Drake's demeanor gave him a taste of what it must have been like.

"Where's your weapon?"

He meant Ross's M16; the Glock 9 holstered at his hip and the KA-BAR tactical knife sheathed at his ankle were clearly visible. Drake carried his long gun and wore the same sidearms.

"In the car," Ross said.

"We'll get it on the way out." Drake shot his wife the briefest of smiles. "Look for me when you see me coming, Tiffany Marie," he said, then abruptly about-faced. Ross had to scramble to keep up.

"Happy hunting!" Tiffany called. "Don't let the vampires bite!" Ross didn't look back, but he was sure that smile was still pasted in place, and there was probably a "Fabulous!" ready to erupt from behind it.

———•———

Sharla waited down the street until she saw Drake's Hummer exit the property and drive into the twilight. She only caught a glimpse of her husband in the passenger seat because she was hunched low behind the wheel of her Audi. Not that there was anything wrong with her presence here—it was as much for his benefit as hers—but she still felt strange about it, even after several visits. She gave the Hummer a few minutes, to make sure the men hadn't forgotten something and wouldn't come straight back, then scooted into driving position and pushed the start button. A few minutes later, Tiffany ushered her inside.

"Answering your own door tonight?"

"Ascención asked for the day off," Tiffany said. "Some Mexican thing, a festival or something. They have them all the time."

"I thought you said she was Peruvian."

"Right, a Mexican from Peru." Tiffany looked her up and down, as if fitting her for a shroud. "What do you need?" she asked. "You look good."

Sharla's "good" and Tiffany's were never likely to be the same. Tiffany—and most of her Scottsdale crowd—were perpetually thin and tanned, blonde and gorgeous. Ross called them the Golden Girls because

143

they almost seemed to glow, like small earthbound suns in orbit around Arizona's wealthiest enclave.

Sharla had her own private name for them: the Real Housewives of Scottsdale, which she mentally abbreviated Real HoS and pronounced "hoes." Her hair was black, her eyes dark, and she burned if she went out *sans* sunscreen. Her roots were Slavic, not Nordic or Californian or whatever the Real HoS' were. Sharla had curves, which Ross appreciated, but spending time with the Housewives, she felt walrus-sized. She pinched her stomach, tapped her hips and behind. "A little off here and there," she said. "To fit into my dress tomorrow night."

"Stomach, hips, ass," Tiffany said. Sharla could almost hear the adding machine whirring in her brain. "Two-fifty."

Sharla knew the going rate, and had the cash in a pocket of the loose-fitting warm-up suit she wore. She passed it over. Tiffany gave it the briefest of glances before making it disappear somewhere in her own outfit. "Come on," she said. She started up the stairway on the right, and Sharla followed.

"I hope he's hungry," Sharla said.

"I've never seen him *not* hungry. I don't know how much they eat normally—if you can even call something like him 'normal.' But he's always ready for a meal."

"I guess they're normal," Sharla said. "They're all over, right? That's what they say."

"Vampires, yes," Tiffany replied. "But I've never heard of any like Cherry. Most of them drink blood."

"I'm glad you have the kind that sucks fat instead." Tiffany had told her early on that he was called a *lik'ichiri* in his Andean home, and that was why she'd named him Cherry.

As Tiffany unlocked a door that led into a seldom-used wing of the house, Sharla caught a whiff of the pine-scented air freshener she sprayed around the vampire's room. His smell was disconcerting, there was no doubt about that; he smelled sour, like meat left on the counter too long, with an added soupcon of gym sock. The pine odor covered it in the hall, but inside his room, nothing could overcome it.

"That's strange," Tiffany said.

"What?"

"The door didn't feel like it was locked."

"Does anybody else have a key?"

"No. Maybe I didn't lock it the last time?" The tone of her voice suggested she considered that unlikely.

They hurried down the hushed hallway to another door, one Tiffany had installed for this purpose. Tiffany stopped and said, "Damn it!"

"What now?"

Tiffany stepped aside so Sharla could see. This door was steel and had an old-fashioned hasp, a big one, affixed with dozens of screws. The padlock had been cut. "How…?" Sharla didn't finish the thought.

"Someone's been in here," Tiffany said, urgency tightening her voice. "He couldn't have done this from the inside."

"Who would do that?"

"I don't know." She pulled open the door and passed through, Sharla close on her three-inch heels. There was only one more door, the one into Cherry's room. When Sharla heard Tiffany suck in an exasperated breath, she peered around the other woman and saw that it was open, the jamb splintered around the lock.

Tiffany dashed into the room. Sharla looked past her, already pretty sure of what she would see.

Cherry was gone.

His room looked much as it always had. Tiffany's customers lay on a hospital-type bed, in restraints, while availing themselves of Cherry's services. Shelves across the room held medical supplies. The door to the half-bath that Cherry used was partly open. But the heavy steel chains that held him in place, connected to D-rings bolted into the walls and floor, had been cut.

"How…?" she began again.

"Shit!" Tiffany said, cutting her off. "Shit, shit, shit."

Sharla's hands went automatically to her hips. Though she was already turning back toward the door, eyes wide and panicky, Tiffany saw the motion. "Your butt is the last thing on my mind, Shar. We've got a bigger problem. Much bigger."

Tiffany led her back downstairs and into a niche just off the kitchen. There she had a desktop computer, which she used to run the household systems. She tapped a few keys and brought up a grid pattern dividing the monitor screen into six blocks. In another moment, each block filled with a different image, except the one in the top right corner, which was dark. Sharla realized she was seeing security footage from cameras stationed about the property.

Sharla tapped the dark one. "What's this?"

"Service entrance. Whoever took him must have known there was a camera there and covered or disabled it, but didn't know about the others. They're well hidden."

Tiffany worked the keyboard and mouse until only one screen showed. Sharla recognized the location as the corridor leading to Cherry's room, in a view looking down from above the padlocked door. A timestamp in the lower right corner showed the current time. Explaining that she and Drake had been out of the house playing tennis earlier, Tiffany hit one more key and the timestamp started counting backward, too fast to follow. After passing over footage of herself and Tiffany in the hallway—an unsettling moment; Sharla had never realized that her treatments were being recorded—the image remained stationary for a while. When there was more motion, Tiffany slowed the rewind, then stopped it when the hall was empty. When she started it again, it advanced in real time.

Seven people dressed in dark clothing and hats passed beneath the camera. This angle didn't show their faces, but some carried tools— flashlights, huge bolt cutters, a crowbar, other things. Nobody spoke; Sharla heard only the shush of rustling fabric, the soft thump of sneakered feet. They stopped in front of Cherry's door while someone employed the crowbar, and then they disappeared from view.

Tiffany let the video run. After almost six minutes had passed according to the timestamp, Tiffany sped up the video until a shadow approached the doorway, then returned it to real time. The group emerged again, and this time Sharla could see faces. They were dark-skinned, mostly, with dark hair and eyes. Short of stature, broad of face. She had seen at least one of them before.

"*Ascención*," Tiffany hissed.

"Isn't that your—"

"My maid. Former maid, now. Her ass is *so* fired."

Sharla started to respond, but then Cherry came into view. His wrists were handcuffed. A gash in his brow dripped blood into his right eye, which was already swelling shut. He was a good head taller than Drake, who was two or three inches over six feet. Cherry's body was lean but muscular, all long arms and legs, with a short, solid torso. Where he should have had fingernails there were instead sharp, curving protuberances that she could only think of as claws.

147

The most notable thing about him, though, was his face. His skin was pale and pockmarked, his hair an unruly mass of coppery curls. Under a heavy brow were deeply sunken gray eyes. His nose was barely there, and it receded more in contrast to his mouth. His jaw jutted forward, pushing out his lips so they were beyond the line of his nose or even that pronounced forehead. Behind them were many small, sharp teeth. When he went to work, he sliced the patient open with those claws, then bent forward, clamped those rubbery lips around the opening he had made, and sucked with a sound like someone drawing the dregs of a thick milkshake through a straw. When he had fed enough, he bit, and his teeth acted like a zipper, tugging the flesh back together and binding it so it would heal without scarring.

He was so hideous that "ugly" didn't begin to suffice. Yet, seeing him stumble along in chains, Sharla couldn't help feeling sorry for him. He wasn't evil, or at least didn't seem so. He did what he could to survive. That was what she told herself, anyway, when she was having fat sucked from her body—that she was doing him a favor, providing essential nutrients, not simply giving in to societal standards of slenderness.

While Sharla was fixated on poor Cherry, Tiffany was listening to the words picked up by the microphone. "My Spanish is rusty," she said, "but I think I got the gist of it. They're meeting a truck tonight. From Chicago, I think. It sounds like they're selling Cherry for a lot of money. They're worried about the guys with the truck—they were promised what they wanted a month ago, and they didn't get it. If Cherry isn't delivered tonight, it's going to be very bad for this bunch."

"Who are they? Besides your ex-maid?" Sharla asked.

"I recognize a couple of the others. Servants at some of the neighborhood homes. They sound really worried."

Sudden motion on the screen caught Sharla's eye. Cherry tried to yank free of his captors, but somebody hit him with a Taser. His handcuffed arms shot into the air, his back arched, and he let out an agonized wail. After the shock passed, he was docile again, and they led him out of the frame.

Tiffany rewound one feed after another, playing them forward enough to see what became of Cherry. He was taken through the house, down the stairs, and out the service entrance with the disabled camera. Outside, a truck waited, barely within the camera's view. Three men standing around it were nothing but shadows in deepening gloom.

Sharla bit her lip. The vampire was homely, and she had not established any rapport with him—he was a tool, nothing more—but she hadn't disliked him. She didn't want him mistreated.

She was as surprised as Cherry's captors when he slumped forward, causing those nearest him to move closer, trying to hold him up. As they did, he yanked his arms apart, snapping the handcuff hinges. With the same motion, he drove a fist into the face of the nearest man. Another reached for him and Cherry opened his hand, slashing with those thick claws. Blood flew and that person dropped. Someone fired a Taser; Sharla could see pain register on Cherry's face, even with the poor video quality. But he didn't slow down. He bulldozed Ascención and vanished into the darkness.

The group took off after him. When the scene was vacated, Tiffany sped up the video until the people reappeared, twenty minutes later. Sharla held her breath until everybody was in the frame, empty-handed.

Cherry had escaped.

Sharla almost let out a cheer, but caught herself. Tiffany didn't seem at all elated. "Let's call the girls."

"Why?"

"We need to find him, Shar. Before *they* do." She blew out a breath between her teeth. "I don't know why they want him, but he's ours, and we're keeping him."

Ross sat in Drake's Hummer, watching the gated estates of Scottsdale's elites roll by and wondering at the lives of the people inside. How many were like Drake, drunk on their own perceived power, bullies in business suits whose main goals in life were protecting their wealth and acquiring more? And how many were like him, wearing this lifestyle like an ill-fitting costume at a masquerade ball they'd never wanted to attend and couldn't figure out how to leave?

149

Ross had a feeling if he were to take a poll, the Drakes would win by a landslide.

"Why so serious?" Drake joked as the silence between them dragged on, only intermittently interrupted by the static of the police-band radio mounted to the dash.

"Just trying to get geared up for some action," Ross said, somehow managing to keep the irony from his voice. The only action Drake's moneyed militia ever saw was when they ventured into Tempe to pick up college girls, who might actually be impressed by their uniforms and bearing.

Well, that wasn't exactly true. The Scottsdale elites were often dazzled by displays of authority. As long as they were also accompanied by displays of wealth—the more ostentatious, the better. Drake's uniforms served the first purpose; the Hummer he drove and the Range Rovers and the Mercedes G-Class SUVs the others piloted served the second. Ross's own Beemer sat in Drake's driveway, too conservative a vehicle for their outings.

The radio crackled to life, sparing Ross Drake's reply. "All units in the vicinity of North One-thirteenth Place and Beryl. 10-V reported. Approach with caution."

As responses filtered back, Drake looked at Ross and smiled, an expression a little too reminiscent of the creatures they hunted for Ross's liking.

"Looks like you're going to get your wish!"

They pulled into a neighborhood a few miles south of Drake's, full of customized McMansions and luxury cars. A few homeowners in the streets toted the sorts of guns you'd expect wealthy Arizonans to own—HKs and silly gold-plated things that probably had never seen a shooting range, much less been used to protect the lives and property of their owners. They were more than happy to wave Drake's convoy through to where the real action was, an impeccable two-story at the end of a cul-de-sac with a pair of towering crested saguaros flanking the paved walkway.

Drake's Hummer screeched to a stop behind a military Humvee, up-armored with bullet-resistant glass and a machine gun turret on the top, currently manned by an Army National Guardsman. There were other Humvees on either side. The one on the left had a remote-controlled grenade launcher mounted on top, pointed straight at the front door.

As he and Drake piled out of the Hummer, Ross could see uniformed Guardsmen advancing toward the house on foot. It looked like they were carrying flamethrowers.

The machine gunner glanced at them as they moved up, Drake in front, Ross a step behind, Carl and the others crowding in after. Mark brought up the rear, his AK-47 at the ready, sweeping back and forth, looking for a target. The guy was ex-military—dishonorably discharged, Ross suspected, though he hadn't seen Mark's records, because most of the man's missions had been classified. He was even more anti-vampire than Drake, if such a thing were possible. And more gung-ho, which Ross found infinitely more frightening.

Ross didn't like having the man at his back, but at least he had the comfort of knowing Mark would have to shoot through several other bodies—many plumper than they ought to be—before he got to Ross's. Not much of a deterrent with the gun he was carrying, but Ross had always been a silver lining kind of guy.

"What unit you guys with?" the Guardsman called down, clearly not recognizing them. But reservists were activated on short notice all the time these days, so that didn't necessarily mean they didn't belong, and in the darkness all camo looked the same.

Then he got a good look at Drake's Hummer and any semblance of camaraderie drained from his bearing.

"Goddamned wannabes," he spat. "Stay the hell out of our perimeter!"

When it looked like Drake might ignore him, taking a step forward, the gunner swung his turret toward them.

"Look like I'm kidding, boys?"

Drake shook his head, red-faced.

"Good. Now stay put before you become collateral damage."

Then he swung back around to face the house, just as the grenade launcher on the other Humvee fired.

A streak of light sped toward the house, and the door—along with the entryway, and most of the front half of the structure—exploded in a burst of fire and smoke worthy of any Michael Bay film. Flaming shrapnel flew, pelting the Kevlar-wearing Guardsmen, the Humvees, and the two saguaros, turning them into blazing torches.

Three figures burst from the ruins, shrieking and charging the soldiers. Ross could make out long, lanky hair, twisted faces, and six-inch claws sprouting from their fingers. Then the vampires were engulfed in fire as the Guardsmen let loose with their flamethrowers.

The scent of barbeque filled the air, making Ross's mouth water for the milliseconds it took to connect the smell with its source. Then he tasted bile and looked away. Most of the others did, too, though he couldn't help but notice that Drake stared longer than the rest. Mark watched the whole thing, rapt, a grin that Ross hoped was unconscious lifting the corners of his mouth as the vampires' wails reached operatic levels before dying off into groans and whimpers and, eventually, silence.

As the soldiers sprayed the charred corpses down with fire extinguishers so they could transport them to wherever they took such things, Drake turned to his men, his face despondent. Ross couldn't tell if it was because they'd been rebuffed or because the show was over.

"Come on," he said, forcing cheerfulness that Ross was sure he didn't feel. "Got here too late to help on this one, but there's bound to be action somewhere else."

But he knew as well as Ross and the others did that there wouldn't be. Tonight was the only time since Drake had begun these patrols that they'd even seen real vampires in the blackened flesh. Sooner or later, they would have to face the truth. Scottsdale was no hotbed of vampire activity, and it never would be.

151

"When I found it—*him*," Tiffany corrected, "he was in the pool house, so many chains wrapped around him he couldn't budge. I didn't know who had put him there, or why. Honestly, I was scared shitless when he snapped at me. All those teeth."

She eased the Escalade around a sweeping curve as she spoke. They had spent about ten minutes at the house mobilizing the HoS. Now they were fanning out across Scottsdale, keeping in touch by cell.

"How did you know what he was?"

"I took a picture with my phone and uploaded it to Google's photo matching page. I didn't get an exact match, but there were enough close ones that I figured out he was a *lik'ichiri*. I ran to the market and got a bunch of pork fat, loaded it up with Valium and Ambien, and tossed it close enough for him to eat."

Sharla peered out through the Escalade's window. Judging from Tiffany's frequent complaints, driving so slowly must be physically painful, but even at that reduced speed it was hard to see into many of the yards they passed. Some were walled, others screened by hedges or dense stands of cactus. Searching in the dark seemed hopeless.

"What did he do?" Sharla asked.

"He ate it. Like it was Halloween candy and he was sugar-deprived. After a little while, he started drooping, and then he was out cold. I had to call a couple of the girls to help, but we got him upstairs and into the room where he does his thing. Or, *did*."

Sharla eyed a Mediterranean-style manse with ground-level lights beaming up its every surface, wondering who thought so much of a building that they kept it on permanent display.

"Who put him in the pool house?"

"Well, Ascención and her little friends, obviously," Tiffany replied. "But once he was in my house, he was mine. Finders, keepers. Anyway—"

She jammed on the brakes so hard that Sharla was rocked forward against her seatbelt, despite their leisurely speed. Sharla turned toward the front just in time to see an ancient blue pickup truck rocket past a stop sign. As she was braking, Tiffany cried, "Ascención!"

"What?" Sharla leaned back in her seat and peeled the belt away from where it had cut into her breasts.

"In that truck! I'd swear that was her."

Tiffany smashed her foot to the floor and the SUV bolted forward. As she cranked the wheel hard to the right, Tiffany's profile looked almost orgasmic; her lush lips were parted and the tip of her tongue was a pink triangle at the corner, her chin slightly raised and her eyes wide and liquid. She *was* beautiful, Sharla allowed. But that beauty had been sculpted, not grown, and her flawlessness made her look as vacant as a department store mannequin.

The turn pressed Sharla against her door, then the sudden acceleration out of it forced her back against the seat. "Easy, Tiff," she said. "Won't do us any good if we get killed looking for him."

"She's one of the bitches who stole him!" Tiffany snapped. "Maybe they caught him again."

Sharla decided that keeping quiet and letting Tiffany focus on driving was the best idea. They hurtled down the winding road too fast for her to scan for Cherry, so she watched for the pickup's taillights.

When they found the truck, though, its lights were off, and Tiffany almost tore right past it. "That's it!" Sharla shouted.

Tiffany slammed on the brakes again, bringing the Escalade to a shuddering, screeching stop. "What? Where?"

Still swaying in her seat, Sharla pointed. The old blue truck was nosed into the shadows beside a garage that could have doubled as an airplane hangar. The massive garage doors were open, splashing light across the roadway. "Right there."

Tiffany reversed, then nudged the Escalade into place beside the truck. "This is Allen Ashman's house," she said. "You like football, Shar?"

"Not especially." Sharla wracked her brain for the name of the local team, wondering at the abrupt topic change. Tiffany might seem like a vapid blonde to someone who only judged on appearance, but Sharla had learned that there was a reason for pretty much everything that came out of the woman's mouth. Usually a self-serving one, but, still.

The Cardinals, that was it; as if there were any similarities between hulking brutes throwing each other around the field and those brilliant, graceful creatures.

"Does he play for the Cardinals?"

Tiffany shot her a pitying glance. "Darling, Allen *owns* them. I've always wanted to get to know him better."

They climbed down from the SUV and headed for the open garage doors. Sharla expected that they would sneak up, maybe peer around the corner until they knew the coast was clear, but Tiffany just walked into the light as if she owned the place.

She stopped there, hands on her hips, mouth gaping open.

When Sharla caught up, she understood why. The garage looked like an automotive museum. Gleaming cars were spaced out on a spotless white floor. She recognized some: a 1960s-era Corvette Stingray and a Jaguar XKE of the same vintage, a Rolls Royce seemingly as big as an ocean liner, a bright red Ferrari Formula 1 racecar.

The garage was so clean that when she spotted an oil spill, it was as out of place as wedding cake at a funeral. She bent down for a closer look, and the sharp tang of fresh blood reached her nose at the same moment that her eyes told her it was not oil at all. Too red, and the splash was uneven, with drips all around the central mass. Droplets led toward a door at the rear. "Tiff."

"What?"

"There's blood here. A lot of it."

Tiffany came around the Ferrari. "God!"

"I know, right? There's a trail. Looks like it goes through that door."

"Then I guess we do, too," Tiffany said.

"But… all that blood."

"We're looking for a vampire, Shar. They like blood."

"Not Cherry. He likes fat."

"Sometimes you have to break a few eggs," Tiffany said. "Come on."

Sharla let Tiffany take the lead. She was beginning to regret being mixed up in any of this. Letting Cherry suck out her fat in the first place. Helping Tiffany round up "the girls," as she called them. Going with her in search of her missing *lik'ichiri*. Dieting and exercise had always worked before. Eventually.

Mostly.

They weren't as targeted as Cherry was, obviously. And she had never been as skinny as Tiffany and her friends. But curvy was okay, wasn't it? Especially when it meant you didn't have to go hunting for escaped vampires.

She realized that she'd let Tiffany get out of sight. As she hurried to catch up, she heard a gagging sound. Was someone choking Tiff? Would Cherry *do* that?

"Tiffany?" Fighting the temptation to turn and run, she rushed through the doorway.

Tiffany was doubled over, supporting herself with one hand against the wall, head down. Light spilling through the open door fell on what looked like a bundle of empty, bloody clothing at her feet. It took Sharla a moment to realize that there were two bodies amid the clothes, and a few more to process the fact that they were emaciated almost beyond belief. Her stomach heaved.

When Tiffany looked up, tears were tracking down her cheeks. "This one's Allen," Tiffany said. "I don't know the other."

Finding her voice, Sharla asked, "Did Cherry…?"

"Who else?" Tiffany replied, a bitter edge in her voice.

"Why?"

"Who knows? Maybe running took a lot out of him, and he had to replenish his energy supply. But… I never knew he was capable of… of *this*."

"We should call Ross and Drake," Sharla suggested. "They'd know what to—"

"No!" The ferocity of Tiffany's response was almost as frightening as the desiccated corpses. "They can't know about this. Drake would kill him in a heartbeat."

Not to mention what he might do to us, Sharla thought. From what Ross had told her, the man might be just as likely to shoot vampire sympathizers as he was to shoot the vampires themselves.

Tiffany made a "follow me" gesture. "The blood leads toward Allen's house. Let's get the girls over here and find that damn monster before Ascención does."

Drake's Badgers stood around their vehicles, car doors open to catch the staticky bursts from police-band radios and expensive scanners that picked up mobile phone signals. Flasks came out and were passed around. Drake accepted each one, taking a healthy slug every time. Ross only pretended to drink, sloshing a few drops around in his mouth whenever a container came his way. He would need his wits about him if he had to rein Drake in. The more booze Drake consumed, the angrier he became, and that reining-in looked more probable all the time.

"What's the fucking point?" he was saying. "We gear up and patrol and try to take responsibility for keeping our neighborhoods, our families, safe from harm. And then the cops and the soldiers fucking laugh in our faces. The average response time for the police in this town is *five minutes*. Think what a vampire could do in that time."

"I know, Drake," Ross said. "Preaching to the choir, bud."

"'Course, if you're a cop, your backup is there in no time flat. They watch each other's backs, but—"

"Drake!" A ruddy-faced guy with a strawberry blond crewcut was walking toward them, holding a cell phone. Ross didn't know his name; everybody called him Jocko, but that could have been because he had the build of a high school football player gone to seed. "Drake, listen to this, dude! Just grabbed it off the scanner."

He thumbed a button on the phone, and an anxious, heavily accented voice said, "...the vampire has been seen on East Wingspan Way, off Saguaro Canyon. Everybody get over there, pronto. *Todos ustedes*."

Drake's eyes had been dulled by disappointment and drink, but when he caught Ross's gaze, they were lively and alert. "You think it's real?"

"Sounded real to me," Jocko said. "I lost the call before anybody answered."

"Guy didn't sound like he was joking," Ross added.

That was apparently all Drake needed to hear. "Mount up, men!" he shouted. He called out the cross streets as he slid behind the Hummer's wheel. "Come on, Ross."

Ross climbed into the passenger seat and drew the seat belt across his chest, wondering if Drake could still operate the vehicle. He was still wondering when Drake slammed it into reverse and peeled backward, spraying sand and gravel, then shoved it into drive and whipped the wheel around. Once the vehicle was racing forward, he seemed to have a handle on it, and Ross breathed a little easier.

A few minutes later they were rolling slowly down a quiet desert road, the Hummer in front and five other vehicles spaced out behind. Ross tried to scan his side of the street and wondered what it was like to have so much—or to be so fearful—that you had to live behind locked gates and high walls.

He was lost in thought when Drake let out a grunt and stomped on the accelerator. The Hummer lurched forward.

"What is it?" Ross asked, head snapping forward, alert now.

"They just ran across the street up here," Drake said, cutting left into the oncoming lane. "Just beyond the headlights. Almost missed 'em." He braked and cranked the wheel hard, turning into a dirt track between two walled properties that Ross hadn't even seen.

Now the headlights picked out two humanoid forms, running away. With the walls on either side and open desert ahead, they had nowhere to hide and couldn't outrace the Hummer. As Drake bore down on them, they stopped and turned and held out empty hands.

They were kids, Ross realized when Drake finally hit the brakes and came to a sliding halt. Seventeen, maybe. Thin and pale and fanged, wearing dark clothes and terrified expressions. Drake slipped out his door, hit the ground, and brought his M16 up, all in one smooth motion, Ross following suit.

"Freeze!" Drake commanded.

The kids had already frozen, so Ross wasn't sure what more they could do. Pinned by the Hummer's headlights, they glanced anxiously at Drake's gun.

"You've sucked your last pint," Drake said. "We don't want your kind around here."

Ross saw his finger slip from the guard to the trigger. "Drake, don't!" he shouted, moving into the line of fire.

"What the hell are you doing, Williamson?" Drake barked.

"These aren't vampires," Ross said. "Are you?"

The taller of the two kids answered. "No. No, sir, we're not. Not really."

"What are you, pseudo-vamps?"

"That's right," the kid said.

"You want to become vampires?"

"Sure. It'd be cool. All that power. No school, no responsibility, just do whatever you want all the time."

"Open your mouth."

The taller kid obeyed. Ross grabbed one of his fangs with two fingers and wiggled it loose. Then he held it up for Drake and the others to see.

"They're wannabes," he said. "They dress up and pretend, that's all." *Not so different from you,* he wanted to say, but didn't. Instead, he turned his back on them and walked to Drake's side. "Forget them. They're not what we're after."

"You kids wish you were vampires?" Drake asked.

"Sometimes," the tall one said.

"Fair enough. You want to live like them, you can die like them."

His finger started to tighten on the trigger. Ross grabbed the barrel of Drake's gun and yanked it hard to the left. When Drake squeezed, the rounds tore chips from a wall but missed the kids.

"What the fuck?" Drake demanded.

"We're supposed to be protecting our neighborhoods," Ross said. "These are probably the kids of one of your neighbors. If we don't look out for them, what kind of protectors are we?"

"Hey, listen," the shorter kid said. He had a bit of a lisp, which Ross thought probably came from trying to talk with fake fangs in. "If you're looking for a real vamp, we saw one." The tall one punched his friend's shoulder, but the other stood firm. "Not far from here."

"Where?" Drake snapped.

"Just down the street. We tried to get his attention. In case he might turn us. Instead, he ignored us and ran away."

"Ran where?"

"Into that big garage over at Mr. Ashman's place."

"When? How long ago?"

"Maybe fifteen minutes. We were just coming from there."

"Come on, Drake," Ross said. "Let's check it out."

"How do we know they're not shitting us?"

"Chance we'll have to take," Ross said. "Besides, they're from the neighborhood. You really think they're stupid enough to send us on a wild goose chase?"

Drake scowled, indecisive.

"Come on," Ross repeated. "Before the vampire moves on."

"Fine," he said. "But don't you ever get between me and my target again, or I'll shoot through you. Understand?"

Ross nodded, hoping that would placate the man, but the look Drake shot him as he walked past made it clear they weren't done with the subject. Not by a long shot.

———•———

The HoS arrived far more quickly than Sharla would have anticipated, and she couldn't help looking for strobing red and blue lights, considering the traffic laws they had broken en route. Hoping for the cavalry to arrive, truth be told, so she didn't have to go into that huge house searching for a creature who could do... *that*... to people. A creature she'd let close enough that he could have done it to her anytime he wanted.

She wondered why he hadn't.

Then the women gathered round, and Sharla didn't have time for musing or vain hopes of rescue.

"...either the alarms weren't set," Tiffany was saying, "or one of the domestics worked here and knew the codes, because the cops would have been here ten minutes ago otherwise. But we don't know who all might be inside, so if you're wearing heels, take 'em off. Phones on vibrate and keep the chatter to a minimum. Oh, and I hope you all remembered your guns?"

Sharla was dumbfounded to see every one of the eight well-dressed women pull a small pistol of some sort out of their Coach, Gucci, and genuine Louis Vuitton bags. A couple of the women had Tasers and chains, which Sharla assumed were for recapturing Cherry once they found him.

The girls looked at her expectantly—maybe a little accusingly—when she didn't produce a weapon of her own, but to her surprise, Tiffany came to her rescue.

"Shar's is in the shop," she said, and the others relaxed. Sharla flashed her a grateful look, which Tiffany barely acknowledged as she continued. "Obviously, we don't want Cherry hurt. But anyone else who gets in the way? Well, it's up to you decide if they're worth more than the lipo scars and cleanses you currently don't have to deal with."

From the thin lines of Ravishing Red and Perky Pink on the faces around her, Sharla was pretty sure she already knew what the decision would be.

There was a brief clatter of heels hitting the ground, purses being slung across their owners' bodies, and rounds being racked into chambers. Little stars began winking into existence as the girls thumbed on their phone flashlights, then Tiffany led her strike force into the darkened mansion.

Ashman had apparently been a hunter—taxidermy animals and mounted heads took the place of expensive statuary and art, their dead, glass eyes reflecting the light from the women's phones, making it seem as if the animals were tracking their movements. Sharla knew it was just an illusion, but it made her shiver and move closer to Tiffany, whose little pink-gripped .22 looked less silly and more reassuring by the minute.

Oversized western furniture provided plenty of cover as they made their way through the house, dodging fringed lampshades and barbed wire accents. Their bare feet made little noise on tiles or carpet, and the women moved with surprising grace. Well, all except Sharla, who felt like her breathing was deafening and the sound of her sweat-slicked thighs moving past each other with each step could be heard throughout the entire house. But Tiffany didn't frown at her more than once or twice, so maybe she was just self-conscious, the curvy girl in the midst of models.

And then they entered Ashman's study/man cave, complete with a huge desk and throne-like chair in front of a fireplace, trophy cases bracketing it on either side, pool table in one corner, a flat-screen TV the size of a smart car and a handful of leather-upholstered recliners in the other, and two high, arched entryways in addition to the hallway they filed through.

And some of the biggest taxidermy animals yet, including a lion, a tiger, and, of course, a bear.

"Oh, my," Sharla murmured under her breath, and not even Tiffany glared at her for the comment.

The women fanned out through the room, and Sharla moved toward the enormous bear, fascinated and a little frightened. The thing stood erect, front claws extended, gaping maw full of sharp teeth, as if it were about to attack. She could almost imagine the drool puddling on its lolling tongue, then dripping to the wooden base it was mounted on before sliding down to the cold tile and... what was that?

A clawed foot, hastily withdrawn into the space between the bear and the leather recliner it guarded when the light from her phone touched it. *Cherry.*

Sharla motioned frantically to Tiffany. When she got the other woman's attention, she pointed to where she'd seen the movement. Tiffany nodded and caught the attention of the women who'd brought Tasers and chains—Melody and Nanette—who extracted said items from their bags as quietly as possible. When Tiffany was in place, she nodded and shone her light into the small space where Cherry was hiding. The other women rushed forward, and there was an electrical sound and a small cry of pain, followed quickly by the clanking of steel links. By the time Sharla made it to Tiffany's side, Cherry was trussed up like a criminal, with cuffs on wrists and ankles and thick chains connecting them all.

"All right, let's get him up."

Melody and Nanette pulled him out of his hiding spot while the other women gathered close and trained their guns on the vampire. Cherry had only been stunned by the tasing, but he didn't struggle as the women got their shoulders underneath each arm and began half-carrying, half-dragging him across the floor—he might be able to over-power them, but he'd take a chest full of lead before he made it a step past them, and he knew it. Sharla recognized the look of defeat that crossed his features.

She'd seen it often enough on her own.

"Okay, Cherry," Tiffany said, her smile triumphant—and, Sharla thought, a little relieved. "Time to go home."

There was the unmistakable sound of a shotgun being pumped and then a heavily accented feminine voice spoke from behind them.

"I don't think so, Missus."

"Ascención!" Tiffany shouted. "You put that down right now!"

Her maid didn't lower the shotgun, but raised its stock to her shoulder. "I don't work for you. *No más.* And he"—she indicated Cherry with the barrel of the gun—"belongs to us."

"Back away," a man said. Sharla didn't recognize him, but judging from his olive skin, dark hair, and discount-store clothing, he was another domestic servant. He held a big revolver that looked like an antique. There were ten or eleven of them, she thought, and a couple of them—big, muscular guys holding big, scary guns—looked like the thugs from the truck.

"Possession is nine-tenths of the law," Tiffany shot back. "And we have him. Let's go, ladies."

Sharla took a tentative step backward, not quite trusting legs that had suddenly turned to rubber, but unable to tear her gaze from the people pointing guns at them. Someone moved beside her, Cherry's chains clinked, and then someone else—she couldn't say who—pulled a trigger. In an instant, the room was full of bright flashes and roaring guns, and acrid smoke stung her nostrils and eyes.

Her first instinct was to freeze, but when a bullet whistled past close enough to hear it, she decided that was a mistake. She needed cover. She took a step to her right, thinking the bear might be dense enough to stop bullets. Before she could go any farther, a burst of automatic gunfire caught Nanette, who stood between her and the big beast. The rounds stitched across her midsection, cutting her almost in two, like paper torn along a perforation. Blood and tissue splashed Sharla. Reeling away, her foot slipped in a pool of blood on the tile floor and she went down, landing hard on her left hip and elbow. From that angle she saw a shadowed niche, between a stout wooden column and an antique globe. Staying low, she scrambled toward it.

Reaching relative safety, she allowed herself one deep breath. As she let it out, she heard a metallic sound in the shadows beside her. Startled, she snapped her head around and peered into the gloom.

Cherry cowered there, visibly terrified.

"Believe me," Sharla said. "You're not the only one."

Approaching the Ashman mansion, Ross heard muffled reports from inside and grabbed Drake's arm. "Hear that?"

Drake nodded. Through an upstairs window, light strobed erratically. Muzzle flashes. "Lock and load, men," he said. "It's hot in there."

He took point, dropping to a running crouch with his M16 at the ready. The other men followed. Ross tried to hang back, but a couple of the guys moved in behind, as if wanting to keep an eye on him. He had agreed to join Drake's militia because he cared as much about the vampire threat as anyone, but he doubted that vampires were shooting at each other inside Ashman's home.

The place was a multimillion-dollar showpiece with an aesthetic that smacked more of Aspen than the desert Southwest—a hunting lodge inflated to gargantuan proportions. Ross didn't have much chance to be impressed, though; the sounds of battle made their course obvious. The men thundered up a sweeping staircase with polished log railings. At the top, through a short hallway, gunfire illuminated hanging smoke like lightning in the clouds.

When Drake strode down the hallway, Ross wasn't sure whether to credit him with incredible courage or call for mental health professionals. He stayed close to the wall himself, in case lead came flying his way. The idea of racing back down the stairs made more sense every second, but before he could, Drake stopped short. "*Tiffany?*"

Ross emerged from the hallway in time to see Drake's wife spin around. With the arrival of the armed men, the gunfire came to a blessed pause. "What the hell are you doing here?" she demanded.

"I was just going to ask you that."

Before she answered, Ross spotted Sharla, protected from the enemy on the far side of the room by a massive pillar, standing next to a chained creature the likes of which he had only seen in nightmares. "Shar!" he cried.

His attention drawn to her—and the monster—by Ross's outburst, Drake asked, "Is that a vampire, Tiff?"

"He's my vampire, and those—those *menials* are trying to *take* him!"

"We can fix that," Drake assured her. He raised his weapon and sighted in on the creature. "This is it, men," he said. "Do your duty, and help me put this abomination down."

"No!" Tiffany darted between her husband and the chained-up monstrosity. "Leave him alone!"

"Fire when ready," Drake commanded. He lowered his rifle's barrel just a hair, so it was aimed at Tiffany rather than the vampire.

"Drake, don't!" Ross implored. "That's your wife!"

"If she's protecting a bloodsucker," Drake said, "she's no wife of mine."

Knowing it would forever sever any ties between him and his one-time friend—and might get him killed—Ross lunged. As Drake's finger tightened on the trigger, Ross plowed into him. The shots went high, sending down shards of glass and antler from a chandelier.

Drake slammed the rifle's stock into Ross's ribs, knocking the breath from him. "That's twice," Drake said, his expression grim. He snatched the M16 from Ross's grip and tossed it to one of the other guys. "You're done."

He was turning his weapon toward Ross when Tiffany fired.

———— • ————

Sharla's first instinct was to rejoice that Ross had found her, but that evaporated when some of the HoS turned their guns on the Badgers. Tiffany fired first, narrowly missing her own husband but distracting him long enough for Ross to scrabble away. The other men flattened themselves against the walls or the floor, or sought cover behind big, chunky furniture, and started firing back.

As if the gunfire had awakened them, the domestic servants on the other side of the room resumed their assault, too. Guns were going off all around, the racket deafening, the ever-thickening smoke savaging her eyes, nose, and lungs. Another of the girls fell, blood spurting from her throat, and then one of the Badgers went down. Sharla took a step back—and felt a solid bulk behind her, with chains wrapped around it. Anxiously, she stepped away again, braving a peek over her shoulder. Cherry stood there, trembling.

She felt the same way. Afraid of being shot, but also of Cherry. She had been prone on a table, nude, while he sliced her open with those razored claws, then bent forward and sucked the fat from her. The feel of his mouth on her had been oddly erotic, and after the first couple of times, she had looked forward to the experience as well as the results.

But he was still a vampire, and she remembered those withered husks he had left by the garage.

She looked away just in time to see one of the men aim a hunting rifle at Cherry. He sighted down the barrel, intending to make his shot count. Cherry saw the threat but, bound as he was, could not move to safety.

The man squeezed the trigger and Sharla reacted instinctively, moving between him and Cherry. The flash seemed overly bright, and she felt an impact on her right shoulder, as if she had been punched. Suddenly woozy, she watched the floor tilt up toward her. White heat spread from her shoulder, and then she saw the spray of blood and realized she'd been shot.

———•———

Ross knew the sound of his wife's agonized cry. He couldn't see her through the dark and smoke and press of bodies, but he tried to push toward her anyway. Drake snarled a command, and strong hands yanked Ross back and slammed him against a wall.

Jocko and Carl. Over the course of the evening, whatever respect Ross might have had for them had vanished. They were executives playing soldier, because it allowed them to exhibit cruelty and machismo they couldn't in the boardroom. As Ross tried to break their grips, Drake left his cover and walked toward Tiffany. She pointed her little handgun at him with both hands, but he raised his M16 again, saying, "That's cute, but it's got no stopping power. This, on the other hand…"

Uncertainty flashed across her features, and then Tiffany made her decision. She lowered her gun and stepped back. He continued—more of a swagger in his step, now that he had cowed his own wife—toward the vampire. Somehow, Sharla remained on her feet, although blood ran down her arm and rained onto the floor.

She held firm where Tiffany had not. Unarmed, she planted herself in front of the monster, wearing a look of fierce determination. Ross had never loved her more than he did at that moment. Drake lowered his weapon, and for an instant, Ross thought she had won. Then Drake swept the stock across her face. She tumbled to the floor, blood seeping from her mouth.

Ross tugged against the men holding him, to no avail. "Drake will deal with you later," Jocko said in his ear. "After this part's done."

"Drake can go fuck himself."

The man laughed. "Maybe after he does your wife."

Ross had had enough. He jerked his head to the side, smashing his skull into Jocko's nose and feeling cartilage give. Jocko's grip loosened, and Ross lashed out with his right foot, catching Carl just below the knee. The kick wasn't hard enough, and Carl's response was a quick, hard jab in Ross's gut. Carl was bringing his 9-mil around when an impact staggered him and pink mist blew out the side of his head. He collapsed in a twitching heap. Jocko still leaned against a wall, hands cupping his nose as if trying to hold it together. Panting, Ross looked toward Sharla.

With her down, there were no obstacles remaining between Drake and the vampire. Drake shifted his body weight, as if preparing to aim his weapon at the beast, but then he paused. Ross saw his head turn toward Sharla, who was trying to rise, her hands slipping on the bloody floor. He shifted again, and pointed the M16 at her head.

Too far away for Ross to do a thing about it.

—————•—————

Panic coursed through her. How did she ever wind up here? All she'd wanted to do was shave off a few pounds. She would never be skinny and glamorous like Tiff and the others, but she wanted to look good for Ross. Now she was in a three-way gunfight, and Ross's best friend was pointing a rifle at her. The gunfire had come to a stop, and all she could hear was ragged breathing and shuffling feet and the clicking of Drake's jaw as he worked it. He seemed to be considering something—probably whether to shoot her in the brain or the heart.

Somebody shouted in Spanish, and she realized it was Ross. She had no idea what he was saying. To her surprise, it wasn't one of the domestics who answered him, but Cherry. She had never heard him utter a word.

"Don't cross me, Williamson." Drake said.

Ross ignored him and talked with Cherry. After another couple of moments, he called out louder, and one of the thugs, with long hair and a goatee and a body that could have been chiseled from stone, crossed the room, mindless of the danger. He and Ross conversed in rapid-fire Spanish.

"You want to watch her die, Ross?" Drake asked, "I don't blame you, man, she is on the chunky side."

Ross paid him no attention. He shook hands with the big man, who crossed back to his side. Ross didn't look at Drake or Sharla. "Tiffany," he said. "We need to talk."

Tiffany's eyes narrowed as she looked from him to Drake and back again.

"So talk."

"He wants to stay with you. Keep doing what he's been doing— against all odds, he actually *likes* you and the other women. But free; not a slave. No more chains."

Tiffany frowned thoughtfully.

"What about them?" she asked, nodding toward the domestics.

"They're on bo—"

"What the *hell*, Tiffany?" Drake interrupted, gaping at his wife in fury and disbelief. "There's no way you're cutting some deal with these assholes to keep a *vampire* in my house. *I'm* in charge here, not y—"

"Shut up, Drake," Tiffany said flatly. She turned her back on her husband, giving Ross her full attention. "You were saying?"

"They're good." He looked at the man he'd brokered the deal with, saw him nod. "They don't want—Cherry?—specifically, just a *lik'ichiri*. I still have contacts in South America from my defense contractor days.

I'll get them a new one—a steady supply of them—and we'll throw in a hundred grand for the inconvenience. And they'll let you keep Cherry. And, of course, stop shooting at us."

Ross watched her chew on her too-pink lip as she mulled it over, then she nodded.

"Okay. I—"

Whatever she'd been about to say was lost as Drake made an apoplectic noise and launched himself at her back.

Ross wasn't sure what he meant to do—though the rage on Drake's face made murder a safe guess—but whatever his intent, he didn't get far.

Tiffany began to turn, raising her gun, but before she could, the *lik'ichiri* snarled and lunged, looping the chains connecting his wrists around Drake's neck and twisting them.

Drake dropped his gun and brought his hands to his throat as he tried to pull the heavy links away, but Cherry only pulled them tighter. Drops of bright blood appeared as the metal bit into Drake's flesh, mirrored by the reddening of his face as he struggled to breathe. There was complete silence in the room as he fought futilely against the vampire's grip, his visage darkening from crimson to purple as his writhing slowly weakened, then ceased altogether.

Finally, the vampire loosened his hold and Drake slumped bonelessly to the floor. The thump of his head against the tiles echoed in the quiet room.

Tiffany stared down at his body for long moments before turning back to Ross, expressionless. "You'll pay the hundred grand?"

As Ross nodded, there was a commotion behind her, and Sharla yelled, "Tiff! Watch out!"

Tiffany spun and put three bullets in her husband's body as he tried to rise—two in his chest, the last one in his head.

She lowered her gun and shook her head. "Bastard never did know when to quit."

———◆———

Outside the Ashman house, Ross's agreement sealed, Tiffany ushered the now-unchained Cherry into her late husband's Hummer. Behind her, the men from Chicago loaded bodies into their truck, "cleaning" apparently having been part of the arrangement Ross had brokered.

"I still can't believe he's… gone," Sharla said to Tiffany, placing a comforting hand on the other woman's arm. "I'm so sorry."

Tiffany shrugged.

"I can always get another husband. My figure's harder to replace."

Sharla's sympathetic smile faltered and she dropped her hand, stepping back into Ross's waiting arms.

"You guys need a ride to the hospital?" Tiffany asked.

Ross answered. "No, it's just a graze. I can take care of it at home. It's not far; we'll walk."

"Suit yourselves." She climbed in the driver's side and slammed the door, revving the engine and beginning to back down the driveway. After a few feet, she stopped and poked her head out the window.

"You want to come over later and have Cherry do his thing? You already paid for it."

Sharla shook her head.

"No, thanks. I think I'm done with that," she said, earning a tight squeeze from Ross.

Tiffany frowned. "Suit yourself," she repeated, then disappeared back into the Hummer.

Sharla and Ross watched her drive away. In the east, the sky was already edging toward light. She shifted in his arms.

He gazed down at her, reaching up a hand to gently wipe Drake's blood from her cheek.

"You're the most beautiful woman I've ever known," he said softly, reverently, and for the first time, she believed him.

She smiled.

"Come on. Let's go home."

As they turned, hand in hand, Sharla reflected that, despite everything else, it really was a lovely morning for a walk.

WET WORKS PART 7

By Jonathan Maberry

Global Acquisitions LLC
Pittsburgh, Pennsylvania
Day 17 of the Red Storm

"**K**ill her!" screamed Anatoly.

The woman named Violin raised her knives and smiled. She was beautiful but it was not a pretty smile. It was a viper's smile. A scorpion's. A killer's.

The Red Knights rushed at her.

Swann yelled a warning for her to run. She did not.

Instead she did as Ledger had done earlier. She moved into their charge. Except she did it with so much more speed, so much more grace. Her hands became blurs tipped with silver. As talons clawed at her she turned and was not there. As hands grabbed for her there was a swirl of motion and those hands clutched air as they flew up, no longer attached to the reaching arms. Throats opened to her and spilled blood and life into the air.

Anatoly roared like a lion, but he did not attack the woman. Instead he leapt into the air to try and smash Ledger to the ground. He battered the gun from Ledger's hand and locked his fingers around the man's knife-wrist as they crashed into the wall and then fell to the bloody floor. Swann rushed in and lashed out with as powerful a kick as he could manage and caught Anatoly in the ribs. It was like kicking a brick wall. Pain detonated in Swann's foot and he fell, feeling agony from several shattered toes and metatarsals.

Violin leapt like a dancer, turning in the air to kick, landed still pivoting and slashed at the legs and bellies and groins of the Red Knights as they tried to surround her. She was laughing as she fought, filled with a red delight that seemed to conjure terror in the eyes of her enemies.

Ledger rolled as he landed, jamming a foot hard against the floor to give him leg power to add to his hip twist so that Anatoly's body turned instead of crashing straight down. As the vampire landed hard on his hip, Ledger drew his knees to his own chest and kicked out, catching Anatoly in the chest. Between the force of the fall and the power of that double heel-kick, the big vampire lost his grip and reeled back. However, the knife flew from Ledger's hand and went spinning away into a pool of blood.

Anatoly made a reflexive grab for it and Ledger punished him for that by chopping the vampire across the throat. It was a powerful blow but the angle was bad. Even so, the big vampire coughed and sagged back for a moment, giving Ledger an opportunity to escape. He did not take it. Instead he rolled onto one knee, braced himself with his hands and fired off three very fast chopping kicks at Anatoly, catching the monster in the chest, collarbone, and on the side of the head. The last blow really rocked the Red Knight backward and Swann realized that Ledger must have some kind of steel reinforcement in his shoes. As Anatoly scrambled to reclaim his balance and reset himself for an attack, Ledger pressed him. He spun on that braced knee and dove forward, grabbing the vampire's hair in both hands and slamming the creature's head backward and down. The fact that Anatoly's neck did not immediately snap spoke to the immense power in his neck muscles and shoulders. He hooked a punch over and down and connected with Ledger's forehead, dropping the man flat.

Violin must have seen this for she cried out, and that split second of inattention nearly cost her the fight and her life. A bulky Knight with a face like a gargoyle lashed out with a huge fist and struck her a savage blow across the face. Violin staggered and bright blood flew from her torn lips. She reeled backward against the wall, her knives loose in her trembling hands, eyes glassy and momentarily unfocused. The other Knights gave malicious, hungry grins and closed on her. There were five of them and Anatoly made six. Ledger was hurt, too. The world seemed to suddenly dwindle down to this moment. All of the politics, the pain, the struggles, the hope, the sacrifice… it all blew away like dust to reveal a hard truth that threatened to bring Swann to his knees.

We're going to lose.

We.

Not the humans. Not the vampires.

We.

As if a window opened up to let him look from today into a certain tomorrow, all Swann could see was a wasteland. Drained of all life, burned to ashes, wrecked and ruined and dead. The end result of ten thousand years of civilization, of millions of years of evolution, of all struggles to come down from the trees and rise up to build something, to *be* something. To create, cultivate, and curate a world worth living in.

Gone.

And all of it, every last bit of grace and beauty and potential torn down by maniacs like these. Fanged and unfanged, monsters all.

The moment of silence held. Held.

And then Luther Swann screamed. Not in fear. Not *only* in fear. He screamed in rage, with a fury hotter than anything he had ever felt before. In all of the battles and struggles since Michael Fayne's transformation set the world to burning. He ran straight at the group of vampires surrounding Violin—a woman he did not know and had never heard of only minutes ago—and slammed into them. The pain from his broken foot only threw gasoline on the fires of his anger. He had no words, no threats, just a continuous and inarticulate howl of fury.

The vampires turned, hissing, laughing, reaching for him with their black talons, and Luther Swann knew that he was going to die. At least now, after all this time, he would die fighting for something rather than yelling and not being heard. He would rather go out this way than live to see everything fail and fall and perish.

He did not inflict so much as a scratch on any of them. One of them turned and punched him in the chest hard enough to pick him up off the ground and hurl him ten feet backward. Swann could feel his sternum crack. He fell hard and fell badly and the lights in the room suddenly seemed to become far too bright and then fade quickly. He

172

skidded fifteen feet through blood and lay there, gasping, thinking he was dying.

But he saw what happened.

He saw what he had accomplished.

A moment of chaos, a moment of distraction. That was all it took. Everything changed. The world had slipped a gear and now it caught again.

The Red Knights had made the mistake of turning away from Violin and looking at the screaming, stupid human. They had swatted him like a fly, but it cost them. Violin sprang at them, her knives moving, her eyes focused once more, her mouth frozen in a hard smile of pure joy. It was the most ugly beautiful smile Swann had ever seen, and somehow it reminded him of the Crimson Queen.

The knives cut and cut and cut. The Knights turned back to fight her, but the advantage they had was gone and the red room became redder still.

A scream made Swann turn and he saw that Ledger was on his feet, blood streaming from a scalp wound, one eye puffed nearly shut. Ledger had Anatoly down on the ground with a knee on the vampire's throat as he systematically smashed the Red Knight's face with a series of powerful blows to nose, eyes, temples. Shattered bits of broken teeth flew up as Ledger's hands hammered down. During the distraction he, too, had seized the slim advantage and turned defeat into a brutal attack.

Swann tried to get up. Tried to help. Ledger's knife was ten inches from Swann's outstretched left hand, but it might as well have been on the far side of the moon. He watched as Ledger straightened, lifting his foot, and stamped down on the Red Knight's throat. The sound seemed very far away.

"Stay down, Doc," yelled a voice. Maybe it was Ledger. Swann did not know. The darkness closed in around him and opened up a big hole into which he fell. He did not remember striking bottom.

THE THINGS THEY MURDERED

from Vampire Team Eight's Records of War
transcribed by Nancy Holder

THE TARGET:
    East Slav vampire cell, *ereticy* vampires embedded

THE MISSION:
    Doomsday is confirmed, and V-8 is going in to stop it.

THE FIELD:
    Outside Moscow

'm too old for this, Gunnery Sergeant Nestor Wilcox, AKA Big Dog, thought as he fought to see something. It wasn't snow, it was fucking sleet, and the wind wanted to grind it into Big Dog's eyes. No such luck; the team didn't need to know that their night vision goggles and body armor came courtesy of the death benefits of Porkchop, Dingo, and Genghis, who had designated Big Dog their beneficiary with the intention that their savage destruction at the hands of the enemy—goddamn bloods—would mean something.

No such luck.

Parachuting in had gone total FUBAR—recon had the arboreal canopy at the wrong height and Gonzalez was down with a broken leg, sucking up the medic's time when far worse injuries were surely on the way. Gonzalez was green; hell, they were all green, except for the remnants of V-8—him, LaShonda, and Taurus.

But they were in the drop zone, and maybe Big Dog should take a victory lap because *motherfucking shit* it had not been easy. Everything was harder and stupider because there was no more V-8, just the trio, plus some fresh blood—make that *beats*—and he didn't even know who had sent them on the mission. As far as he could tell, Colonel May had been benched and the so-called "One World" dream team had gotten as much accomplished as any limp-dicked band of liberals in any man's war. And these were the V-Wars. Armageddon with a bite.

Taurus had moved forward into the trees and now he came back and gave Big Dog the thumbs-up: *Target acquired.* At least their informant had given them better intel than the faceless dickheads who no doubt had more wrong stuff in store. He signaled to LaShonda to gather up her ten baby chicks and she nodded. Taurus approached and walked right past her without acknowledging her. He never so much as looked at her anymore. The Dog had taken each of them aside and grilled them, threatened to boot them off the team if they didn't tell him what the hell was wrong. Couldn't be a lover's quarrel; they weren't like that and never had been. Secrets weren't just bad, they were fatal. Of course he wasn't sharing the information that he had a killer hangover. Thing was, these days he always had a hangover. He'd probably fuck up if he didn't have one.

LaShonda, the Dog's number two, had refused to spill, insisting that nothing was wrong; she also reminded him that she and Taurus *were* the team so if he booted them, well, it would be like burning down his own house. She had no idea how much that had stung, didn't know that he drank the nights away wondering if the two of them were safer with him or released from their V-8 tour of duty.

Big Dog held up a hand and crossed to Gonzalez and Mandell, their medic. Gonzalez was unconscious. Mandell had doped him up so that he would stop moaning, which made the kid an even greater liability because now he was just cargo. But the Dog was damned if he was going to leave any of his people behind again. Even if they left in body bags, they were coming with him. Not that a broken leg was anywhere near a fatality. But the Dog had learned not to underestimate the Reaper.

"We get him out, he'll be fine," Mandell told his leader.

Big Dog nodded, gazing down at the slack-jawed grunt. The kid looked like he was twelve. His pain threshold was for shit. "Keep your weapon close."

"Yessir."

Taurus led the way into the Russian woods. Dog and LaShonda had discussed salting the foliage with a few of the grunts to provide cover and possibly surprise but neither of them trusted the babies to do anything but screw the pooch.

From the road, the HQ of Butterfly, a gang of East Slav vampires, looked like an abandoned *dacha*. It was fronted by a rounded brick turret; behind it, a stone porch served as the platform for pitted, worn gingerbread. According to their mole, the turret contained five armed vampires at all times, just itching for a home invasion. The entire structure was fortified six ways to Sunday and the main works was below ground. Dog's inside man—make that woman, make that *eretica*—was supposed to keep the light burning for him, and now he activated the tracker. Sure enough, it caught the beacon and the pulse in his earphone beeped in his ear like old-fashioned sonar.

The grunts crept through the forest, making a godawful racket. He could practically smell the flop sweat on them. He didn't know how they'd been picked for the mission, and neither did they. Soldiers didn't question orders; they followed them. The Dog had his orders, but he sure as hell was questioning them. He half-suspected he'd been sent here to fail. That would be typical of humanity's war effort—politicians and dictators making backroom deals with the filthy monsters who had murdered his people.

The East Slav vampires had acquired the capability to murder millions more. They had stolen one of the three Russian *cheget*, or nuclear foot-balls—portable command systems built into protected suitcases that could launch Russia's nuclear arsenal—as well as the current launch codes, called biscuits. The only good news for humanity was that there was a split over how to use the *cheget* and the codes—deploy the nukes themselves or sell the means to do so to the highest bidder?

The members of Butterfly were a species of Russian vampire that did not drink human blood. In the ancient mythology about them, they had "two souls," one of which rose at night to murder and ravage (much like Vampire Zero, Michael Fayne, when he began to transform, so Dog had heard). The butterfly had been associated with these vampires as the manifestation of their extra soul, and these terrorists had taken on the image as their logo. Pre-Event, their brutal "other self" was usually diagnosed as multiple personality disorder.

Butterfly was disordered, and ruthless in the extreme. They had zero loyalty to anyone but themselves, did not see themselves as part of some great vampire world order, and would do whatever they damn well pleased with the *cheget*. Their confusion had bought humanity some time to get the *cheget* back. Enter V-8 the next generation. Ha fucking ha.

V-8's informant was Katya Ivanova, who was embedded in Butterfly with her two henchwomen, Maria and Svetlana. Katya and company were a different kind of Russian vampire—*eretica*, "heretic" in Russian—genetic psychopaths, the "bad seeds" of stage and screen. After their junk DNA triggered their vampiric natures, they became psychopaths on steroids.

In the olden days, *ereticy* were said to be witches who had made pacts with the Devil. Parents who wanted their children to be good Christians would warn them that if they sinned, they would become *ereticy*. They were said to be old women who dressed in rags. But the fact of the matter was that the three women were babes.

Katya had originally hooked up with Butterfly because of her interest in their leader, Vladimir, and because she wanted safety in numbers for her people. There were hardly any *ereticy* in existence. They were only female, and their secret weapon was their "evil eye." They could mesmerize people into doing their bidding. They got the Minister of Defense of the Russian Federation to set himself on fire, and were only too happy to torture and maim every human they came across, especially the ones Butterfly targeted in their quest to obtain the *cheget*.

According to the Dog's briefing, Katya told the good guys that she was betraying Butterfly because of the infighting and instability. She figured Vladimir was going to fall and it was time to cut loose. In return for leading V-8 to the *cheget*, she wanted assurance that her people would be relocated and protected. That wasn't up to the Dog, but for him, the enemy of his enemy was not his friend. She was a fucking blood.

Of course everyone on the planet wanted the *cheget*. Russian mafiya was after Butterfly, as were old loyalists who want to reestablish the

Soviet Union. It was not the time to screw around with emotional baggage. It was time to get 'er done.

A figure stepped from the shadows and if God was good, thirteen M16s raised in salute. Actually, God's fitness for duty was not at issue: Big Dog was great at what he did.

Svetlana, Katya's number two, was wearing a form-fitting black snowsuit and a fur hat over a thick white braid that was coiled like a cobra over her shoulder. As agreed, she was wearing goggles to hide her eyes. The Minister of Defense had begged the doctors to put him out of his misery. The man said that Katya had never stopped laughing the entire time her two lackeys dipped his every cell in misery. Svetlana being one of those two.

In old Russian times, it was said that the *ereticy* could send their evil eye through the night to do their dirty work. Given all the things that Big Dog had seen, he believed that that was entirely possible.

LaShonda did not give her chicks the order to lower their weapons either. One move and this vampire bitch would be shredded. She was pointing a Kalashnikov straight at LaShonda and Dog bristled with fury. A need to protect his soldier warred with the mandate to move the mission forward.

Stomach sour, he walked up to her. She sniffed the air like a bloodhound, then smiled, revealing sharp fangs in the moonlight. He waited for the code even though it was obvious that this was their contact.

"'Whose woods these are, I think I know,'" she said in heavily accented English. It was from some poem. Typical egghead bullshit.

"Yeah, okay," he grumbled. "'His house is in the village, though.'"

She lowered her Kalashnikov. "They think I am in the village buying vodka." She gestured to a backpack looped over her shoulders. "It is laced with cyanide. Just in case."

Who for? Big Dog wondered.

"Don't lower," he ordered his soldiers. Then he said, "On the record, we have backup, and you cross us, I'll dig your fucking eyes out of your head."

Her smile chilled him. The goggles made her look like an insect and he clamped down yet more rage. Fucking non-humans. Goddamn global warming.

"We have the codes," she said. "Katya mesmerized Vladimir to get them. Once you extract us safely, we'll give them to you. You'll be a hero."

Her voice was silky. He wondered if she was doing some kind of mind game on him.

"Let's go."

"This is not a parade," she snapped, blank gaze taking in the cluster of recruits whose weapons were still pointed at her.

He looked at LaShonda. "Taurus and I will go in. Fall back. Then bring up the rear and create a second front."

"Yessir." She turned to the grunts. "You heard the CO."

If he was a praying man... but he wasn't. He and Taurus flanked Svetlana as she headed down the western exterior of the dacha. Shadows covered them but surely there were eyes on them—cameras and infrared. The way Taurus held himself—ramrod straight, cocked pistol, Defcon One—Big Dog got mad all over again wondering what he and LaShonda were hiding from him.

Halfway down, he pinged LaShonda. She pinged back: *situation nominal.*

Like hell it was.

Because suddenly flashbangs exploded and machine gun fire kicked up snow and gutted the row of trees to their right. Blinded, deafened, the Dog sprayed the entire fucking world with lead. Then someone clamped a hand on his shoulder and half-ran, half-dragged him toward the left. That was his dacha side. Pressure buffeted the edges of his silhouette; he was being shot at. The ground heaved beneath him. Grenade, he figured. Or mortar.

The effects of the stun grenade faded as he and Taurus—had to be Taurus—were running through utter darkness. They were being shot at. Then a figure dropped from the ceiling and slammed against Big Dog. A less seasoned soldier would have been dropped; the Dog stayed on his feet, then almost lost his balance when his assailant seemed to fly off him. They had been assured that there was no such thing as flying vampires. Nor could vampires change into things that could fly. Then maybe the man had been plucked off him and heaved away from him. Maybe a circus strongman could do that. But no one on his team was that strong, not even Taurus.

A second figure came at him from the right. Big Dog whipped a quarter turn and kept his finger on the trigger mechanism. His hearing was coming back: *ratatatatatatatat*. Maybe there was a cry of agony and a thump as the body fell. He didn't stop to verify. He just kept running forward. *A trap*, he thought. Or else Vladimir was not as malleable or stupid as Katya had believed.

If LaShonda was on her game, then the second front had already launched a counter-attack. The mission could still succeed. As he kept running forward, his eyes began to adjust to low-level ambient light. Twenty feet in front of him, Taurus and Svetlana were attacking a Butterfly vamp. Each had hold of an arm and as he aimed his weapon at the bastard, the blood's body was ripped in two. He silently whistled, impressed that Taurus had been able to hold onto the arm as Svetlana did the dirty work. Guy had to be bench-pressing in his spare time. Maybe he was juicing with steroids; maybe that was why LaShonda was so pissed off.

Another Butterfly launched himself out of the darkness toward Taurus, but the soldier used his assailant's weight against him as he pivoted and dropped. His attacker went sailing. Svetlana hurtled herself at the blood and tackled him, driving him to the ground. Without hesitation, Dog aimed and blew off his head. He missed Svetlana, but barely, and she snarled up at him. He was glad she still had on her goggles. He had a feeling her looks could kill.

She held up a hand and he realized she'd slipped on a glow-in-the-dark gauntlet. He followed it as she tipped downward at breakneck speed. This was the gangplank into the basement, where the vampires kept the *cheget*. This would be more heavily fortified and they would meet with the most resistance. He focused attention to the rear, attentive for LaShonda's arrival. A sharp, feral grin creased his face when footfalls thudded and body heat and sweat stink wafted around him like a fog.

Ahead, a light beamed and in the blurry oval he made out figures holding weapons. Then a fucking hail of gunfire decimated the world and Dog flattened himself against the wall. Screams echoed and blood gushed everywhere like a broken water main. He looked over his shoulder. The grunts were dropping like flies. LaShonda whizzed past him in a crazy-ass assassin ballet. He pushed away from the wall, busting his own moves. Some fucking anonymous puppet master had sent those kids to die under his watch. There would never be enough payback. But the sooner he got the *cheget* and the codes, the sooner they could get the hell out of there. He swore that some of the baby chicks would make it all the way through. How many he didn't know, but he would be damned if he'd give them all up. Gut-churning images of the eviscerations of Porkchop and Dingo blotted out his clear and present danger; he forced the flashbacks out of his head and pressed forward. LaShonda was in front of him, and then Svetlana, and in front of *her*, like an idiot, Taurus was on point. He should let the vamp go first; she was stronger and also expendable.

A Butterfly vamp leaped in front of Taurus and—*holy fucking shit, what the hell?*—Taurus grabbed him up, threw him down, and began stomping on him with his thick, metal-toed boots. The vamp was helpless against Taurus's fury and Big Dog tried to make sense of what he was seeing. Taurus could not be that powerful. A stronger case was made for some kind of steroid use.

Goddamnit, he thought. *That shit is evil.*

But if it worked this great, maybe he would use it, too. After all, alcohol was evil.

More bombardment; he didn't know how he wasn't hit but he didn't have time to wonder. The way was forward and he did that, blasting and punching and weaving through the deafening roar. Suddenly the entire wall burst apart, brick by brick by brick, the debris every bit as dangerous as bullets. Svetlana was barreling through and Taurus charged after her. Dog made it in. Someone collapsed behind him and he turned to look. All that he registered was that it was not LaShonda.

On the other side of the destroyed barrier, he was brought up short by what he was seeing: Vladimir, the massive vampire leader of Butterfly, all six-foot-five of him, on his knees with his head thrown back, staring into the eyes of a beautiful woman with wheat-colored hair hanging loose and curly down her back. Body armor made her look like Robo-

Cop; her right index finger was piercing Vladimir's jaw and blood was streaming down his neck. A third woman was standing on top of a pile of inert bodies. The face of the topmost one was contorted with horror.

A couple of shapes moved in the dusty haze and Svetlana blew them away. Behind the Dog, there was a volley of shooting, a scream, and then silence.

"Katya," the Dog said, and then he averted his gaze when she turned to look at him. Coming up beside her commander, Svetlana began to remove her goggles.

His people could be in deep shit.

"Don't look at them," he shouted. "Do not fucking look."

"Been there, done that, more or less," Taurus muttered, and LaShonda glared at him. Big Dog didn't have time to ponder that, but he filed it away.

"He has revealed the launch codes to me. We are ready to leave," Katya said in English. "You will provide escort." Her accent was very cultured, like from the British upper classes, and he wondered what her deal was. Not that he had time to find out.

"Where's the *cheget*?" he demanded.

She spoke in rapid-fire Russian to Svetlana. Svetlana crossed to the back of the room, savagely kicked one of the vampires she had shot just a few seconds prior, and disappeared.

Vladimir said to Big Dog, "I make deal. I give you codes."

"I can get them from her," the Dog replied.

"She will lie. She is most evil. Say she love…" He began to gurgle as she coolly pushed up hard with her fingernail, then slid it backward toward his neck. Blood gushed out; she grabbed the back of his head and kept ripping.

"Tell me you love me," Katya whispered to Vladimir.

"*Da*," he ground out, and his voice blazed with adoration. His flickering eyes were locked onto hers.

"Tell me you'll die for me."

"*Da*." He meant it with every fiber of his being. His slumping body arched and he struggled to raise his hands toward her. He looked like he was praying to her.

The Dog cocked his weapon. "I want the fucking *cheget now.*"

LaShonda and Taurus flanked him. He looked over at LaShonda and she held up a full hand of fingers. Five grunts had made it. Fifty percent losses. He was enraged.

Just then Svetlana appeared carrying the briefcase that housed the launch system. Could be a fake. Could be they were lying about the codes and so much else.

"You said you had a second front," Svetlana sneered.

He looked anywhere but at her. At the squirming Vladimir, as Katya unzipped his throat with her fingernail. "Yeah, they're still out there waiting to blow you away, you fuck with us." To Katya's general vicinity, he said, "Stop. I want to hear Vladimir's version of the codes before you kill him. See if they match up."

"Oh, sorry." She inched her finger into his neck and yanked out his Adam's apple. "I just killed him."

The dead vampire toppled to the floor. The Dog felt nothing but hatred as he studied the tortured body. Vladimir could have fried the earth to a crisp. His thugs had murdered LaShonda's baby chicks and countless other humans.

"Give me the *cheget,*" he said. On cue, Taurus and LaShonda raised their weapons. A brush of movement behind Big Dog suggested that the surviving soldiers had copied the actions of their betters.

Katya, Svetlana, and the third *eretica* conferred. Big Dog began to count to ten and at seven, Svetlana sashayed toward him and held it out.

"Sir," LaShonda said anxiously, and he figured the blood was trying to get him to gaze into her eyes. He grabbed the suitcase.

"Let's go." His voice was as sharp and cold as ice chips. "No tricks."

"Why would we trick you? You are protecting us," Katya pointed out. "Are you not?"

No clue. Don't care.

"Those are my orders," he lied.

They began to move. LaShonda swept up beside him and murmured, "It's too quiet."

Because everyone's dead, he thought, and he remembered his promise to take all his people home. He was going to have to come back, maybe.

But he wouldn't leave anyone here to rot. He had to get Mandell and Gonzalez, too.

"Keep your weapons on them at all times," he ordered. To the *eretic*y: "Put on your goggles."

"But—" Katya began.

"Put them on, goddamn it."

He heard a bunch of rustling. Then Katya said, "We've complied." He was in a fix: how to verify without turning into a zombie.

"You three take point." He'd examine the backs of their heads for goggle straps.

They exited the dacha through a labyrinth of subterranean tunnels clogged with electronics and dead vamps, coming back out into the sleet and waving pine trees with needles made of ice. He had ordered his people to put on their infrareds and check their gear and now, as they wove past boulders, he thought of all the things they didn't have— weapons, ammo, warm enough jackets—sufficient equipment to fulfill the mission. If they weren't being fucked over, they had three GAZ Tigr 4x4's courtesy of the Russian Federation Armed Forces waiting down in the valley. Justice would suggest that the undercarriage of one of them would be packed with C-4, but that was just wishful thinking.

Jesus, he was tired. A year ago—shit, six months ago—the thrill of victory would be juicing him with endorphins. He'd probably have a hard-on. But he was too angry and cynical.

So when they entered the woods and human soldiers and half a dozen *eretic*y dropped from the trees, he was in no mood to grab his ankles. As his team—low on ammo, exhausted, yet truly valiant— engaged the enemy, he made straight for Katya, clocked her over the head with his M16, and forced her to kneel. He slammed the barrel of his weapon against the back of her head, practically sensing her frustration as he planted a boot between her shoulder blades and pushed her facedown into the snow. He held her there, battling his own instincts to mix it up in the fracas, accepting the grim reality that the best thing he could do was keep her contained.

Bullets zinged and he did not move. Ghostly green shapes dropped from the trees; others gave chase. One arm around the *cheget*, he kept track of every detail; maybe Katya did too, because when the roar died down to a few screams and then it was just the wind and crunching boot soles, she said, "I'll give you the codes now. Just don't kill me."

That was when he knew for certain that she had planned this ambush. He had no idea why he cared. He was a hardened soldier. He was used to betrayal. War was always ugly, brutal, and usually immoral.

"We have only one *cheget*," she reminded him. "There are two more. And the launch codes are the same for all three. If you find them, you will control them."

That was stupid, but given the chaotic nature of the world, it made a kind of sense. He indented her flesh with the muzzle of his weapon, remembering the delight she had taken in slicing open Vladimir's neck and yanking out his larynx.

"I swear they are the right codes," she said. "I swear it."

Nothing ventured. "Okay," he said.

She opened her mouth and recited the strings of letters and numbers. He listened hard, absorbing them despite his utter fatigue.

"Say them again," he ordered her, and she obeyed. He kept his mind on the sequence, concentrating to see if she altered it, which would mean she was lying to him.

Then suddenly he became aware that his vision was telescoping. He was seeing *inside* himself—that was the only way to describe it—and looking down at his brain. There were iridescent strands attached at one end to his invisible fingertips and on the other, to various parts of his brain. When he moved one of the strands, his head raised, and he knew then that he was staring directly into Katya Ivanova's eyes. His weapon was in his hands; he was tightening the grip, turning it so that he was pointing it toward himself. She had him; she had him. He didn't know how it had happened but she was going to fucking kill him. And the horrible thing was part of him was willing to let that happen. It would be a relief, wouldn't it? Just let it be all over.

He saw again the faces of his dead team. He didn't yet know which of the troops under his command had died tonight. He hadn't had time. But there would be more. There would always be more. He was racking up a body count.

Murder.

What the fuck was he thinking, drinking to shut it all down? Weak, sloppy.

Murder.

"Do you have the code?" Katya asked silkily.

"Yes." His voice was so heavy he could barely speak. Much heavier than his assault rifle. He did not see her eyes. All he saw were dead soldiers.

After he shot her in the face, he saw fewer of them.

He didn't know how he had managed it. Everything in his brief had emphasized that once the *eretiсy* cast their evil upon you, you were a doomed man. Maybe he'd been spared because he was already a doomed man.

Maybe a few years ago he would have felt some satisfaction over her death. But as with the night's other victories, he remained untouched. Mesmerized by the darkness, he supposed.

A sweep of the landscape revealed inert white figures sprawled on the ground. One was writhing, and he crossed over to it. He squatted down. Another fucked-up-factor of this mission was that he didn't speak Russian.

The dying enemy was a human being. The Dog took off his goggles. He couldn't really see the guy.

"Who are you?" he demanded.

"Loyalist to Soviet Union," he said. "Give power back to the State."

"You asshole," Dog said, but the moron didn't respond. The Dog got up. This one wasn't going anywhere, and he wasn't going to be killing anyone today.

He put his goggles back on and hailed LaShonda as she approached. He said, "We have to get the fuck out of here."

She got the grunts back together—miraculously, they still had five—while Taurus stripped weapons off the dead and distributed them to the team. The Dog ordered them to go back the way they came, figuring there could be another surprise waiting for them at the Tigrs and this was as good a time as any to collect Gonzalez and Mandell.

He kept them out of the tunnels, preferring instead the open space. They presented better targets only in the sense of square footage; in the tunnels they would be cramped, confined, and sitting ducks if someone threw in a grenade. He swore again they would come back for their dead.

Then the dacha exploded in a fireball of stone and steel and plaster, wires, sensors, computer components. Everyone flattened against the snow, not out of an instinctive reaction for self-protection but because the roiling earth threw them off their feet. Heat and massive fragments rose into the air like a mushroom cloud. Dog knew that what went up would come back down and he shouted at LaShonda, "Move move move!"

Springing to their feet, weapons in hand, Taurus, LaShonda, and Big Dog formed a revolving triangle with the grunts inside. M16s cracked and reported as they hustled into the trees but continued to skirt the perimeter of the burning building. Smoke coated the sleet and the world stank of burned things including people—the planners of the attack, Big Dog surmised. He shot into the fire, then laid down a path of lead between his people and the dacha. They charged up an incline, Big Dog loathe to take such a chance, compensating by heaving grenades that threw pounds of snow up into the sky. Taurus followed suit; the snow reared up like a tsunami.

He thrust himself behind a tree, using it as a breakwater as the sopping slush crashed back to earth. Ignoring the biting cold, he pushed away as soon as possible, scrambling over a boulder the size of a Mini Cooper and then darting around another, this one twice as large and jagged along one side, as if someone had run the tines of a rake through clay, then allowed it to dry. Brushing his hand along the fissures, he closed his hand around a bloody, detached human finger. When he picked it up, he found a smashed human eye beneath it and recoiled, fearing that it was a traveling *eretica* evil eye.

He aimed his M16 up at the canopy and let it rip. As if on cue, the sleet stopped. The last drops fell and Big Dog's vision began to clear at once. Ahead of them were two Tigrs with their doors open, attackers behind the doors.

The fusillade spewed a nearly infinite number of rounds. Thick trees were cut in two. Fresh adrenaline coursed through the Dog's body, lending him the boost he needed as he wigwagged among the trees so as not to present too easy of a target.

A hand clapped his shoulder and he recognized the sensation. Taurus held out a rocket launcher and Big Dog dropped into the snow. Taurus set it up, and Big Dog gave him the word. The projectile as it rocketed forward made a whooshing sound, eleven hundred Hammer units looking for home sweet home.

Blam. Be it ever so humble.

The two rose as one, crab walked, set down, shot again. The Dog yelled, "How many do we have?"

"Two more," Taurus shouted back. Gunfire punctuated every syllable.

The launcher went off, sizzling before it arced into the sky and blew something to kingdom come. In the ensuing chaos, the pair shot forward again. A trio of grunts zoomed past them as agiley as mountain goats, and the Dog allowed a fleeting thought about the criminal wasting of youth on the young.

LaShonda and two more grunts caught up to them. He pointed to the slight northwest, where the turret room used to be, and LaShonda leaped like a fucking gazelle.

Mortars were incoming; the concussion threw up divots in the slush that momentarily stole Big Dog's balance. Vertiginous, his arms began to pinwheel and he gave thanks that the *cheget* was so well protected. Still, everything in this world had a shelf life, and all this wear and tear could not be good for it.

Then his foot crashed through what he immediately recognized as the thin, frozen surface of a pond. His points were waterproof but pinpricks of aching cold skittered all over his foot, shin, and knee. Taurus yanked him out and the Dog gritted his teeth as he hobbled on his frozen feet. At once his body began to cave, all the accumulated insults and exhaustion taking a toll that adrenaline could not ameliorate. He was beginning to fall apart. He needed whatever Taurus had, or some other wonder boost their medic had. His legs wobbled and he lurched from side to side like a drunk. Then one of the grunts grabbed his arm and righted him.

"Sir, are you all right, sir?" the man asked courteously.

Big Dog grunted a yes, but his joints were freezing up. He half-walked, half-trotted, this time avoiding the counter-measures their foe had in place.

A large piece of the dacha stove in, collapsing into the fiery pit, matter shooting back out like a million little comets.

It took him a second to realize that some of the bright yellow flames were actually streaks of sunshine. The sun was rising and black night had just transformed into gray dawn.

And silhouetted against the rosy horizon was a tank.

Its turret swiveled toward Big Dog, and in that second, a figure in a helmet popped up and took aim straight at Big Dog.

"I will drop him," the figure said to the group at large. Big Dog recognized the voice. "Lay down your weapons."

Shit, Big Dog thought. Unless he was mistaken, this guy was big in the Russian mafiyah. His name was Mischa Putin.

Everyone had come to the party, and each person wanted a goody bag. Trouble was, the Dog had just the one.

"You have the *cheget*. Good," said Putin. "Please to give it here."

"No fucking way," Big Dog growled.

"It is not a problem. I will get it myself," Putin said. He took aim, and Big Dog heard a dozen weapons clack to alert behind himself.

Mexican standoff.

Maybe. Who was going to shoot first?

"Putin," Big Dog grumbled, and Putin, a tall Cossack, bowed.

"Don't feel bad about giving me the *cheget*," he counseled in a mockingly sympathetic voice. "You wouldn't be able to deploy the football. You don't have the correct codes."

Knew it. There was no shock value, just boredom and detachment from the entire thing. He wasn't at all surprised that his mission had resumed its current status of situation head up ass.

"We just got the new ones," Big Dog lied, but it was unbecoming. The lie was just too fucking weak.

"We worked a long con on the government," Putin said. "We fed them disinformation for *years*. Memos, briefs, pillow talk..." He shrugged. "It worked. They programmed in codes *we* inserted into reams of memos and orders."

Big Dog's stomach clenched. "To do what?"

"Nothing. Not to work," Putin said. "Once we acquire them, we'll reprogram them. Until then, we cannot be hurt by them."

With a wave of his hand, two dozen soldiers moved from the trees, Kalashnikovs aimed at Big Dog, LaShonda, Taurus, and the chicks.

"Don't," Putin said gently.

If we die, we can't get the cheget *back*, Big Dog reminded himself. Someone trotted up to him and yanked the suitcase out of his arms. The same henchman pirouetted over to Putin's tank and the football was handed up.

"Watch this," Putin said. He did things to the suitcase—Big Dog had no idea what—and it popped open. He did things to the interior—the Dog still didn't know what—and Big Dog heard a whine. Something was activating, warming up.

"Holy shit," Taurus muttered close behind Big Dog. His tone was gravelly, menacing.

Different.

The whining faded. Putin shrugged and shut the lid. He smiled.

"Failsafe. The nuclear device received no instructions. It's so simple." His smile faded and he said something in Russian. All his solders took aim at all Big Dog's soldiers.

"You do know that your superiors are corrupt," Putin said. "That they can be bribed."

I fucking knew it, he thought.

"That you are alone now that your Colonel May has been castrated. You have no friends, no one to protect you. The loss of life you incurred in your most recent missions—"

"Shut the fuck up," LaShonda said.

To their credit, none of Putin's soldiers reacted. No one tried to hit LaShonda or take her insolence out on the Dog. They stood stock-still.

"Since I'm dying anyway, just tell me who set us up," Big Dog said. Holy shit, did Taurus *growl?*

"That only works in the movies," Putin said. "Buying time, getting the answers, escaping to fight another day."

"Well, that's appropriate since we're living in a fucking horror show."

Putin cocked his head. "You sound tired and bitter, my friend. And old. Day is done, gone the sun."

"Climb out of your tank and say that." As slowly and discreetly as he could, he activated the same tracker that had led him to the football.

Putin only smiled.

Right before a clutch of F-35s, B-1 Lancers, and A-10 Thunderbolt IIs pounded his tank, strafed the field of engagement, and laid down death.

Big Dog's people knew to scatter. He knew he had to risk it all to get the football. Probably no one was expecting him to run directly into the line of fire but as he did it, he felt like he was eighteen and he *did* have a hard-on and he let out a whoop. Since the bad guys were busy ducking for cover, he leaped onto the smoking, half-crushed tank, crashed the barrel of his M16 into Putin's face, and grabbed the *cheget*.

Second later, bombs found the tank and the Dog leaped wide, his body buffeted, his eardrums bleeding, and his teeth cracking. No matter; he kept hold of the *cheget*, kept hold of it. Kept hold.

But it sure hurt like hell.

———•———

He woke to beeps and boops, but he woke. With a groan not of pain but of frustration, he opened his eyes to find LaShonda and Taurus seated by his bed... and sumbitch, Luther Swann too. V-8's former friend half-rose when he realized that Big Dog's eyes were opened.

"Report," Big Dog ordered him, although technically, Swann was now his superior in the new world order.

"Gonzalez is fine. Mandell is getting a field promotion." His somewhat cheery demeanor sobered. "Putin survived. And he's acquired the second of the three *chegets*."

"But he doesn't know the real codes?" LaShonda said, moving forward and holding a plastic lidded cup with a straw to Big Dog's mouth. He sipped through cracked lips.

Do I look like Frankenstein? he wanted to ask someone. But that was pussy talk. The answer to LaShonda's question was what men craved.

"We don't know." Swann shrugged as if in apology. "Nuclear force... this changes things."

"Can some kinds of bloods survive a nuke blast?" Taurus asked. He still sounded off. Big Dog was going to get to the bottom Taurus's weirdness. He was tired of it.

"We were set up," LaShonda persisted.

Swann pointed to his lips then gazed meaningfully around the room. Big Dog translated: it was bugged.

"You're going to be up in no time," Swann said to Big Dog. "First down. Easy. Don't even sweat it." Then he mouthed, *And then... payback.*

Big Dog pursed his lips and narrowed his eyes at the civilian. From start to finish, civilians were responsible for this whole mess.

He thought of the dead members of V-8. Of the grunts who had died tonight. Of all the soldiers and civilians who were going to die as a result of this escalation.

Payback, he thought. And, *I need a fucking drink.*

Yeah, like a hole in my head.

"Payback," he said, and LaShonda and Taurus shifted and grinned, looking more relaxed than he had seen them in, well, ever.

We'll kill those sons of bitches. All of them.

His vow was made. And suddenly, for reasons he was not exactly clear on, Big Dog Wilcox felt... young.

WET WORKS PART 8

By Jonathan Maberry

Global Acquisitions LLC
Pittsburgh, Pennsylvania
Day 17 of the Red Storm

S wann heard voices.

Only voices, and only parts of the things they said. He tried to open his eyes, but either he was blind or the world had turned to shadows and ashes. There were only vague shapes that moved through the blackness. A man shape. A woman shape. Other shapes lay sprawled, unmoving.

"Fuck," said a man, "I think they killed the poor son of a bitch."

"No," said the woman. "He's alive. Barely, but alive. His chest is crushed. The sternum's in pieces. I think one of them is pressing down. Here, let me see what I can do."

Then there was pain.

So much pain. White hot pain, though the brightness of the pain did nothing to push back the darkness. All it did was fill his mind with an unbearable glow of pain and then it switched off all of the lights.

———◆———

Swann did not remember waking up. Awareness of consciousness came slowly, reluctantly, and incompletely. It was still dark, but then he realized that he was seeing actual shadows instead of the darkness of injury and disorientation. He tried to blink his eyes clear but clarity was elusive.

The voices were still there, though. Nearby.

"The hell'd you even know I was here?" asked a man. Was it Captain Ledger? Swann thought so.

The woman, Violin, laughed. It was strangely musical. An odd thing for so horrible a place. "I did not, Joseph. I followed Anatoly Grigorson and his team."

"So, you're saying it was your plan to attack them all by yourself?"

"There wasn't time to wait for my team," she said.

Swann heard footsteps. Wet footsteps as the big soldier and the strange woman walked through blood toward him.

"He's breathing," said Ledger.

"He's awake," said Violin.

He saw them now, shapes in the darkness, but they became more visible as they squatted down on either side of him. They were smiling, but it was the kind of smiles people wear when visiting the sick, or the dying.

"Hey, Doc," said Ledger with surprising gentleness. "How we doing here?"

Swann tried to speak. Failed. Managed a weak mumble.

"What did he say?" asked Violin.

"Doc," said Ledger, "hold on, okay? We have a medical team on the way. You're hurt but you're going to be okay."

Swann thought Ledger sounded false. Lying or uncertain. Trying and failing to encourage him; offering no believable comfort.

"He's saying something else," said Ledger as he leaned close.

"...*Fayne...?*" whispered Swann. It cost him a lot to force out that one word.

Ledger leaned back and Swann could see the answer in the man's face. Defeat, fear, anxiety.

"Gone," said the soldier. "Sprull's people got the body out before we even got here. Maybe more of the Red Knights, I don't know. But we lost, Doc. The Red Empire has their fucking messiah."

Swann heard the words and felt them punch him back down into the darkness. This time he didn't try to stop his own fall.

THE UNFORTUNATE CASE OF SISTER RUTH

By Jennifer Brozek

I have… we have… Merciful Lord, Bishop James, we need to talk."
Father Eduardo's words came out in a burst of emotion and exhaustion. "Now, Most Reverend. Please." This last came out in a whisper.

The bishop's brows furrowed in concern as he stood and gestured for the priest to enter his office. "Come in, come in. What is it, Eduardo? Are you all right?"

The priest closed the door behind him and moved with exaggerated care as he walked to the sitting area of the office. There, he set his laptop on the coffee table in front of the couch, placed his slim briefcase on the floor, and sat. Rubbing his face, he gathered his thoughts. "There's a problem, James. A big one. I must confess, my faith is shaken."

James cocked his head as he watched the Italian priest move through the room. He hid his surprise at Eduardo's choice of seats. "I take it, then, that is not to be an official report?"

"No. Not yet." Eduardo shook his head. "I don't know what to do. I'm at a loss…"

James walked to the chair opposite the couch but stopped at Eduardo's raised hand. "Yes?"

"Here." The priest patted the space next to him. "I have much to show you, my friend. Then you can advise me."

"As you wish." James took a seat on the couch. "Perhaps you should begin at the beginning."

"Yes." Eduardo rubbed his cheek. "Yes. The beginning." He took a breath and let it out slowly. "I went to investigate the miracles reported at the Servants of Saint Lucy, a convent in Arlington, Washington. We've been hearing quiet rumors of such for a few months now—spring flowers in the fall and the winter on a nun's gravesite, maladies and afflictions cured by a touch of the gravesite soil or the flower, little things. Nothing so gauche as a statue crying blood. But enough that I heard."

"I've heard these rumors as well." James kept his opinions and questions to himself. For now, it was best to let the younger man speak. When a priest confesses that his faith is shaken, all a bishop may do is listen until everything has been said. Then, ask the questions.

"What I found was… is… either a miracle or heresy and I don't know which it is."

Eduardo stopped speaking and gazed at James for the first time. His eyes begged for the help of his mentor and James could not deny that. "That is a strong statement." James let his words hang in the air and then nodded to Eduardo, encouraging him to continue.

"Strong. Yes." Eduardo returned the nod. He shifted to his laptop and opened it. Again his movements took on the sense of something fragile. "You will see." He unlocked the laptop and opened up a folder called "Sister Ruth."

Within the folder, James saw a series of folders. Each folder had a name attached to it: Mother Superior Phoebe Lake. Nun Rachel Kilmer. Nun Alicia Ebarra. Sister Heather Mead. There were at least two dozen in all. When Eduardo opened the folder called "Mother Superior Phoebe Lake," James saw that the folder was filled with videos—too many to count in a quick glance. He sat back and gave his attention to Eduardo again.

"When I arrived at the Servants of Saint Lucy Convent, I noticed that the nuns and acolytes were polite and nervous around me." Eduardo's voice took on the strength of a man used to giving reports. "This usually means one of two things: Either the miracles are a sham or the miracles are real and there is a fear of losing the miraculous. Most of the time, it is a sham. And yet, most believe the miracles to be real. The thought of being taken in by a sham shakes the foundations of faith. Part of my job is to investigate *and* to reaffirm faith."

James nodded but said nothing. He was pleased that Eduardo seemed to have regained his emotional footing.

"Unfortunately," Eduardo shook his head, "I don't know what to think in this case." He looked up. "It seems that Reverend Mother Phoebe and her charges kept a secret from the diocese. It is this secret that has caused me such heartache. But I will let her tell you as she told me."

With that, he double-clicked on the video icon labeled "Confession."

———— •••• ————

"Please state your name for our records." Eduardo's voice is heard from off screen.

The elderly woman before the camera is slender, wrinkled, healthy-looking in her white scapular, a black veil, and large silver cross on her breast. At her feet is an open file box with a dozen folders peeking out. She shifted and settled as she spoke. "I am Mother Superior Phoebe Lake, Abbess of the Servants of Saint Lucy Convent." She paused. "I know why you're here."

"Why is that, Reverend Mother?"

"You're here about Sister Ruth. Only, you don't realize it." She glanced away from the camera then back again. Mother Phoebe smiled a gentle smile. "I fear this will be a difficult investigation for you, young man."

"I will do my best. Tell me about Sister Ruth. Start at the beginning."

"No." She shook her head. "You need to understand what it is you're actually investigating. Sister Ruth Davis was a vampire. It is her miracles you've come to investigate. I now am petitioning for her to be declared a Servant of God."

Eduardo paused for a long time and Mother Phoebe waited with the air of one who would wait for the Second Coming. *"Sister Ruth was a vampire and you wish to have her canonized?"* His voice was soft with awe and horror.

"Yes. Now you understand the enormity of your investigation and I may begin, as you say, at the beginning." She clasped her hands together, palm to palm. "Sister Ruth Davis was thirty-six years old when she came to me and confessed that she'd become a vampire—afflicted with I1V1. I remember the day as if it were burned into my soul. She said to me, 'Reverend Mother, I'm frightened. I believe I've become a monster.

I don't know what to do. I've prayed for guidance but all I can think is that I must protect my sisters and this convent.'"

Mother Phoebe took a breath and shrugged. "You might imagine the kind of courage it would take a nun, just months after taking her vows, to come and confess that she was a vampire. It took me a bit but she confessed the changes in her mind and body to me."

"Tell me about these changes." Eduardo's voice still held a note of horror.

"She was sensitive to sunlight. Not because it hurt, but because it was so bright. She likened it to being at the beach on a bright day without a hat or sunglasses. The light did not hurt her skin, though she was fair. She also saw colors beyond what we normally see. For example, a green leaf fallen to the ground is nothing more than green to you or me. But to Sister Ruth, she could see colors at the edges of the leaf—reds, blues, yellows—where it had begun to die." Mother Phoebe smiled. "She could even see how the beehives were doing. It helped us understand that one of the Queens was ill."

"Expanded vision? Is that all?"

The Abbess shook her head. "No. She was stronger and faster. She worked harder because of her affliction. She did not sleep. Not as we did. She confessed that she spent most of her sleep hours praying for her soul and for guidance. By the end, it appeared that she only needed two hours a day of meditation to recharge. She began to request more tasks to fill the evenings when the rest of us slept. Tasks that had long lay fallow for wont of time and energy—which Sister Ruth had in abundance."

"How did the rest of the convent react to Sister Ruth's condition? Or, did you keep it secret from them as you kept it secret from the diocese?"

Mother Phoebe's eyes flashed with indignation. "Do not speak to me in that tone of voice, Father Eduardo. I understand what I did... what we all did... and why. Do not judge me until you know all." Her voice, sharp and commanding, softened. "And yes, every single nun and acolyte within the convent knew. We spoke together and decided *together* what to do."

"My apologies." Eduardo paused. *"Every nun and acolyte? Were there no dissenters?"*

"There was fear, yes." Mother Phoebe admitted, glancing away from the camera. "But, Sister Ruth had been among us and changed for more than six weeks before she came to me for help. We knew we were not in any danger. Even though Sister Ruth needed to feed. We were never in any danger. Foremost in her mind was her devotion to God and to doing good works. Even when she needed to feed. Perhaps, most acutely when she needed to feed."

"What did she feed on?" His voice was barely a whisper.

"Blood, of course."

———•———

James reached out and stopped the video. "This is about a vampire nun?" He stopped and shook his head then looked heavenward. "I cannot believe I just said that."

"Yes, Most Reverend. Now you understand my state. Not only are the miracles coming from the gravesite of a nun who became a vampire, Mother Phoebe wishes to formally begin the process of declaring her a Servant of God."

The bishop shook his head. "Such investigations cannot begin until five years after death. Sister Ruth died when?"

Eduardo pulled a thick manila folder from his briefcase and opened it. "She died about fourteen months ago."

"Then we have time and that will be a debate for years to come." James gazed at the laptop, not really seeing it. This was not what he expected when he rose for the day. *Nothing is ever put in my path that I cannot face. God be praised.* He turned his attention to the younger man beside him. "But, one afflicted nun could not have shaken your faith. There is more for you to tell me." He gestured to the laptop. "To show me."

"Yes, there is." Eduardo navigated through the folders until he came to Nun Sofia Cantor. "There is the devotion the others took to protecting the vampire. Sister Sofia was the one in charge of collecting the blood to feed Sister Ruth."

"You had no problems or second thoughts about having Sister Ruth in your midst?"

"You mean to ask me, was I afraid of a vampire living with us? No. I wasn't." A middle-aged Latina woman sat before the camera in the convent's traditional habit. The interview already in progress, she was comfortable speaking to the camera. "I miss her and her serenity. I think I knew her best. I was the one in charge of making sure she was fed."

"Could you tell me what that was like? What you did? How often you did it?"

"Of course. Sister Ruth needed no more than a pint a week. I collected this from a sister, a volunteer, each week. She never knew who it was from. On Mondays, I would collect and deliver the blood in a collection pouch—though I didn't use the anti-coagulants. There was no need. She would feed and dispose of the pouch, cleaning up after herself."

Sister Sofia gestured to the camera. "You see, we volunteer at a blood bank once a week. I believe that's how Sister Ruth survived before we came up with the system to keep her safe."

"What do you mean? You and your Sisters volunteered to feed her?"
"Yes."

"She didn't ask you to do so?"

"No." Sister Sofia gazed at the floor. "It was my idea. After the meeting. After all of us understood what had happened."

"Was she there at that meeting?"

"No. Sister Ruth excused herself so we could speak privately and candidly. And after so much talk—none of it about having her leave—we came up with the idea of the anonymous weekly donation. She never knew who she was feeding from."

Eduardo paused the video. "Sofia didn't know it, but Ruth always knew."

"What do you mean?" James tried to keep his voice level and neutral, though the thought of the situation turned his stomach.

"She knew. She always knew." Eduardo flipped through the stack of papers—pages of photocopied handwritten pages, notes, and pictures—until he came to one highlighted in pink. He looked down at the passage, started to speak, then shook his head. "Read."

James took the page without comment. He cleared his throat. "*I feel wonderful. I always do after I feed. It is the feeling of life coming into me and radiating out in waves. I know intrinsically that I must feed every two weeks to live without any drawback and once a week to ensure I am comfortable enough to pose no danger to my sisters. Though I know I could feed daily or every other day and be completely satiated. But that would be sinful. Gluttonous. And I will not do so. This affliction tests me but not in ways I cannot manage. God is merciful in this.*"

The bishop paused as his eyes scanned the next passageway. Then he continued. "*Yet, I cannot stop thinking about how good I feel. I believe it's because of the blood—Josephina's blood—that I feel this well. I've come to understand that like regular food, which I still enjoy, there is good blood and bad blood and favored tastes. I don't know if it comes down to blood type. I should investigate. I swore I would record everything about my condition for posterity.*

"*I hesitate in my investigation because of my sisters. They believe I don't know who gives me blood each week. But how can I not know? I smell it in the blood and on them. I sense their fresh wounds no matter how small. Each week, a different sister is my donor and my salvation. Each week, I must keep my gratitude to myself. Were I to look up their blood types to correlate to how good I feel after each feeding... they would realize their sacrifices were not as anonymous as they wished them to be.*

"*Does this mean I lie to them? I don't know. All I want to do is protect them as they protect me. I know so little and all I can do is pray each night for guidance.*"

"She knew," Eduardo repeated.

"Apparently so." James handed the sheet of paper back to the priest. "Did you interview everyone in the convent?"

"Yes."

"Did any of them object to feeding Sister Ruth?"

"Not as such." Eduardo navigated through the folders as he consulted his notes. "But one, Sister Alicia Ebarra, wanted to shift from human blood to animal blood." He found a video and fast forwarded it to the halfway mark.

———————•———————

A small Latina woman with gray streaks peeking out from under her veil nodded to something said. "Oh, yes. We did discuss how to f— ensure sustenance for Sister Ruth. The discussion went on for months." The nun bowed her head. "I… am afraid that it was my suggestion that caused her so much suffering."

"What do you mean?"

The woman shook her head and continued to gaze at her clasped hands.

"Sister Alicia?"

There were tears in Alicia's eyes when she looked up, but they did not fall. "I, like all of my convent sisters, was shocked to discover that Sister Ruth was a vampire. But, as she had not harmed anyone and was looking to us to guide her, I thought that, perhaps, we could… that she could consume animal blood." She took a breath. "I was wrong."

"What happened?"

"Sister Ruth was willing to do whatever we suggested. But she said the cow's blood tasted terrible to her. She said the same thing when we gave her sheep's blood the next week. At that point, she confessed to feeling ill when she fed. By the middle of the second week, she looked… terrible."

"How so?"

"So tired. Like she hadn't been sleeping. Deep circles under her eyes and a gauntness that wasn't there before." Alicia shook her head. "But she went on. We had pig's blood to try and we gave that to her before the week was out. She got violently ill. Her cell looked like an abattoir. She begged us to bind her to the bed. She didn't want to hurt us. She was hungry but not yet to the point of losing control." Alicia looked away. "She wanted to know how long she could last without human blood and how long she could control the inner beast."

"What did you do?"

Alicia looked at the camera with a sharp jerk of her head. "Me? We. What did *we* do? is the question."

"What did the sisters of the convent do?" Eduardo's voice was level and patient.

"We voted and the decision was to allow Sister Ruth her test of will." Alicia paused for a long time. Then she shook her head. "It was terrible."

"Did she become a monster or hurt any of you?"

Alicia shook her head so hard she had to readjust her veil. "No. Of course not. Nothing like that. Sister Ruth suffered but she suffered in silence and prayer. She took on the look of a very ill person but she never once attacked anyone. Not me, the Reverend Mother, none of us. In the end, Mother Phoebe declared Sister Ruth's test of will at an end after a full month. Then she fed our sister herself."

"Directly?" The horror was back in Eduardo's voice.

The nun gave him the look a disgusted teacher would give a student who had done something inexcusable. She straightened up and answered in a firm tone. "No, Father. She did as we have always done. With a needle and blood drained into a pouch. Though Sister Ruth was too weak to feed herself. Thus, Mother Phoebe fed her the blood from the pouch, pouring the blood—two pints for the sake of your archives— directly into her mouth. The effect was immediate. Her glow of health returned. As did her physical strength. Through it all, her will never wavered."

"Do you have her journal notes from that time?" James asked as Eduardo stopped the video.

"Yes, Most Reverend, I do." Eduardo shifted through the folder again, then handed the bishop two pieces of paper.

James skimmed them, without reading them aloud. He nodded to himself, thinking hard. This was going to be a difficult situation to deal with. "She did fight with bestial thoughts of murder and gorging on blood but her faith in the Lord strengthened her. Even when the sisters inadvertently put themselves in harm's way."

Eduardo nodded as he took the pages back. "They never knew how close she came to killing them all."

"But she didn't give in to temptation." The bishop shook his head, clearing it. "How did she die? How is all this linked to the supposed miracles at the convent?" *And why is your faith shaken?* James did not ask the question. Eduardo would confess that in time.

"She sacrificed herself to protect the convent."

———•———

Mother Phoebe gazed directly at the camera as she spoke in a dry, neutral voice but the brightness of her eyes and tiny hand twitches spoke volumes of her true emotions. "Just over a year ago, Sister Ruth did not appear for Morning Prayers. This was unusual. She was as devout as any nun I have seen. Her faith only deepened with her affliction. When I investigated, I found her in her cell, dead."

The old woman's brow furrowed at the memory. "She had moved a bench into her room, laid upon it with her arms down, and bled out into two buckets of water. I remember… her wrists… rather than cut, were torn as if by teeth. But no blood showed upon her teeth, her tunic, or the floor."

"She committed suicide? Why?"

Eyes flashing, Mother Phoebe corrected Eduardo. "Sister Ruth sacrificed herself for us." She took a breath and let it out slowly. "On her table was a letter and her journal. They explained everything. You see, Mother Superior Mary Theresa was coming to stay with us for six weeks. She was to guide us in the ways of providing succor to those who'd lost loved ones to vampires and how to spot the fiends while we did our good works… and who to report them to."

As Mother Phoebe paused, Eduardo leaned to James and whispered, "Mother Superior Mary Theresa had been an adherent to Reverend Josiah Mann's belief that the bible states that we should all kill vampires, werewolves, and other such 'magic users' on sight. However, after her visit, the Reverend Mother cancelled all her appearances with Reverend Josiah and has become cloistered."

———•———

On the video, Mother Phoebe shook her head. "Sister Ruth knew that it would be difficult for all of us to hide what we knew of her. That she was not the godless, soulless creature so many of the faith proclaimed them to be. She knew it would be too much to ask of us to continuously lie to the visiting Mother Superior. And she knew the moment Reverend Mother Mary Theresa discovered our secret, all of us would be denounced and excommunicated. We all remembered what Mother Mary Theresa had done to the convent in Oklahoma. How she had publicly humiliated the sisters and felt no remorse when the townsfolk burned the convent to the ground, killing all the sisters within."

"You're saying that Sister Ruth committed an unforgivable sin in order to protect this convent?"

"Perhaps before you judge as you have continuously done, you should hear the rest of what we have to say." Mother Phoebe gazed at the camera with her head tilted. "Or, should we end this now as you have already made up your mind?"

"No. Please, go on."

"We gave Sister Ruth a simple burial within our convent cemetery. There was no embalming. Nothing more than placing her body in the casket with prayers and burying her. From that week forward, the gravesite has sprouted shooting star flowers. If you are unfamiliar, shooting stars are a spring flower and go dormant for the rest of the year. Not so here. They have not stopped blooming. It was something Mother Mary Theresa commented on. She spent no little time in contemplation, walking the grounds of the convent and, after a single aborted lecture, apologized and excused herself. She left the next day, saying only that she needed to renew her faith in the Lord. That she'd gotten too wrapped up in politics."

"Do you have a theory as to why she left?"

"Some of the sisters have reported dreams of Sister Ruth. All of the dreams show her in a golden glow and she assists with a question they are wrestling with."

"Have you dreamt of her?"

"No, Father. But I have felt her blessings in other ways."

Bishop James pulled in a breath at the word "blessings" and darted a quick glance at Eduardo. For once, the younger man seemed at peace. He decided not to interrupt the video. Instead, he counseled patience to his suddenly racing heart.

"Tell me?"

"I'll show you." Mother Phoebe picked up a folder from the file box at her feet. "It's been well documented that I suffered from facial scarring from my childhood." She pulled a photo from the file and handed it to Eduardo.

There was a long pause, then the camera zoomed in close on Mother Phoebe's unscarred face. *"You have no scars."*

"No. Not anymore. The flowers from Sister Ruth's gravesite took them away. In my grief, I had picked one of the flowers and rubbed it on my cheek. When I returned to my duties, the other Sisters were shocked. I didn't understand why until I looked in the mirror."

———— ◆ ————

Eduardo stopped the video and slid a photo to James. It was of Mother Phoebe. But, instead of the clear-skinned, wrinkled woman in the video, it showed her with a livid scar running up the right side of her face. "This is how she looked until that moment. This is the first known miracle. Though, if Mother Superior Mary Theresa would speak to us, we might discover what made her seek isolation and silence."

"I see." James fought to keep his voice neutral. The photo of the Abbess shook him. *This could have been photoshopped,* his skeptic's mind whispered. *Also, there is no telling what sends a member of the clergy into hermitage.* "Are there more miracles?"

"Yes. From the sisters themselves and from some of the visitors to the convent." Eduardo pulled a small stack of papers from within the thick folder. "All documented. Sister Rachel no longer gets blinding headaches. Sister Isabel's cataracts are gone with no medical explanation. Sister Maria received a vision of her nephew, lost in a ravine. She called her brother and told him where to find the boy. Sister Lata no longer needs her asthma medicine." He paused at James's shaking head.

"Photos can be manipulated. Cataracts could have been secretly fixed by people with a story to sell. The vision is nothing more than hearsay. Asthma can be healed by good living." The bishop shrugged. "All of these can easily be explained away."

Eduardo stopped. "You don't believe the sisters of the convent?"

"They lied for a vampire for months. Who's to say that she didn't manipulate them?"

"Most Reverend…" Eduardo gazed at his hands. "I've dreamt of her myself."

"Oh?"

He nodded. "She told me that I had a long, hard road before me. But, as God is merciful, he would help me in one small way. Then, in the dream, she took an iron band from my head—one that I didn't know I was wearing. On the inside of the band were small spikes. I've not had a migraine since that dream, three weeks ago."

James pulled in a long slow breath through his nose, held it as he squared his shoulders, then let it out. "There must be other miracles for me to consider beyond the word of women who have something to gain from the story." He raised a hand at the darkening of Eduardo's face. "I speak only as others within the diocese will speak."

Eduardo nodded, still scowling. "I will give you three miracles that were not based on the word of another. First, there are the spring flowers. They were there when I visited in fall and then again in the winter. I had an expert tell me about the flowers. Yes, they were shooting stars, a spring flower. Second, there was an undefined but pleasant smell about the gravesite that had nothing to do with the flowers. Third, I had Sister Ruth's body disinterred."

"Ah." The bishop nodded. "After the request for Sister Ruth to be named a Servant of God. A decaying body is not a miracle. An intact one is."

"Yes." Eduardo shifted a photo to James. "She was not decayed and the pleasant smell came from her body. I had a mortician examine her while Sister Alicia and Mother Phoebe watched. He declared her whole."

James gazed at the picture of the nun in full habit. Sister Ruth looked very young for thirty-six and, most definitely, still alive. She didn't have the gauntness she wrote about when she was starving, though logic dictated that she should have. Her hands were clasped together. He could see the white bandages wrapped about both wrists to hide the wounds of her suicide. He had seen images of the dead before. In this case, if he had not known she was more than a year dead, he would believe her to be sleeping.

Finally, he lifted his head. "Are you certain she was dead?"

Eduardo shook his head in confusion. "I don't understand."

"She was a vampire. Are you certain that she wasn't... isn't... in some state of suspended animation?"

"In every way that I know how to tell if someone is dead, she was dead to me, Most Reverend."

"Who else knows about Sister Ruth?"

Eduardo threw a hand skyward. "Who knows? The rumors reached us over the months. There was a steady stream of people coming to visit the convent and its candle shop." He touched the stack of papers. "There are visitors claiming to have been healed of an affliction and others claiming to have dreamt of her. It is out there. The real question is... what do we do now? How can a vampire be blessed of God? How can she deliver His miracles?"

That was the question. No doubt about it. "For now, re-bury Sister Ruth at the convent. And we will watch for the next several years. You need to leave all of this with me. I need time to go through it and determine if, when it is time, to begin the process of declaring her a Servant of God. Finally, I think you need some time in contemplation. You have become too close to the situation to be objective. You need time and distance."

"But..." Eduardo began.

James narrowed his eyes and raised a hand. "I understand that you did not want this to be a formal report but, unfortunately, I must take it as such. I need time to consider all you have told me, brought to me."

"Yes, Most Reverend."

"I believe you should return to where you began, Father Eduardo. Go to your home seminary school in Italy. Go for a visit and I will follow up with the transfer. We will speak about all this again in one year." He stopped Eduardo from cleaning up the table of papers, photos, and laptop. "I'll do that. I will need to go through it all anyway. Is there anything of yours, personally, in all this?"

The younger man thought for a moment and shook his head. "No. It's all church business."

"Good. Good. Why don't you take the rest of the day to settle your affairs at home and get ready for the transfer? They'll be expecting you within the week." James watched the younger man with a keen gaze. There was both relief and defiance in his stance. It was to be expected.

"Yes, Bishop James. Thank you for seeing me." Eduardo paused as he stood.

James let the pause stretch out into something awkward and uncomfortable as he shifted through the papers and photos, looking at them but not seeing them.

Finally, the priest nodded to the bishop, "Good afternoon, Most Reverend."

"Good afternoon, Father Eduardo."

James sat up and waited to a count of ten before he stood and walked to the open office door. He watched Eduardo disappear down the hallway. He hated the defeated hunch of the man's shoulders. He wanted to reassure Eduardo that he was not in trouble. But the truth was, the bishop didn't know what would happen to Eduardo now.

Sighing, the bishop closed and locked his office door. Then, he pulled out his cell phone and dialed. He shifted into Italian when the phone on the other end picked up. "It's Bishop James Kovak. I need to speak with the Archbishop as soon as possible. It is urgent."

"One moment please."

There was a pause and the sounds of conversation in the background before the phone was picked up again. "Good evening, James."

"Good evening, Your Grace. My apologies for this late call... but it's happened again."

The archbishop paused and there was the sound of a closing door. "I see. Is it worse than Oklahoma?"

"There are verified miracles. Oh, all of them could be discounted and disproved in one way or another but...," James glanced at the pile of documents, "verified."

"Ahhhh. Well, my friend, you'd better start at the beginning and let me know how much work I will need to do tonight."

For the next ten minutes, the bishop explained what Father Eduardo had brought him—the videos, the documents, the photos, and the priest's dream. James sat on the couch and gazed at the mess of documents with no little resignation as he finished up. "As you can see, this isn't one that we can sit on. Too many people have had experiences. Too many laymen have heard the rumors."

"That will be our salvation. Miracles do not happen every day. Clearly, something else is at work."

"Do you really believe that, Your Grace?"

The archbishop clucked his tongue a couple times before answering. "I believe that something of importance is occurring at the Servants of Saint Lucy Convent. I believe that, perhaps, Sister Ruth was touched by God in some small way. But I know that the conversation of whether or not Sister Ruth will become a Servant of God is a question for years from now. An argument for another day."

The archbishop sighed. "I also know that since the outbreak, people have returned to the faith in numbers never before seen and that is something we do not want to hinder. The question of a blessed vampire is something we need to treat with utmost delicacy. Lord knows we don't want someone to come up with the idea of 'Saint Ruth, patron saint of vampires.'"

"I understand and agree. But what do we do now?"

"We do our due diligence. I will assign Sister Tabitha to the convent. She is a scientist and has the skills to determine whether or not the nuns there have been chemically affected by Sister Ruth—unknowingly or not. She can also determine if Sister Ruth's body is giving off pheromones that inspire loyalty or dreams or a magnetic field that affects flower growth. There is much we can do. In this case, science is our ally. As are hidden cameras which I will have installed to watch the gravesite to make certain that fraud isn't the source of these supposed miracles. Sister Tabitha will report directly back to me on her progress. I will let you know what you need to do should action be required."

James nodded to himself and felt the tension in his shoulders loosen. "What of Father Eduardo? He's been greatly affected by his investigation. I've sent him back to Italy but I believe he needs to be examined and then watched very carefully. We need to know if he is cured of his migraines or no. We need to understand how much he has been affected by his investigation and time at the convent."

"Ah, yes. The investigator." The archbishop considered this before he spoke. "Assign him here. I will take him on as a mentor. I need a new junior secretary. That will keep him close. Also, after you examine all of the evidence, I need you to do two things: call out anything that could be used to prove the vampiric condition is so evil that even a good woman like Sister Ruth could not resist. Anything to fight the afflicted. Second, package up all of it and send it to my office. I will have my own people go over it as well with your notes as guidance."

James paused, uncomfortable with the directive but aware that it was the right course of action for the time. "It will be done."

"James, how are you feeling about all this?" The archbishop's voice radiated care.

The bishop paused before he answered. "In truth, intrigued and frightened. I don't know what it means. This is the second such case of its type. It makes me wonder how many more afflicted are hiding within our ranks and what, if anything, we should do about it."

"You mirror our concerns. There are good people and bad people in every race. But remember, we are fighting a war for humanity and humanity's soul. At this time, know that we are doing everything we must do to protect the innocent."

"I know, Archbishop Mateo. I know."

"Thank you for your vigilance and candor. Now, I have much work to do. Good evening, Most Reverend."

"Good evening, Your Grace."

James held the phone to his chest for a long time as he considered the task before him and the man who'd brought it to his attention. He did not like the idea of creating a smear campaign against a godly woman. But the archbishop was correct. The masses had returned to the faith and it would not do to destroy that by acknowledging the fact that God had blessed some of the afflicted—clergy or not. The whole of humanity was at stake.

"Saint Ruth, patron saint of vampires..." he mused and shook his head. "Perhaps someday... but not today."

RED EMPIRE PART 1

By Jonathan Maberry

The Oval Office
The White House
Washington, D.C.
Day 18 of the Red Storm

The president leaned back in his chair, legs crossed, thin fingers steepled, dark eyes fixed in a long and silent appraisal of Dr. Luther Swann. The president did not look at anyone else. Not the two generals, not the secretary of state, not the director of national security. He continued to stare at Swann for what seemed like an hour. No one spoke.

When the president spoke, his tone was calm, measured, precise, revealing none of the emotion he had to be feeling.

"And you are absolutely certain of this, Dr. Swann?" he asked.

Every eye in the room was on him. Swann swallowed. He could feel sweat running in slow lines down his body beneath his clothes. His hands were balled into icy knots at his side. He sat in a wheelchair, his foot in a cast and his entire upper torso encased in a plastic shell. It would take weeks for his sternum and right clavicle to heal, and then there would be months of careful, painful physical therapy. The stitches had been removed from his mouth and when he was better he would see a dentist to replace the teeth he did not remember losing. His eyesight was getting better every day, though, and the double vision was nearly gone. The headaches persisted, however.

"I am, sir," Swann said.

The president nodded. "Since the V-Wars began, doctor, we have seen threats hitherto unimaginable to the modern mind. Vampires. Many *species* of vampires. What's the current total?"

"Counting newly discovered subtypes and hybrids?" said Swann. "Six hundred and thirty-eight."

"Six hundred and thirty-eight different kinds of vampires," said the president slowly, as if he could taste each syllable. "Even now it's hard to process that fact. And the I1V1, the so-called Ice Virus... all of the original estimates, the computer models are wrong. That's what you're telling me, doctor. Instead of one to three percent of the population being infected, you're here to tell us that it could be as high as ten percent."

"Y-yes," said Swann, tripping over the word.

"*Ten* percent."

"Yes?"

"Of the global population?"

"Yes."

"There are seven and a half billion people on this planet."

"Yes."

"Ten percent would mean that there are seven and a half *million* vampires out there."

"Yes, Mr. President, that's what I'm saying."

The president waved a hand toward his staff. "You're saying that despite all existing medical evidence. You're saying that despite everything the best medical experts in this country—in the *world*—are telling me."

Swann swallowed again. "Yes, I am."

"Bullshit," said one of the generals under his breath, then immediately muttered an apology. There was nothing genuine about the apology and he fixed Swann with a harsh, unblinking shooter's stare. Swann was used to being glared at by soldiers. For the first three years of the vampire wars he had rolled out as advisor to V-8, a special ops team. He had never managed to bond with the members of that team, especially with their leader, a gruff gunnery sergeant named Nestor Wilcox who everyone called Big Dog. Since deciding to step away from an official involvement with the United States military and most of the political and law enforcement departments, Swann had still run up against men and women in uniform who looked at him as if he was the cause of all of this. That was absurd, of course. The cause was climate change melting billions of tons of polar ice and releasing dozens of ancient diseases into the air. People called it the Ice Virus, though it really wasn't a virus from the ice. Bacteria from the ice melt had caused a mutation in an influenza A virus, transforming it into a new disease that targeted genes that lay dormant in all human DNA. The so-called junk DNA. One of those genes coded for a transformative mutation and this bacteria-virus cluster—known as I1V1—and unlocked the genes, which in turn activated a string of others, returning to the human gene pool ancient disease forms that were the historical and medical basis for the legends of vampires. No supernatural curses, no demonic possession, nothing like they used to show in Hollywood movies. Real vampires.

Hollywood wasn't making vampire films anymore. Not in the same way. Now they were making war films. Humans against vampires. Vampires against humans. Sometimes vampires against vampires. Hundreds of iterations. Countless potential variations, though it all came down to the same thing. A percentage of the global population was changing, transforming, acquiring new abilities. Turning into monsters.

Some looked like monsters, with oversized fangs, hideously distorted features, misshapen bodies. Others were so subtly changed that only they could pass without detection. The kicker was that there was no real way to test for vampirism. Everyone had the V-gene. Everyone. But until the change manifested, no one knew who was infected by the activation virus. Sometimes not even the infected knew. Not at first, anyway.

The math was further complicated by the variety of ways in which the transformations impacted brain chemistry and behavior. Some of the vampires, like the first known case—Michael Fayne—had lost his humanity entirely and turned into a killing machine driven by a bloodlust so powerful that he had no free will when the thirst was on him. Others developed new personality traits, ranging from a kind of violent misanthropy to a dangerous type of pack hunting instinct. And some—even most— experienced no measurable behavioral changes. They were who they had always been; however, they were no longer *what* they had always been.

Outbreaks happened in pockets and they happened quietly in isolation. They tore families apart with fear and aggressive hatred, and they brought families together in sympathy and support. The same was true of neighborhoods, schools, towns, cities, countries. There was no pattern to how people would react to either becoming vampires or seeing friends and loved ones transformed. Paranoia burned in the air, and because of it sometimes whole cities burned.

What tortured Swann was that most of the violence was unnecessary. Sure, there were times when the police and the military were forced to take action against an individual or group who either were slaves to their new predatory nature or reveled in it. Isolationists and extremist groups emerged among the vampires. V-cells, as they were called, were cells of terrorist vampires who believed that the Ice Virus was proof of an evolutionary jump and that the new species needed to fight in order to ensure its own survival. And some were just assholes who liked to kill, liked to burn, liked to tear it all down.

For every one of the vampires who wanted to go to war there were at least as many humans, though Swann thought it was more like ten to one. Or a hundred to one. Humans feared the vampires. Old fears and new fears. Rabble rousers and hawks screamed out a message that the vampires were rising to kill them all, and that the only path to survival was genocide.

A bad and terrifying policy at the best of times. Worse still when anyone could turn at any time. And when many of the vampires could hide among humans as easily as a terrorist could hide among civilian populations. There were rumors—and Swann believed them—about human sleeper agents who pretended to be vampires so they could infiltrate the Red World.

That was the war.

So far there had been four phases to it. After the first outbreaks groups of V-cells launched terror attacks on the human establishment, and the pushback was brutal. Back then the humans possessed all of the weapons, all of the power, all of the advantage.

There was a peace that was fragile as glass and which shattered when bombs were detonated across the country, tearing down bridges and monuments and buildings. Vampires were blamed and a second wave of the war exploded. But fresh rumors began circulating that a group of humans were behind the attacks, that they had reignited the war so that they could continue their fight with the full support of the population. Hundreds of thousands died on both sides.

The second peace lasted longer.

And then more bombs went off, destroying huge chunks of New York City. This time it was a radical human group behind the attacks. Swann had been in New York on that long, dreadful night. He had been there through the days of shocked awareness and expectation. Waiting for the other shoe to drop.

It dropped so hard. The response from the militant vampires was immediate and appalling.

Since then there had been a steady escalation. Not just in America, but globally. The battles in Germany, Italy, Russia, the Czech Republic, China, Saudi Arabia, and elsewhere were unlike anything that had come before. And yet some cities went untouched. There were places where humans and vampires lived in peace. Paris, Las Vegas, Cardiff, Shanghai, Baghdad.

Over the last five weeks, though, the fury of those battles had begun to ebb. There were fewer deaths, fewer terrorist attacks. And notably fewer cases of active infection. The scientific community had begun to whisper of a possible end to the virus, a stopping of the spread of the Ice Virus. Luther Swann knew that this was not the case. It was the Red Empire. It was out there, rising slowly, gaining power, gaining followers, uniting many of the disparate bands of vampire terrorists and even drawing in some infected in the middle ground, people who saw them as something stable and maybe as something that could protect them.

The trick was convincing the president of what he knew.

"Should we assume your source is confidential?" asked the president dryly.

"It is information passed along to me through what I can best describe as reliable."

"'Reliable,'" said the president glumly. "Why not just come out and say that you have this from the Crimson Queen?"

Swann took a moment to compose his features. The woman who called herself the Crimson Queen was a vampire, that much was true enough. She was also militant, but militant in defense. Her people had never once launched an attack on the human population. Not directly. She had, Swann knew, very quietly had people on *both* sides of the war removed. Hawks and killers who wanted the war either for ideological, religious, political, or monetary reasons. Sometimes for all of those reasons. The Queen herself did not want a war. She wanted some kind of new society, one where diversity in all of its manifestations was accepted. Race, religion, political views, and even species. It was a lot to ask from either of the two human races—*homo sapiens sapiens* and *homo sapiens vampirus*. Humans were a predator species. The history books and even the holy books of the world's dominant religions were filled with accounts of conquest, slaughter, genocide, persecution, xenophobia, and mass murder.

So far all that the Crimson Queen's empire had managed to accomplish was a holding pattern. It did not defuse the bomb as much as it simply added time to the clock every once in a while. Maybe peace and cultural evolution was naïve. Swann didn't want to think so, but he had little evidence to support any optimism.

"Because," said Swann, "I didn't get this information from her."

"Oh? From whom, then?"

Swann said nothing. He had been advised not to let himself get tricked into trying to defend the name of his confidential informant because those kinds of conversations were filled with tricks and traps. He was in a room filled with politicians and military strategists. They were all better at subterfuge than he was, so silence was his safest option.

The president nodded and even smiled, acknowledging Swann's tactic. "Can you offer any proof?"

"None," said Swann. "Absolutely none. As you know there is no scanner, no reliable blood or genetics test that can—"

"Thank you, yes, I'm aware of that. Which makes a claim like yours hard to buy."

"Sir," said Swann, "I think you misunderstand why I'm here. That's my bad, that's on me for not making myself understood."

"Then, pray, enlighten us."

Swann looked around at the hostile eyes and frowning faces. He licked his lips and took a steadying breath. "I'm not here simply to give you numbers that I can't support. What would be the point of that? You already have statistics that work for you, and you have a slightly different set that your press people trot out during press conferences. I *know* the difference, Mr. President. I know that you elevate the threat level when it's useful to do so and dial it back when you think that's best. I saw those numbers go up and down during the last election cycle, and frankly I'm appalled at the manipulation of the public, especially when candidates in *both* parties trotted out completely different sets of numbers on the same day depending on how red or blue the state was, or on which bias was fueling the camera shoved into their faces."

"Now hold on a goddamn—," began an aide, but the president cut him off.

"Dr. Swann knows he's right," said the president. "We all do. He also knows he can't prove it in any useful way. He knows that my saying what I'm saying isn't something he can repeat because he is aware that my staff will deny anything he says. Let's hear him out."

The eyes, already hostile, seemed to all burn a little hotter, which made fresh sweat pop out on Swann's face.

"I came here at the request of cooler heads," he said. "My source for this information tells me that contact will be made, so I can only assume that facts and assurances—if there are any to be had—will come from them. I'm here because I've been a part of this whole thing from the beginning. Before any of you. Before the government. I've seen this grow and I've seen it go out of control. I've watched what happens when political agendas are allowed to trump the actual best interests of the American people and the people of the world. I've watched that happen from the inside. I've been privy to conversations that would shock the nation, and yes, I know I signed reams of nondisclosure agreements. I know that breaking those agreements would get me arrested and also lose me all constitutional protections. I know all that and it scares me. But, more than that it offends me. It sickens me that this is required of someone like me. I'm not a soldier and I'm not a politician. I was a college professor before this. I wrote scholarly textbooks that no one but my students read. I was tenured and happy. Then the world changed and I lost my job and a lot of my faith in the system."

"Boo hoo," said one of the aides.

"Hush," snapped the president, giving the aide a stern look. "Have some respect."

The aide began to speak, thought better of it, and clamped his jaw shut. He gave the president a single nod but made no apology to Swann.

"I'm here because the *majority* of people on this planet do not want this war to get worse. They—no, *we*—want it to stop. We want sanity. We want common sense. We want a sophistication of response appropriate to a livable future. There are only three choices left to us anymore, Mr. President. Either one side succeeds in committing wholesale genocide, or we continue fighting to the point where someone—blood or beat— gets their hands on the nuclear codes, and then it's all over for everyone. We both know that is a real possibility. *You*, of all people, have to know that it's true, even likely."

The room was deadly quiet. The president uncrossed and recrossed his legs. He rested his folded hands in his lap.

"There were three choices," he said. "What's the third?"

"Peace, of course."

"Between humans and vampires?" said one of the generals. "You can't be that stupid, Dr. Swann."

"General Cole, please," began the president, but Swann shook his head.

"No, it's okay. I'd like to respond to that," said Swann. "Stupid, general? No, I'm not stupid. Nor am I as naïve as I once was, or as optimistic as I used to be. Right now I feel like I'm clinging onto the edge of the world by my fingertips. I came to you to make a request and to give a warning."

"What's the request?" said the president. "To meet with the Queen? She's refused that offer a dozen times."

"I told you, this isn't about her. Not directly," Swann countered. "I spoke with her, sure, but I spoke with a lot of people and a lot of groups. Before and after the attack at Global Acquisitions. The Queen won't meet with you, Mr. President, because she doesn't trust that any such meeting can be safely arranged. That concern is shared even by some of the celebrities in OneWorld with whom I've been working since the attacks in New York. George Clooney, Shaq, Jennifer Lawrence… there are a lot of people who have risked quite a bit to speak out in favor of a new direction but they stop short of meeting with the military on either side of the conflict. And I can't blame them."

"And yet you're here," said the president.

"I am. Not as a representative of any party, though. I don't speak *for* the Crimson Queen and I don't speak for you. Not anymore. I'm not here to try and advise anymore. Not in the way I had been doing because that was a waste of my time. I think I may even have done more harm than good because my knowledge wasn't used to try and understand the vampires, it was used against them. From the very beginning they were regarded as monsters and the response from your government and other governments was cliché. Kill what you don't understand. Use force instead of reason. Well, Mr. President, hatred as a policy has gotten us all into a lot of trouble, hasn't it? Now we have the Red Empire to worry about."

"A handful of radicals calling themselves an empire doesn't make it so," said the secretary of state.

Swann gave him a long, pitying stare. "Surely you can't be that dense, Mr. Secretary."

"Now just a goddamn minute—"

And the president's phone rang.

The president snatched it up. "Carol, I thought I told you to hold all—"

He stopped. Listened. Said, "Very well. Wait until everyone leaves and then send him in."

The president replaced the phone very carefully and sat back, staring at nothing for long seconds.

"What is it?" asked the secretary.

The president glanced at him. "I would like you gentlemen to leave," he said quietly. "No questions and no arguments. Everyone except Dr. Swann. Out."

"Mr. President," began the secretary, but the commander in chief shook his head and waved him away. The aides and the generals scowled and exchanged looks of confused annoyance, but they left. Swann watched them go, then he turned back to the man behind the desk.

"You knew he was coming to see me, didn't you?" asked the president.

He rubbed his eyes and looked very old and tired. "This was all a set up."

"Yes," said Swann.

"Shit."

There was a discreet knock on a side door to the oval office and then it opened. The middle-aged man who entered was big and blocky. He had dark hair going gray, wore tinted glasses and thin black silk gloves. Swann did not know why he wore the gloves, but when the man declined to shake the president's hand he assumed that they hid some kind of damage or injury.

"Good afternoon, Mr. President," said the big man. "Thank you for agreeing to see me."

"Did I have a choice?"

"You always have a choice. You've made quite a few already, which is why things are as bad as they are."

"I thought you agreed to stay out of this matter."

"I was *ordered* to stay out," said the visitor. "I can no longer do that."

The president sighed and flapped a hand toward a chair. "Have a seat. I assume you two already know each other."

The big man stopped in front of Swann's chair. "Only by reputation," he said. "Captain Ledger speaks very highly of you, Dr. Swann. He said that you offered crucial assistance at Global Acquisitions. He is grateful and so am I."

Swann laughed. "My assistance was getting beaten half to death."

"But at the right time. Captain Ledger said that you endeavored to help at a critical moment, which created a much-needed advantage. That's what matters. You have my gratitude and admiration."

"I don't even know your name," said Swann.

The big man smiled. "Church," he said. "You can call me Mr. Church."

He settled himself in a chair, crossed his legs, folded his gloved hands in his lap and studied the president for a full five seconds before he spoke.

"The world is burning, Mr. President," he said quietly. "Let's talk about keeping it from burning itself out."

By Lois H. Gresh

"Pull the testes to the bottom, dimwit."

"I'm working on it. This ain't easy, you know." My brother, Tonio, grabbed Vasito's scrotum as close to the base as he dared. The bull's testes squeezed into the bottom of the scrotum, which bulged like a blown-up balloon. The thick hide stretched, the coarse hair bristled.

Beyond the field of dead brush, blood-red rock whirled in spires and stabbed the sky. A wisp of cloud hung beneath an orange sun. So hot and dry today, even the howls of the wolves cracked.

Vasito clearly didn't enjoy having his balls clenched. His eyes fogged and his lips curled back. He strained against the chains that held him to the iron post. His massive shoulders heaved, and then he hurled himself upward and crashed back down, a thousand pounds of angry muscle slamming to the earth. A dust cloud rose, and I fell back as one of Vasito's horns slashed my arm. The pain spread like fire and radiated into my shoulder and chest.

Tonio rolled to the right, avoiding the bull's hooves. The sun shot down, a red sizzle across iron chains.

My arm was coated in blood and dirt. I rotated my shoulder, crooked my elbow, and flexed my fingers. Nothing was broken. I'd suffered much worse over the years. This was minor, I told myself, and scrambled to my feet.

Tonio rolled back into place and clutched the bull's scrotum again.

Vasito glared at me. Bulls always thought they were the alpha males, and bulls were always wrong. I glared back at Vasito. He hadn't met his match yet, and it wouldn't be long now, would it?

"Hurry up and measure it, Manuel. We ain't got all day," Tonio said.

"This is a big moment," I said. "Vasito's a rare one."

My brother shrugged.

"Get on with it, would you?" he said.

"Keep your pants on. Like you have something better to do?"

I stared my brother down, and he had to look away. I wrapped the scrotal tape around my right fist, and I held the end of the tape between my left thumb and forefinger.

Vasito lowered his horns and grunted. His hooves cleaved the dirt. Carefully I moved closer, tensing my legs so I could crouch and quickly take the measurement.

I'd been measuring bulls for as long as I could remember. My father had raised and fought bulls in Spain, as had his father and all my ancestors. Most New Mexico ranches raised livestock for meat and milk. But my brother and I, the Freire brothers, we raised *fighters*. My Vasito was born of a special breed of Cabrera crossed with Jijona, the females all artificially inseminated near the Manzano Mountains to the east.

"I can't hold his balls forever," Tonio said.

I slipped the tape over the scrotum and pulled it snuggly across the largest part of the bulge. Vasito bucked, but I held on tightly. The pain in my arm didn't help, but like I said, I was accustomed to much worse.

"Forever's a funny word," I told my brother. "There's been no forever, no tomorrow, no today, no nothing, since Hell Night." The V-Wars had taken care of any plans we'd had. Our only hope was to survive… and pulling that off would be a miracle.

The only good thing about the damn V-Wars was that nobody gave a rat's ass what hicks like us were doing in the middle of New Mexican nowhere. But you know, they really hadn't given a rat's ass about us *before* the bloods, the vamps, and the wars. They just didn't pin as many laws on us now. They were too busy trying to survive, too.

I squinted at the tape, then rose.

"A full 16 inches," I said. "I've never seen a sack so big. You're just bucking to pump that semen into a lovely little cow, aren't you, boy?"

Vasito was, by far, the most powerful we'd ever had. Scrotum size was directly correlated with dominant alpha superiority, and only alphas got females and only alphas got to fight. Tonio and I had no use for weak bulls.

"*Finally.*" Tonio released Vasito's balls and hopped to his feet. He rolled his shoulders, reminding me of how Vasito had heaved his muscles only moments before. But while Tonio was six feet four and packed with muscle, he was nothing compared to the bull.

My brother and I scrambled from the pen into the field, and I clicked the gate shut.

"I think Vasito's the beginning of a new line, something special," I said. "I mean, the scientists were breeding these bulls for decades, crossing the lineage this way and that. How many balls have you seen that measured this big, eh?"

"You might not want to fight him, Manuel. He could crush you."

"Yeah, well, my balls are big, too," I said, and I thought, *Tonio's such a dimwit.* "Go get the horse, Tonio. It's time to test the bull's strength. Besides, he needs a way to release all that anger. We just put him through hell."

Tonio knew the routine. He nodded and ambled off toward the stable. He was older by a year but I made all the decisions, and how many times had I beat off the stray Hispanics and Native Americans who picked on him at every chance? Tonio was too easygoing and kind. I hadn't known our mother, but I always figured that my brother took after her while I clearly was my father's son. Girls always loved Tonio's gentle brown eyes and warm smile, but they never told *me* that I had gentle eyes and a warm smile. Oh, no. They got off on my cockiness and swagger.

I watched my brother's gait, relaxed as if he had no care in the world. Scruffy jeans and a work shirt, straight black hair streaked with the dirt of the pen and ragged on his shoulders. My hair was a thick brown, and I was anything but relaxed. I was always on the move, taut and tense like a live wire. Sometimes, I could barely believe we came from the same bloodline, but we did.

Grandma had told me so.

I rested my elbows on the rungs of the bull pen and stared at Vasito. Black fur mottled with patches of red and white, enormous girth and height, horns sharp as daggers and strong as steel.

I fuckin' loved this bull.

I heard my brother's voice and turned. A stallion—Samson, I saw—trotted into the field behind him. Samson was one of our best. Rippling muscles, glossy mane, and a proud trot. He was a damn fine horse. I hated to lose him, but unfortunately, no other horse was strong enough for our purpose.

Vasito roared and slammed his horns against the metal fence, and the whole structure shuddered and rattled. The bull smelled blood. He knew the horse was for him, and this excited him. He needed the kill.

I hopped on top of the fence, reached over, and unlatched the gate. I couldn't wait to watch Vasito, how he shifted his weight when he lunged for the kill, how his horns dipped then plunged into the meat of the horse. I needed to see and analyze everything. Or maybe I just needed the kill, too.

The bull thundered out of the pen.

I leaned forward and nearly fell off the fence, grabbed the top rail with both hands.

The blood-red rock receded farther into the distance. The scrubby trees and weeds disappeared. I saw nothing but the bull.

The horse's eyes grew wild. He screamed and raced around the field.

The bull's head went down. The horns dipped.

Samson careened into the fence, *clang*, and for a moment, didn't move.

The sun stabbed down like knives. My mind whirled. Blood surged, and I felt faint, dizzy. The world slowed. I looked at Vasito, forcing my eyes to focus, and I felt the sun pierce his hide.

I didn't *see* it.

I felt it.

I fought down the panic, but my heart was racing.

I smelled animal meat, *the horse*, and I needed to kill it. I smelled animal meat, *the bull*, and it was sweet as if emanating from my own body.

But how was this possible?

Vasito charged, his horns aimed directly at Samson's left side.

Neighing, screaming, roaring: the sounds washed over me in waves. In that moment, I knew: *this was what the bull heard, too.*

Samson batted his front hooves at Vasito, but his efforts were futile. It was like watching an ant try to crawl away before you crush it beneath your boot. The horse twisted, exposing his belly and heart.

Tonio yelled from the other side of the field. He ran in slow motion across the weeds toward the animals.

"No," I tried to call, "don't hurt him, don't interfere!" but there was no way Tonio could hear me over the screams of the horse, the stomping, and the bellowing of the bull.

The air buzzed. All the way from my face to my crotch to my toes, my flesh tingled. My stomach lurched. My back arched.

Twin horns slammed into the horse's belly. Steam of blood rose into the dry heat. I smelled it, a nectar, a fragrance like honeysuckles in spring.

Red spires stabbed the sky.

Red horns rammed meat against the fence.

Ecstasy surged. The meat, the blood.

Red horns wrenched out, then slammed back in.

I tasted the kill, and I wanted more.

The horse flailed, and as his body twisted into unnatural shapes, his bones cracked, and I knew that *I* had killed...

No, I knew that the *bull* had killed the horse.

A tall figure, arms outstretched, lasso in his hands: Tonio stood halfway across the field, not approaching Vasito and Samson, knowing it would be certain death.

I slipped off the fence. My legs wobbled, my head reeled.

Chestnut hide sopped in blood, chunks of meat littering the weeds, bones jutting from the ripped torso. Samson's head smashed open, brains dumped out, brains smearing the eyeballs and lips. Heart exposed, bull hoof squashing it, squirting blood, pulverizing the life essence. Intestines draped over the bull's horns. Bull bellowing and stomping on the meat.

With a start, I realized that I no longer *felt* the bull; I only saw him now. I was alone, tiny, a human in a weed field with a thousand-pound beast.

The beast turned, saw me, and charged. Fury in his eyes. Red rage.

So weak, sapped of strength, still dizzy, I couldn't move.

The air vibrated with death. *My* death.

Tonio raced after the bull, then threw the lasso around his neck. "Get back, motherfucker!" he screamed.

My throat went dry. I couldn't swallow. I tried to call my brother's name, but it came out as a croak.

I'd saved Tonio countless times and never given it a second thought. I'd never considered it possible that I could die saving him. And yet, in reverse, Tonio could easily die trying to save me. Tonio wasn't strong and smart enough to act quickly, with confidence, and know he was right. A bull like Vasito could kill him in seconds. This is why I'd never let Tonio fight in the ring.

Tonio tripped on a rock and almost fell, staggered momentarily, regained his balance. His eyes widened in horror. He dropped the lasso.

The bull swerved and circled back.

I couldn't let Tonio die, not without a fight. I forced my legs to move, but it took all my strength to limp.

Tonio was screaming and running, the bull on his heels, bloody horns ready to skewer him to the fence.

I didn't have time to close my eyes.

It was that fast.

Certain death, I felt it. I would lose my brother, I knew it.

But in that moment, Tonio hurled himself over the fence, and the bull smashed into the metal links and recoiled, dazed.

I limped backward, keeping my eyes fixed on Vasito. When I reached the pen, I wrenched myself to the top of the fence and flipped to the other side, where I lay, panting and watching the sky spin. My fists clutched the weeds.

But then—

Crash!

Vasito slammed into the fence a foot away from me.

My heart lurched, and my breath died in my throat.

The bull glared at me. He was the alpha male, and he knew it.

I lowered my eyes, and I trembled before him.

Static rolled on the TV screen.

"Pretty good picture," Tonio said.

He had a point. It was unusual to see even vague outlines of anyone on our TV.

A woman's voice intoned the latest statistics about junk DNA outbreaks, murders, robberies, rapes, cannibalism, and insanity. The world had gone mad, but what else was new?

"She's the sexy one, Yuki Nitobe," said Tonio, and he hunched closer to the set to get a better look. Again, he had a point. Huge breasts jiggled on a thin frame that rolled from the bottom of the screen to the top. Yuki Nitobe had been reporting on the vampire outbreaks and resulting hysteria and wars since Michael Fayne, the so-called patient zero, was at Bellevue Hospital.

Grandma slinged a platter of horse meat onto the floor next to me.

"Here's your TV dinner, boy."

It was a good night when we had dinner *and* a movie. Not that Yuki Nitobe's news show was a movie, but it was as close as we were going to get.

But—

"I don't have any appetite," I said.

My teeth were chattering, my body trembling. I lay on the floor like a rag doll. The gash on my right arm was already closing. I hadn't washed off the dirt or blood, but there seemed to be no sign of infection.

Tonio grabbed a fistful of meat and crammed it into his mouth. Bloody juice ran down his chin. He wiped his fist on his shirt. In better times and in better places, people would have said the meat was char-broiled, a fancy term because in our case, Grandma cooked it over the trash barrel behind our mobile home.

"…manifests itself via dormant DNA present in wide swathes of the population," said Yuki. She droned on about wild animals busting out of former zoos and eating city people.

"Like we care about them city folk. This woman's a *dimwit*." Grandma slumped in her chair, a wooden frame with springs and no cushion. She was darning my socks. Her needle flashed in the glow from the TV screen. Behind her, hanging from rods that used to hold curtains, were my underpants and a few of Tonio's t-shirts. She had hand-stitched the curtains into a thin dress that bagged over her emaciated frame and hung below her knees. A pink-and-yellow gingham, hideous really, with the thin fabric leaving little to the imagination.

Tonio swallowed hard. He reached for more meat. "Well, I don't have no ancient stupid vampire crap in me," he said. "No V-Genes in my junk DNA."

"You wouldn't know," I said.

"Well, how come I wouldn't know? Of course, I would."

I pushed my plate away and propped myself into a sitting position. My ribs felt bruised, as if I'd been punched, and my stomach burned with acid.

My fingertips tingled. That wasn't normal, was it? In fact, *all ten of my fingertips tingled.* A fine tremor ran down my skin, pulsing like soft waves in a secluded cove. I could see the blood in my veins.

I stared at my hands, mesmerized.

"You ain't gonna eat? Can I have yours?" asked Tonio.

"Sure." I curled my fingers into fists. I didn't want my brother to see me shaking. I kept my voice steady. "You wouldn't know if you have V-Genes, Tonio. They might be dormant, and besides, you don't know what it would be like in us." Hadn't he been paying attention to Yuki Nitobe all these months? Everyone knew, the V-Gene load could hit at any moment and would be different depending on ancestry.

Grandma's needle flashed.

"You don't look so good. You feeling funny, boy?" she said.

…like my fingertips tingling? Like weakness, shortness of breath, blurred vision, *weird* vision, like seeing the blood pulsing in my veins?

"No, Grandma. Nothing funny."

I shifted my attention back to the rolling static of the TV.

"No point applying for welfare or unemployment insurance. People keep writing in, and we keep telling folks that the government as we knew it no longer exists. Only skeletal police and military are functioning. We don't know of public schools that are still open. There are few hospitals left. No food stamps. Nothing. Don't expect help, folks, from anyone. The best advice Dr. Phil can give you today is, *Don't get sick and don't need anything you can't provide for yourself.*"

"You should eat," said Tonio. "You look awful. You need strength. We got things to do tomorrow, gotta schedule a fight for Vasito, gotta make some dough."

"There's nobody else who can fight that bull."

"Yeah, well, you can't do it."

Sure enough, I thought. Even thinking about Vasito scared the living hell out of me. Something had happened to me. Something had hit me, weakened me, changed me. It seemed unlikely that I'd been socked by the V-Gene, or rather, had my V-Genes suddenly switch on and turn me into a genetic vampiric freak. After all, I felt no need to sink my teeth into my brother's neck and suck his blood.

No, whatever was wrong with me had to be something else.

But what?

Grandma cursed. My eyes focused on a bubble of blood on her wrist. The bubble collapsed and turned into a thin trickle that dripped to her dress, staining it red.

Suddenly, she dropped her needle to the floor and doubled over, clutching her stomach.

"What's the matter?" Tonio scrambled to his feet and hurried to her side. He caught her before she fell off the chair.

I crawled past Tonio and looked up at her. Her thin body quivered. The hair was almost gone from her head, and just a few gray tufts remained. Brown splotches littered her scalp.

I couldn't bear it if something happened to Grandma. She was the one who kept us together. She'd saved us, Tonio and me. If not for her, we'd have died before we were five years old.

My arms stretched toward her. Fingertips tingling, blood pulsing, white white skin red red splotch spreading on gingham...

Tonio gently pushed me aside.

"You ain't well," he said.

Grandma's head lolled to one side, and she sputtered blood.

Tonio lifted her from the chair. She was so skinny, I feared she might break in his arms.

"She needs—" Tonio's voice broke. "She needs a doctor."

I nodded and then limped after him down the short hall into Grandma's room, where he set her on the cot.

Grandma groaned, and she coughed up what looked like stomach fluids and blood.

"Manuel. My beloved Manuel," she whispered, and I felt so very loved, as I always did when I was with her. I glanced at Tonio, but his face was blank. It must have hurt him every time Grandma favored me, which was all the time, but he was so used to it that he was a pro at hiding how he felt.

Grandma started choking again, and Tonio took off his t-shirt and mopped her face with it. "She needs water," he said.

Was he joking? We didn't have drinking water. But we did have beer and it was right on Grandma's nightstand, so I tipped the half-drunk can of flat beer over her lips and a few drops made their way down her throat. The rest splashed over her chin onto the stained sheet.

She moaned, her face pinched in agony, her skin gray.

"We ain't got no money or nothing for the doc." Tonio looked at me with those gentle eyes the girls all loved. "What're we gonna do?"

I leaned over and held my grandma's limp hand. Her eyelids fluttered. "Manuel." A love note, and then she curled into a fetal position.

I placed my hand on her forehead. She was hot, feverish, sweating. She retched again, her body jerking with the spasms. Blood splattered into a quickly widening pool on the astro-turf floor.

I felt her life drain from the blood, drop by drop, as it splashed to the floor. She was being drained, bit by bit, and the essence of what she'd been was soaking into the astro-turf. My head started pounding to the rhythm of the drops. The blood in my own veins pulsed with the rhythm. Gray gray skin red red life… spreading…

"You're shaking!" Tonio grabbed me, but I jerked free. Snapped from my trance. Glared at him. He flushed and lowered his eyes.

"Go get Doc Hermanos," I said. "Tell him he can have horse meat. I'll give him Samson. Doc'll fix her."

Tonio's eyes lit, and he raced off to fetch the doc.

"Manuel, I'm dying," Grandma whispered.

I clasped her hand. I should have told her that she'd be fine. Isn't that what people say at times like this? But instead, I said, "Yes, I know," simple and true.

I watched her life soak into the floor. I feared she was no more. And I admit that while I'd always loved my grandma, in that moment, I thought that perhaps this was for the best because I didn't want her to know what I had become.

Yes, it was better this way. She would die and never know.

And yet, I didn't really want her to die. Another death in the family would leave only Tonio and me.

I still hadn't forgiven myself for my mother's death, and I'd never forgotten how my father died, either.

A blistering day, much like today. My father, one of the finest bull fighters in Spain, stepping into the ring with Raso of the fierce Cabrera bloodline.

My skin prickled from the memory: the bull Raso bleeding from the picadores' lances, bleeding from the *banderillas* thrust into his neck and shoulders. Raso, weakened. Me, a little boy, my heart pounding like crazy, so proud of my father. I wanted to grow up to be just like him, to fight the biggest bulls, to hear the crowd cheering for me, to win the most beautiful girl in my village. My father had won my mother this way.

I'd glanced up at her. She squeezed my hand just as I was now squeezing Grandma's. Tonio held onto her other hand, and the three of us watched my father in the ring.

He wore his finest red and silver outfit. He swung his finest red cape, he flashed us his finest smile. And then Raso charged, and the bull didn't swing left like he always had in the past. Instead, at the last second, the bull veered right. My father jumped, his expression fading to fear.

But it was too late, and the thousand-pound bull, as big a brute perhaps as my own Vasito, slammed into my father, horns stabbing him straight through the stomach. My father's head fell to his chest, his arms slackened, his legs went limp.

My mother screamed and raced into the ring.

"No, don't leave us!" I called to her, but she was already gone.

Tonio had burst out crying.

I did not cry.

I watched, tears frozen in my eyes, refusing to spill, as the bull gored my mother and stomped her into a bloody pulp. People were screaming, everything was chaos. I grabbed my brother and hauled him through the crowd.

I stole enough money to buy the boat tickets that brought us to the United States. I knew from my father that Grandma lived in New Mexico. We hitchhiked here and showed up like two vagabonds.

I should not have allowed my mother to run into the ring. I should have held onto her. I should have been stronger.

What hardened me had softened my brother. I vowed never to be afraid of anything, never to falter and slip. Tonio melted, determined to bring more happiness into the world. We had evolved into near opposites.

And here we were in this new land, and it was now infested with vampires. If Grandma died, I had to protect Tonio at all costs.

By the time Tonio returned with the doc, Grandma had almost slipped away. Only a flutter of life trembled in the hand I still held.

The doc glanced at Grandma, and his face clouded. He knew the score.

"I can give her something for the fever and to reduce her pain. I can give her antibiotics. But that's about it. Is that what you want?"

He fumbled with an old briefcase, vintage junkyard. It swung open to reveal a few vials and hypos, some swabs, and various bottles and boxes. His fingernails were chipped and filthy, his hands thick and gnarled. He smelled like an overripe fruit rotten with age. But Doc was all we had, so I said, "Yes, do what you can."

I didn't care that Doc was filthy and unwashed. You see, when you live nowhere and you're nothing, it doesn't matter if you shave or bathe. And besides, water had always been hard to come by in these parts. I'd been known to wash my face with beer and a chip of soap. So it didn't matter that Doc was past his prime and smelled like garbage, we all understood and we didn't care. What mattered was that Doc would give Grandma medicine for the right price, and there were no other doctors, not even veterinarians, left in these parts.

"I'll need payment," he said.

"You can have Samson's remains, the meat." Doc looked puzzled, so I added, "He was one of our best horses. He died today. A bull got him. The meat is safe."

"I'm inclined, but it's not enough," Doc said.

"What then?" asked Tonio. "What do you want? I ate the horse meat. It's fine."

Doc cocked an eye and shrugged. "Yes, and your grandmother got mighty sick from that meat, didn't she?"

My brother scowled at him. "No, she didn't eat the meat. She had no appetite. Only I ate it. And nothing happened to me, so the meat is perfectly fine."

"I knew your grandmother her whole life," said Doc. "She was older than me by ten years, but she was always nice to me, she was, and I've always felt kindly toward her. You say a bull killed the horse?"

"Yes," I said, "a bull, Vasito."

"Has it occurred to you that the bull is contaminated, that perhaps your grandmother was infected by this bull?"

"That's absurd," I said. "She was nowhere near the bull."

The doctor plunged a needle into a bottle and extracted fluid, then tapped the needle with his fingernail. He squirted liquid from the tip of the hypo.

"She's been near that bull since its birth. I believe that whatever's in the bull got into her and triggered her vampirism, long dormant in her genes. This is how it spreads. People get infected, sometimes with a simple cold, sometimes with the flu, and before you know it, they become vamps."

Tonio burst out laughing. I just shook my head. I was dismayed.

"She's just old," I said.

Doc ignored my comment. He positioned the hypo over Grandma's neck. "My payment," he said. "I want you to kill that bull, Manuel. I won't risk the horse meat. It might be contaminated with whatever infected your grandmother. The bull has to die. It's like a rat during the Black Death."

I wasn't myself. I was too weak to slaughter Vasito, and my brother didn't have the skill.

…and my Grandma as a vamp?

I'd heard about people who went vamp, but they always suffered for a long time before fully turning. If Grandma was going vamp, it was striking her like a sudden and extreme case of the flu.

Whether I was vamping or not was irrelevant to Doc's request. I simply didn't have sufficient strength to fight any bull, much less Vasito.

Grandma rasped from deep within her lungs. I wondered if she had pneumonia.

"Please," I said, "just give her the injection, whatever medicine is needed. Please, just save her." Grandma was the closest thing I'd ever known to a real mother. She'd always taken care of me and Tonio.

"Of course, I will, Manuel. I'm a doctor. But as a favor to the medical profession, we who have to care for *all* the infected, I ask that you put down that bull. Fight him. Kill him, Manuel, like the man you are."

"Why can't we chain him up and kill him?" Tonio interjected.

Yes, why? I thought.

Doc shrugged. "Nothing's free. You have to pay for what you want in this world."

Some favor to the medical profession or to the people who might get infected with whatever Doc thought the bull carried. The doc was like everybody else, and everyone has a price.

So I had to agree. Doc was willing to tend to Grandma as much as necessary—that is, if I fought and killed Vasito.

What choice did I have?

———•———

A tangerine haze drifted overhead strung with cloud baubles. The sun drooped low, fat and syrupy, its tendrils caressing the horizon of blood-red rocks, the spires jutting at odd angles like broken bones.

I staggered, the world spinning before me.

I'd had nothing to eat or drink for the past day and a half. I knew what I had become. My legs felt as if they could crumble at any moment. My hand rested on the hilt of my dagger, the one I would thrust into the neck of the bull between his shoulders. But that would be the finale, the death blow. First, I would tease and enrage Vasito, I would see the blood foaming on his hide, the pain frothing on his mouth. I also had three *banderillas*, each wound with strips of pink-and-yellow gingham. Three would not suffice to bring the bull down to his minimum strength, but we hadn't had time to make more *banderillas*.

I waited in the center of the field. My fingertips tingled. From afar, blood pulsed in rhythm to mine. I *felt* the bull, I *felt* his heat, I *felt* his blood. He was born of an ancient bloodline, a fierce one unmatched by no other. But so was I.

Generations of Freires, we beat to the pulse of the bulls. Whatever was dormant inside of me, whatever was triggered, whatever they called it—V-Genes, junk DNA—it had driven the finest bull fighters in Spain. My father's *banderillas* always hit their mark. My father's dagger always killed. No mistakes, not ever. The swords never wavered. They always sliced into the bulls' necks at exactly the right place. My father knew when to jump, to swerve, to duck, to thrust. *He knew...* as if he knew the bulls' moves as they happened.

And now, I felt Vasito as if we were intertwined as one. We beat in rhythm.

Doc Hermanos clung to the fence rails by the horse stable. I could smell his excitement. He should have cured my Grandma without insisting upon this blood feud. He should have done the right thing. How cruel to keep my Grandma alive, just barely, to force me into the ring. I already saw the death of Doc Hermanos.

Click.

I swiveled. Tonio had unlatched the gate between the bull stable and pen. Vasito lumbered into the sun, which shimmied orange-red across his black fur. He gazed about and then his eyes, gorged with blood, focused on me.

He glared.

I glared straight back, unwavering.

The air crackled like the static on the broken TV.

Back in the mobile home, Grandma lay twisted. Her weak heart beat slowly, and it called out to me.

This is what it meant to be a Freire, a fighter of great bulls. I knew that my father must have felt this way when he fought Raso and lost his life. I knew that my father must have felt my mother's heartbeat, and possibly mine, as he swung his finest cape and flashed his finest smile. At the last second, Raso had veered right, and why hadn't my father felt that, too? What if Vasito out-maneuvered me in this way? What if Vasito was smart enough to break the rhythm of blood?

My mind flicked to Grandma, struggling for life on her cot. The doc's medicine could not cure the virus that raged through her feeble body. She was old, yes, but she was probably infected with whatever had hit me. After all, Grandma was my father's mother, a Freire, born of my bloodline.

Tonio climbed on top of the fence, stared at me once, eyes brimming with fear, and then he unlatched the gate of the pen.

The gate slammed against the fence, and in a burst of dust, Vasito roared into the field.

The static rolled red.

My fingertips vibrated. My hands felt like iron. I swung toward Vasito, my arm high, my hand gripping a Grandma-gingham lance.

Tonio, knees scraped. Warm Grandma embrace.

Me, starving. Warm Grandma stew.

Tonio, crying. Grandma lullaby.

Me, screaming *Dimwit Tonio Dimwit*. Grandma soothing, hush hush, both of you, everything will be all right.

Weak, lack of food, big bull racing at me. Orange streamers in the sky. Cloud bullets.

Blood staining the dirt, shreds of Samson clinging to the weeds.

My fingertips split in agonizing pain. Bull rushed in. Red haze. Red blur. And static rising, static buzzing, blood rushing to my head.

Suddenly, everything came into focus, and I plunged the lance through thick meat. Right between the horns and between the bones of the skull. *Crack*. Bone shards splintered into flesh.

My body twirled up in a spire as twisted as rock spires. Higher I went, and I whirled and landed yards from the bull. Strength surged like winter wind through my muscles. Like a blast of cold air, I whooshed, my body self-propelled and driven by something innate and far beyond my mental control.

Grandma shrieked and arched her back. I felt her.

Doc staggered back and pointed.

Tonio, my brother, *dimwit dimwit*, Tonio jumped off the fence and raced after the bull, as if a lasso would do any good.

My body soared, whirled, and now slammed down onto the bull, my legs straddling his shoulders, my hand gripping a lance, the second lance, and driving it hard into the meat.

Now two Grandma-ginghams wobbled in the flesh.

He bucked, Vasito did, his haunches kicking up the dust, his horns stabbing air, eyes feverish, but my legs held tight, and I rammed the third and final lance right between his eyes. Dead between those eyes, and they flooded red and fogged.

My left leg slipped, and I started falling off the hide. My arms lashed out, my fingertips hot with pain. The bull swerved and bucked. Tonio ran close, too close, the lasso high and whipping toward the bull's neck. I flipped off the bull and rolled across the dirt. The weeds were thorny on my back, but I didn't care. I smelled blood, and I needed blood. It gave me strength, just the smell and the knowledge that it would soon be mine.

I ran toward Doc.

My Grandma shivered.

In a flying leap, I soared and landed squarely on the fence right where Doc stood, and he clasped a hand over his mouth, his eyes wide, the blood screaming in his veins.

You should have saved my grandma. You greedy, greedy man. You didn't know what you were screwing with, did you?

His throat, his eyes, his heart... *where?*

My left arm stabbed down, all five fingertips ruptured into sharp tubules, fine as hairs and hard as horns. Thrust, and a loud crack and a *swish*. Forefinger in the right eye, middle finger into the forehead, ring finger into the left eye, pinky and thumb into his cheeks. I curled my fingers into a fist and squeezed until the nose popped off, then I clutched his brain until the mush oozed. His life flowed through the tubules into my blood, the essence crashed through me, surged to my head. Venom trickled from my fingertips into what was left of the doc's head.

Tonio strained on his rope, lasso around Vasito's neck. Warm brown eyes, kind smile. Tonio the weak. Tonio the dimwit. Tonio, the one with compassion. Tonio, who thought he could save me.

But it was I who had inherited the bloodline.

"Manuel," whispered Grandma, "my beloved Manuel." I felt the life flutter from her. She was too old to withstand the ancient virus that triggered our V-Genes.

The doc should have saved her.

You see, even I had compassion, even I had love. Strength doesn't necessarily mean we're heartless. But in the moment that compassion and love gripped me, the bull struck.

His horns slammed into the fence, but like Grandma, he was weak. The lance had hurt him badly.

I plunged my right fingertips into his neck by the Grandma-gingham, and the venom stunned him. It seeped death through his veins. His eyes glazed in a tangerine sheen.

Vasito, the great Cabrera bull born of the fiercest bloodline, he fell before me, and his blood soared through my tubules and into my head. We Spaniards had always had a thing for blood, and now I knew why. Only a great Spaniard can fight a bull with precision. We were alike, that bull and I. We were of ancient bloodlines joined tightly through the ages.

Vasito's blood whipped through me. I staggered from the impact. The sky whirled.

Had my father felt this power, this feeling that nothing could stop him? Is this what drove the great bull fighters into the ring time and time again?

As a thousand pounds of angry muscle fell, my brother tripped, tangled in his own ropes. Vasito crashed down on him, then rolled off. Tonio's head lolled back, his arms slackened, and his legs went limp.

It all happened within a split second, though it has always felt like eternity. I lost my grandma and brother in the ring that day just as I had lost my father and mother long ago. This time, I couldn't run away. The wars raged everywhere between humans and those like myself. I realized that I didn't need to run away. I could hide on the ranch, and when the urge hit me, I could grab a stray human for the ring and satisfy my blood lust. It wouldn't be the same as fighting a bull of the Cabrera line, but it would have to do, wouldn't it?

SILVER OR LEAD

By John Skipp and Cody Goodfellow

23:57 EST;
Gelabert International Airport
Panama City
Republic of Panama

I n the new world, nothing could get you killed faster than trusting the wrong people. But without someone watching your back, you were almost certain to end up dead, sucked dry, or worse.

Lt. Isela Diaz learned this the hard way when her tactical police unit responded to the first vampire outbreak in San Jose. One of her partners got bit and slaughtered the rest of the team.

How the world had changed. Less than a year later, her new tactical team came from every country in Central America, her leaders said, so they would have to learn to trust each other. But two of her team were vampires, and now, they had stuck their necks out even further for the only thing on two legs she trusted less.

An American.

They had come down to Panama to raid a Chinese freighter in the canal, trusting the American's word that there was something worth all this trouble waiting onboard.

And now, she had put her trust in the vampire warlord of Panama City to accept their generous gifts and turn a blind eye to their activities.

But Diaz had also changed in the last year, and she wasn't done changing. She knew how to trust completely—or appear to—until things changed, and trusting gave way to shooting.

You could trust General Innocente Gamboa to sell you out at the earliest opportunity, but no matter what kind of treachery you prepared for, the vampire warlord of Panama City somehow always managed to catch you out.

Ninety-eight degrees at midnight in January. The heat sat on your chest like bricks, radiated up from the cracked, weed-infested tarmac of Gelabert International Airport's cargo zone. The Pig, the team's Gulf War–surplus Tomahawk, grumbled as it chopped the torpid air with its rotors, but Lt. Isela Diaz felt no cooler for all its wind at her back. The humidity felt like sweat, like the oily, diesel-stinking sweat of this tortured, filthy city.

The general could not quite contain his drool as he perused their offerings again. He ran a curled talon over the pressurized plastic bubbles to make condensation beads drop onto the pale, serenely sleeping faces. Ever since he seized power after the American collapse, Gamboa straddled the canal like a greedy spider and took what he wanted from every passing ship. But they'd brought the one thing he couldn't get enough of.

"I want to see their pedigrees," he rasped through a forest of fangs. A student of the classics in his profession, Gamboa's particular fetish was for pure European vampire blood. Maybe he thought drinking enough of it would make him a purebred Aryan like his idols.

Diaz looked at her silent partner, Hidalgo Soto, tensed and ready beside her, felt the rest of the team in the chopper watching her. "Austrian passports are all there," she said, laser-pointing the vacuum-sealed packet on the back of each wheelchair from a safe, sane distance. "They're not show-dogs." Expat brothers retired to Belize to run a hotel, they had always been cannibals, eating small children procured in the slums, and turned eagerly to vampirism as the next logical step. They and the general deserved each other.

They had little choice about meeting Gamboa and paying him off. Panama still had plenty of American anti-aircraft hardware lying around, and loved to use it. Blowing off the local warlords would make their mission unthinkable, instead of merely impossible.

Gamboa's taster punctured the bubble and spiked the oldest brother's earlobe, licked the ruby blossom that swelled from it. "It's pure," he said.

"If you can control yourself, you can make them last for years." She wasn't the only one who laughed at the joke. Even among the bloodsuckers, Gamboa's gluttony was legendary.

"This is very generous, yes," the general hissed. Like a serpent's tongue, his arm flicked out and lifted her off the tarmac by her throat. "But you know, I have to wonder... what is making you so generous?"

Half her team came running and ordered Gamboa to put her down. Soto crouched and unsheathed his knives. Struggling to breathe, she ordered them back. "You wouldn't know it if you saw it," she told him, "and you couldn't use it if you had it."

"But you want it very badly, so now... I want it, too. Of course, you understand..."

His honor guard circled under Diaz on all fours, gurgling feline growls and bloody foam spilling from their blunt snouts. Indian tribes from Mexico to Guiana believed in jaguar-men. These had spotted pelts and claws that gouged the cracked tarmac as their circle drew tighter.

"Just tell me what it is," Gamboa said. "Maybe we can share it."

"Accept our silver," she said through gritted teeth, "or you'll take our lead."

His smile bore witness to the Taino creation myth that their god made them from the piranha. "I already have the silver. "

"Not all of it," she said. It took all her strength to bring both legs up and kick the General in his sagging belly. The silver combat knife she kicked out of its ankle sheath sank up to its hilt into the monstrous sack of guts and disappeared, the slurping hole nearly swallowing her leg as it sealed itself.

Gamboa dashed her against the tarmac, then flung her away from him as hard as he could, cursing and clawing at his belly.

Diaz had only started to fall when Hidalgo Soto caught her and laid her flat on the tarmac beside the pair of wheelchairs. She screamed and nearly blacked out when she put the slightest weight on her left leg.

"So much for going in the front door," said a voice that somehow muted even the chopper's roar. Villalobos introduced the jaguar men to his son.

The first fully automatic salvo of silver and uranium buckshot carved two of their assailants into airborne cube steak and severely antagonized the other two. Gamboa's soldiers in the three jeeps parked in a semicircle around them opened fire on the Tomahawk from mounted sixty-caliber machine guns. Gamboa picked up one of the wheelchairs with its Austrian cannibal sleeping in his bubble, and flung it into the rotors whirling above their heads.

243

Up until then, the situation was still what Diaz would have classified as containable. But the storm of red sleet, graphite, and steel that rained down on them was only a warm-up for the shrieking whirlwind of shattered blades. The chopper flipped over like a dog playing dead. Villalobos leapt out the loading door with son and daughter chattering away in his hands and spraying phosphorus rounds at everything that moved.

Diaz turned to Soto to find him gone. She was searched for weapons before this farce, but ordinary firearms probably wouldn't do much more than harass most of Gamboa's death squad. Feeling naked with a spotlight on her back, she rolled to take shelter under the front of Gamboa's bulletproof limousine.

Over a dozen vampire *sicarios*, cartel gunmen, had them pinned down at the wreck, and more were coming. Gamboa had retreated behind a jeep to direct the troops. Soto was stalking, somewhere. Paz and Kiko and Chuy, their pilot, were still in the chopper with McClintock.

Diaz shouted, "Guerrero!" and drew a flurry of rifle fire down on her position. She felt the heat of a bullet sear the close-cropped hair on the crown of her skull.

Villalobos popped a fistful of smoke bombs at the jeeps and chased them with a couple grenades. Paz Guerrero sprang out of the chopper in a blur, firing wildly into the red curtain of smoke with her MP5, but damned if every round didn't make someone on the other side of the smoke scream.

Paz flicked her sidearm at Diaz and swapped magazines on her own rifle, licked her teeth and swallowed, tweaking on the blood from her slashed tongue. Taller, leaner, with fine European features that radiated arrogance, Paz could work her CO's nerves like few of their enemies. Her boot brushed Diaz's leg, making her bite back a scream. "Ready to get bit yet? Better you get it from a friend…"

"I'm ready to go home," Diaz said, "but we're still working. Go find some wheels."

Paz's mocking laughter could shrivel sheet metal, but she sprinted off in the direction of the hangars.

Somewhere amid the carnage, Villalobos roared, "*Villalobos!*" and something exploded. Chuy and Kiko bolted from the chopper during the ensuing lull, and found Diaz just as a jaguar-man bounded out of the smoke to pounce on her. It shrugged off their bullets, snapping and slashing at her, driving her farther under the limousine. She rolled under its weight, talons mauling the Gore-Tex shell of her body armor, and drove her pistol up against its throat, emptying the clip of silver flechette rounds into its soft palate and brain.

Chuy pulled her out from under the corpse. Kiko went to work splinting her leg. McClintock crawled up, looking like a turtle in a flight crew helmet and off-the-rack flak jacket. "Lieutenant, we're losing time."

"*Pura vida...* thank you..." She so hated the sound of his Boston-accented Spanish that she reflexively answered in English. "Even if we still had wings—"

"We won't catch it out on the open water..."

Diaz caught where he was going. "But we can still intercept it at the locks. Yes, I thought of that, and it's suicide. The Chinese still control the locks, and without local protection—"

"It's the only way—"

"No! This is not a suicide mission. I'm not throwing away lives for whatever you say is on that ship..."

"It *is* there, and it's..." He looked away, calculating how much to declassify. "I spent my whole career sending native cutouts into meat grinders, so I know better... but *I'm* here, aren't I? What does that tell you?"

She stared harder into his flinty blue eyes. This pencil-neck expat came to them only weeks ago out of nowhere. Ex-CIA, and willing to bargain a headful of intel for a place in whatever they managed to build out of the bloody rubble, and protection from his old bosses.

Paz screeched up to the downed chopper in an Escalade. "Move it, piglets."

Diaz bit her lip standing and waved Paz out. "You, Chuy, and I will find another helicopter, preferably armed, and be ready to pick the others up."

Paz said, "Splitting us up is stupid..."

"It's not even the stupidest thing I've done tonight. The rest of you…"

"*Villalobos!*"

"Intercept the freighter and get Mr. McClintock's precious cargo, then be ready to get extracted."

"My part is already boring," Paz said. "I'm trading with Hidalgo."

Soto's shadow shook its shaved head, even if he didn't move.

"How're we going to fly out of here?" Kiko asked. "They'll shoot us down…"

"Not if someone cuts the head off the missile command, which is in this airport…"

"I like my job again," Paz said.

Diaz gave her back her pistol. "So go do it."

One of the ragged carcasses off across the tarmac sat up and started shooting at them with a soldier's rifle. "Which of you whores wants to be my favorite cow?"

Villalobos leapt onto the roof of the limousine and emptied his daughter into Gamboa without slowing him down. Just as the shambling vampire warlord seized him by the throat, the Guatemalan lunatic jabbed a plastic squirt-gun up Gamboa's nose. "How d'you like holy water, *cabron*?" he shouted, spraying the general's face. Before Gamboa could finish laughing at Villalobos's ineffectual gesture, his smoking, sizzling face melted and slid off his skull like foam off a beer.

Villalobos disentangled himself from the spasming corpse and kicked it off the hood of the limo.

"Not all vampires are Catholic," he said, "so Villalobos simply had a priest bless a jug of muriatic acid. Just to be sure."

———◆———

00:12 EST

Avenida Omar Torrijos Herrara

For Bolivar "Kiko" Pech, it all depended on what you called a thing. If you called what had happened to the world a plague, then you could fight this plague with a clean conscience, even though the disease had human names and faces. If you called the things more and more people had become monsters, then you could kill them without guilt. Trained as a doctor, his passion for folklore and mythology made him, in this strange and terrible new war, an ideal soldier.

He nervously polished his glasses, cursing the American who got him thinking on all this, when he asked Kiko how he could serve alongside vampires. He didn't call them vampires, he called them partners.

Soto drove the Escalade. Villalobos rode shotgun with his son resting on the rearview mirror pod, his daughter parked barrel-down between his knees. Kiko watched their progress on GPS and monitored local military and emergency channels on his headset.

The plan was to intercept the target ship after it cleared the Chinese-controlled Gatun locks on the Pacific side, but General Gamboa had misled and delayed them for hours, until he could get the ship into his own domain. The airport was only a mile from the canal, but five miles from the Miraflores locks, their last hope of intercepting the ship before it hit the open Atlantic. The Escalade crashed a barricade and veered onto a modern four-lane highway, headed north.

They cut through a jarring mix of high-end residential enclaves and freight yards before the road came within sight of the canal. The far shore was pristine rainforest, a wall of darkness even deeper than the moonless sky. They passed a steady stream of cargo ships and even a cruise liner, though passengers in open cages on deck screamed piteously as they drove by. It should hardly come as a shock, though, should it? The world turned and things were bought and sold, even in war. Especially in war.

When the bombs went off across North America, Mexico was already a war zone with hundreds of thousands dead and unbelievable atrocities and institutional genocide everywhere. As once-human *chupacabras* and the dominant vampiric strain, the Blood Mothers, spread out from the cities and became gods to worshipful drug cartels, the ragtag assortment of Central American nations had remained in varying states of denial until the plague was in their midst. For the poorest in every country, the displaced Indians toiling or just hanging on, the transformation was a whole new form of life that many leapt into all too eagerly.

Each country had faced its own nightmares, and had its own shameful responses to account for. Guatemala's military junta clamped down on vampire and human alike and paved the streets of the capitol with headless bodies. The European elite in Belize took to the virus eagerly and worked to turn the cities into plantations and stockyards before a rebellion of human and vampire peasants brought them down, along with most of the coastal resorts. Nicaragua's Sandinista regime preserved a semblance of order that only muted the spread of vampirism through the population. In El Salvador and Honduras, chaos reigned in the cities, and most of the peasantry had returned to the jungles and the old ways. Only in Costa Rica had the government actively sought a peaceful solution to the Great Changes, as they politely called them. Diaz had cut her teeth on raids on vampire colonies in the highland cloud forests, at resorts turned to human farms, at schools where rampaging bloodsuckers went through classrooms full of children like a birthday feast.

Horror and barbarity cast a pall over the entire region, but none of Central America's children were strangers to horror. In the months that followed, the people slowly began to adapt, as they always had, and in less than a year, this all began to seem normal. For some, it offered the promise of something that no one, from peasant to president or dictator had ever enjoyed in their lifetime—autonomy.

From the moment the vampires came out in the US and the civil war began, the Americans had lost contact with the outside world as never before. As media outlets and satellite networks went dark or switched allegiances according to the convoluted politics of the plague, the overriding terror was that no one from the north was coming to save them. None of the magical solutions that America was famous for, in their movies if not in real life, appeared to restore normalcy. Nor did they raise a voice against the proclamation that went out from San Jose at the beginning of the year, declaring a union of Central American States and challenging whatever leadership survived in each of her neighbors to rise up and restore order and prosperity.

It was only a paper union, for much of the region was still terra incognita, with dragons and tigers everywhere on the map. For the indigenous peoples, the transformation to vampirism had restored the magic of the otherworldly lost to the Spaniards and Catholicism and Coca Cola. Most of the coastal vampire strains were docile goat-suckers, no more threatening than before, but the rest...

Like the one behind the wheel. Hidalgo Soto—not his real name—was short, whip-skinny with sharp Indian features, and covered from the chin down with Salvadoran gang tattoos, with names, perhaps the names of his countless victims. He never spoke, seemed broken in half by whatever he lost at home. Kiko had seen Soto feed, and still didn't comprehend it.

And then there was Paz Guerrero... about whom it was not even safe to think, in the privacy of one's head. But she was right. "This is a bad idea," he complained. "Splitting us up."

"What are you afraid of?" Villalobos laughed, roasting a cigar stub with his lighter. "Divide and conquer."

"You don't divide and conquer the enemy, you divide *them* and then you conquer—"

Grinning, blowing smoke in Kiko's face. "What I said."

"There's nothing to worry about," McClintock assured him. "It's a milk run."

"Where I come from," Villalobos said, "to get the milk, you have to get past the bull."

With any luck, Gamboa's junior officers would try to kill each other all night, and there'd be no dragnet, but they'd left behind a lot of dead people—*dead monsters*, he corrected himself—at the airport. Along with half their team...

The American pointed out at the canal. "Look at all those boats out there. They don't care what's going on, they just know the markets are always open."

"You saw how business is done in Panama now."

"All I'm saying is, you've got your weapons, and I've got mine." He tapped the briefcase on his lap. It was actually handcuffed to his wrist.

Kiko didn't elaborate on the local situation. The urban mestizo population in Panama City was like too many Latin cities; driven out of the rainforests generations or just months ago and dropped into the slums, they had nothing to lose by embracing the plague. They had by and large forgotten the gods, monsters, and animal spirits of their ancestors, but their blood remembered. Some tribes held that the Creator made them from jaguars, or snakes, or piranha. And who could say now that they were wrong?

The local Cuna Indian vampires tended to be docile albino animal-bleeders, until a lunar eclipse. But strange strains from all over the world washed up in Panama to make the city far more dangerous than the jungle across the canal. From the "water children" that frolicked in the Caribbean shallows and drank victims dry before they could drown, to the vicious "Amazons" on Hispaniola, who raged round their tiny island rending and devouring anything that looked or smelled like a man, this land was more savage and lawless than before the Europeans "discovered" it.

"Your ship is approaching the Miraflores locks now," Kiko said. "So you are quite familiar with our part of the world?"

"You could say that, yes... Hey, we were on the same side."

"Allies against Communism, yes. And now, you are our friend. And what about your old friends? Are they as forgiving as we are...?"

Think about that, *Yanqui*. McClintock tugged his hair, looked out the window. "You can't imagine what it's like up there, right now. It's worse than this mess... The bombs that went off, we did that to ourselves... I couldn't go back after that. This pickup, if your people don't blow it..."

"It is all that important?"

"It is. And in the right hands," McClintock let his eyes swivel to bounce off Soto, "it could change everything."

———————

Villalobos shouted, "No more political bullshit!"

Red and blue lights in the rearview, closing fast.

Climbing up to sit facing backward on the windowsill of the passenger door, Villalobos dropped a grenade in the road and introduced the cops to his daughter.

The lead police car flipped on its side and skidded onto the shoulder, but three more came up from behind it. Soto floored the Escalade, making Villalobos drop back into his seat.

The highway cleared a rise and they passed a turnout lit by torches, choked with bodies dancing around a couple of burning trucks in the middle of the road.

McClintock snapped, "Hey, you passed it! We need to get down there," pointing at the Miraflores locks, but Soto continued north on the highway after a quick glance at Kiko's notebook screen.

"It's especially dangerous for foreigners tonight in the city," Kiko said, "and if you knew this place, you'd know why. It's Martyr's Day."

"What the hell is Martyr's Day?"

"In 1964, the students in Panama City demanded that the Panamanian flag be flown alongside the stars and stripes in the Canal Zone. The US Army cracked down and killed twenty locals."

"Twenty people? They're still sore about *twenty* people?"

"They are still 'sore' because Panama still does not control the canal. These Chinese we are to do business with, they still hold the locks and Gamboa is—or was—a puppet of the Colombian cartels."

They went another mile up the highway and turned onto a narrow suspension bridge over the canal. Three police cars were gaining on them when Soto hit the brakes and fishtailed to a stop on the center span of the graceful arch.

"What the hell are we doing?" McClintock screamed. "You can't surrender…"

Villalobos jumped out and braced his son and daughter on the open door. When the cop cars came over the rise of the bridge, spraying bullets that pinged off the Escalade's body armor, he opened fire on their engine blocks and tires. One veered wildly to slam into the railing, another slewed sideways and rolled four times to rest on its roof within spitting distance, and the third hit its brakes and reversed back up the bridge with its lights and front grille flying apart under Villalobos's withering fire.

Soto took another look at Kiko's screen, then put the Escalade in gear and drove into the railing.

The cheap steel gave way under the hurtling weight of the SUV and they tipped nose-down, plummeting into the dark…

McClintock screamed and threw his arms around Kiko, who was only less afraid because his partners had done more foolish things than this, and survived.

The Escalade tumbled less than ten feet and crashed on its front axle on top of a mountain of bright, gigantic children's building blocks.

Villalobos slashed the airbag deployed in his face, kicked his door off its hinges and jumped out. Soto had already gone out the open window.

"What the fuck did you just do?" McClintock moaned, holding his face. He'd broken his nose against the headrest in front of him.

Kiko jumped out, stowing his notebook. "Isn't this your ship?"

They were parked on top of the highest tier of cargo containers on a Panamax cargo ship, a gargantuan flatbed freighter maxed out to fit through the locks with only a few feet to spare.

Cradling his busted nose in one hand and his briefcase in the other, the American got out and took stock of their surroundings. "OK, we're back on track. Find me the captain."

* * *

00:12 EST
Gelabert International Airport

No emergency crews came to put out their burning helicopter. They all had bigger fires to put out, all over the city. But Gamboa's uniformed *sicarios* buzzed the airport like flies over their master's corpse.

With nowhere else to go, they'd broken into the nearest hangar. Chuy supported Lt. Diaz, but she still nearly blacked out with each agonizing step. Kiko had adamantly refused to leave her, but McClintock insisted he was needed to verify the "goods" they'd come for.

Inside the hangar, a pair of old Bell Little Birds sat under tarps, blocking a G-6 private jet with its belly open for luggage. A gang of men in expensive suits and mechanic's coveralls looked up from their work loading big refrigerated cases into the plane. Nearly all of them produced and pointed guns.

"I'm very sorry to disturb you," Diaz called out. "We will leave…"

"No, it is all right," replied a short, stocky man in a *guayabera* shirt and jeans. He sat on a director's chair at a folding table laden with vials and blood-testing equipment. An open refrigerator beside him was stuffed with blood in plastic pouches. With a sleepy-eyed smile, he beckoned them closer. "Please, we were just waiting for the unpleasantness outside to be over. Please, join us…"

The beautiful woman sitting on his knee strolled closer to them.

"Fucking Colombians," Paz hissed. Her knife fluttered in her hand at her side. The beautiful woman came up to Diaz. Chuy went for his sidearm, but then froze.

"I beg your pardon, doctor," Diaz said. "We would not want to disturb you."

"Oh, but it's too late for that," purred the don. Your rudeness outside has disturbed our schedule. We demand recompense."

Paz strutted closer to the Colombian. "You want that one?" She pointed at Diaz. "You can have her—"

"I already have *all* of you." The don's *sicarios* chuckled dutifully.

Chuy stared, shaking, at the stunning lady vampire. "Ynez," he said, "what are you doing here?" His voice sounded far away, stupefied…

"Chuy," Diaz said, "*that's not your wife*—"

"Who is that bitch on your arm, Esteban?" The vampire pouted, making the pilot whimper.

"She's nobody, *mami*…"

"I don't believe you." The vampire turned away.

Chuy brought up his arm and threw it across Diaz's throat, crushing her windpipe, but he was already growing weaker. "She's nothing, *Ynez*… look, I'll show you…"

Diaz's vision went blurry. "Chuy, let me go! It's feeding on you…" She tried to tell him he was in the grip of a *tunda*, a Colombian vampire that took on the likeness of a loved one to drain the life essence almost in the form of love itself. But she couldn't even rip free of the pilot. Her broken leg betrayed her, and she hung from his arm like a noose.

Weeping hysterically, Chuy put the gun to her head. Diaz elbowed him in the groin and slammed him into the sheet-metal wall.

Diaz faltered as Chuy made a choking sound and fell against her. The vampire hadn't touched him, but somehow, he was growing lighter, almost hollow.

Diaz took Chuy's pistol and shot the creature in the neck and chest with her eyes averted, terrified she would look into its eyes and see someone she recognized.

Paz drew her MP5 and pistol. The refrigerator beside the don exploded and a torrent of blood gushed across the concrete floor. Of the half-dozen or so vampires in the hangar, only two were able to keep their footing on the sticky, viscous flood. Diaz fell on her hip behind Chuy's horribly empty body, jerking in her arms with the ferocious gunfire.

Paz went down on one knee to slide into their midst on the shallow red lake, placing surgically precise shots into knees, necks, heads. Two men she shot actually jerked and reflexively shot their own mates, like billiard balls banking and going into their holes.

Still sitting unruffled in his chair, the Colombian don licked a blob of stray blood off his hand and smiled sadly, taking out his cell phone. "How much would you like?"

"All of it," Paz said, and ripped out his throat with her teeth.

If I ever have to face an enemy as devious as Paz Guerrero, Diaz thought, *I'll just quit.*

For a second, it sounded like rain. The whole hangar thrummed with it, but then the droplets punched through the corrugated steel roof and began to chew up the concrete floor. It was a monsoon of lead.

00:20 EST
Cargo Ship Ji Lyu Wei

The deeper they went, the colder it got, but Kiko didn't welcome it.

Something green with no ears and a hole for a nose led Kiko, McClintock, and Villalobos down off the tiered castle of cargo containers and a narrow companionway forward of the bridge that led below deck. He thought it would be better down here, away from the stench and the noise of the containers, most of which were filled with people.

In some, he heard weeping. In others, he heard feverish clicking, as of masses of hands typing at keyboards. In one, he heard someone singing a karaoke version of "Twilight Time" in Chinese, but nailing the Johnny Mathis voice.

According to McClintock, this was business as usual in Asia. "These people trying to get out, they work in the factories, they steal, kill, whatever, and they get to Hong Kong or Macau and they pay to come over here, but somebody else always pays more, so a lot of them get drained and dumped out here on the ocean by one of the, uh, first-class passengers. The rest, if they're lucky, will end up in sweatshops or construction projects worse than anything at home, but a lot of human beings are just worth more as a meal than as a worker." He shook his head. "Sad but true."

They turned a corner and the narrow corridor ended in a warehouse-sized compartment filled with more containers. Their guide bowed out and a white-haired vampire in a charcoal tailored suit approached them like a salesman in a high-end showroom. His smile was perfect, but his skin had a greenish cast and something that might be mold grew in thick patches on his exposed skin.

He and McClintock exchanged pleasantries in Chinese, and the vampire, limping stiffly, led them down a passage between stacks of cargo. Kiko and Villalobos exchanged bemused looks, the latter with seething anxiety behind it. After all they'd gone through to get here, to be escorted to their goal like mere customers... This was what the world would be like when the war was over, and vampires became both wolves and sheepdogs, and humans demoted forever to the role of livestock.

"While you guys have been dreaming about a new world, the Chinese are making it happen. The Party elite turned en masse as soon as they saw the benefits. Now, they're trying to lock in their control. Not everybody can be the wolves, so they're working harder than anyone for a cure to the Ice Virus, to keep their herd of a billion sheep.

"They found some people with an immunity to the Ice Virus... something in their junk DNA, whatever... and they isolated it. They think they've got a vaccine that'll stop the virus dead."

Down here, at least, the smell was good clean oil and new plastic, until they rounded a corner and came to another hatch, this one closed, with a massive Mongolian ogre who stood and challenged them.

The white-haired vampire nattered in McClintock's ear. "Oh shit," he said. "Complications."

"What kind of…?"

"Seems somebody tried to drink him on the crossing."

The hatch opened and a rush of fetid air made Kiko gag.

"This is why the Chinese are back to the drawing board on their vaccine. Seems a side effect of it renders human blood toxic to vampires."

"Seriously?" Villalobos said.

"For real. They wanted to kill him, but common sense prevailed… so they just… punished him a little…" McClintock snapped at their guide, who retorted angrily.

Kiko forced himself to step into the compartment. The air was solid with the stench of death, and not just human flesh. *Jiangshi*, the most common variety of Chinese vampire, were prone to secondary infections, even mold and fungi, like their suddenly irate escort.

"What we were going to have to pay," McClintock said, "he just added a zero on it."

"At which end?" Kiko absentmindedly asked, still struggling not to vomit. He strapped a surgical mask over his mouth.

Two bodies lay on the deck, both almost completely engulfed in luxuriant gardens of rot, like a riotous compost pile. Kiko stepped over them to get to the short, gaunt man hunched in the farthest corner.

He was shivering, teeth chattering, but the noise could've been his ribs. They jutted out against sallow, bruised skin. He'd been starved for almost the whole two-week cruise, though he might've got water from one of the dripping pipes overhead. The corpses must've been the vampires who died from trying to feed on him. They'd taken off one of his arms, or maybe he'd done it himself.

Kiko knelt beside the man, who began to whisper in some thick dialect of Chinese. Pleading for his life, or begging for death.

He kept his remaining hand up to protect his long, gaunt face.

Kiko took out his field kit and prepped an antibiotic and a painkiller. "He's not going to be able to leave on his feet."

"Just check him," McClintock snapped, and went on arguing with the *jiangshi*. He had his phone out and was punching the screen as they haggled.

"What am I looking for?"

"Just make sure he's human."

Kiko didn't need any test for that.

"And this." McClintock set his briefcase on his knee and cracked it open, pulled something out. "If he's our boy, he'll have this marker in his blood. Can't miss it."

It looked like a home pregnancy test. You dripped blood onto the receptor at one end of the little wand, and checked the digital counter. Set up so a layman could do it, calibrated to detect McClintock's miracle antibody.

Kiko shook his head. Of course, if it reacted violently with the Ice Virus in the bloodstream… and indeed, the fluid reservoir inside the wand had hardened into a blackish crust. So the vaccine caused human blood in a vampire's bloodstream to coagulate and clot in the veins… Mother of God! The implications of it were staggering. If only he spoke Chinese—

The man left off begging and hung his head, resigned. Kiko tried to reassure him as he took a course of blood samples and stowed them in his knapsack.

"Are we good?" McClintock demanded.

"He appears to be what you say he is, but he's in no shape to travel…"

"So carry him."

Kiko dashed off a quick text to Lt. Diaz, but there was no signal so deep inside the cargo ship. He offered his arm and the man painfully let himself be lifted to his feet. The *jiangshi* moved to block the doorway. Villalobos got close and puffed his cigar until the cherry lit the green vampire's face bright orange.

McClintock stabbed his phone and held it up in the vampire's face. "There. How's that work for you?"

The smiling vampire stepped out of their way. Kiko was dismayed to find the man all too easy to carry. The ogre loped ahead of them out of the hold and up onto the deck. As he maneuvered the sick man up the stairs, a shadow crossed in front of him and lifted the man's arm off Kiko's shoulder. He went for his sidearm, but it was only Soto. Still spooked and mistrustful, yet he gratefully let the silent Salvadoran vampire take the man.

The night sky was washed in orange from the floodlights over the Miraflores locks. Their ship was squeezed into the first lock and waiting for the water level to bring them down halfway to sea level. Beyond the freight yard, the darkness was livid with torches and bonfires, with sporadic bursts of gunfire around the gate where Gamboa's goons held back the angry mob who resented the Chinese flags flying over the canal.

Villalobos went first and jumped easily from the ladder onto the pier running along the locks. Soto came down with the sick man on his shoulder while Villalobos went looking for ground transport.

McClintock stood by the ladder, rubbing his hands together nervously.

"It looks like everything went according to plan," Kiko said.

"Yeah, come on, let's go…"

"Except you forgot something."

McClintock blinked. "What's that?"

"Your briefcase."

"Oh, that. Forget it. Come on, let's go." The American climbed over the gunwale and started down the ladder.

Kiko held up McClintock's briefcase. "So you don't need it?"

"God damn it, why'd you have to do that?" McClintock shook his head angrily. "What was that thing your boss said to that fat Panamanian fuck? *Plata o plomo…*?"

"Silver or lead, yes…" Kiko took a step backward, but it felt like he was going down. "The wisdom of Pablo Escobar. That is how things, down here, are done."

"Yeah, I know. It's a shame you don't." McClintock's pistol came up in his hand as if it'd been up his sleeve all along, and before Kiko could say another word, the American shot him in the face.

———•———

00:17 EST
Gelabert International Airport

"Move it!" Paz screamed, shoving her commander toward the parked G6. Diaz lurched forward but fell, growling, crawling on the concrete to fall down in the shadow of the plane. An attack helicopter circled overhead, and Diaz could hear someone ordering troops to circle the hangar.

Paz sank her teeth into a plastic pouch of blood and slurped greedily. Diaz averted her eyes, but she couldn't miss the spray of bullet holes in the vampire's deceptively willowy frame.

"You're not gonna make it any other way," Paz said, offering her hand. Diaz looked at up at her, at the fangs dimpling her full lower lip.

Diaz recoiled from what she was offering. "I'm not giving up…"

"Giving up what? Your humanity?" Paz shook her long black hair out of its braid so it hid all but her faintly luminous eyes. "You'd rather be dead than end up *like me*?"

"That's not what I meant," Diaz said, but what *did* she mean? She ran the risk every day of getting infected and changing—she and the others joked about it—but she really did fear it more than death, because she just couldn't believe that whatever looked out of her eyes and walked around in her body would be *her*, if she changed into one of *them*.

"Fine," Paz snarled. "But don't expect me to carry you and your precious humanity." She slipped out of sight. Diaz heard her scramble up the steel wall as fast as an athlete could run on open ground. Then the helicopter started shooting again, and she couldn't hear anything.

Diaz rolled up against the nose landing gear and covered her head. Something buzzing against her chest like a second, malfunctioning heart. Her phone vibrating in her pocket. She took it out and saw a note from Kiko. *Gringo found his friend. Ready to go home…?*

The machine gun fire fell off again, but the helicopter still buzzed angrily just above the roof. Diaz heard the big doors slowly sliding open.

She could hide here and pretend to be dead for as long as that lasted, or she could do something. Looking around, she decided fainting from the pain of running on a broken leg was a nobler way to go out than huddling in a puddle of tacky blood under an airplane.

Pushing off with her good leg, she lurched out from under the G6 on both hands and one leg. Risking a brief glance upward, she saw Paz brachiating across the ceiling from the I-beam rafters, kicking out a plastic skylight and slithering out onto the roof.

Crawling for all she was worth, Diaz reached the landing skids of the nearest Little Bird and yanked open the pilot's door, launched herself across the seat. Someone shouted and fired a shot at her, and then everybody started shooting at everything. The bullet-resistant windscreen starred and cracked. Fighting quicksand panic, she made herself go through the rows of switches, slid her broken leg agonizingly over the seat and onto the right pedal. The doors before her stood a quarter of the way open, and about a dozen soldiers stood or knelt in the gap, shooting at her.

Diaz fumbled with the stick, gritting her teeth against the sickening waves of pain, and triggered the guns.

Twin fans of orange hell spooled out of the pods under the cockpit. Half the men blocking the doorway flew apart like red smoke. Pulling back on both sticks, she felt the chopper rise and tilt alarmingly backward. Her left foot pressed the pedal and the chopper pivoted to send the arc of fifty-caliber fire across the line of men and up the wall.

Remember your training, she shouted at herself, but she'd only flown a couple missions with Chuy coaching. Even Paz was a better pilot. She leveled the Bell off and tilted the nose down to charge the open door.

The whirling rotors barely cleared the narrow opening and sent the surviving soldiers scattering back. She cleared the hangar and spun around as she climbed to get a visual on the helicopter that shot up the hangar.

A Black Hawk spun drunkenly a couple hundred feet above the ground. Someone jumped, or was pushed, out the loading door. It wasn't Paz, she noted with something approaching relief.

Suddenly, the larger troop helicopter stabilized and took off over the airport. Diaz picked off stragglers with her machine gun pods as she furiously texted Paz.

The Black Hawk crossed the cargo runways and approached the military hangars. The rocket pods blossomed red-white and the control tower exploded.

Ready to go? She sent.

Follow me, Paz replied, even as the Black Hawk veered sideways to dodge an RPG launched from the ground.

Diaz fumbled off a message to Kiko to pop beacons and find an open space in the Canal Zone, then turned to head in that direction, when the whole southern horizon exploded.

Something in the nearest narrow strait on the canal birthed a hideous fireball over the canal that spread out to hang over the city.

Diaz texted Paz but got nothing. The Little Bird dipped and nearly tipped over. She gave a little scream and fought to stay upright when Paz's Black Hawk dropped out of the sky nose-first to explode on the highway.

"Paz!" Diaz screamed.

"Calm down," Paz shouted as she swung from the Bell's landing gear and climbed into the cockpit. "It's way too big," Paz said, "to be a regular bomb."

Diaz almost reflexively argued, but she was right. A firestorm had swept the locks and the Canal Zone, smashing everything flat and hurling cargo containers like meteors in all directions. The flaming ship blocked one passage but the locks in both channels were seemingly gone. A foamy brown flood was pounding down the canal, wiping away residential neighborhoods and freight yards with a terrible inevitability.

But worse than all that, far worse, was the knowledge that her team was on that ship.

Her phone buzzed. Villalobos. *MY CHILDREN ARE STARVING.* His beacon popped up on her map. He was on the highway outside the Miraflores docks, and he had just stopped moving.

"There!" Paz shouted, hanging out on the skid, the unruly bedspring curls of her black hair ironed straight by the hot, smoky wind.

Diaz swooped down over the lone set of headlights on the highway. Something was blocking the lights, hundreds of something. A white pickup truck was swarming with vampires. A pair of guns stuttered lightning that illuminated one man standing atop the cab.

Paz hit the spotlight and Villalobos stood out in blue-white light that momentarily stunned the vampires closing in on him. Most of them were ordinary Panamanians of more European than Indian blood, but among them was a huge contingent of Chinese *jiangshi*, workers from the Canal Zone. Villalobos regretfully dropped his empty children and drew a machete and a knife to stave off the blood-mad horde.

Diaz nosed down and scoured the highway around the truck with the last of her ordnance. The vampires flew apart like mowed grass, but she'd only bought him a few moments. More were sprinting or hopping out of the blazing freight yards like fleas and ticks from a burning dog, converging on the truck.

"Drop the harness," Diaz shouted, but Paz had already paid out the nylon line. They hovered twenty feet above the truck, Paz picking off vampires as they strayed too close.

Villalobos grabbed the harness. Stomping on the roof, he knelt and helped a sickly Asian man in a soiled white coverall climb out the blown-out rear window. Then he got into the harness, wrapped his arms around the man and waved at her to reel him in.

The helicopter strained, slewed to the right. Diaz compensated and started to climb, but something leapt off the ground like a locust and fastened onto the man in Villalobos's arms with its claws and fangs. Villalobos buried a machete in its face and lost it when the *jiangshi* let go and fell to earth. Another leapt onto him, clawing and biting in a frenzy, and then another, and another. Paz picked some off with her MP5, but more of them kept leaping up to get at the dangling bait. One of them sprang off the knot of bodies to hang from the left landing skid until Paz shot its fingers off. "Climb!"

Villalobos struggled mightily to hold onto the one-armed man, but now four dead vampires clung to his passenger, their seizures causing them to dig deeper into the bloodstream that had poisoned them. The man in his arms was slathered in blood, white as a sheet.

"Let go!" Paz screamed. She had to clout Villalobos on the head a couple times before he released the dead man and his parasites.

Villalobos reached up and pulled himself onto the running board. "All for nothing," growled the Guatemalan. "The fucking American used us! Kiko, Hidalgo, *gone!*" He wept into his arm.

The news had to be repeated into her ear. It hit Diaz like a flurry of blows. All of this lay on her head. She was following orders, but she owned every mistake thereafter. And for what? Was there even a real reason to come down here?

And then her phone rang.

"It's McClintock. I want a deal."

It took all her control to keep her voice steady. "You have everything you wanted, don't you?"

"Yes... I'm prepared to share it, if you'll call off your pet monster before he kills me and himself and the last hope of an end to this fucking plague."

Diaz searched the location of her caller. "I'm listening."

———•———

00:48 EST
Puerto de Balboa

The first thing he noticed after being shot in the face was the smell of cinnamon. Strange, that, but patients had often complained of strange, seemingly random symptoms, just before they died.

And he was most definitely dying...

The bullet had smashed his cheekbone and whipped his head around, but fell well short of the kill shot McClintock wanted, so he popped Kiko once more in the gut, and once in the neck, which was probably a mistake. Then he stripped the medic of his knapsack, dropped his briefcase down a ventilation shaft and made his escape—away from the rope ladder, to the starboard side. Kiko reached out for him or what he thought was him, but he couldn't move or feel his legs, and his hands weren't cooperating, either. But he had to move, he had to get the bastard...

Hands fell on him and lifted him up. He clumsily lashed out, but it was only Soto. The tattooed mute carried him to the rope ladder, ignoring his protests that they had to find McClintock before the bomb went off—

And then it was too late.

Soto was climbing down the ladder with Kiko under one arm when the firewall washed over them. Soto dropped into the muddy canal and they were both swept downstream.

Now, on the bank of the canal several hundred yards from the awesome torch of the Panamax ship, Soto dragged Kiko up onto the mud and fell down beside him. His skin crackled and steamed, and when Kiko spoke, his hand fumbled out and touched the medic's face, like a blind man.

He had never trusted Hidalgo Soto, could never trust someone who chose to feed on other human beings, let alone one who took lives and sold poison to make a living. But Soto had not hesitated a moment when he came to find Kiko Pech.

And now, thanks to that admirable show of courage, they were going to die together.

"Tactical," Kiko said, fighting for breath, "nuke. Briefcase bomb… he has the… blood."

Soto's boiled eyes twitched at him as if he could see. He coughed and put his hand to his throat. His mouth opened, trying to talk.

"No," Kiko said, "it's too late for me. You too, probably… unless…"

He was going to die in a matter of minutes from the radiation, if not the lead poisoning. But he didn't have to die for nothing. They didn't both have to die.

These questions of who was human were moot. If they could not trust each other, then none of them could claim to be human.

"I don't know how you do it… but do it." He pushed Soto with his hand, fumbled, pulled his hand closer, to rest it on his chest. "Tell them what he did."

Soto clenched his hand over Kiko's heart, but he resisted the urge, even though it meant agony such as no human could survive.

But finally, he gave in.

———•———

01:17 EST

The yacht was twice the size of the next largest in the harbor at Balboa, and smothered in armed guards, whose blood was splattered all over everything.

Paz had sprung off the chopper before Diaz landed on the helipad deck. Diaz shouted at her to wait, but there was no point warning her. Even from the air, they could see the dead men on every deck, the arcs of blood from ripped throats and punctured aortas. Even from up there, they recognized Soto's work.

Villalobos helped her down the stairs onto the fantail deck, where a hairless, charred demon sat with McClintock. She did a double-take when she recognized the demon as Hidalgo Soto.

The Salvadoran vampire was scar tissue from head to toe, his tattoos burned away and healed over. The extent of his injuries was unfathomable. He must have been on the cargo ship when it exploded.

"Finally," McClintock said, lighting a cigarette. "Make this animal understand that I'm worth more to you than he is, and we can go home."

"Were you going somewhere with these assholes?" Paz asked, pulling his hair back and snatching the cigarette. Taking a deep drag to get the cherry going, she waved it over his eye.

"That ship has sailed, so to speak," he said, affecting profound boredom. "Listen, I don't like it any more than you do, but relationships have, you know, obligations. You have to do things sometimes to prove your love. To get back in with, you know, the people I used to work for… I had to blow up the canal.

"I know what you're thinking, but think about it. The Chinese still control it, and look what they're becoming. They can pretty much invade both North and South America one superfreighter at a time. The flow had to be cut off. By the time the canal stops glowing, we'll have the Lake Nicaragua passage activated. We've got big plans, this was only a hitch in the road."

"You used *us* to do this, so we'd get the blame…"

"Hell no, everybody's going to blame the Chinese, but who cares? It's war, but it's always been war. But I told the truth about one thing. The man we got out…"

"He didn't make it."

"Too bad," he smirked. "I guess *I'm* your only hope, then."

"What do you mean?"

McClintock slowly, gingerly picked up a knapsack. Kiko's medical bag. "You see, our mutual friend took blood samples, but they're all gone. I injected myself with them. And I'm not dead, which means the antibodies are in there, doing their thing. You want the vaccine, you're only going to get it from one place." He tapped himself on the chest and grinned.

"You can't possibly expect us to bring you back with us…"

"No way. Just drop me off on the nearest island or neighboring country with a phone and a first aid kit, and I'll generously donate a pint or two of Boston's Finest."

—•—

01:47 EDT
Taino Island

They agreed to drop him off on the beach of Taino Island, just off the Panamanian coast. When they told him about the Amazons, McClintock had actually thought it sounded charming, the fucking idiot.

"It's been real, kids," he shot them the finger and made to jump out, when the Little Bird pivoted and dipped low over a shallow lagoon. Looking down into the water, he shouted, "Hey, what the fuck're you doing?"

The tempestuous wash from the rotors roiled the crystal-clear water and brought sleek, silvery-white shapes to the surface.

"Give my love to the mermaids," Villalobos said.

"Mermaids?" The chopper tilted. McClintock lost his footing and tumbled out of the chopper.

The American screamed a lot of things nobody could hear. They hovered above the lagoon until the foam ran red, then took off for home.

Diaz reclined in the passenger seat as Paz flew them over the waves, almost close enough to catch spray on the fractured windscreen. She touched the vials in the pouch between her knees, wondering if it was worth anything that happened tonight, if it even began to offset the unbelievable harm they'd helped to wreak upon Panama. She could not say, and would not until she had to face her commanding officer, when she got home. She had to trust that it was always worth her life, and every life in her trust, every time they went out. She wondered if the vampires in her team would have fought as selflessly if they knew what they were fighting for, what it could mean to the balance of power. Perhaps it was a violation of their trust, but again, such questions were, mercifully, above her pay grade.

She looked over her shoulder at Villalobos and Soto riding on the running board behind her seat. Soto hunched over, intently stabbing his forearm with a needle and a vial of ink. The letters were crude and would need going over, but she could already read it.

It said, KIKO PECH.

RED EMPIRE PART 2

By Jonathan Maberry

The Oval Office
The White House
Washington, D.C.
Day 18 of the Red Storm

"**M**r. President," said Church, "I must admit to being both alarmed and disappointed in your handling of this matter. I know that you inherited this war from your predecessor, and I know that there is a learning curve when it comes to living the role of chief executive and commander in chief. I know there's more to it than sitting behind that desk."

"You're not particularly subtle," said the president. "I was warned about that."

"I can imagine you received quite a lot of cautions about me," said Church.

"I did. A lot of people on *both* sides of the aisle think you're a megalomaniacal manipulator who thinks he's above the law. Some others say that people are afraid of you because they think you have files on everyone, like J. Edgar Hoover."

Church brushed a fleck of lint from his tie but offered no comment.

"I've read the charter for your organization. The Department of Military Sciences. Your group has an absurd, possibly illegal, amount of operational freedom. A great many of the congressmen and politicos I know think that charter should be amended or canceled altogether."

"That has been attempted several times over the last few decades, Mr. President," said Church.

"Is there a threat in that comment?"

"Not unless you choose to put politics before common sense," said Church. "Not unless you marginalize the safety of the American people in favor of political interests."

"Christ, you don't give a good goddamn who you're talking to, do you?"

"This isn't the first time I've been in this chair facing someone on the other side of that desk who was facing a crisis of this magnitude."

Swann sat in his wheelchair and watched the two men. He did not interrupt, but he felt breathless. The president was the most powerful man in the world, but Church was the most powerful man in this room. That was obvious even if it seemed like a contradiction. The big man was calm, focused, and in complete control.

"Don't push me, Church," growled the president. "I could make a lot of people happy by revoking your charter and putting your ass in front of a senate committee."

Church sighed. "But you won't do that, Mr. President. What you will do is listen to me. What you will do is listen to Dr. Swann. What you will do is shift your political and military policies so that your sole focus is opposition to the Red Empire. You will write and sign a series of executive orders that will put an end to persecution of nonviolent vampire citizens. You will close all of the internment camps and release every vampire incarcerated therein. You will schedule an address to the nation in which you will say that you are spearheading a movement toward peace between *all* human species. You will encourage your fellow heads of state to join you in this, and you will find that many will follow your lead. You will also reinstate Dr. Swann as official advisor on vampire affairs, and you will expand his position and powers and make him a member of your cabinet. That, sir, is what you will do."

Swann watched the president's eyes widen until they were almost bugged out and saw his mouth open until it gaped. After a long shocked moment, the president tried to laugh, but it came out crooked. Then his face began to burn a furious red.

"Who the *fuck* do you think you are?" said the president in a low, dangerous tone. "What in hell makes you think you can come in here and say these things to me? To the president of the United goddamn States? You must be out of your mind." He reached for his phone. "I'm going to have you put under close arrest and—"

Mr. Church said, "No."

The president stopped with the phone halfway to his mouth. "What did you say?"

"I said no, Mr. President. You are not going to make that or any call. Not yet. Not until we have reached an understanding."

"I'm going to throw you into a goddamn hole and throw away the hole."

"I *know*," said Church.

He leaned ever so slightly on the word. The president froze. Absolutely froze, and Swann saw sudden, intense fear in the man's eyes. He actually felt sorry for the man. And although he had never met Church before, Swann had received several visits from Ledger, Violin, and others working with Church's organization. Swann knew what Church knew.

"Yes," said Church, "I know. And I also know that other people are aware of the truth and have been using it against you. To control you. You are a prisoner of their knowledge."

The president was as still as a statue. The fear in his eyes turned to terror.

"I am here to offer you a way out, Mr. President," Church said quietly. "Please… put the phone down and listen to me."

The president lowered the phone. "You can't know."

"And yet I do."

"*How?*"

Swann said, "Because I told him."

The president's head snapped around toward Swann. "What the hell do you know?"

"About politics? Nothing, sir," said Swann, "but I know a vampire when I meet one."

YOUNG BLOODS

By Mike Watt

*"People don't want to learn. You could run PSAs night and day
and you'll still see idiots putting garlic on their doorsteps.
You know I still get crosses shoved in my face? I mean, for
real? But that's just dumb racism. I think what's worse is the
fang-shaming. That whole thing is why my sister got hers
filed down. Freaked out all the negs at the office. Had a bunch
of them whine 'religious rights'—'cause we're all the devil,
right? And no, I don't believe for an instant what they say
about 'Code Red.' That's a false-flag set up by the negs. No
vampire would bother blowing shit up. We really wanted to...
one tweet, okay? One tweet and there'd be a thousand-blood
flash mob. Just pick the location. Wouldn't need bombs to take
out the negs of the human race."*
— *Young Bloods* interview subject Carla Washington,
music major, Mircalla Institute of the Arts

Back at the Karnstein Academy, everyone showed their fangs when
they talked. There was no reason to hide them at the school: "Vs
Only" for over a decade and growing. Negs couldn't get in if they
wanted to.

Ray Garfield checked himself, grimacing for even thinking the word
"neg." He was no racist. They didn't call his side of the gene pool
"pozzies." Not this far east, anyway. Maybe in the Midwest they slagged
the hematophageous minority, but that kind of thinking never gets
much accomplished.

"'Human,'" his father had said, standing on the Capitol floor. "What does that word even mean anymore?" He paused and glanced around the gallery, beyond the spectators and at the old white men who had held all the power for decades. "Genetically, Vs are ninety-nine-point-one-six percent identical to naturally born human beings. Even those who were transformed by the so-called 'Ice Virus' only changed a fraction of a percent. A fraction of a percent. Point-eight-four. Point-eight-four, ladies and gentlemen, is the entire difference between a human and a vampire. But this point-eight-four percent means endless debate. Should vampires be allowed to vote? Or drive a car? Or hold public office? Should his point-eight-four percent mean segregation of basically the same species? This is more than a house divided, ladies and gentlemen. From a cosmic point of view, we are but a single cell fighting against itself."

With one speech—quoted and played ad infinitum on television, online— Warren Garfield, billionaire, "came out of the coffin" and revealed himself to be one of the very few naturally born vampires on Earth, predating the I1V1 infection by the span of his entire life. Living as a human, among humans, without feeding on humans: an ideological symbol of peace and unity. Warren Garfield had the power to change the world, for surely those with flattened incisors could see that point-eight-four percent was not a difference at all. If vampires had existed among them all this time, then why should a sudden population increase be so frightening?

No reason at all.

"No reason at all." The primary source of conflict since the dawn of time. Warren Garfield's words shattered very few walls, even though they were only point-eight-four percent thick. More vampires fled east and more V-only schools like Karnstein popped up.

Gradually—however gradually—you stopped hearing about V-students forcibly removed from "human" schools. Howls of outrage grew softer as human and vampire continued to love and marry and reproduce, churning out Vs and Hs and what-have-you's in exponential numbers. Because that's what happens in nature. Disapproval alone never stopped anything.

Did it stop insane beats from breaking into V-homes, armed with stakes and hammers and terrible blank-verse scripture? Of course not. It didn't stop the more desperate Vs from lurking in alleys and pouncing like Lugosis on lonely beat victims. It didn't stop the slander from either side.

"Pozzy!"

"Neg!"

"Bleeder!"

"Bloater!"

It didn't stop taggers from spraying double-Vs on vampire-owned businesses.

But it also didn't stop the voluntary blood drives, which Warren took as a victory. When donations went up, violence went down. It was a statistic that couldn't be shouted away by radio hosts or editorials.

———•———

"No, what I'm saying is, vampires are the new gays, the new illegal immigrants," Ray said at dinner.

"Chew your food," his mother said.

He finished his mouthful to finish his sentence. "We're the new whatever that lives under the bed and to scare innocent, patriotic white humans."

"'New'?" said his brother. "We're not the 'new' anything. If anything, we predate all the other minorities."

"David," their father chimed in, "you're lucky you can even say the word 'we,' okay? Vampires didn't breed often and when they did they didn't send out birth announcements. We were hunted to near extinction."

"That was the torch-and-pitchfork crowd," David said.

"And that crowd is coming back," Ray said, a bit of potato dropping from his fork as he gestured. "Vs need a more positive image."

David argued, "Neither side has learned anything from the ninety-nine—"

"But I think we can all move past that."

"What do you think you can do that Dad hasn't done? Or tried to do?"

"Okay, boys, let's not drag your father's sterling record into this. Eat your steak."

"I was thinking about becoming a vegetarian," said Gracie, not yet fifteen.

"And I was thinking about turning into a bat and flying out that window," said mother Grace. "Neither of those things is likely to happen tonight. Chew."

LOUIS RODWICK, I1V1-positive, nineteen years old, political science major: "You won't hear about any of our charity work on the 'bloodstream media.' They don't report about the vampire attacks that *don't* happen every day. And when's the last time you heard about neg-on-V violence, huh? That shit doesn't get clicks."

RAY GARFIELD, interviewer: "What about Mathias Monroe?"

RODWICK: "Bunch of *rednegs* torture a ten-year-old kid with sharpened stakes for four hours, doesn't matter if he's a vampire. People are going to talk about that."

GARFIELD: "Some of the biggest donors to the Mathias Monroe Foundation happen to be Ice-negatives."

RODWICK: "It was horrible. It got attention. I got a name for you: Shaundra Llewellyn."

GARFIELD: "I don't know who that is."

RODWICK: "Of course you don't. You're not going to hear about a forty-something black human who was raped and tortured by a bunch of negs who *thought* she was a vampire. 'Bloodstream media' covered that shit right up."

PEPPER MALLORY, camera operator: "Do you realize how dumb you sound every time you use that word?"

RODWICK: "And you sound like a self-hating hema-phobe."

GARFIELD: "Pepper, can we stay impartial here?"

MALLORY: [Indistinct mutter.]

RODWICK: "Look, you think I'm biased, but we could sit here all day and talk about neg violence. But I don't know too many negs who'd change their minds after hearing it."

At his father's party, Ray had just popped an entire cheese-and-cracker combo into his mouth as his father swept an arm around him.

"Raymond, this is Mr. Fortesque, one of the founders of the Vampire League of Anti-Defamation. I told him all about your project."

Desperately chewing, while simultaneously begging his body not to spray crumbs onto the delicate man's thousand-dollar suit, Ray accepted Mr. Fortesque's handshake. Finally he managed to swallow and gasp out, "Very nice to meet you, Mr. Fortesque."

White-haired, sharp features, the man's face split into a mannered smile, revealing just the tips of his bleached fangs. "Please," he said, "call me Llewyn. I understand your project is making quite a stir at Mircalla. Sounds like something we might be interested in."

"I'm flattered, Llewyn, but this is just a student project. I was thinking it might be helpful for new student orientation or something. Maybe to follow the anti–sexual harassment message."

Warren's hand tightened on his son's shoulder. "The artist is always his own worst critic, right?"

Llewyn Fortesque clucked a short, low laugh. "Indeed," he said. To Ray he continued, "Nevertheless, I'd love to see a copy when it's finished. If it seems like something VLAD could use in its own programs, it might be worth pursuing with additional funding."

"That would be incredible, thank you. Of course, I can't take all the credit. I'm working with Pepper Mallory on this. She's my camera operator and producer. She's responsible for finding the majority of the interview subjects."

"Mallory… She wouldn't be related to Art Mallory by any chance?"

"Yes, actually. He's her father."

Llewyn gave Warren a quick glance. "Art Mallory is quite the big shot in the photography world."

Warren nodded. "Yes, I caught part of his retrospective at the Sheridan Museum last month. Schmoozing a couple of congressmen. Trying to get Act 988 onto the spring docket."

The two men fell into a discussion of politics, of Act 988's attempt to block another proposed bill gathering traction in the now ironically named "Red States" which would proclaim any Ice-positive vampire legally dead, unable to vote, hold office or property. Basically, 988 was his father's shield to preserve V rights in the United States. A stand against the Elderly White Human Powers-That-Be running the country. As usual.

Unable to gracefully excuse himself, Ray half-listened as he pondered Mr. Fortesque's maybe-offer. Underwriting from VLAD would not only give his doc a budgetary boost, but would give his production more than just an air of validity. It would give the documentary a louder voice to a wider audience. Images of a very bright future for himself sped through his mind.

"I think we're focusing too much on the average suburban vampire," Pepper told Ray during dinner break. They were sharing a half-gallon of Gold Label Goat's Blood Milk. More expensive than the junk stocked in the commissary vending machines, of course, thanks to the higher, purer blood content. His parents taught him at an early age that skimping was admirable, but you didn't compromise when it came to the finer foods.

Ray looked up from his sushi. "As opposed to what?"

"Jesus, Ray, there are as many different races of vampire as there are human. For example, have you ever met a *jiangshi?*"

Ray shook his head, but that wasn't the truth. A family of Chinese vampires had once rented the lake house next door to his family's when he was a kid. Shamefully, he and David had spent much of that summer teasing the younger vampires, mocking their oval eyes and hopping hunting style. "Hey, Kam-bo," twelve-year-old David had said to the eldest Cheng child, "why don't you *hop on home*, and grab some sticky rice for us." It was an epically racist thing to say to a *jiangshi*, referring to their mythological aversion to cooked rice, said to stop them in their place. Other times, David and Ray would simply hold their breath when one of the Chengs came by—the old saw that Chinese vampires couldn't see you if you didn't breathe. Ray was ashamed of himself now, but at the time, it was the height of prepubescent hilarity.

Pepper continued, "We should try to interview at least one. And there's this beautiful *aswang* girl up on my floor. You would not believe how long her tongue is. If I were a dyke, I'd be with her every waking moment. She's like a sexier, less horrible female Gene Simmons."

Ray nodded, "I'd be totally down for that. Both the interview and watching her go to town on you."

"Don't be an ass."

"It's college, Pepper. You're supposed to experiment."

"Okay then. Why don't you get it on with Kristos Stavrakas? He's a *vrykolakas*. I think his family's from Crete. I heard his penis is pointed."

"You know what? Get me drunk enough and I might try anything. Unlike you, Little Miss Prude."

Pepper made a face at him, then snapped off a piece of carrot with her beautifully sharp front teeth. Unlike most of the vampires he knew, Pepper was the first he'd ever met whose fangs rested on either side of her front two teeth. For that alone, he found her to be exotic.

— • —

Abenaa Murkob had just the slightest hint of an Ashanti accent, and to Ray it seemed like her skin was so dark she barely reflected light. As she spoke, she removed her shoes for the camera, revealing the hooked toe that unfolded from her heel. "It's supposed to help our kind sleep upside down in the forest," she said as the camera zoomed in on her strange appendage. "We're descended from the *asasabonsam*. We hunted at night and slept during the day. My grandmother told me that *'bonsam* disguised themselves as a type of large, poisonous fruit to protect us from predators and humans." She preened for the lens, curling and uncurling her special toe, flexing it, displaying the long dewlap claw. "'Course the rich white girls at school didn't care about the history. They just wanted another excuse to humiliate me and my sister in the gym showers. When my hearing really began to develop, I could hear them insulting us from across the football field, especially after I left their skinny asses in the dust during track. I could cross that field in four seconds and bitch-slap them into tomorrow before they finished their shit talk." She gave a big smile, showing two sets of sharp incisors.

"Were you bullied by only humans or other vampires too?" Ray asked from off screen.

"Mostly dumb-ass negs," Abenaa said. "Ámma, my sister, and I changed so fast from the virus, there wasn't time to get us into any other type of school. So we went from being two of ten black kids in the entire school, to two of only three black vampires. They just added to the list of names they already called us. And for a long while, my father didn't want us to mix with any other vampires, either."

"Sounds very lonely," said Pepper, readjusting the close-up on Abenaa's face.

"Everyone's got their *Breakfast Club* drama. But now I'm here on a track and field scholarship and dating this beautiful boy from Little Rock."

"What do you think about the proposal to declare Ice-positives legally dead?"

"That's just more white man paranoia. It'll never pass. How much money would it take to even enact something like that?"

"So you're saying it's just political theater?"

"We got a vampire judge in the Supreme Court and a pending Amendment to the Constitution. They're just wasting taxpayer money."

"It's apparently gaining popularity in the South."

"If the South was gonna rise again, they'da risen by now."

———•———

"It was easy enough for our family because we didn't fit any of the stereotypes," Warren Garfield told Ray's camera phone. The interview was impromptu, thrown together in the family room, lit only by the lamp on the end table. "We didn't need blood to survive, weren't 'allergic' to the sun. Long as we kept our teeth hidden and stayed white, we had a pretty comfortable ride. That tight-lipped smile I use in public is pretty much the same as your grandfather and uncles used while they served as Congressmen. 'The Garfield Smile' means something different in our family than it does to people who read comic strips."

Ray's smile was open-lipped and wide and unashamed of his fangs. At no time in his life had he felt the need to conceal his genetic disposition. "Why didn't you follow in your family footsteps and run for any kind of office?"

"Because I was born into a rich family and had more interest in growing our wealth than making changes. I was still a young man when the Ice Virus spread. It wasn't until after the 'ninety-nine' that I saw the need for any kind of politics."

"Do you have any interest in a government position now?"

"Well…" Warren continued, his eyes drifting downward for just a second, "the idea has crossed my mind more frequently than I care to admit. I've seen a lot of positive change over the last few years, but also numerous steps backward. On the other hand, I'm perfectly content to dip a toe in the pool every now and then, but I don't think I'm prepared to try the high dive just yet."

"What would it take to get you to run?"

"Let's not finish this discussion until after 988 goes up for a vote, okay? Wouldn't want to jinx it."

———•———

By his own description, Duncan DeBartalo was half Italian *vampiro* and half Irish *dearg-dul*. Aside from slightly pointed ear tips, Ray didn't see much of a genetic difference. Duncan was born and raised in Brooklyn and everything he said had a slight con-artist leer to it. Seated in Pepper's frame, he looked relaxed, confident to the point of arrogance. And he never stopped smiling. Halfway through the interview Ray noticed that even Duncan's molars were sharp. His front teeth and fangs wore a nicotine earth tone. He wore a silver crucifix around his neck. *An attempt to be ironic?* Ray wondered. Or was it to make an even sharper point?

"The negs realized very quickly that we're the next stage of evolution. Kind of blows their sky fairy out of Nirvana, doesn't it? They can't play the 'antichrist' card or even any kind of race card. That bill your dad is fighting is pure panic. Not just of vampires. They're terrified of a new world order that doesn't include them. It's an end of an era for the fat, rich white guys of the world."

"Even Norman Gyre?" Ray asked.

"Oh, fuck that guy," DeBartolo said, laughing. "His fangs might as well have come from Hollywood. He's as much a vampire as I am a vegetarian. Plus, he's a Republican. All he cares about is where his kick-backs come from. He's voted against vampire interests as often as he's 'supported the cause.' Dude's a pineapple."

Ray's pause was quite awkward. "What's a 'pineapple'?"

"Sharp on the outside, soft and white on the inside."

"That's a terrible metaphor."

DeBartalo shrugged. "I didn't coin the phrase," he said, and fixed Ray with a narrow glance. "Most people get the meaning."

"So do you feel that vampires are deliberately discriminated against—?"

But the interviewed vampire cut him off. "Okay, the long and short of it is everyone is discriminated against. We're not different in that regard. But that's not the question. The question is, are they right to be afraid of us? The answer is an emphatic *yes*."

Ray studied the man's face, the wide grin that was mostly sneer and baldly disgusted. Glancing back for help, Ray saw he was on his own. Pepper's eye was glued to the camera viewfinder, her slender fingers teasing across various buttons with refined expertise.

"Look, Garfield, no offense to you or your old man or even VLAD, but the rules changed the minute whatshisname did."

"Who?"

"Fuckin' Fame, or Frayne, whatever they called patient zero. Ice-V did a number on him and everyone else. Completely flipped the script. I've heard all kinds of vampires call him weak or deranged. I say he was doing what came natural. He evolved, okay? Into an entirely new breed of species. Ice-V made him into an alpha predator. But all the positives have to go around and act like he was a criminal or a wild animal. Something that deserved to be hunted down and euthanized. But that's an act, man. A scam. It ain't gonna last much longer, either. Say that stupid law gets passed. You think for a minute that vampires are gonna enjoy being second-class citizens? Get our property and holdings revoked? Emphatic *no fucking way*."

"What are you implying?" Ray asked him. He could feel righteous anger creeping down his scalp. "Another vampire revolution?" The idea was disgusting. Uncivilized.

DeBartolo snorted. "Revolution. Shit'll explode and be over in ten seconds. That Vampire Registration Act? All bullshit. They have no way of knowing who registered and who didn't. Half the pozzies I know are still off the books."

"How is that even possible?"

"Are you kidding? We're talking about the US government—who can't even keep the Post Office running—and the UN, which spends the majority of its time rearranging chairs, with all the countries forming and dissolving like soap bubbles. Think their V-database is up to date in the slightest? NSA has no idea how many vampires there are in America, let alone the world. Want a hint? *Way* more than they think. Vampire communities are cats waiting to pounce. And our tails are swishing like mad. Figuratively speaking. I don't know any real vamps that have tails. Though I did bang this *nangina* who has to have surgery three times a year to keep her legs from melting together into a snake rattle. But that, my positive friend, is a story for another time."

"I think we've gone a little off-topic here…"

"Yeah, I see the look of 'bullshit' on your face. Lemme guess, you're from some pristine gated community, right? Central air, indoor pool, servants—am I getting warm? Tennis courts? Year-long school dances. Classes of fine vamp gentlemen and ladies?"

Ray swallowed back a resentful sigh. "We didn't have servants," he managed.

"So an 'x' for the 'servants' column. I nailed the rest of it, right? Pepper was right, you're a sheltered trustafarian and this project of yours is one debutant away from being *Sound of Vampire Music*."

"Don't drag me into this," Pepper said.

Duncan waved her off. "You don't know the first thing about real vampires, Ray."

"What the hell does that mean? I grew up in a family of vampires. My dad doesn't even have the virus. He was born in 1908, fangs and all."

"Yeah, and his father came over on the Mayflower, right? And his grandfather was present at the manger, along with the Three Wise Men. Blah-blah. You ever been to a real Red Party, boyo?"

"No. I try to stay away from *fang fiction*."

"Drop that shit, Ray. Red Parties are no different from tribal celebrations held after a hunt. They're primal and real and the stuff of neg nightmares. You wanna meet real vampires, I'll send you a text with an address next time one comes around. Then we'll talk persecution and discrimination, yeah? Meantime, keep drinking the AB Kool-Aid."

———•———

"That asshole is so full of shit," Ray said, taking his anger out on the microphone cord he was coiling up.

Pepper closed up her tripod with a metallic snap. "Pun intended?"

"Just fucking feeding into the stereotype. He might as well have hovered around in a big black cape. I hate fucking emo vamps!"

"Please. He was so far from emo."

"Now you're on his side?"

"Oh, sorry. I didn't know this was a clique thing. You two gonna snap fingers and dance off?"

With a frustrated growl, Ray dropped the cord and whirled on her. "Don't! Don't make me sound like the petty one here. Fucking 'Red Parties'? Seriously?"

Pepper shrugged. "Seriously, Ray. They're a thing. They're not college keggers either, for your information."

"Maybe you're the one drinking the Kool-Aid."

"Whatever."

"You ever been to one?"

Her response had an edge to it. "Yeah. A ton of them. My stepbrother threw them all the time in our dad's garage."

"Oh for—seriously, Pepper? And what? Bowls of chips and dip arranged around the body of a naked virgin? Were hoods and whips involved too?"

"Fuck you, Ray."

"Did you prowl the neighborhoods beforehand, looking for the perfect victims?"

"You know what? Believe whatever shit you want about vampires, DeBartolo, and me. Won't change the fact that I was right and he was right." She slammed the camera case lid closed. "You don't know shit about vampires."

"So I'm naturally born. So what? I didn't catch the virus, I come from linear gene line."

"'So what' is right. That doesn't change anything either. It doesn't change that this little doc of yours is nothing but cute vampire PR. More PSAs for VLAD and their 'Hug A Vampire' holidays!"

Without looking, Ray knew his face was the shade of boiled lobster, cheeks and ears flushed, red running down his neck. She was dead right, but damned if he could admit it. "Fine, Pepper-from-the-Hood. You're so in tune with Red Parties, I guess you'll accompany me to Duncan's next shindig?"

This time Pepper paused. "I don't go to those things anymore."

"So you're full of shit too."

"They don't play Spin the Bottle at these things. Seven Minutes in Heaven means appetizers. And the food supply isn't always willing."

It was Ray's turn to "whatever." With that one word, Pepper's face mirrored his. "You know what? I'm in. You're basically asking an alcoholic to buy a round, but that's just the fucking asshole in you. Like you give a damn anyway."

All of the strength drained from Ray's body. He sighed and slumped into a metal chair. "Okay, look, I'm sorry. It's been a long day and I'm exhausted. I'm taking his crap personally."

"No. You're acting like a know-nothing neg groupie. You don't know anything beyond your own limited experience. You want to be an ass, I might as well go with you to make sure you don't get hurt."

———•◆•———

"Come on, Raymond, seriously?" his father said. "Some idiot actually invited you to a 'Red Party.' That's the kind of negative stereotype VLAD is trying to avoid."

"So you have heard of them?"

"Yes. It's a popular college rite of passage. Along with hangovers and hazing. Booze, blood, and the vampire equivalent of date rape."

Then his mother chimed in. "I do not want to hear of you going to one of those," Grace said. "It's sophomoric debauchery."

"Well, now you're just selling me on it."

"Don't be cute, Raymond," she said.

"Mandy Tyler's older sister went to one of those and got sucked on by, like, twenty different vampires," said Gracie, playing with her spaghetti.

Mother Grace sighed, "No, she didn't."

"Yuh-huh! Mandy told me. And Lizzie showed me the marks up and down her arms."

"Elizabeth Tyler always ran with a bad crowd," said Warren.

"You never like any of my friends!"

"You don't need friends like that, Gracie. I won't have any kind of feeding going on in this house, do you understand me?"

"Oh, like I said I was gonna do it. And I totally could, too, by the way. Johnny Verbinski said I could drink him any time I wanted to."

Her mother tossed her fork down, clanging metal against porcelain plate. "I don't want to hear you talking like that again. Johnny Verbinski is four years older than you are and a college drop-out."

"So what if he is? He paints vans, mother. He runs his own business."

"Okay, getting back to the subject," Ray said. "I just think my documentary will have a little more depth if I knew about more of the counter-culture side. My world-view is completely sheltered."

"Did we 'shelter' you by keeping you away from heroin?" Warren said. "Did we 'shelter' you by not taking you to biker bars or cross burnings? Those exist too."

"Dad, at no point did I mention heroin or biker bars. This is Mircalla we're talking about. It's one step below Ivy League. They're not going to risk abducting someone against their will. There are more than enough feeders around eager to get their veins drained."

Ray's mother shook her head. Her voice broke slightly when she spoke. "I'm so happy we're spending a fortune to enlighten and educate you. Go to your Red Party. Just keep the details to yourself."

"If I go, I'm going to document it. You'll see it in the movie."

"No, I will not."

"Seriously? I'm the interviewer, mom. It's not like I'm going to participate. I'm a neutral observing party—"

"Maybe you can catch a cockfight afterward. Or maybe your new friends will take you down to the docks to set the homeless on fire. Excuse me." Her chair squealed against the hardwood floor as she got up from the table and left the room, leaving behind embarrassed silence.

"Ray," Warren said. "I'm not going to tell you what to do. I would advise that before you do anything else, you apologize to your mother."

"For what? Stating my case?"

"You upset her and you know it."

"Yeah," said Gracie.

Ray went to bed early that night. Instead of logging footage or doing any studying whatsoever, he flopped on his bed and stared at the ceiling. He had zero interest in attending any kind of a Red Party, let alone going as a guest of DeBartolo. But if he didn't, what kind of documentarian would he be? What was it Akira Kurosawa said? "To be an artist means to never avert one's eyes," or something like that. Or was it, "Gaze long at that which pleases you, and longer still at what displeases you"? If this was going to be his life, he couldn't shy away once things got slightly uncomfortable. He had a job to do. And if what he captured next didn't fit in with VLAD's agenda, so be it.

Just before sleep caught up to him, his phone buzzed. It was a text from DeBartolo, to both him and Pepper. With a time, a date, and an address.

After some debate, it was decided that Ray would dip into his own funds and get Pepper a pair of spyware contact lenses. Wearing them, she'd live-stream footage to a wireless hard drive in her pocket. A separate DAT recorder in another pocket would capture the audio. Worse comes to worst, it would be easier to score forgiveness than permission from the party-holders. And there were a number of things they could do in post-production to blur identities, disguise voices, etcetera.

Duncan's text brought them to an underground parking garage in the South Side. The Italian/Irish vampire met them outside, gave their bona fides to the bulky bouncer hired for the night. Several masked attendees filed past them. "How very *Eyes Wide Shut*," Ray muttered. Pepper nudged him. If Duncan heard him, he didn't let on. The noise from inside was muffled by the thick cinderblock walls, marked with many "Do Not Enter" signs.

After the bouncer let them pass, they followed Duncan through the thick metal entrance doors, where the cacophony increased exponentially. Their host led them down three flights of steel stairs, their clanging footsteps bouncing echoes all around them. Behind them, two other couples, dressed in blacks and reds, added their own foot sounds to the echoes. The stairwell smelled overwhelmingly of mold and "used wine." Both Ray and Pepper felt their sensitive olfactories offended. Naturally, if Duncan was bothered by the odors, he didn't let on. Nor did he drop his arrogant grin.

Opening the terminal door, a wall of sound smashed into and through them. A near-solid wave of industrial noise and pounding bass threatened to turn their insides into gravy, but they soldiered on, following DeBartolo into the thick of the crowd. They waded through undulating bodies and the accompanying fragrances the bodies wore. Patchouli and jasmine and Old Spice and plain ol' B.O. wormed into their nostrils, leaving a trail down their throats. Unable to make himself heard over the din, Ray texted Pepper, standing at his elbow. "You rolling?" his message asked. She nodded at him. They then arrived at their destination, a dilapidated black leather couch, an obvious rescue from curbside trash, wearing a handwritten cardboard sign reading "Reserved."

"Wow, your own booth," Ray half-shouted. DeBartolo simply nodded.

They sat to Duncan's left, on the far edge of the couch. Looking around, Ray saw the strobe of waving glow sticks, the occasional flashes of sweaty, naked torsos of both genders, the DJ's head bobbing in time with the droning music. It was every rave he'd ever been to. In the darkness, lasered frantically apart by spinning disco lights, it was difficult to tell who was vampire and who was human. Not that he'd ever been particularly adept at catching the distinctions. Like his father, Ray prided himself on "not seeing species." Only the glint of fang gave the vampires away.

The only difference from other flash mob events was the sheer blackness of the dark. Like most vampires, natural and V-positive, Ray had exceptional night vision. But here in the garage, there was just the glow worm after-image of the spinning strobe, a blob of gray in its wake. It messed with his head as well as his insides. But damned if he was going to admit it.

"So this is it?" he shouted to Duncan. "An underground rave in a parking garage? *Skinny Puppy* mashed up with *Roxy Music*? The subversion is so daring."

"This is just the pre-show, boyo. Keep your panties unbunched."

They sat. And watched. A razor-thin girl dressed as Neil Gaiman's "Death" brought them red drinks they didn't order. They tasted like Hi-C punch with a shot of rum and a whole lot of half-heartedness.

Seated on the very edge of the couch, Pepper swung her head slowly back and forth, like a literal surveillance camera. She was taking it all in, but Ray doubted that the camera was calibrated well enough to pierce the darkness. They'd likely get back a stream of footage ruined by blocky blacks and low-light greys, shot through with neon-bright color. The sound would be worse, blown out by the excessive decibels. If something big *did* happen, it would require narration. Perhaps even an animated mascot.

He turned again to DeBartolo, whose own head bobbed in time to the bass. "How long before anything actually goes down?"

"It's still early. Relax, Spielberg."

"So far I'm not impressed!"

"And I'm ever so shocked to hear it."

Ray put his mouth close to Pepper's ear and shouted, "This seem familiar to you?"

"Yep. Loud and garage-y, just the way I remember. Only thing missing is my stepbrother vomiting on his date."

If all Red Parties were like this, Ray thought, he wasn't so much "sheltered" by his parents as "spared."

Over the course of an hour, they sat and watched. Pepper recorded. DeBartolo drank and grinned and flirted with the various "Deaths" serving as waitresses. The bar was on the other side of the DJ stage, positioned behind the hula-hooping girl dancers in black bikinis flanking the turntables. Ray never got a good look, but the bar seemed to be a pair of card tables stocked with empty booze bottles of a variety of labels.

Most of the partiers were dressed in the *hautest* of Lestat *couture*, which seemed to Ray a warning light of human poseur wannabe pozzies. He felt his repressed classism rising with every near-identical throbbing "song." Every now and then, a vampire would break through the crowd and greet DeBartolo with a hug or a fist bump. DeBartolo never bothered introducing them, but occasionally Pepper pointed out those she recognized.

"That's Savin," she said, as *sotto voce* as physically possible, pointing her chin toward a young woman dressed all in white, blouse, jeans, and boots. Her hair seemed to mimic the near-total blackness. "She's one of the heads of the V-Defense League."

"The what?"

"They were a kind of street gang that became socially conscious. They spend the bulk of their time escorting vampires after dark, protecting them from any teeming mobs of hateful negs that might be lurking about."

"Noble," Ray said.

It continued like that for most of the evening. People would come up to Duncan, Pepper would explain who they were. At no point did Duncan attempt to make introductions, nor did the visitors pay Ray any notice. An enormous black vampire stopped by, obviously bred for football excellence. At least a foot taller than Duncan, he nonetheless embraced the smaller man.

"Blue," Pepper whispered.

"What is?" said Ray.

She nodded at Duncan's muscular visitor. "He's like the king around here. Ganger from New Orleans, but his boys ran him through the gauntlet when he caught the Ice. He came north, found some V-brothers, and then he took them on a visit home. Wiped out seven or eight negs. Dropped on the rest and got them locked up. This is pretty much his town, his party."

Maybe Blue heard her over the impossible din, or maybe he just noticed her sitting with the stranger. Whichever the case, Blue turned his attention on Pepper. "Is that my girl Pepper?" With a surprising quickness, he stood in front of her and swept her into his arms. "Been too long a time. Where have you been hiding?"

Still wrapped in his Tarzan carry, Pepper did something that dropped Ray's jaw. She blushed. And giggled. In Ray's experience, Pepper melted for no one. She was all about the lens and the light and the shot. No time for play at Mircalla. But there she was, in the hairless giant's arms, eyes goggled like a tween at her favorite boy band concert. "School, you know."

Blue laughed, delighted. "You still shooting pictures? That's wonderful, Pep. So proud of you." He set her down on her own very wobbly legs. She actually gasped, ran a hand along his muscular chest, unhidden beneath the navy tank top. Ray felt his last meal rising. He suddenly realized how little he knew about his director of photography and producer. But she seemed to know everything. About everything. How?

"Um…" she started, testing Ray's gag reflex further. "This is… uh… this is my friend, Ray Garfield."

And then Blue's eyes were on him. The man still smiled, wide and friendly, but his eyes were narrow, and almost red in the near-absent light. The spinning lights found his face with a shocking frequency, then darted away just as quickly. Even the music seemed to be flirting with this particular danger. "Oh yeah," Blue said. "I heard all about you, Mr. Garfield. You're working on some sort of V propaganda, right? Gonna show the world that the bloods are just like them, only fangier, right? Just a different diet. Gonna tell them all that we're, like, gluten-free or something?"

Fear began stumbling around in Ray's mind and heart. If Pepper were to be believed, this vampire was a criminal. A danger. The thing lurking beneath every V-negative's bed. Enormous African-American monster, with a tendency for blood-drinking and revenge. He was the poster child for white fright. It took all his strength, but Ray forced himself to his feet and extended his hand. "Point-eight-four percent. That's all that separates us from the V-negatives."

"Well, yes, that," Blue said, "and these." He showed his fangs. Top and bottom, from the front teeth on back. They were all sharp. Blue's mouth was a ceramic bear trap. Before Ray could even flinch, Blue's enormous hand wrapped around his and held firm. He didn't squeeze—there was no brash display of strength or power. Just a nice, solid hand-shake that didn't release.

"Some friends of mine," Blue said, "and I are very interested in this movie of yours."

Ray's voice caught on its way out. "Are you a member of VLAD?"

Blue smiled wider than Ray would have thought possible. "My friends and VLAD have a similar agenda, but there's a point where they split and go their separate ways. But we both really like your intentions. We'd love for the beat communities to stop seeing us as a threat. Invite us to block parties. Show us where the spare keys are hidden."

Ray felt the blood rush from his face and for an instant wished he'd fed recently to replenish what the spurt of fear just cost him. Then Blue released his hand and chucked him on the shoulder in a friendly, non-terrifying way. Like an enormous, dangerous older brother. "I'm just kidding around, Ray. Can I call you Ray? I'm just playing a role here. In all seriousness, I can't wait to see your movie when it's done. I'm sure it'll be a real eye-opener." He smiled then at Pepper. "And with my girl Miss Mallory's talents, I'm sure it'll be as gorgeous as a sunrise."

"Well… um, thank you, Mr. Blue, is it?"

"Just Blue, my good man."

"Oh, okay. It'll be mostly talking head interviews, Blue. We'll have some on-the-street stuff, of course. Like the blood kitchens down in the Strip, for the homeless vampires. Things that emphasize the positives and the negatives really working together for change."

"Sounds *tres* nifty," Blue said. "Pity you're not shooting here tonight. With all the colored lights and stuff, might jazz things up a little. Interrupt the talking."

Ray nodded. "That's something to think about."

"Too bad cameras aren't allowed in here, though." That came from Duncan, rising to his feet for the first time in hours. "But don't worry about that, Blue. Pepper knows the score."

Blue's glance bounced from DeBartolo and back to Pepper, skipping Ray entirely. "That she does. That she does." Without looking at him, Blue said to Ray, "You stick with Pepper, Ray. She'll show you all the ropes." His demeanor changed entirely without even a breath or a pause. "Well, if you gentlemen—and lady—will excuse me. I must finish up my rounds before the main festivities begin. It was very nice to meet you, Ray. Again, please keep me informed as your production develops."

It was as if Blue simply dissolved into darkness. Once there, then not, swallowed by the frantic swirl of lights knifing the nothing. Blue became one with blackness and music. Before he could process it, he felt Duncan's hand on his shoulder, gently prodding him forward. "Come on, Coppola. We have a table waiting for us."

DeBartolo didn't so much lead the way as simply guide them, with hands at Ray's neck and at the small of Pepper's back, toward empty space, past the crowds. As if the blackness surrendered suddenly, they found themselves in a small banquet area, round tables draped with white cloth, lit with candles, lined with plates and silverware. Completely overlooked when they entered, it was as if the table settings had appeared by magic, unfolded from the darkness. Or perhaps it all rose from the floor like a magician's illusion, or a spy's secret lair. It made all the fear in Ray's body bunch up in his chest, filling his skin with crawling ants.

"Yeah, yeah, yeah," came the DJ's voice, filling the room like God's command. "It's time, boys and girls. We're now gonna put the 'red' in this Red Party. Let's have a round of applause for our hosts and give thanks for what we are all about to receive."

The room exploded with the sound of clapping hands, cheers, whistles, genuine excitement, and gratitude. Blue's name was not mentioned. Nor Savin's or any of the vampires Pepper told him about. The identity of the hosts was implied, self-evident. If you didn't know who was providing the feast, the applause hinted, you had no right to be there. Just as Ray realized that he had no right to be there. Upper-class vampire in a party thrown by a secret society. He was a fish flopping on the pier.

A "Death" unfolded from the darkness, wheeling a cart on which was placed a giant silver dome covering a platter. There were four other vampires at the table, none of whom had stopped by to greet Duncan, so their faces were foreign to him, just eyes and fangs glinting in the candlelight.

The DJ's voice of God boomed again. "Ladies and Gentlemen: thy bounty."

Across the room, the Deaths placed trays on tables, as magnificent polished centerpieces. Once in place, the lids were lifted.

Ghoulish. Something out of a Charles Addams cartoon. The main course, on a bed of cabbage and roasted potatoes, wrapped in a flowered tortilla and tied in place—each table had its own squirming, struggling infant child. Tears flowed down the chubby cheeks, but its open, toothless mouth made no noise. Ray didn't have to ask to know that the baby's vocal cords had been severed in preparation. Applause erupted again, appreciative noise straining to burst the concrete walls.

A prolonged "f" sound escaped Ray's lips, as if he were leaking air. The sound gave way to words, "*Fuck no!*" His eyes couldn't leave the struggling infant. "Fuck no! No fucking way." Finally, in self-defense, his gaze shot across the fangs and smiling faces of his tablemates. Only Pepper had the grace to look slightly ashamed. "You people are—"

Someone dropped an iron bar across his neck. It was Duncan's vice-grip on his shoulders. "'Hungry.' That's the word you're looking for, Garfield. But the good news is, it's time to dig in."

He tried to shake his head. DeBartolo's hand wouldn't let him. "There is no way I'm taking part in this! This is… this is fucking *evil!*"

The weight on his neck increased, forcing his head closer to the table. He could feel DeBartolo's breath on his ear. "Get off your high horse before someone knocks you off. You are a vampire. Just like us. All of us."

Ray strained to look at Pepper. Her eyes were down, avoiding his. Then suddenly, she too was entranced by the sweating, red-faced, trussed-up baby.

"You are going to eat like a civilized, cultured being," DeBartolo whispered. "When you've finished everything on your plate, you and Pepper can go. Put this all in your little documentary. We know all about your hidden cameras and we'd just love it if you got the word out."

"Forget it! And if you do anything to either of us, my father… and… and VLAD and the government will rain fire on all of this!"

"Christ, you're such a comedian, Ray. We throw a party like this at least once a month, and we're a very… small… community. Think about the vampire population in Shreveport. In Albany. In Pittsburgh. In D. *fucking* C., where all your lovely laws are created. Doesn't matter if the V-Pozzies declare us legally dead. Get what I'm saying? We can mobilize at any time, way faster than anyone in Congress can even say 'filibuster.' But you keep on telling people that we're not monsters. And you keep telling vampires that humans aren't monsters. One day, we're all going to gather, en masse, and clear the world of pozzies like locusts."

Struggling against the grip only made DeBartolo press harder. Ray's cheek touched the table, inches from the bucking, thrashing dinner.

"It does not matter what you do from this point onward, Ray. But you don't leave here without having something to eat. You really don't want to insult our hosts. You get it now, right? You greasy little yuppie human wannabe."

Across the table, one of the anonymous vampires moved, steak knife in hand, ready to carve. "Tell you what," Duncan told him. "All you have to do is eat point-eight-four percent."

———◆———

Ray left the garage alone, vomiting and shaking, but managing to keep the sobbing under control. During the long subway ride back home. Only once his bedroom door was closed behind him did the floodgates open.

Alone. Pepper stayed behind. With DeBartolo. With Blue. With all of the others. She wouldn't meet his eyes. Wouldn't answer his pleading, helpless eyes. For back-up. For support. For even a hint of a lie that this wasn't happening. She never looked up. From her plate.

He spent the rest of the night staring at his ceiling, desperately working to clean his mind of the evening. Of the baby. Of the baby's terrified bright blue eyes.

Of the tiniest bit of effort to stop its struggling and silent wailing.

Of the wonderful, wonderful taste.

Tomorrow morning, he'd face a digital mile of Pepper's footage and a variety of choices equally horrific.

Very young blood, still cooling on his chin, delicious and forbidden and hateful—as he was forcibly shown the door.

Should he turn the footage over to VLAD?

To his father?

To the police?

The flavor—the aftertaste—still lingered at the back of his mouth. Tender strands caught between his teeth.

To the news?

Should he stream it on the internet for all the world to see?

Should he bury it? "Trim it out for time"? Leave it on the cutting room floor and simply let the show go on?

Forget the footage, what would the *world* look like tomorrow? What would Pepper look like, to him, tomorrow?

It was all so big, too huge to comprehend. Who would the truth benefit? Who would it destroy? Certainly, it would change the thrust of his father's entire life's work. Certainly, it would dredge up terror and fear and hatred and even more violence.

Where had the babies come from? There was nothing on TV or the web of massive natal kidnappings. Maybe he'd imagined it. Maybe it wasn't a baby. Just a piglet, the dark tricking him into seeing an infant. But what piglet had he ever seen with blue eyes.

The weight of the world had taken up a comfortable residence on his chest. Ray Garfield was not equipped to deal with these choices.

He had to admit to himself: until this evening, he had never before met a vampire.

CHOP SHOP

8

By John Dixon

McClellan blocked the haymaker and countered with a right cross, clipping the big hillbilly on the jaw and dropping him to the muddy ground. The musclebound redneck sat there, rubbing his chin and shaking his head, obviously trying to clear the cobwebs and likely struggling to comprehend just how this hundred-and-sixty-pounder had gotten the best of him.

"You have the right to remain silent," McClellan said, snapping cuffs over the young man's thick wrists. "Anything you say can and—"

This brought the guy around. He staggered to a knee and glared up at McClellan, who continued to read him his rights. "Hey," the redneck said. "You can't do that. You're not a cop."

"That's where you're wrong, son," McClellan said. "I'm a game warden. That's law enforcement, and you're under arrest."

"What charge?"

"Poaching deer," McClellan said, "and assaulting an officer."

The guy cursed and struggled to his feet. "I didn't poach no deer. I got my uncle's tag right here in my shirt pocket. Pull it out and see for yourself."

McClellan pulled the tag. "Well, then," he said, pausing to read the name, "I'll see that *Otis Yates* gets a citation, too. This is hunting, son, not baseball. No pinch-hitting allowed."

McClellan was just leaving the police barracks when a gray-haired officer stepped between him and the door. The man was obviously ex-military: short gray hair, squared-away uniform, ramrod posture, and hard-glittering eyes. He'd seen action. Undoubtedly against bloods in the V-Wars. Probably against beats, too, before that. Afghanistan, Iraq.

McClellan himself had waged war in these countries and others, first as line infantry, then with the 75th Ranger Regiment, and finally with Delta, before getting reassigned to a Homeland V-Team back in the States, where he'd seen enough action to last him ten lifetimes and had lost everything—including most of his soul—in the process.

"Officer McClellan," the gray-haired policeman said, extending a hand. "I'm Dave Garrity, Harmony Hollow's chief of police. Spare a minute?"

McClellan nodded, and Garrity led him into a small room that smelled strongly of new carpet. There was a metal desk and chairs and a mirror on the wall. Garrity sat on a corner of the desk. McClellan remained standing, took out his cigarettes, and offered one to Garrity. A few years earlier, smoking would have been strictly forbidden in a government office—and perhaps it still was, technically speaking—but the V-Wars had provided more pressing concerns than secondhand smoke. Thank God for small favors.

Garrity said, "That's the fourth man you've brought us in… how long have you been here?"

"A week," McClellan said. "Three days in the field."

Garrity squinted over the cigarette. "Your predecessors… we didn't see them often."

"Perhaps if you had, I wouldn't be here."

Garrity took a deep drag, nodding and shrugging at the same time. "Perhaps."

McClellan waited. He had an idea of what was coming but wanted to see how Garrity would handle it. He didn't have to wait long.

Garrity said, "Harmony Hollow isn't like other places. Its citizens are ridge runners to the core. You know the term? They have their own ways, largely settle their own disputes. Country justice, you might call it. And some don't have much respect for the law."

McClellan ashed his cigarette on the new carpet. "I can understand that."

Garrity narrowed his eyes. "You have a dog in this fight, McClellan? What I mean is, is this personal for you? Off the record. Are you trying to start a war?"

McClellan said, "I'm just upholding the law, Chief."

"Did you know Tartakower?"

McClellan took a long drag, looking Garrity in the eyes. "I'm not here to avenge his murder, if that's what you're getting at, but I'm not a passive man. It's my duty to enforce the laws of the Pennsylvania Game Commission, and if these boys step out of line, I'm going to run them in."

Garrity considered this for a second, then offered what seemed to McClellan a measured smile. "I believe you might be suffering from a degree of culture shock. These folks aren't bad, not really. They just take some getting used to. If you let your foot off the gas for a while, you'll—"

"The law is uniform," McClellan said. "If we can't agree on that, we can't agree on anything. Poaching here is just as illegal as it is in Philadelphia. No exceptions."

Garrity rapped his knuckles on the desk. "When Hurricane Katrina hit back in '05, I watched thugs on TV looting New Orleans and strutting around the Superdome with AK47s, and I thought, *Nothing but a bunch of goddamned savages.* Here in Harmony Hollow, we have problems— mostly DUIs and fellas knocking each other's teeth out—but watching that mess on TV, I knew that if a Katrina-sized crisis hit my town, we would come together and take care of each other. And then the V-event hit and proved me right."

McClellan listened as Garrity told how the townsfolk had come together, one and all, not with torches and pitchforks but with shotguns and deer rifles, to root out the common enemy and end the conflict between beats and bloods forever. There was no hiding among such a united population.

"We take care of our own here, McClellan," Garrity said. "Ease into the job. Back off these good old boys for a couple of weeks, see how things work. In the meantime, I'll ride out to the mountain and give them a talking to. All right?"

McClellan exhaled smoke as he shook his head. "My job is to manage wildlife and maintain a healthy herd."

"I could say the same thing," Garrity said, leaning forward. "And trust me: you'll manage best if you work with me, Officer McClellan."

Enough of this horseshit, McClellan thought, reaching past Garrity to stub out his cigarette in the ashtray. "The way I see it," he said, "we're both sworn to uphold the law. That means we *are* working together. And I plan on holding up my end of the deal."

"Fair enough," Garrity said, almost managing to disguise his annoyance. "I just want you to understand who it is you're dealing with. People here in town are civil enough, but these boys you're riling up are strictly backwoods, through and through. Dog-patch mean, most of them. Wouldn't think twice about using a jackknife on you, and there are some that might even come after you with a double-barrel... if you provoke them."

"They'd better hit me pretty good the first time," McClellan said, and turned to leave.

"McClellan," Garrity said.

McClellan turned in the doorway.

Garrity laid a hand on his shoulder. "Don't fight a two-front war. I'm with you. Just take your time and watch your back."

"I'll take that under advisement, Chief."

"I knew Tartakower," Garrity said. "Hell of nice guy. He got in on our card game, Friday nights. You might even like to join us yourself."

"I'm not much for games."

Garrity spread his hands. *Suit yourself*, the gesture said. "The sons-of-bitches shot him in the back and dropped him in an old well, way out in the woods." He shook his head. "According to the coroner, Tartakower survived for two days out there in that well. I can't imagine dying that way. The pain, the despair, the feeling of abandonment."

McClellan controlled himself. "That all, Chief?"

"One more thing. This Johnston boy, he might be a special problem. He's kin to the Yates family. Heard the name?"

McClellan nodded. "Otis Yates?"

"The boy's uncle... or maybe his cousin. They're all tangled up, the Yateses and the Johnstons. Anybody by the name of Yates, you take extra special care. There's a whole clan of them out on the mountain,

297

8

and they've got one foot back in the Stone Age. They're wily as bobcats and meaner than rattlesnakes, the Yateses. You'd do well to steer clear of them. We've got plenty of other poachers to keep you busy."

"Where, exactly, do the Yateses live?"

Garrity gave him a hard stare.

McClellan forced a smile. "So I can avoid them."

"They have a junkyard off of Fire Tower Road, up on top of Barstow Mountain. You see a sign for Yates's Scrap and Salvage, you'll know it's time to turn around and come back to town."

McClellan turned his back on the man and walked out.

He pushed through the station door and into a crisp autumn evening. The waxing moon, nearly full, was already peeking over the mountains. The good smell of wood smoke tinged the air, and all up and down the wide street, trees blazed in a stunning display of yellow and orange and red. From an adjacent playground came the shrill and gleeful voices of children, a sound that never failed to bring a smile to his face and an ache to his heart.

Don't start, he cautioned himself. *You can't afford to hurt until this is all over.*

Harmony Hollow was a beautiful town, almost perfect, with wide streets lined in stately Victorians with wraparound porches and black shutters and neatly manicured lawns boasting mature oaks and maples and sycamores. From the streetlamps hung nostalgic banners showcasing the pictures of local veterans who'd served in various conflicts down through the ages, from the Civil War to the V-Wars, the latter of which, although ongoing elsewhere, had obviously been put to rest by this little town. No MRAPS prowled these streets, nor even foot patrols of troopers in full battle-rattle. Also missing were boarded windows and caution tape, brick walls pocked by gunfire and scorched by flames, and shop windows covered over by metal gates writhing in graffiti propaganda. *Stop the genocide! Beats 4 Bloods!* People moved freely and fearlessly here, and Harmony Hollow appeared very much like some quaint little town straight out of the blessed days before the V-event had washed the world in blood.

Couldn't Garrity see all this? Not just the beauty of Harmony Hollow but also the threat posed by the belligerent rednecks from its mountainous outskirts?

He couldn't figure the man's reluctance. Was the police chief afraid? It didn't seem possible, given his hard-ass comportment and military background, but if fear didn't have him by the balls, what did? Something even more loathsome than cowardice? Did Garrity have kin up on Barstow Mountain? Could he be on the take?

"Son of a bitch," McClellan said, reaching his Ford. Someone had shattered the windshield. Lying in the driver's seat, surrounded by pebbles of broken glass, was a brick, onto which someone had tied a note—as if this crime was the work of some unimaginative cartoon character.

Fuming, he picked up the brick and read its message.

YOU ARE A ASSHOLE!!! GO HOME FUCKFACE!!!

It's "an" asshole, you illiterate bastards, he thought, and tossed the brick into the passenger foot well. It would take more than a brick and a broken windshield to scare him off. He hadn't been entirely truthful with Garrity. This assignment was personal to him.

Jonas Tartakower had been a friend and more: a mentor, first in the army, showing McClellan the ropes and putting him in for Delta, then stateside, making a place for him on the V-Team. Later, after everything happened with Sara and the baby, and McClellan couldn't do it anymore, couldn't carry on another day on the V-Team, killing, killing, killing, he'd confessed his emptiness to Jonas, who had by that time "retired" to the Game Commission. Jonas had opened a Commission door, nudged McClellan through it, and, in doing so, saved his life. Organization to organization, McClellan had followed his friend and mentor, leading him at last to this place, where he would sooner die alone in the woods a thousand times than leave his friend's murder unsolved.

I will make these animals suffer, he vowed.

He brushed away the broken glass, and as he hoisted himself into the seat, he noticed the square of light that was the small window toward the back of the police station, and the face framed there, peering out at him. A second later, Garrity stepped back out of view, allowing the drape to fall shut—but not before McClellan had registered the delighted smile on the police chief's face.

———•———

The next morning, McClellan dropped off his truck at Paulson's Garage, where they told him it would take a day to replace his windshield. Then he walked across town to the Game Commission office, which was nothing but a converted house trailer conveniently adjacent to Ladrido's Boarding House, where he'd rented a Spartan room.

"You sure do have the diner in a stir," Desiree said. She was young—twenty-two or twenty-three, McClellan figured—but a competent office manager nonetheless, and he was glad to have her.

He gave her half a grin. "Happy to give them something to chew other than those third-rate pancakes."

"Some of them think you're just what the doctor ordered," Desiree said. "Others call you the Cowboy." She made a face. "I don't think they mean that in a nice way."

"Well," McClellan said, "I'll try not to let it hurt my feelings." He straightened the framed photo of Jonas Tartakower that hung by the door, then returned to the counter, where he'd been leafing through Jonas's old notebooks… to little avail.

The door slammed open, and into the office stormed a red-haired man with a squat pumpkin head set atop a mountainous body. He wore a ratty green-and-brown flannel with the sleeves rolled up, exposing meaty forearms matted in orange-red hair dense as orangutan fur. He waved a citation at McClellan, his upper lip lifting in a snarl. "You McClellan?"

"I am," McClellan said. "You must be Otis Yates."

"You're goddamned right, I'm Otis Yates!" The gigantic redneck crumpled the citation and slammed his fist onto the counter. "I want to know what you mean, putting my name on this thing."

"I cited you," McClellan said, keeping his voice level, "because your nephew informed me that you had given him your deer tag."

"Bullshit," Yates said, poking the air between them with a stubby finger. He leaned forward, and the stink of the man slapped McClellan in the face. Not just sweat and cigarettes and booze but a rank animal odor, too, as if the burly man had spent the morning wrestling a wet dog. "He *stole* it from my house. Confessed to Garrity and everything."

"That's not the way he told it when I arrested him," McClellan said.

A grin stretched grotesquely across Yates's wide head. His teeth and eyes were yellow. "Garrity released him on his own recognizance this morning."

Released him? McClellan thought. What was Garrity up to?

"My kin's lived up on Barstow Mountain for two hundred and fifty years. We've had outsiders come here before, trying to boss us," Yates said, and turned toward the framed photo of Jonas Tartakower. "They never last long. Do yourself a favor, city boy, and leave my kin alone."

McClellan said, "I'll tell you what, Mr. Yates. I don't know what kind of arrangement you've got with Garrity, but you so much as fart sideways out in those woods, and I'm going to haul you back to town and toss you in a cage."

Yates's smile curdled. His yellow eyes burned with menace, and tufts of red hair jutted like flame from his flaring nostrils. "Come out to my mountain and see what happens!" He slapped the counter and marched out, slamming the door so hard that the framed photo of Jonas Tartakower fell from the wall, shattering its glass. In the silence, McClellan could hear the crumpled citation Yates had left on the counter transforming, spreading out from its compressed state like a thing emerging from a chrysalis.

Desiree pushed her hands forward on her desk, fingers splayed, and released a shuddering breath. "I've never been so frightened in all my life," she said. "That man scares me to death."

"Don't let him," McClellan said. "He's fixing to run head-on into a stone embankment."

Desiree nodded but didn't look convinced. She rose, went to where the picture had fallen, and started to whisk broken glass into a dustpan.

"Stop," McClellan said. He knew now what he had to do. Tomorrow, when he had his truck back, he would pay a midnight visit to Barstow Mountain. With the cold snap, Yates would almost certainly have fresh meat hanging. And if McClellan spotted so much as a poached squirrel, he could get a search warrant without interference from Garrity. "Give me that broom," he told her. "I clean up my own messes."

———•———

The sun was just rising when Desiree pulled off the dirt road and parked beside the police cruisers. McClellan double-checked his sidearm, told his officer manager to stay put, and crossed the hilltop field, his boots brushing the frosty hay stubble until he joined the rough circle of men hunched like vultures around the carcass.

He shook hands with Garrity, who introduced his deputies and the aggrieved party, an old farmer named Orville Foskins. Shaking with palsy, the white-haired farmer nodded at McClellan then glared at the remains of his dead cow—what little was left of it—through eyes foggy and blue with cataracts.

McClellan crouched. The cow's ribs had been pulled apart at the sternum, which, like nearly every scrap of flesh and hide and many of the bones, was missing. Several feet away lay a large femur. He got up and walked over and rolled it with the toe of his boot. Deep grooves in the bone there.

"Looks like a goddamned crocodile chewed on it," Foskins said, fixing McClellan with his rheumy gaze. "What the hell did this?"

McClellan looked at Foskins, looked at the yawning ribcage between them, and looked back at the farmer.

Given this mess, the bite marks, and the previous night's moon—nearly full—he figured he knew exactly what they were dealing with here.

So what's the call?

If he shared his suspicions, Central would call Homeland. A W-Team would rush straight here, and he'd spend God only knew how long bolted to that investigation, when he needed the freedom to hunt Jonas's murderers. So what he said was, "A big enough pack of wild dogs could clean a carcass like this."

"And drag my heifer halfway across the damned field?" Foskins jerked around and jabbed a gnarled finger across the field to the hedgerow fence line and forest beyond.

"Could be a bear," Garrity said. "Last season, a guy just south of here bagged one close to eight hundred pounds. Animal like that could drag your cow all the way to town."

"Let's walk over to where you say this thing was killed," McClellan said. "I want to see what you're talking about, Foskins, the *abomination*."

"No need to hike across the field, Officer McClellan," Garrity said. "Once the offices open, I'll call in the evidence team." He offered one of his fake smiles. "They'll see things that guys like us might miss."

McClellan wanted to tell the police chief to go to hell, but Foskins had initially called the police station, so this was a crime scene first and a wildlife conservation matter second. The word *obstruction* rose in McClellan's mind like a bad moon. He put on his own false smile, saying, "I won't mess up any of your evidence—and besides, I might notice something your boys don't see every day… a track or a bit of fur. Might save them some time and"—turning to Foskins—"get this man any possible *compensation* as quickly as possible."

The old man nodded sharply. "Let's go, then," he said, and marched jerkily across the field to the fence line, where another patch of field was beaten down and dark with blood. McClellan saw bone fragments and bristly cow hair and bits of unidentifiable tissue, buzzing with flies. Drawing nearer, he winced at the smell, a blend of coppery blood and cow manure and something else, something rancid and musky and hormonal, like a buck in ruck, only stronger, sour, and sharply offensive.

McClellan spotted the fence post. Foskins hadn't exaggerated. Dark with blood and flies, it really did look like someone had painted the thing.

This is real, he told himself. *You must face that—even if the timing is inconvenient.*

But not yet. Not tonight. If Homeland got involved now, he'd be tied up for weeks. This could wait for a day. Full moon or no full moon, tonight he had to drive out to Barstow and see about catching the sons of bitches who'd let his friend suffer for two days before dying alone in a well.

All at once, McClellan was pointedly aware of the nearness of the trees. A stand of pines overhanging the barbed wire fence. Dark as midnight in there. It felt like the woods were staring back at him.

A cold wind moaned across the field, and McClellan thrilled with gooseflesh.

That's not cold making you shudder.

"There's your abomination," Foskins said, pointing at the post. "Painted up just as red as a stop sign in hell," he spat in disgust. "Think a pack of dogs did that, too?"

McClellan studied the scene. It was still dark here in the shade of the forest. A solitary fly landed on his face. He swatted it away, then thumbed his flashlight to life and panned across the matted hay. The ground around the post was covered in blood, too, almost as if...

He leaned over the post and lifted his beam, carving a tunnel of light into the branches overhead... and managed not to flinch when he saw it.

The other men gathered around, looking up.

"What in the hell?" someone said.

Twenty feet overhead, strung through the branches like strands of Christmas lights, the ropy entrails of the cow shone greasily in the light.

"That's how the post got painted," McClellan said. "Last night, it rained blood."

Foskins stared up, all the color gone from his face. "Vampires!"

"No," McClellan said. "Vampires wouldn't waste so much blood... even cow's blood."

"A werewolf, then," Foskins said.

Garrity chuckled. "Let's not get crazy, Orville. Werewolves are rare. We've never had one in these parts before, and I doubt like hell we have one now."

McClellan nodded in false agreement, thinking, *Oh yes, we do have one... and judging by that fake smile, Chief Garrity, you know it.*

———•———

He awoke just before midnight and sat up as stiffly as a robot, blinking in the half-darkness of his boarding house room. The light of the full moon fell silver-white through the open curtains. Automatically, his eyes went to his phone on the nightstand, and just as automatically, he thought of calling her.

But that would be a mistake.

Even if it wasn't midnight, he knew what would happen. A cheery nurse answering, "Whispering Pines, this is so-and-so speaking, how may I help you?" Then a long wait for the nurse to return and tell him, "I'm sorry, Mr. McClellan, she doesn't want to talk today."

Sara... poor, broken Sara... come back to me... we can rebuild our life together...

But the room was small and cold, and he was alone, and he would remain alone until the impossible happened, and the V-Wars ended, allowing Sara to escape catatonia.

He rose and put on his black V-Team jumpsuit—sans insignia—his boots and body armor and holsters. He did not call. Instead, he picked up his phone and keys and left the room.

He pulled off Fire Tower Road onto a rutted log road, hiding the Ford from anyone who might drive past.

He slid the H&K MP7 machine pistol into its thigh holster, patted the Desert Eagle .50-caliber hand cannon on his hip, double-checked the .38 in his ankle holster, and pulled the stubby Mossberg 12-gauge from the truck. He'd loaded his pockets with first aid supplies, extra magazines, and two grenades. Overkill? Almost certainly. But as they said in the teams, *Better safe than sorry, and better sorry than dead.*

McClellan locked the truck and breathed in the good, crisp night air. Overhead, rags of cloud glowed silver in the moonlight. An owl hooted down in the hollow.

He walked back downhill to the Yates's Scrap and Salvage sign. Duct-taped to this was a sheet of paper sheathed in kitchen cling wrap that caught the glare of his flashlight. In bold font, it announced, *No Trees Passing!!!*

He chuckled. *Redneck auto correct at its finest.*

His levity passed swiftly. On an eerie night like this, with the dark pines bending in the wind, sighing and creaking and groaning, it didn't seem entirely impossible that some ancient elm might be walking, bent and black and hungry, through the forest.

He climbed up the driveway until the pines flanking it gave way to broadleaf and scrub, and off to the left, he could see a moonlit field. He went in this direction, wading through weeds and snagging against briars until he topped a rise and broke through a hedgerow onto a wide, mown field, where he whistled low, stopped by the sight awaiting him there.

Row upon row of cars stood deserted in the field, a maze of metal and glass and chrome shining in the moonlight. This was no rust bucket graveyard, however. Many of these cars were in great shape, practically new.

He saw plates from all over. Mostly Pennsylvania, but plenty from Jersey and New York. Others from Maryland, Ohio, and farther... Virginia, Maine, even one from Arizona.

Yates is running a chop shop, he thought. *And one hell of a big one.* And the fact that they were just sitting out in the open was additional proof that Yates knew that he had nothing to fear from the police.

Wonder what kind of car Garrity's wife's driving these days? McClellan thought.

But he wasn't here to investigate auto theft.

At the edge of the car lot sat an unmarked tow truck. Beyond that, a road of sorts was beaten into the dirt. McClellan followed this through towering stacks of scrap. Approaching the mountaintop, he saw lights through the trees and heard dogs barking.

Good, he thought. *Keep barking.* That way, if the wind shifted and they scented him, they couldn't sound the alarm—they would already be barking.

He reached the end of the scrap yard and stared out into the open, where the full moon washed the Yates compound in silvery light. At the center of several outbuildings stood what must have been the ancestral Yates home, a dilapidated farmhouse badly in need of a paint job and general rehabilitation. The wide wraparound porch sagged, held up at one corner by a pile of cement blocks... and in another, almost unbelievably, by an engine block. One shutter hung loose, reminding McClellan curiously of a winking eye. There were lights on in nearly every room.

Across the wide patch of matted weeds that passed for a yard stood a chain-link kennel filled with barking dogs—German shepherds, pit bulls, a Doberman—all going crazy, banging against the fencing. The dogs hadn't noticed him, thanks to his concealment and the direction of the wind, but something sure had whipped them into a frenzy.

Across from the house was the chop shop, a hangar-style half-pipe garage of corrugated aluminum perhaps thirty feet high and four times as long. That's where the deer would be hanging. The wide doorway and small windows glowed yellow. There was a big Dodge Power Ram parked on the gravel drive.

His attention was stop-punched, however, by a sight that made absolutely no sense. Between the hangar and the farmhouse, a massive blue silo jutted into the moonlit sky like the enormous phallus of some pagan god lying just beneath the soil of this sour ground.

Why would Yates have a silo up here? There was no farm, no herd.

He crept to the silo. Up close, he realized that it was ringed in caged HVAC units. *Weird...*

A spigot protruded from the silo over a catch grate. He crouched down, keeping the silo between the house and him, twisted his penlight to life, and grinned at the rusty brown stains beneath the spigot.

This wasn't really a silo at all but a disguised meth factory, likely a multi-level operation that cooked, packaged, and readied the drug for distribution. The HVAC units controlled the temperature and vented the poisonous fumes, and the spigot allowed them to route away toxic run-off and spray down any residue, preventing any casual observer from discovering evidence. Well, McClellan was no casual observer.

He was going to break this syndicate wide open. Burn them for stealing cars, running a chop shop, cooking meth, and, yes, poaching animals. Much of this would be up to the police—*the state police*, he thought, *not that crooked mother-shepherd, Garrity*—but McClellan would push for prosecution of everything, including the dumping of toxic chemicals. Get the EPA involved, the IRS, everybody. But what he really needed was evidence that these assholes had murdered his friend. Jonas would have justice at last. With this in mind, he used his phone to start filming seconds later, when the pair of rednecks emerged from the hangar.

Despite the cold, Yates was shirtless, his naked upper torso a pale barrel furred in orange, jiggling with fat, and heavy with muscle. His face and chest and arms were splattered in blood. Were they butchering deer in there?

The squirrely looking slip of a guy with him had to be family, given the straggly orange hair and goatee. A son, maybe.

Something clanked overhead.

McClellan leaned back into the shadows and saw another man—Johnston, the burly nephew, by the look of his silhouette—crawling around on top of the hangar. "All set," he called down. Yates said something to the skinny guy, who jogged across the gravel and climbed the silo ladder like a monkey until he was level with Johnston.

"Coming your way, Skeeter," Johnston said, and there was a groaning of metal on metal as a long metal tube swung stiffly away from the top of the hangar.

The red-haired guy—*Skeeter*, McClellan told himself, thinking that was one name he wouldn't need to write down to remember—reached out, grabbed the end of the pipe, and affixed it to a section of pipe that ran like a massive downspout the rest of the way up the silo.

Only it wasn't a downspout, McClellan thought. It was an *up*-spout... a blower pipe, the tube farmers used to fill their silos with grain. Yates must be storing chemicals in the garage, then piping them over to his cleverly disguised meth lab as needed.

"Secure?" Yates called up.

"Tighter than a weasel's asshole," Skeeter called down.

Yates said, "Well, get down here, then. We don't have much time."

Johnston disappeared over the other side of the hangar, and Skeeter started his descent.

McClellan stayed very still, running his fingertip over the trigger guard of the shotgun.

He was filming again by the time Yates sent the others inside the hangar, telling them to get everything ready. Then Yates reached into the bed of the truck, grunted, and backed away, tugging. A black mass the size of a couch fell heavily to the ground.

It was a dead cow. A massive Angus... just like Orville Foskins raised. The animal had a length of blood-stained cloth wrapped around its neck. Yates grabbed the hind legs and started singlehandedly dragging the dead animal—which had to weigh close to a ton—across the gravel into the hangar.

That's when McClellan understood. Yates wasn't just a poacher and a car thief and a drug dealer and a probable murderer. He was a werewolf. Only that could explain his incredible strength. Lycanthropy mutated muscle architecture, surrendering fine motor skills for accelerated reflexes, explosive gross motor commitment, and superhuman strength. And what about the others? Were they fangs, too? Likely at least some of them, McClellan figured. After all, the condition was hereditary, just like vampirism.

After Yates dragged the cow into the garage, McClellan circled back into the deeper darkness and placed the call.

Desiree answered, sounding groggy. Once she understood who was calling, she woke quickly.

"Sorry to call so late," he whispered. "I need your help."

"No problem," she said. "Anything."

He told her where he was, what he'd seen, and that he needed her to contact Central Command and the state police, who were twenty minutes away in Towanda. "I'm emailing you some footage. Share it with them."

"What about Chief Garrity?"

"No," he said. The man was obviously dirty. No way could he have overlooked this operation otherwise. Remembering the police chief's behavior in Foskins's field, he wondered if Garrity had known all along that Yates was the werewolf.

"If he's a…" Desiree said, "…a werewolf, you'd better get out of there, sir."

"I'll be okay," McClellan said. The girl was right—staying was dangerous—but when the state police arrived, he wanted to take Yates down personally, look him in those yellow wolf eyes, and ask him point blank about Jonas Tartakower.

Within the hangar, a motor kicked on, low and rumbling. Then he heard the whine of power saws.

He thanked Desiree and hung up, then hurriedly sent the video clips her way.

From inside came a loud rattling clatter like someone feeding rakes into a wood chipper. Overhead, the chute that ran from the top of the hangar to the silo started to vibrate.

309

S

What the hell?

He double-timed it toward the nearest window, keeping the silo between himself and the barking dogs.

If Yates is a werewolf, why are the dogs contained? Everything McClellan had read on the subject said that werewolves let their dogs roam free. So why were Yates's dogs locked up?

Can't believe everything you're taught, he thought. *Especially when it comes to bloods and fangs.*

Reaching the hangar, he peered through the window at a grisly scene. The bloody cloth that had been wrapped around the cow's neck lay on the floor. The three rednecks stood, drinking beer and looking at the cow, which hung upside down at the center of the garage bay, draining blood like motor oil into a floor grate. After a time, they set down their beers and took out knives, and McClellan watched as they eviscerated the animal. Yates wrangled the tremendous gut pile a few feet away, where it oozed a stream of bright red blood across the bowed floor and into the grate. Johnston used a power saw to decapitate the cow, and the men worked in unison, skinning the carcass.

Behind them idled the grumbling machine with a stocky frame and a wide-mouthed hopper, like a wood chipper on steroids. From its base ran a pair of thick tubes. One disappeared out of McClellan's view, toward the rear of the hangar; the other attached to a brass fixture in the floor near the drain. As gore oozed into the grate, the tube vibrated. A heavier hose rose from the top of the machine to the center of the ceiling—right where Johnston had swung the silage pipe to Skeeter.

McClellan filmed it all. What were these bastards up to?

When they finished flaying the cow, Skeeter rolled the hide and carted it off and tossed it onto a nearby workbench.

The saw whined again as Johnston powered it up the spine, cutting the carcass in half lengthwise, so that the halves wobbled back and forth like punching bags.

Yates leaned in and took a big bite out of one haunch. He let his head roll back and gobbled the meat, barely chewing before he choked down the flesh like a gorging hound.

McClellan considered stepping into the hangar and putting the scat-tergun on them, but if they didn't respond well, this would quickly turn into one hell of a mess. And besides, who knew how many people—and werewolves—were in the big house?

Better to wait for the cavalry to arrive. Fifteen minutes had passed since he'd called Desiree. Only five or ten more minutes until—

Somewhere inside the hangar, a woman screamed.

McClellan jolted with surprise and watched Yates bark toward the back of the hangar, which was out of McClellan's line of vision.

He crept to the back of the hangar, peered through the window there, and went cold. Hanging from the crossbeams were people. Not cows, not deer, but people. Living people, twenty or thirty men and women, naked and shackled by the wrists, hanging so that their toes barely touched the cement floor. Some struggled fruitlessly, while others hung still with eyes closed, as if praying. They were all gagged, save for the screaming woman whose gag had fallen away from her mouth.

McClellan stared in horror and revulsion. All those cars out there. Yates had been stealing not only vehicles but drivers. Why, though? Ransom? Sex trade?

Then, with a chill, he noted the floor beneath them. It was bowed like the floor beneath the cow, complete with a drain, near which the grumbling machine's other hose vibrated. In a kind of slow-motion nightmare, he leaned, widening his field of vision and tracing the crimson trail from the mouth of the grate back to the red mess hanging in chunks, the modest-sized gut pile underneath, and the raven-haired human head lying decapitated beside it.

They were butchering not just beef but human flesh. McClellan felt his gorge rise, and with it rose his rage.

Johnston marched into view and slapped the woman hard in the face, yelling at her to shut up. He lifted the decapitated head by its long, black hair and leered at the woman, who started screaming again. He carried it out of view, and seconds later, McClellan winced at the rattling clatter of the chipper and the chunky tumbling sound as the tube overhead carried its unspeakable silage up into the silo.

And in that second, McClellan no longer cared what they were doing with their mysterious silo. The state police would be here any minute, but he could wait for them no longer. He had to stop these monsters.

Fingers tingling madly, he jogged into the hangar and put the Mossberg on Yates, who stood perhaps ten yards away—can't-miss distance with a shotgun. "Hands up!"

Skeeter stuck his hands into the air, but Yates grinned his yellow smile. He didn't even look surprised. "The game warden. Didn't think you'd have the balls to actually show up here."

"Hands up!" McClellan repeated. "Get them on top of your head." Then, with a half-turn toward the rear of the hangar, "You, too, Johnston!"

But Johnston had dipped behind the shackled captives.

Shit.

McClellan could see his big shape moving behind them into the very back of the hangar.

Shit, shit, shit.

"Johnston," McClellan shouted. "I see you back there. Come on out with your hands up. "And you two," he said, swinging the barrel back toward Yates and Skeeter—the former of whom still hadn't put up his hands. "I said to get your hands on top of your head."

Yates took a step forward. His yellow eyes glowed brightly. "Or else what?"

"Or else this," McClellan said, took three steps forward, and pulled the trigger. The shotgun boomed, and the side of beef swayed, a fist-sized hole blown through the ribs.

Skeeter half-squatted, whining with terror.

Yates laughed, but raised his hands slowly, looking bored and amused all at the same time.

"Look out," the shackled woman called, "he's got a gun!"

As McClellan broke for the door, he spotted the rifle barrel sticking out from between two frantically jerking captives and saw the muzzle flash.

Crack-crack-crack!

One round went wide. Another snapped close by his head. The third ricocheted off the hangar wall as he sprinted out the door. McClellan couldn't return fire, not when Johnston was using the captives as human shields. Yates's laughter roared and receded. He was on the move, no doubt getting a weapon… or transforming into one.

Johnston fired another burst, punching a line of holes in the aluminum hangar mere inches from McClellan. Time to move…

Then a sound caught his attention—approaching sirens—and glancing downhill, he saw a long line of vehicles winding up out of the valley.

Yes!

He just had to survive a few minutes until they arrived—no small feat in a gunfight.

He ran back to the silo, rounding its corner as behind him, a shotgun went *boom!… chug-chug… boom*!

McClellan hollered as pellets burned into his shoulder and lower leg and pinged off the silo. He'd caught two or three pieces of what felt like white-hot birdshot.

He leaned out from the silo and blasted away with the Mossberg—fire-pump-fire-pump-fire-pump—and watched Skeeter spill backward till only his boots and twitching legs were visible.

Served the dumb bastard right, matching birdshot against buck at fifty-some yards.

As McClellan thumbed more shells into the magazine, a tremendous bellow shook the hangar. It was unlike anything he had ever heard, more akin to a lion's roar than any noise a dog or wolf might make. The roar was so loud and primal that he took an involuntary step backward, every hair on his body standing on end. The Yates-monster was coming for his blood.

Behind him, the penned dogs yipped and howled madly.

He glanced toward the steep driveway. He could hear the sirens growing louder and see lights bouncing uphill but still at range. *Hurry, hurry, hurry!*

A horrible racket, the barking and yowling of a wolf pack, erupted within the farmhouse, and turning in that direction, he saw silhouettes moving quickly behind the windows.

What kind of a hornets' nest have you kicked?

He slung his shotgun over one shoulder, yanked the MP7 from its thigh holster, and twisted in the direction of the hangar doorway, which remained empty, save for the unmoving legs of Skeeter.

Good. He needed every second he could buy.

The farmhouse door slammed open, and the pack of abominations clambered onto the porch. He'd seen videos of werewolves during training, but he had never seen—and could never have anticipated the terror-inducing power—of actual fangs. They were horrible humanoid beasts, some on all fours, others tottering like dancing dogs on thin lower legs that swelled into massive thighs covered in dark fur brindled with orange. Some were lean, others fat. All possessed muscular frames and vaguely human hands sprouting wickedly curved claws. Their yellow eyes stared out from wolfish heads with bright fangs and lolling tongues. They yipped and snarled and howled as their muzzles bobbed, scenting the air.

McClellan wrestled against a primal urge to run. Coming here alone had been a colossal blunder—the act of a stupid man so distraught by the unraveling of his life that he'd ignored even the most basic tenets of not only police procedure but self-preservation—and now he was going to die for his foolishness.

Then—Oh, God—they had scented him, were looking this way, were coming off the porch, coming for him…

He opened up on them with the MP7, raking it back and forth. Werewolves hunched and tumbled and yipped and turned away, packing injured legs and retreating, but the core of the pack, several strong, loped straight at him, growling and barking. He dropped the empty magazine, reloaded, and blasted into the pack.

Fifty yards, forty…

He saw hunks of fur and muscle spinning away like bloody divots.

Thirty yards…

Another dropped, and another, and another, but two pressed on, eyes glowing and jaws snapping.

Twenty yards…

He shot one between the eyes… and his weapon was empty.

Ten yards.

Reflexively, he threw the empty machine pistol at the remaining wolf-thing, a massive dark-furred monster streaming blood from its dark coat streaked in orange as with flame. The weapon bounced harmlessly off its shoulder as it leapt growling for him.

He had just enough time to free his Desert Eagle .50-caliber from its holster before the wall of fur and muscle slammed into him. His hand bucked as the pistol fired, but then he was off his feet and tumbling through the air like a bull-tossed matador.

He crashed windless to the hard ground, half-paralyzed and expecting any second to feel the thing's teeth sink into his flesh. But he lifted his head and saw it a few feet away, struggling to all fours and panting, streaming blood from an abdomen wound. It snarled, licking its fangs, glared with its bright yellow eyes, and lurched once more toward him.

Filled with pain, McClellan dragged his arm around and fired again, and half the thing's head exploded in a red mist. The monster dropped, very dead, and instantly started to transform, fur reeling back in, muscles withering… a sight uncanny and terrifying and revolting and yet mesmerizing.

On the other side of the silo, he could hear the sirens arrive and go silent—they'd made it!—and their lights flip-flopped crazily, wobble-rolling across the farmhouse and the hangar and everything in between.

"You're done for," McClellan called to the werewolf he saw slink past the engine block and under the porch. Then, suddenly, the Desert Eagle was batted from his hand.

Before he could turn to face his attacker, something latched onto the back of his jumpsuit and hoisted him into the air like a puppy by the scruff of the neck. Struggling wildly, he lashed backward with an awkward kick. It was like stomping a mossy brick wall. Then his assailant spun him, and he was face to face with a slavering orange muzzle and yellow eyes that glowed like windows onto the fires of hell. Its lips peeled back, and its jaws opened slowly. McClellan smelled the beast's horrible breath as strands of thick and bloody drool stretched from its yellow fangs.

"Yates," McClellan said, and jabbed his fingers at the hateful yellow eyes—but the werewolf's jaws snapped down on his hand like a bear trap. He screamed as fangs crunched through his flesh and bones.

Then the werewolf jerked its arm, and McClellan flew through the air, slammed into the silo, and crashed down on top of an HVAC unit. The impact knocked the wind from him, and fire lanced from his newly broken ribs.

"Help!" he cried breathlessly. The police were just around the silo, but they would never hear his urgent nightmare whisper. "I'm back here!"

The werewolf inched forward, licking its snarling lips, savoring McClellan's pain.

McClellan couldn't expect help, couldn't wait for it. Feigning resignation, he rolled away to face the silo—and shoved his good hand into a cargo pocket. He gripped the cold globe inside, shoved the sphere into his mangled left hand, wrapped his right over this for strength, lifted the grenade to his teeth, and pulled the pin.

When the Yates-thing leaned over him, chortling, McClellan lashed out with his left, as he had before—and again the werewolf chomped down. McClellan shoved forward, pushing his fist deep into the thing's mouth, and splayed his fingers as explosively as he could, propelling the grenade forward.

The Yates-thing released him and reared away, choking. McClellan bolted.

He'd just made it around the other side of the silo and into the full wash of the flip-flopping police car lights, when the grenade detonated with a muffled thump.

McClellan saw the shape of the state policemen coming toward him but focused on freeing the .38 from his ankle holster. The Yates-thing was certainly dead, but others might be lurking. With the small pistol drawn, he backed away from the nightmare scene to the front of the silo.

"You can drop that pistol, Mr. McClellan," a familiar voice said.

McClellan whirled. "Garrity. What the hell are you doing here?"

"I could ask you the same thing," Garrity said, "considering the warnings I gave you." Beside the police chief stood three of his officers. Each pointed a shotgun at McClellan. "Please disarm yourself. I'm not supposed to shoot you, but I will if you don't comply."

McClellan let the pistol drop to the ground. Behind the police cruisers, a line of headlights stretched all the way down the long driveway. He heard doors opening and closing, saw people coming out of their cars and trucks and minivans.

Something was wrong.

Townspeople were emerging from their vehicles, chatting excitedly, all of them dressed strangely—and uniformly—in tight, black, leather bodysuits. High-pitched laughter trilled out of the darkness.

"What the hell is going on here, Garrity?"

Garrity spread his hands and offered one of his fake smiles. "I told you that Harmony Hollow takes care of its own problems. I only wish you'd listened. You've caused a problem."

"Caused a problem?" McClellan said. "Yates was a *werewolf.*"

Garrity shrugged. "He served his purpose. That silo behind you... it isn't really a silo."

"I know," McClellan said. "It's a meth lab."

Now Garrity offered a genuine smile. "A meth lab? That's good."

One of his deputies chuckled. They still hadn't lowered their weapons, McClellan was dismayed to see.

"It's not a meth lab," Garrity said, "though you do make a good parallel. That silo's full of blood. Some of it human, some of it from animals run down by the werewolves. In fact, you might say that the Yates clan 'cut' the pure blood with other 'agents'... cow blood, deer blood, whatever. The silo has a separator and an extractor, and it keeps the blood at a scrumptious 98.6 degrees."

"You're all vampires," McClellan said. His insides had gone icy.

"No," Garrity said. "Some of us are vampires... but we're all in what you might call cahoots."

"Well, you're screwed now," McClellan said. "I've been sending regular reports to Central. I disappear, they're definitely launching an investigation."

Garrity laughed. "Is that right? You've been delivering these messages yourself?"

"I—" And then he understood. After all, why else would Garrity be here?

Desiree stepped from behind the cruiser. In her tight and shiny black leather bodysuit, she looked like some nightmare twin of his innocent office manager. "Oh, sure thing, Officer McClellan, sir. I'll send that right over to Central, honey," Desiree said in a sugary sweet mocking voice.

"You, too, Desiree?"

She laughed with cruel delight.

"I'm sorry it had to go down like this, soldier," a familiar voice that McClellan hadn't heard for a very long time said. And his old mentor and friend, Jonas Tartakower, stepped from the darkness and put his arm around Desiree.

"Jonas," McClellan said, and a tornado of emotions—elation, confusion, dread—spun within him. "I thought you were dead."

"I apologize," Jonas said. He was a small, slightly built man, with intense eyes that hinted at his brilliance and steadfast focus. He wore not black leather or game warden green but his old uniform from their V-Team days together. "I hated having to mislead you, Tommy."

Tommy...

How long had it been since someone had called McClellan by his first name. He took a step toward his old friend. "It's great to see you, Jonas."

But then he noticed Jonas staring at his bloody hand—and saw the fangs descend.

No...

"Cover that injury, if you will," Jonas said, gesturing toward the hand, his voice betraying none of the excitement suddenly burning in his eyes. "The smell is enticing enough, but the sight of all that blood might prove entirely too provocative."

McClellan shoved both hands into his pockets. The left hand roared with pain. The right closed around his last grenade.

Townsfolk were coming uphill in pairs and trios, murmuring eagerly.

Garrity and his men blocked the gathering crowd. "Hold on, folks," Garrity said. "We'll tap the blood soon enough."

"You're having a blood party?" McClellan said.

Jonas's eyes twinkled in the moonlight. "I've established an orderly, sustainable community. Everyone serves a purpose. Harmony Hollow has achieved a peace that shames the rest of the world. Bloods and beats live harmoniously side by side."

"Oh, yeah?" McClellan said. "What about the people inside the hangar?"

"Outsiders, mostly," Jonas said, "and a few locals who... failed to adapt. An unfortunate business, but times of great change sometimes necessitate extreme measures. The same goes for bloods who can't pass. Everyone you see here," he gestured behind him to the bright-eyed crowd, which vibrated with enthusiasm, "can pass as a perfectly 'normal' beat."

McClellan panned the crowd. Dressed in skin-tight black leather and eying him hungrily, they looked like a wayward convention of fetishists. He saw his landlord, Mrs. Ladrido; his mechanic, Joe Paulson; the pretty young checkout girl from the supermarket, who always seemed so timid and soft-spoken and who now stared at him with eager eyes and fangs that flashed in the moonlight.

"As a *wurdulak*," Jonas said, "it's my pleasure to oversee these midnight ceremonies." He didn't have to explain. McClellan understood. A *wurdulak* would want no part of silo blood. Jonas would feed only on loved ones, family and close friends. "No worries, old friend. I didn't recruit you as food."

"Good to know," McClellan said, thinking, *How do I get out of here?*

"On the teams, you and I worked together brilliantly," Jonas said. "We knew our roles and shared a common mission. The citizens of Harmony Hollow are a team now, and we share a mission, too: the establishment of a unified, sustainable future."

"And these others are just, what... collateral damage?"

Jonas smiled. "Exactly. You always were a top-notch operator, McClellan. That's why I engineered your move here. I knew you would hunt my murderers."

"Only they didn't murder *you*," McClellan said.

Jonas spread his hands. "The Yates clan has been very valuable to us. We don't feed on the local population, but we still have our needs. This is our place for community. When we come here, we can let it all hang out."

McClellan's mind whirred, trying to devise a way out, but he could see none. There were too many of them. Dozens. All he had was a single grenade. Jonas and the police were armed, and the other vampires—all of them gyrating and giggling and transforming now—

319

S

would happily tear him apart.

Around the silo, the dogs barked incessantly. Well, that was one mystery solved, anyway. The werewolves had been expecting these guests, and dogs hated bloods.

Jonas smiled. "This is what you've been looking for. We have order, rules, peace for beats and bloods."

"I don't understand peace that includes butchering people."

"Oh no? You didn't butcher in Iraq, Afghanistan, the V-Wars? Remember the William Penn Projects in Chester?"

McClellan suppressed a shudder, remembering how he and Jonas had stood ankle-deep in blood and fought back to back in a stairwell-become-oubliette. "That was different."

"No, it wasn't," Jonas said. "In both cases, we shed blood to avoid bloodshed."

McClellan opened his mouth but said nothing.

Then Jonas said, "Think of Sara."

Her name hit McClellan like a punch to the gut. "I'm sorry the war broke her, Tommy, but we can put her back together. We'll have her transferred here, to Harmony Hollow. She won't need to know what's happening. All she will know is that you've escaped the violence. All she will see here is tranquility. You can build the life she deserves."

Jonas's scenario stopped McClellan. Poor lost Sara. Here, he really could insulate her from the V-War, coax her from her catatonic state, and nurse her back to health. His grip loosened on the hand grenade. He pictured Sara smiling... the two of them living not in a Spartan boarding house, but sitting on the wide porch of white Victorian with black shutters, flowers in pots on the front steps, an American flag fluttering overhead, the whole scene suffused with good mountain air and beautiful fall foliage and...

"You were always like a son to me, Tommy," Jonas said, outstretching his hand. "Join me now. Harmony Hollow will provide a template for the world. Together, we will finally end the V-Wars."

That's all I ever wanted, McClellan thought.

Inside the garage, the woman screamed again. The chilling sound hit McClellan like a bucket of ice water.

Laughter rippled across the crowd, drawing his attention... and he watched in terror as Mrs. Ladrido hissed and took a step forward, and an impossibly long tongue whipped from her mouth, writhing snakelike in the air. His landlady was clearly an *aswang*... the exact type of monster that had robbed Sara's womb, stealing their unborn child, destroying Sara's sanity, and ruining McClellan's life.

"Go to hell," McClellan said. He pulled the pin, hesitated, eying Jonas— a dangerous, dangerous man, despite his friendly demeanor and slight build, a lifelong special teams operator strengthened now through vampirism. This grenade could kill him and maybe even Garrity and his men, but there were so many others. The humans might flee, but the bloods would charge after him. So many of them. If only he could distract them...

Then he had it.

He lobbed the grenade—not toward Jonas and the vampires but against the base of the silo—and sprinted off, injuries be damned.

Behind him, the grenade exploded, and a nightmare chorus erupted as dozens of vampires cried out in gleeful bloodlust, surging at the torrent of blood rushing from the breached silo.

That's it, McClellan thought. *Come and get it!*

Glancing back, he saw them diving greedily into the crimson flood, spilling onto the ground and squealing like kids on a gory Slip'n Slide.

He skirted the gory remains of Yates and stepped toward his shotgun, but there was a sharp *crack*, and a bullet snapped past his head. Reflexively, he backpedaled away, realizing he'd stepped briefly into Jonas's line of fire.

"Forget the blood, you fools!" Jonas shouted at the blood-mad townsfolk. "Stop the intruder!"

Of course Jonas could resist the blood feast. As a *wurdulak*, the blood of random people would do him no good. He could only drink the blood of loved ones.

McClellan was his silo.

He couldn't reach the shotgun, and there wasn't time to search for the MP7. He could only run. Still backpedaling, he glanced at the piles of gleaming scrap. He could run that way, but they would hunt him in the junkyard and run him down in the maze of dead cars.

"Gluttons!" Jonas shouted. "I'll do it myself."

Here he comes…

McClellan had backed all the way to the kennel, where the dogs pounded against the chain link gate, insane with their own bloodlust.

That's it!

As Jonas came around the silo, pistol in hand, McClellan threw the latch. The chain-link door banged into him, and the dogs, wild with rage, raced across the yard. Jonas got off three shots before the shepherds hit him. Then the pit bulls had him, and his screams knifed the night air.

Watching his former mentor die, McClellan felt a consuming emptiness as cold as the void of space. Jonas was gone, the baby was gone, even Sara—yes, he admitted to himself for the first time—even Sara was gone. His life was gone.

But he had found his purpose.

Tragedy had taken from him again and again, honing him to a lethal edge. He would exist forevermore in pursuit of only one shade of order: *genocide*. He would kill every last vampire on earth.

The woman in the hangar was screaming again, but she could wait. They all could. The world could…

All that mattered to him now was the slaying.

Calmly, McClellan retrieved the MP7, replaced its magazine, and charged the weapon. Then he went around the silo to where the monsters were lost to their feeding frenzy and opened up with all the hellfire burning in his soul…

RED EMPIRE PART 3

By Jonathan Maberry

The Oval Office
The White House
Washington, D.C.
Day 18 of the Red Storm

"**W**hat do you know?" asked the president.

"Enough," said Mr. Church. "You are a hybrid of Slovenian *pijavica* and Bosnian *tenatz*, with some qualities of the English *revenant*. What Dr. Swann calls a 'melting-pot' vampire. Uniquely American, drawing on more than the cultural connections of your immigrant ancestors."

The president said nothing. He sat with his hands on his desk, palms flat, eyes wide, color bad.

"We know that you presented as a vampire after your candidacy but before you won the election. Once Dr. Swann shared his observations with Captain Ledger I had my people run every minute of facial recognition footage through our computer systems. The facial tics common to the *tenatz* are there, as are the slight skin changes of the *pijavica*. There are other things as well, but what matters is that we know."

The president said nothing.

"It was Captain Ledger who reasoned that someone in your administration knew, too. There is a pattern to the shifts in your policies, a movement away from your former tolerance toward a more militant stance. A stance, in fact, that favors the use of certain combat systems, weapons, and support equipment manufactured by a small group of companies. Once we identified those, it was not particularly difficult to work backward to the congressmen and high-ranking generals who were in the pocket of those corporations. This being Washington it wasn't a stretch to assume that such corruption was in play. The cause and effect of those people getting the support of your administration and you making decisions that continued to support them was there to be seen for whoever looked. We looked. None of those power players are pro-vampire, and yet here you are, a vampire cooperating so completely with them." Church spread his hands. "I don't need to lay out all the math. They own you, Mr. President, and no one should be allowed to own the president. Any president. It offends me."

"Offends you…?" echoed the president.

"Yes," said Church with the ghost of a smile on his lips. "Idealists are rare in my line of work, but we exist. And Dr. Swann is proving to be a useful ally."

The president looked from Church to Swann and back again. "It's not just me," he said hollowly.

"We know," said Swann. "Your youngest son is a vampire, too. That's why you took him out of school and put him in that private academy. To hide him."

"Y-yes…"

"We can protect him," said Church. "We can protect your whole family."

"They'll kill us all."

"No," said Church. "They won't."

"No, I mean they'll tell people. The public. They'll know what I've done."

"No. Once you agree to make the right choice then my team will take each of those men out of play. It will be done very quickly and very quietly. No fuss, no press. No arrests. Quiet conversations."

"How? That's impossible."

Church's smile grew very cold. "You said that people warned you that I have files on key people in government. I *do*. Not because I play politics or because I enjoy abusing power. I have gathered information because situations like this happen far too often. I have those files because sometimes the good guys need a weapon to protect themselves against their own government."

The president stared at him. "What... what happens now?"

"When you give me your word, I will send the go order. We will wait here until I get an all-clear from Captain Ledger. At that point you will tell your press secretary that you wish to address the nation tonight. You'll tell your speechwriters to prepare something on the increasing tensions between human and vampires. That speech will be uploaded to your teleprompter. We will hack that system and a different speech will be there for you to read. You will announce that the United States of America is changing direction in this war."

Church opened his briefcase and handed the president a thin sheaf of papers.

"This is a draft. Feel free to re-word it."

The president read through it, then frowned, "But... this says that Maria Giroux will be with me on the podium during my speech. There's a part here where I introduce her and let her make some remarks, but there's no text for her. What's she have to do with this?"

"Senator Giroux has been one of the strongest advocates against the V-Wars, Mr. President. Her presence there will be an act of unification."

"Yes, but how? Why?"

"Because," said Swann, "Senator Maria Giroux is the Crimson Queen."

FROM GERMANY WİTH LOVE

By Weston Ochse

T he funny thing about regular people is that they automatically discount the fat guy, the small guy, the ugly guy. They think the agent of action should be the classic Hollywood action hero. But the fact is that Bruce Willis went bald, Schwarzenegger fucked a maid, and Steven Seagal became an asshole. Even heroes can't be trusted to be heroes anymore. So in this faithless hero-less world, even the small, fat, ugly guy has a chance.

Such was Schwarz's siren song and he sang it every day.

His phone pinged from where it lay so that only he could see it beneath his customer's chair. Someone had sent him a picture. As he applied black polish with his right hand, he used his left hand to open the picture and it showed a woman standing in a market holding up the largest zucchini he'd ever seen, her eyebrows raised, her mouth curled into a suggestive smile. The caption beneath read *100% Organic Sex Toy*.

Schwarz snorted.

Klara was already the craziest bitch he'd ever pimped, so crazy he'd considered losing her. But she was the only one who could rally her kind. Plus, she was balls out the prettiest of the lot, verging on heart-stoppingly beautiful. The only mar was the scar he'd given her, a thin slice across one cheek, because no one wanted to fuck a perfect girl. They were too intimidating. Too unearthly.

She'd thanked him for it.

"Herr Schwarz," came a shrill voice from behind him. "I'd like to speak with you after you're finished with this gentleman."

He didn't turn, but instead glanced up at the man whose shoes he was shining—a US Army lieutenant colonel assigned to Patch Barracks named Bradford. Schwarz had yet to approach him. The LTC was on Klara's list and had already been fucked by one of the other girls, but he had no idea of Schwarz's link to the process. To the lieutenant colonel's credit, he gave Schwarz a pained look.

"Herr Schwarz, did you hear me?"

"I'll be there, Ms. Clark," he said, lowering his eyes once more to shining the lieutenant colonel's boots. He could feel her standing behind him and knew she was staring with that look that conveyed absolute intolerance. He had to give the over-efficient micromanaging bitch credit too. She was an equal opportunity hater, and treated everyone with the same disdain.

He felt her searing gaze shift away, but made no indication he knew. He just kept on shining.

Finally, the lieutenant colonel asked, "She that uptight with everyone?"

"Equal opportunity hater," Schwarz reprised.

LTC Bradford sighed. "I guess their kind is everywhere. Had one of those as the mess hall director back in Afghanistan. Actually commented to me once about taking too much salad. And in front of the entire dining facility nonetheless."

"And what did you do?"

LTC Bradford grinned. "Stopped taking too much salad. Had he been in my motorpool, I would have behaved differently. But that was his territory and I knew to step lightly." He was silent for a few moments, while Schwarz put the finishing touches on the shine. Then added, "I swore to myself that if he ever came and requisitioned a car, I'd pay him back in spades for his attitude." He chuckled. "Payback's a bitch and then you die."

Schwarz stood, his head barely coming up to the lieutenant colonel's waist. He had to crane his neck to look into the man's face. "That'll be five bucks, sir," he said.

LTC Bradford handed him a ten. "Keep the change."

Schwarz nodded and shoved the money into his apron. Once the lieutenant colonel had departed, he produced a notebook and jotted down what he'd just learned, underlining the anecdote about the mess hall director. He wasn't worried people would read it because he was using an old-fashioned Elizabethan substitution system and without the key or an NSA computer, no one would ever break it.

"Herr Schwarz?"

He glanced up and saw Ms. Clark looming over him. Her mass was easily four times his own. Beneath a head of unearthly red hair, her blue eyes glowed with loathing. But he had to comply. After all, if he wanted to keep his job shining shoes at the largest American Exchange in Stuttgart, he had to be a good worker. At any time, she could take away his workers card and hand it to another upstanding German citizen. The only reason she hadn't was because he'd made friends with her bosses above her and several colonels on the post.

He smiled, knowing that he'd have his moment with her and it would be sooner than she ever would have wished.

"Yes, Ms. Clark. What can I do for you?"

He saw her fingers rubbing against each other and knew she'd have preferred to grab him by an ear and drag him.

"We really need to speak with you," she said.

"Then let's get about it, then." He closed his notebook, shoved it into his apron, and followed her into the office.

Soon, he was standing in front of her desk, his head barely able to see across it to the woman who sat, her hatred so obvious that it was palpable. On the wall behind her were pictures of what could only be her grandchildren. Beside these were certificates identifying her as Exchange Employee of the Quarter. The newest was more than five years old. And then above them all, framed in gold, was the standard picture of V-8's heart and soul, Big Dog. His rock chest and jutting chin made him look more comical than real. And in gold ink in the bottom corner it read "For Grace, With Love, Big Dog." If that was her idea of the epitome of what it was to be human, then no wonder she hated Schwarz—born to a German mother, African-American father, dwarf.

"There have been complaints," she began.

"I can't imagine who would complain. I'm just a poor shoe shiner," he said, letting German consonants slip into his American.

"Yet there have been complaints," she said, a twinkle burning in the corner of her eyes.

Schwarz pretended to care and consider her words. Then he said, "Are you sure it's not just because the sight of a dwarf offends them?" He lowered his head. "I know how the sight of me can disturb those too shallow to see the good in people."

Her eyes narrowed. "That's something we couldn't possibly know, now, could we? Not unless they told us."

He leveled his gaze. "Trust me. It's pretty obvious when it happens." When she didn't respond, he took the advantage. "What exactly was said?"

She clucked her tongue. "That you have been seen consorting with… ahem… how can I say… prostitutes."

Schwarz rolled his eyes. "Oh, that."

A smile bloomed on her face. "You don't deny it?"

He shrugged, then crossed his arms and jutted out a foot. "No. Do you think I should?"

A laugh escaped her painted lips and she rushed to cover it with a hand. "You seem proud of your consorting with—"

"Troubled young girls," he interrupted. He sighed. "I know. I know. Some wouldn't understand that they've been abused and are victims. Some would be shallow and think that just because they feel the need to sell themselves to earn even a smidgeon of self-worth that they're somehow terrible. But the fact is that they've been used and abused and need someone to help guide them."

"Guide them?"

"To a place where they can feel good about themselves," he said.

Her shock was replaced with skepticism. "And this is a place you take them too?"

"Indeed."

"Herr Schwarz, you expect me to believe that you consort with prostitutes in order to help them?"

He blinked innocently. "Of course. Why else would I *consort* with them?"

She sighed heavily and pretended to rearrange papers on her desk. After a few moments, she said, "You must understand that working at the American PX is a privilege. It's my job to ensure that only the best and most trustworthy retailers are retained."

"Which I appreciate." He added. "I also appreciate the Americans' careful concern to hire minorities, as I am sure you are, Ms. Clark." He glanced at the picture of Big Dog once more and prayed that he'd be allowed to one day be in the same room with the man.

She sighed again and he silently cheered her exasperation.

"You will need to keep your activities more private, Herr Schwarz."

He nodded and smiled, not a fake smile, but one that beamed. "I'll keep that under advisement." He kept smiling, but he knew then and there that she was his enemy and that she'd not stop until she saw him ruined.

When he was certain she had nothing more, he turned and trudged away, knowing he'd need a plan, lest she figure out a way to supplant him before his pogrom was enacted. After all, the Red King was depending on him.

Her name was Gloria and she was his latest and last piece of his plan. She'd been kept in a barn south of Bremerhaven, used as a plaything by a family with three boys, who'd kept her tied up, hanging by her arms until her shoulders had dislocated. Ever careful of her transformation, when she showed signs, they'd cage and leave her to her suffering for days. All they had to do was feed her. Plus, she'd had no one to explain to her that she could direct her thermiomorphy.

One of the boys had bragged a little too loudly while drinking with some friends. With Schwarz's girls stationed at bars throughout the country, one had heard, relayed the information to Klara, who'd soon put together a team to save the young fraulein.

That had been three weeks ago.

Now that she understood she could control her own change, dear Gloria was no longer malnourished, although a hollow still lived in her cheeks, one which he doubted would ever leave. Her dull eyes had taken on a furious edge, his words, and the words of his girls, boosting her, supplanting the feelings of inadequacy the boys had drilled into her, the self-loathing they'd curated. She was hardly the same young woman at all, except for the razor cuts that crisscrossed her neck—a lasting evidence of what mean boys could do when they thought they could get away with things.

The young man's name was Adalard. It meant brave, which was laughable, because right now he was anything but brave. He was twenty and played professionally for one of Bremerhaven's soccer teams. Schwarz didn't know which and didn't care. Soccer held no interest for someone of his stature. He'd never kicked a ball, nor had he ever wanted to.

His designs had always been different than others'. Not just because of his dwarfism, but because of the way he viewed the universe. It was a funny thing, really. Normal people viewed everything from top down. They saw the good before they saw the bad. They saw intention before they recognized reality. Schwarz saw everything from bottom up. He lived in the mire of societal mediocrity. He saw what people kept hidden. He saw the lies for what they were and knew that there was little he could do for them, other than allow them to recognize their own misguided notions of good and bad.

Not only was Adalard a star soccer player, but he went to church three times a week, volunteered at an animal shelter, and was attending university to become a civil engineer. Anyone observing would think he was a substantial young man with a promising future. They wouldn't know it was his hand that had designed the latticework that now decorated Gloria's neck. They wouldn't know it was his cock that had choked her, keeping her from breathing, gagging her, reveling in his ability to dominate something weaker, something smaller.

Young men like Adalard believed that they could do these things because of all the other good things they did. After all, what's a little badness on the celestial scale of good and evil?

"Gloria, dear," Schwarz said, his level gaze both loving and stern.

She looked up at him from where she sucked blood from the nipple of young Adalard. He lay naked beneath her, his head lolling back, eyes all but closed. Her mucus held a potent tranquilizer, allowing her to feed at leisure, which she did, her head laying in his chest.

"I think he's ready, dear," Schwarz said. "Time for you to sit for a while."

She looked away and continued sucking.

He walked over and petted her hair. "Gloria, dear. It's time to sit."

She sucked once more, then licked the nipple she'd been suckling. She sat up and shuddered. The change had already come upon her. No longer was she the slender young woman. Now she was the same size as Schwarz, her skin replaced by a coat of soft brown fur. Her feminine features remained, but were sharpened as the bones in her face had transformed into the female version of the mountainous *alp*. She drew her feet under her and crawled onto the boy's chest, where she sat, her knees drawn up, her arms hugging her legs, chin resting on them, her red eyes locked with Adalard's. Her long elfin ears twitched with interest.

Schwarz watched the boy's breathing and noted that it was becoming faster and shallower. His mouth opened as he began to wheeze. His eyes gained a little focus as the tranquilizer began to wear off. He stared at Gloria, his forehead wrinkled with concern as if he almost understood what was happening.

He and his brothers had to know. *Alps* were sexual beings. They metabolized orgasm. It sustained them like nothing else. But what they didn't know, or at least didn't believe, was that given enough time and proximity to their victim, their love would inexorably turn them toward sitting and pondering, growing heavier by the moment, until finally the weight of their sadness would cave in their victim's chest, collapsing lungs, and eventually stopping the heart. It's not that they wanted to kill their victims, it's just that they continued to grow heavier as they realized that their love could never last. The *alp*'s excitement for love inexorably turned to depression, and with it, the heaviness of an impending loss.

Adalard tried to sit up, but the weight was too much. He gasped, trying to call out.

Gloria cocked her head and stared at him like he'd done something utterly fascinating.

The first rib cracking sounded like a gunshot.

The next three sounded like a battle.

Schwarz nodded absently. He glanced once more at Gloria, whose face was now inches from the dying boy's, her interest intense as his ribs cracked around her. Then Schwarz turned away. He had a plan to hatch. Ms. Clark was causing him no end of problems. But how was he to be rid of her without anyone knowing?

Ms. Clark was waiting for him when he arrived at work the next day. Since he'd shown up to his booth ten minutes early, it couldn't have been because he was late. He wondered if there'd been any more "complaints."

"*Guten morgen*, Ms. Clark," he said, as he began unlocking the drawers of the shoeshine stand.

"Herr Schwarz," she said simply. He thought she might be done, when she added, "The MPs came by earlier. They're working with the *polizei* and wish to speak with you."

He stopped at the mention of the MPs, then continued, hoping she hadn't seen it. Without looking up he asked, "Do you know what they want?"

"Not in the slightest," she said. "But if there is a problem, we need to know about it immediately."

He nodded. "I'll let you know when I find out."

"Oh, and Herr Schwarz?"

"Yes?"

"If there is a problem, you'll have to find a new place of employment."

He nodded, but didn't reply. Instead, he took his phone and stepped away. Once he was out of earshot, he called Klara. The conversation was short. Everything was alright. No police had been by. They were still ready for the operation tomorrow night. When he hung up, he narrowed his eyes. What could it be then?

Walking back to his stand, he spied two MPs marching toward him through the aisles of the mini mall. He stood back and waited for them.

One was black. The other was white. They wore army uniforms with pistols at each belt.

"You Schwarz?" the black one asked. He had sergeant stripes and the name Jones was taped over his right breast.

Schwarz nodded, pulled out his identification and AAFEES work card, and then passed them over.

The white one took them—another sergeant, this one named Wisnewski. He checked them, then passed them over to Jones.

"What's this all about?" Schwarz asked.

"We're looking into the whereabouts of Lieutenant Colonel Bradford," Jones said. "We understand that he had his shoes shined here yesterday. Were you in attendance?"

Schwarz blinked, then remembered the man. He nodded. "Yes. He was here."

The MPs exchanged glances.

"Did he seem nervous to you?" Wisnewski asked.

Now Schwarz was really intrigued. "What do you mean by nervous? Do you mean was he agitated?" He shrugged. "I don't know. I shine boots and shoes. I don't judge people."

"Did you speak at all to him?" Wisnewski asked next.

Schwarz glanced back at the office. "We just talked about what a bitch my boss was."

Jones grinned slightly, but Wisnewski didn't flinch.

"Did he mention where he was going?" Jones asked.

Schwarz shook his head. "Not so much as a word."

Wisnewski brought out an electronic notepad, and with the stylus marked something, then returned the notepad to his cargo pocket.

"What is it he did?" Schwarz asked.

Neither of the sergeants seemed willing to say, but Jones at least said, "It's not what he did, but rather where he went that's concerning us."

When they'd left, he called Klara back and asked her a simple straightforward question, one he hadn't asked before. When she gave the answer, he locked up his booth and left.

———— • ————

Klara opened the door almost before he knocked. He didn't even look at her as he swept inside. He turned, hands on hips as she closed the door. She turned and pressed her back against it.

"Come on now, can't a girl have some fun?" she asked demurely.

Totally. Bug. Fuck. Crazy.

"I can't believe you did this on the eve of our greatest moment. What were you thinking?"

She moved across the room and knelt before him so that her head was even with his. He normally hated when people did this, but with her it was different. It was always different.

"I had to, darling. I had no choice in the matter."

He shook his head. "There's always a choice."

She lowered her eyes and bit her lip. "Not this time. He changed his password."

"What does that mean?" Schwarz had come up with the plan himself, based on a single conversation with the Red King. He knew it would work and he knew it would get the attention he desired. He'd arranged for funding, found the women, and organized them around Klara, who he'd assigned as the project manager. His position was too public for him to be involved with the day-to-day operations, but without the contacts his position afforded them, they wouldn't have had the appropriate access.

"It means we can't access his schedules. We're not going to be certain where seven of the targets are, three of those being generals and one of those being General May."

General May. The commander of V-8 and Big Dog's boss. Once he'd found out that May would be in Germany for a Council of Generals, it was game on. Schwarz knew that they'd never have this opportunity again.

"Don't the girls we have assigned to them know?" he asked.

She shook her head, her eyes still down. His eyes found the scar he'd given her. If anything, at moments like this, it made her more beautiful.

"These were the seven who were traveling." She counted on her fingers. "Five are on temporary duty and two others are on vacation. It had always been the plan for the girls to follow them, then just show up. The previous hitch had been General Flowers, whose family was scheduled to travel with him. After we arranged for his daughter to get hit by a car, the mother and her son had to stay home, so that problem was solved. Now we can't be sure if there were any last-minute changes to the transportation plan. And since Bradford was in charge of US

Army Europe VIP Transportation, he was the person whose account we hacked."

Schwarz inhaled sharply. "Was?"

"Was what?" she grinned, an insane light creeping into her eyes.

"You said *since Bradford was in charge of US Army Europe VIP Transportation.* He still is, right?"

"Do you mean did I kill him?" She giggled. "Only a little."

Schwarz sighed and began walking toward the kitchen. "How the hell do you kill him a little? Is he in there?"

She remained where she was. "Oh, you know. A little here and a little there."

Bradford was laid out on the kitchen table, completely naked and covered in blood. He'd been cut everywhere. His nipples had been sliced off. The shaft of his penis had been cut in two. His ears were missing. Clearly he'd been tortured. Schwarz rolled his eyes. It wasn't that she'd killed a man. It was just that he was the one who had to clean up this mess. Klara certainly wasn't going to do it. It was all the more difficult with the MPs breathing down his neck.

"Did you get the word to go?" she whispered, coming up behind him.

Red Hand had their own plans and wanted to use what Schwarz was doing as a propaganda tool, strike fear into every military officer on the continent, which would make their next target easier to take out. "I spoke with the Red Hand last night. He has someone in place at the armed forces television station. As soon as the feeds come in, he'll start broadcasting them."

"Yes." She pumped her fist into the air, then leaned down and snuggled her face into the crook of his neck. "So you're not mad at me?"

He sighed. "No, I'm not mad at you. It's just that you made my job so much harder."

"How so? We can just leave him here."

They could. In fact, after tomorrow night, it wouldn't matter anyway. Why not?

———◆———

The next morning he discovered why leaving the body in Klara's home had been a bad decision when he found the MPs waiting for him. He tried to look innocent, but they slapped cuffs on him and took him away. The last he saw of the inside of the Patch Barracks PX was Ms. Clark, beaming as she stood by his shoeshine stand. Fifteen minutes later he was in a holding cell at the MP station sitting next to a snoring drunk marine wearing a pink tutu and with the still fresh tattoo of a penis on his head.

An hour later he knew how they'd found him. They'd traced Bradford's phone, which was still among his things in Klara's house. Then when they saw Klara's phone records, they saw that Schwarz had been the last person she'd spoken to.

"Of course I know Klara Hanneman," he said, sitting awkwardly in a chair. On the other side of the table sat Sergeant Jones and a polizei inspector who'd yet to introduce himself. Schwarz suspected Sergeant Wisnewski was the one behind the glass. "What does that have to do with anything?"

"What's your relationship with Ms. Hanneman?" Jones asked.

"She's my… we were romantically involved."

Jones gave him an appraising look.

Schwarz rolled his eyes. "Not everything is small."

"I'll take your word for it." Jones checked his notepad. "Where were you last night between sixteen hundred and midnight?"

"I brought dinner home from your Kentucky Fried Chicken. I ate it, drank some scotch, and went to bed."

"Is that all?"

"No, I watched the Station Agent for about the hundredth time."

Jones raised his eyebrows.

"It's Peter Dinklage's greatest film."

Jones gave him a blank look.

"Peter Dinklage. Tyrion Lannister. *Game of Thrones*. He's the prince who fucks everything he can get his small hands on."

The light bloomed in Jones's eyes. "Right. Saw that on HBO. Do you have anyone who can verify your whereabouts?"

Schwarz and Klara had fucked each other's brains out after the movie. She'd been delicious.

"No. It was just me."

"That could be a problem," Jones muttered.

Schwarz looked to the German and spoke to him in their own language. "No one has told me what this is about? Should I be concerned for Klara? Has anything happened to her?"

The inspector stared at him with heavy lids, then crossed his legs. When he spoke, it was with a Bavarian accent. "She's wanted as a person of interest in a murder."

Schwarz widened his eyes and sat back. "*Mord?* Murder?" He turned to Jones. "My Klara is involved in a murder? Is she alright?"

"I'm not sure if—" He glanced toward the one-way mirror, then turned back to Schwarz. "A body was found at her house."

"A body?"

"And it was in a state unlike anything we've seen before."

Schwarz just stared open-mouthed because there was nothing else he could think to do.

The inspector addressed him in English. "Is Fraulein Hanneman a *vampire*, Herr Schwarz?"

"A *vampire*? Klara? Never."

The inspector nodded. "I thought not, because she hadn't registered in our database. Neither have you for that matter."

"It's because I am not a vampire," Schwarz said, allowing hurt and surprise to fold into his words.

"So you say," the polizei inspector said in English. Then he switched to German. "I'm Inspector Schenk from German Vampire Information Office. We're going to take a ride downtown." He turned to Jones and switched to his English-accented English. "Are you done here? I've allowed you to speak with this German citizen. Now it's time for us to take him."

"But we still have questions," Jones said.

"Do you really think he has the answers to them? And if he did, do you really think he'd tell you?"

Inspector Schenk rose and approached Schwarz. "Get on your feet."

Schwarz climbed ignobly out of the chair and onto the floor.

"Hold out your hands."

When Schwarz complied, Schenk snapped cuffs around the wrists. He nodded to the door and it buzzed and clicked open. "Auf wiedersehen, gentleman. We'll take the case from here."

Sitting in the back seat of the inspector's Mercedes, Schwarz knew what it was to fear a government agency. The German Vampire Information Office was the modern incarnation of the old Nazi gestapo. That the people of Germany let it function was a condemnation and acknowledgment that little had changed since Hitler had commissioned the program to exterminate the Jews. The influx of hundreds of thousands of Turkish migrant workers had already set the majority white German citizens on edge. While they claimed that the only issue was the lack of a common language, and even offered free German language classes, the issue ran far deeper.

And now there were vampires, so not only were German citizens concerned with this new growing minority, but they also had hundreds of years of mythology and fear to contend with. It was one thing to be a beautiful woman who transforms into a mythological *alp*, but another thing altogether for an ugly little black dwarf whose vampirism was inherited from an African-American father who left the moment he discovered his son wasn't perfect.

His people came from the Ashanti—a proud West African tribe of hunters spread across modern Ghana, Cote d'Ivoire, and Togo. Until recently, they believed in a vampiric creature called the Sasabonsam. The Ashanti mythology had it that this ogre-like creature had hooks for feet and hung from branches to fall on those beneath them. Its teeth were made of iron and were capable of biting through anything.

Schwarz wasn't sure where the hanging from trees belief stemmed from, but he knew that the iron teeth reference was completely true. Combined with the average human jaw's ability to exert over one hundred and seventy pounds of pressure, it was but a little thing to bite through the chain that held his cuffs together. Since he sat so low in the seat and the inspector had failed to adjust the mirror, he did so completely unnoticed.

It wasn't until they were stuck in traffic that Schenk adjusted the mirror to address Schwarz.

"I saw the bodies and I know the signs of alpism. The crushed bones and the torn nipples has always been their signature." Schenk's gaze was firm and filled with pride. "It's no doubt that Fraulein Hanneman is a vampire and since you'd had relations, I find it hard to believe that you'd fail to know this."

"Herr Eichman was the head of the Office of Resettlement before he was the head of the Office of Jewish Affairs. They used the same *Shultshaft* that you're using—this non-judicial process of holding people. Concentration camps were the next step, you know, a place to detain people en masse."

Surprise changed to sadness as Schenk looked away so he could inch a few feet farther in traffic. "Your people always bring that up. The Turks have made it their siren song which is giving the liberal media a field day."

"So I'm free to go then."

"We have some questions for you."

"Which you'll compel me to answer."

"We'd hope for cooperation."

"If I say I'm cooperating, you won't believe me because I don't have the answers you think I have." Schwarz flexed his hands. "Then you'll invoke your precious authority to detain me."

"So you say you're cooperating?"

Schwarz nodded. "I absolutely am."

Schenk sighed. "Then I do believe we will have to detain you."

"On what grounds."

Schenk's eyes smiled in the mirror. "*Shultshaft.*"

Schwarz smiled. And now for the unexpected. "The Red King will change all of that."

Schenk's eyes narrowed. "What do you know of the Red King."

"If the Red King had been around in the 1930s, the Jews wouldn't have been murdered like they were."

"What rubbish are you talking about?"

"If you knew that bad things were going to happen to you against your will, do you think it would be morally right to defend yourself ahead of time?"

Schenk snorted. "You're daft."

"The Red Empire is coming and you can't stop it."

"Jesus, man. Are you saying the might of Germany can't stop an upstart wannabe modern-day vampire emperor?"

"No, I'm saying that *you* can't stop him, Herr Schenk."

Schenk looked a question at the same moment Schwarz leaped from the back seat. Schwarz's mouth opened wider than any human's could ever manage and he sunk his teeth into the back of Schenk's spine, biting down and through bone, connective tissue, and finally the spinal cord like he was merely chewing into a steak. Schwarz shook his head and came away with a chunk of Schenk's flesh, then sat back in his seat to chew.

He watched Schenk's head fall back against the headrest, then the whole body fell over as he began to gasp.

When Schwarz had finished eating, he stood on the back seat, then pulled himself into the front. He got down to eye level to stare into Schenk's dying eyes.

"You are right to be afraid of us. We will kill you all to defend our right to exist."

Then he opened the door, got out, closed it, and walked away.

He knew Schenk had died when the car began to roll forward of its own accord, crashing ever so gently into the car locked in traffic in front of it. But by then, Schwarz was on the sidewalk, unassuming, ugly, certainly nothing anyone wanted to look at.

———◆———

Schwarz grabbed his burner phone from where he'd stored it in his safe deposit box, then went to his emergency apartment and spent the rest of the morning and afternoon speaking to his girls. Klara had come by and they'd spoken awhile before she went off to rendezvous with Colonel May herself, then he'd called the Red Hand to give them the thumbs up. By tomorrow morning the world would be on fire. America and Germany would be at each other's throats, and Schwarz's status would be on the rise.

He had his own part of the process to complete, a personal thing, really. He'd known the address for weeks and easily found a way to let himself in. He'd searched and found the WiFi network, because he'd need it to watch the feeds, when they began coming in in a few hours. Finding the pass key wasn't difficult. He got it on the third try—*Big Dog*. Then all he had to do was familiarize himself with the house and wait.

It wasn't long. She came home at six, right after her water aerobics class at the gym. He let her get in the shower before he made his presence known, and it was to her screams that he laughed and laughed and laughed.

Ms. Clark owned an old-fashioned four poster bed which made it convenient for him to tie her too. Then he took off his own clothes and straddled her, his cock and balls laying on her chest, pointing to the inevitable.

She'd stopped screaming out of pure exhaustion and merely sobbed.

Then he made her feel him inside her. Every place he'd fit, he went. Every place he went, he stayed until spent. He reveled in the feeling of her. He laughed as she cried, her wracking sobs making the feeling all the more delightful. He only stopped when the first feed came in and he watched as Gloria sucked on the nipples of the commander of the 2nd Cavalry Regiment. Their motto was *Toujours Pret*—Always Ready— and as his prostitute's phone broadcast the live feed from a hotel room to Schwarz's computer it was clear that the man was ready.

Schwarz queued it on his laptop and readied it for transmission.

Then came another and then another.

His girls were doing what they were made for, seducing, envenoming, crushing, all through love and intention. He knew the men were dead when the *alps*, now a third of their original size, sat on the crushed chests of their marks, faces inches from their victims', staring intently at what could never ever be.

The commander of the 173rd Airborne Brigade Combat Team stationed in Vicenza, Italy, whimpered as he went, as did the commander of the 7th Army Joint Multinational Training Command in Grafenwoehr.

The white-haired boss of the 12th Combat Aviation Brigade, a man who'd always complained to Schwarz when he was getting his boots shined about his wife and girlfriends, and how they were always wanting too much of his time, let out a sound like air screaming from a punctured tire as his ribs buckled and burst through his chest.

The commander of the 10th Army Air & Missile Defense Command in Kaiserslautern had been a gentle man. Soft-spoken and thoughtful, he was always concerned about the second and third order of effects of his commands, not second-guessing, just concerned, sometimes bouncing ideas off of Schwarz, even though he should have been beneath his attention. Schwarz considered his feelings, and couldn't stir a sympathetic thought, even though the man deserved one.

They were coming in two and three at a time now. Schwarz grinned in amazement how it was important not to discount the need for great men to feel important. Their addiction to adulation made them weak, made them a target, allowed his girls to get past their defenses. Even the great General May wasn't impervious. Commander of V-8, he was the most prominent of the targets, his face on the news, the face of hatred and condemnation to all vampires. To the Red King, May was the Hitler of the modern world, his intent to destroy and or detain all vampires no different.

So it was with a special glee that Schwarz sat with a cup of tea on the now still chest of Ms. Clark, watching as Karla bit into one of May's nipples, then the other. The general's head languorously lolled on a jowly neck, the camera even catching his eyes closing in a special *alpine* ecstasy.

Schwarz blew on the surface of the tea to cool it, as he watched this great man succumb to his baser instincts. A man who'd stood with presidents and kings of the world, now brought down by Schwarz's own queen. By the time she was ready to crawl on the man's chest, Schwarz's tea was cool enough to drink. He sipped as ribs cracked. May gasped as air failed to fill his lungs, the weight of the *alp* crushing like the early American settlers did to their supposed witches when they placed rock after rock on the poor women's shallow chests. Like a fish out of water, May's mouth opened and closed, comical to watch, but terrible to experience. When the chest finally caved, Schwarz lifted his tea cup. "Cheers to you, Big Dog. From Germany with love."

Then Schwarz pressed send.

Within minutes, the Armed Forces Network Germany began broad-casting the feeds over their air, replacing bad American sitcom reruns with the sexual scenes of manipulation and death of most of the commanders of the US forces in Germany. The scrawl at the top of the screen gave credit to an ultra-right-wing German nationalist group. The Red King didn't need the credit, didn't want the credit. They'd get far more traction if Americans believed that the fifty murders were a political statement.

Within minutes, CNN and Fox News picked up the feeds and began broadcasting them worldwide. CNN called this a vampire terrorist act, while Fox news decried Germany for being complicit in killing so many fine American soldiers. The death of General May was replayed over and over. The still photo of his stoic face in the upper left-hand corner of the screen was a droll juxtaposition of his guppy-faced gasping.

Soon, CNN changed their tune when they found a skinhead to interview who claimed ownership of the plot, his spitting comments and biting remarks… his utter hatred for anything American, cowling him in a guilt he deserved but had never earned.

Still, Schwarz was elated to give it to him.

The funny thing about regular people is that they automatically discount the fat guy, the small guy, the ugly guy. They think the agent of action should be the classic Hollywood action hero. They see fat and ugly and small and they avert their eyes. They don't want such a person to be in their mental space. Which means that even an ugly black dwarf has a chance to be a certified action hero, especially if he's a vampire.

Especially if he has a cause.

LEGACY

By Yvonne Navarro

The night-sky sparkles overhead, reminding Mooney Lopez of the way her twins sometimes throw glitter at glue spotted black poster board. Beautiful, serene in the way that only something vast and unemotional can be, infinitely removed from the grievances of earth's creatures. The moon is just as distant, deceptively warm looking in the abyss of the overhead universe, all the while casting its true, icy blue light on the desert below. God's eye, perhaps—dispassionate, judgmental, condemning.

Her boyfriend, Tyler McKinzie, stands beside her but doesn't break the silence. He knows intuitively that this is her time, to reflect, to plan, to question which path might lead to what future. Thanks to the war most of the human scientists are immersed in the study of the virus that activates junk DNA and triggers vampirism, but some still work on other medical conditions, industry, physics. Not too long ago, one claimed to have found proof that a person's soul continued after the body's death, as energy that passed into an alternate universe. Mooney finds it particularly interesting that humans have grabbed onto this theory with the same tenacity that the spine-covered joints of a cholla cactus sink into the skin of a careless hiker. How can they not realize that their alternate universes have already arrived?

Humans.

When had she started thinking in those terms? Humans: them. Vampires: me, my children, Tyler. For a long time she'd fought the notion, asking herself how could she suddenly not be human when that's what she'd been born. In retrospect, the change hadn't been all that fast, like some sort of then-that, now-this thing. It just felt that way in her memory. She still looked human, could pass for a normal woman anywhere as long as she stuffed her rattlesnake-patterned hair under a hat. When she'd turned, her ability to see at night had improved tremendously, and for a while she'd been worried that her pupils would change and take on the vertically elliptical shape so common in nocturnal snakes. Ultimately her pupils had remained round, although her nearly black irises had lightened to a rather lovely golden brown. Some folks even think she's pretty.

But… no. She isn't human. Not anymore.

"There," Tyler says suddenly.

Mooney turns her head and follows the silhouette of Tyler's pointing finger. In the distance, too far away to get there on foot, are moving lights, so small they look more like candle flames than spotlights or, more probably, headlights. There are six… no, eight of them, but there are no roads that far out and night driving is treacherous. One second you'd be inching around a boulder or across a rock-filled wash, the next your front end could drop two feet into a ground fissure and you'd have broken the axle. Whoever was out there would be long gone before Mooney and Tyler could close the distance, and she couldn't spot any landmarks that were clear enough in the dark to call for a helicopter.

"No way to catch them," Tyler says, confirming her thoughts. Then, "What the hell are they doing all the way out there? It's close to the border but there are easier spots to cross." He sounds irritated at his inability to decipher this middle-of-the-night mystery. They've been watching less than two minutes and four of the six lights have already disappeared; as they watch, the last two wink away.

"So much for that." Mooney stares into the blackness for another few seconds, then turns back toward the truck. "Let's head out. It'll take us an hour to get back to town." Tyler follows her without saying anything. That's one of the things she likes about him—he's a quiet young man who doesn't feel the urge to always talk.

They are almost to Mooney's truck when someone steps out of the overgrown mesquite brush six feet to Tyler's right.

Tyler goes into an instinctive crouch at the same time Mooney hisses, the warning sound sliding up from somewhere deep in her lungs and incorporating a vibration in her throat that mimics the shake of a rat-tlesnake's tail.

"Hi," says a childish voice. "I'm lost. Can I go with you?"

⊕

The little girl tells them her name is Geneva and that she's five years old. She doesn't reveal it, but Mooney and Tyler know immediately that the child is a vampire, although she hasn't yet manifested any kind of characteristic. Mooney's own children, twins Sitol and Judum, are the same way—still externally featureless as far as their true ancestry but wild and dangerously untamed in their immaturity. Like most untamed young, Geneva instinctively submits when in the presence of those of her own kind who are larger and superior. Had Geneva been exposed to the ice virus by a bite? Born of a vampire mother? Or sired by a vampire father? Would a human woman be able to survive such a pregnancy? Mooney shudders at the sudden notion of an unsuspecting human woman being consumed from the inside out.

Mooney shakes herself, then walks over and starts the 4 Runner's engine so she can turn on the headlights. She and Tyler study the girl in the paltry illumination; the glow seems to be eaten by the darkness that surrounds them, compressed by something so much bigger. Mooney thinks of that old science fiction question about what happens when an unstoppable force meets an immovable object. Nowadays the darkness has become unstoppable but there's no immovable object.

"What's your last name?" Mooney finally asks. When Geneva looks at her with a blank expression, Mooney tries again. "Where do you live? You know, when you're with your mom and dad?"

That same blank look.

And finally, "How did you get here?"

Not a word.

"I don't like this," Tyler says. "Something's not right."

Mooney scans the area around them, but the glare of the headlights makes it impossible to see anything. There is no sound above the slightly whiney hum of the Toyota engine. She pushes two fingers into the center of her forehead, tries to rub away the spot of tension that has suddenly settled there. "She had to come from somewhere," she says. "Kids don't just magically appear out of nothing."

"I say we leave her and get out of here."

Mooney's mouth falls open. "You can't be serious."

"She's a vampire child. You know she can take of herself." Tyler's gaze focuses on Mooney. "This is some kind of a trap."

Mooney thinks of her own children. "No," she says. "She's just—"

"Please don't leave me," Geneva suddenly says. Her shrill voice almost makes Mooney jump. "I'll be good, I promise."

Mooney's mouth snaps shut. She'd been about to say She's just a child, but there is something odd about the combination of Geneva's words and tone of voice, almost mechanical. Practiced. Her eyes narrow and she backs away from the girl. "Get in the truck," she tells Tyler. "Now."

"Not a good idea."

Mooney freezes at the voice and figures slide from behind the brush and rocks surrounding the small clearing they're in. She counts three, four… a total of five shapes strategically placed at the points of a star around the 4 Runner. They are blacker silhouettes against the shadows except for their faces; those are pale, blurred ovals. Even if they are unarmed—which is a stupid thing to assume—there is no way to take all of them out at once. Their stealth alone makes her know they aren't human. Geneva has sidled backward until she blends in with the dark and stands at the side of one of the unidentifiable shadows. Tyler was right: this is a trap.

"Who are you?" Mooney's right hand starts to creep toward her Beretta, then halts at the voice's next words.

"We're just as fast as you are, Agent Lopez. Faster, perhaps."

Her vision catches movement just outside the circle of light only a fraction of a second before a new figure steps into view. She doesn't have time to contemplate how unnervingly swift this man is, only sees that he's tall and heavily armed, dressed like some sort of Mexican bandito. She has no idea whether this guy is authentic or not because she's only seen them on television, but he has the bandoliers and oversized pistols hanging off each hip, old dusty boots, baggy faded jeans. The only thing he's missing is a sombrero; instead, his head is uncovered and his hair, which looks black in the headlights, hangs straight to mid bicep.

Instead of the swarthiness so common in the poorer Mexican ancestry, his skin is startlingly white, the shadows on his face a deep, unrelenting gray. His skin is pitted with acne scars and his eyes focus on Mooney as though there's nothing more important in the universe. A small cross-bones—no skull—is tattooed on his left temple.

It's the last thing she wants to do, but Mooney lets her hand drop. "What's this about? Do I know you?"

"My name is Heitor Nicanor," he says in heavily Mexican-accented but excellent English. He takes a shallow bow and makes a gesture that is similar to an Arabic salaam, which Mooney finds vaguely insulting considering she and Tyler are unquestionably prisoners. "You may call me Heitor. I feel certain you have never heard of me, but you will certainly remember me in the future."

"Can we just get on with this without the game playing?" Tyler suddenly asks. "What do you want?"

Nicanor fixes his black gaze on Tyler and raises one eyebrow. "Ah, a man who is direct. An admirable trait provided it is not mistaken for impatience."

Mooney doesn't flinch. "We're waiting."

Nicanor sighs. "Very well. And I was so looking forward to more of a conversation." He inclined his head to the side and another man, dressed a little differently but just as heavily armed, steps into the light. "There is me," Nicanor said, "and there is my family. As you have no doubt figured out, we are vampires."

"Your family," Tyler repeats.

"Being related by blood is not the only way one becomes family," Nicanor says. "Please do not interrupt me again." From somewhere in the blackness it sounds like at least two rifles are cocked. "As I was saying, my family and I run a business. This—" he sweeps his hand from left to right, seemingly encompassing the entire desert "—is our factory."

Mooney's eyes are hooded. "I never would have guessed."

"I have no time for your sarcasm, Agent Lopez," Nicanor snaps. "I am here to present my terms."

Mooney is taken aback, both by what he's said and by the fact that he knows who she is. "Terms?"

"The lights you saw a few minutes ago were my employees, doing what I pay them for."

"Which is?" Tyler interjects.

"Not your concern, Agent McKinzie," Nicanor replies. "It is enough for me to say that the two of you will not return to this part of the desert, and my workers will remain unmolested by you. You will not speak of them to other Border Patrol agents, or to your superiors."

So he knows Tyler, too. Mooney scowls as a double shot of anxiety winds down her spine. "That's absurd."

Nicanor sighs, as if this entire conversation is tiresome and something he would like to be finished. "This is not a negotiation, Agent Lopez. You will be well compensated for your silence." The Mexican's gaze flicks to Tyler, then back to Mooney's face. "Although I am afraid your companion will have to be satisfied enough on your behalf."

"We don't take bribes," Tyler says.

"Right. I am sure that you would rather die than be dishonest, protect the Border Patrol, save America, and all that bullshit." Another sigh, but this one has an edge of impatience to it. "Agent Lopez, you will not be paid with money."

Before Mooney can think of a response, Nicanor pulls something small and black from his pants pocket, then tosses it to her. Reflexes take over and she snaps it out of the air. When she looks down at her palm, she sees a battered cell phone, an older flip model. It's obviously an untraceable burner. A small LED light at the top left indicates it has power. She looks at Nicanor incredulously. "You think I'm going to call you? To what—give you information or something?"

"There is something on it that you will want to see," Nicanor says. His melodious voice is almost gentle. "It is the reason you will not only leave us in peace but steer others of the lawmaking variety away from our area."

Mooney opens the phone and presses the ON button. A PIN number screen appears.

"What's the number?"

"There is a war going on," Nicanor says, ignoring her question. He sounds absurdly like one of Mooney's high school history teachers. "The biggest in history, with the highest stakes. The winners will take everything, but don't doubt for a moment that there will be disagreements along the way as to who truly wins. New societies are already being born and bred and... nurtured." His mouth stretches in a smile, the first she has seen. Behind the dark slash of his upper lip is a double row of shark-like teeth. Mooney has never seen anything like it; Tyler's shoulder muscles go tight beneath his shirt, so he hasn't either. She suddenly realizes that although she thought being isolated in Sells was an advantage, it's a disadvantage, too. Beyond what she hears on the news, she knows nothing of the other types of vampires out there, what they can do, how they feed. The ones who stayed in Sells after Josh and Rose died weren't much to contend with as far as violent tendencies—after all, they'd come to Sells on Josh's fake promises of building a vampire utopia in a town that was accepting and free of danger. They are modern-day hippies who are happy to hunt in the desert and do menial work for the humans in exchange for the few material things they need. They have adapted to their new lives, and the humans in Sells have accepted them.

But in the rest of the world...

"What are you?" She wants to demand they tell her but she doesn't; instead she intentionally modulates her tone so that it's filled with admiration.

It works, and Nicanor's expression turns arrogant. "We are Cihuateteo," he says. "Born of the Aztecs and their belief in the goddess Cihuacoatl, to whom many sacrifices were made. In fact, we still make offerings to her every day." He chuckles unpleasantly. "The ancients built many wondrous things, but they also made many mistakes. Such as believing Cihuateteo were only women."

Before Mooney can ask any more questions, Nicanor suddenly flicks his hand. "Enough with the chit chat. I have things to do, and you do, too. The PIN number is 2012."

He pauses, then the gaze he fixes on Mooney somehow intensifies. She feels it as an almost palpable, energy-sapping thing. For the first time since she turned, she suddenly knows what it's like to be on the other side, prey instead of predator. His next words stab her with so much terror her knees nearly buckle.

"The number should be easy for you to remember. It's the year your children were born."

And as quickly and eerily as they appeared, Nicanor and his companions are swallowed up by the surrounding dark. One second they're just inside the light cast by her truck, the next second they're not.

Stunned, Mooney stares after them, the phone clutched in her hand. She can't move, can't breathe, can't think. In another second, she blinks as Tyler pries the phone from her stiffened fingers. Her mind registers that his hand is shaking as he punches in the number—2012—then stares at the screen.

"Oh my God," he whispers.

Tyler offers her the phone and for a long moment Mooney doesn't want to take it, doesn't want to know what he's seeing that makes his cheeks go pale and his eyes widen in a way that she's only seen in late-night horror movies. Even so, she doesn't seem to have control of her own body, because her hand reaches for it anyway, somehow holds onto the black plastic, then brings it to where her eyes can focus on the tiny screen. The image is in color, and—

Everything in Mooney's universe just…

Stops.

Her daughter, Sitol, has a mesquite branch and pokes at something on the ground. Her brother, Judum, peers at the ground with a look of intense concentration on his chubby face. The trailer is behind them, so the photograph was taken from somewhere in the desert, looking at the back yard. Taken without her children, who have exceptional hearing and smell, knowing someone was watching them. Taken with the photographer getting close enough to clearly discern the individually embroidered flowers across Sitol's blouse, count the number of portholes in the pirate ship image on Judum's T shirt.

Without consciously knowing what she's going to do, Mooney's thumb finds the right arrow button on the keypad. Despite the high buzzing in her head, she taps it. Another image flicks onto the undersized screen.

Her children, asleep on the pull-out sofa bed in the living room. Tangled in the sheets with them are the two new toys she bought them last Saturday, only three days ago. Their faces are relaxed and they look like little angels, with their long, dark eyelashes and pink, cherubic mouths. The photo was taken from above and at a slight angle. It's twilight so the living room lamp is on but neither she nor Tyler is in the picture, which means they are relaxing out front or, worse, sitting at the tiny kitchen table while someone climbs up the backside of the trailer, looks in the window, and takes this picture.

Mooney presses the arrow button again, but the screen only goes back to the first image. So that's all there is... perhaps. The number of photos doesn't matter, she knows that. What matters is that someone—no, the eerie men and women who just seemed to melt into the darkness—knows about her children and can get that close to them, even with Mooney right there.

Close enough to kill them.

———•———

Mooney is waiting for Chief Delgado as soon as he walks in with his Starbucks coffee. She'd swung by the trailer to check on the kids, then headed right over to the station. He eyes her warily as she settles on the hard wooden chair in front of his desk. She's seen him in town occasionally but not spoken to him face to face since the day he brought the Border Patrol to recruit her. Except for a deepening of the wrinkles in his forehead and around his mouth, he hasn't changed.

"So," Delgado says with false cheerfulness, "how are you doing, Red Moon? Word around town is that you have a boyfriend who's also joined the Border Patrol and your kids are growing, uh..." He stumbles a little here and Mooney grins inside and doesn't say anything, forcing him to admit what he knows. "Growing quickly," he finally finishes. Then he brightens. "People are talking about how you're doing a fantastic job."

Delgado thinks he's moved the conversation to safe territory, but Mooney is about to show him just how scary that can be. She leans forward. "I need your help, Chief Delgado."

He blinks. "Me?"

She flips open the burner cell phone, enters the PIN, then pushes it across the calendar blotter in front of him. "These are my kids."

Delgado looks even more confused. "Okay. Uh... cute." When she says nothing, he scrolls to the second picture, then frowns. He is just as smart as she thought he was. "Who took this?"

"I don't know."

"Someone looking in the window." It's a statement, not a question.

"Yes."

Suddenly he's all business. "How did you get the phone?"

So Mooney tells him the whole thing, starting with the lights she and Tyler spotted along the border and all the way to the white-faced Cihuateteo vampires who disappeared. He asks a few questions and she answers the best she can; the truth is, she knows next to nothing that she didn't pick up from the web when she got back to the trailer this morning. She asked around, but no one at Border Patrol or ICE seems to have ever heard of this new breed of vampire, and no one has ever seen them except her and Tyler.

Delgado listens and finally leans back. "So what can I do? I can put a couple of officers on your house, but only for a few days. And let's face it, even with guns, my guys are probably no match for these things. I don't want to see people get killed."

"I understand."

"You tell your supervisor about this?"

Mooney shakes her head. "They'll flood that area of the border with agents but they won't find anything unless Tyler and I go with them. And that's not happening."

"Why not?"

"Because I'm not gambling with my kids' lives. Yeah, they're both vampires." The look on Delgado's face as she says this is priceless. "And yeah, they've grown really fast and they can fight, but they're also just children. The equivalent of three-year-olds." She gives him a sideways look. "Unless…"

It's all over Delgado's face that he doesn't want to ask, but he does anyway. "Unless what?"

Mooney lifts her chin and meets his gaze steadily. "Unless I can leave them here at the police station while we raid that location."

The chief's eyes almost bulge in surprise. "Red Moon, you know that's impossible."

"Why?" she demands. "The only safer place in this entire county would be with me, and you know I can't haul them around in the desert. That would be insane."

"And babysitting a couple of vampire kids isn't?"

"Look," she says, "we're all nice and insulated here in Sells, but in case you haven't noticed, the human-vampire war is going on full strength in the rest of the world. Bombs, terrorists, probably the same kind of deceit and corruption that's been in every war ever fought. Maybe you need to catch up, spend some time on the Internet. I'm thinking that something is building over the border and it's about to spill over. I don't want Sells to get crushed when it does, but I have to know my babies are safe before I can even think about moving to fight it." When he doesn't say anything, Mooney spreads her hands. "That's it," she says. "That's all I've got."

Delgado sighs. "So unless I figure out a way to look out for the kids—"

"In the station," Mooney interrupts. "In a nice, locked cell."

"—you're going to look the other way on what you guys saw out there."

"I don't have any choice. Chief, these are my children."

Delgado says nothing for a time, just drums his thick fingers on the desktop. When he exhales, Mooney knows she's won. He squints at her. "You really want me to lock your toddlers in a cell?"

Mooney decides not to tell him that doing so is protecting both the toddlers and the humans in the building.

———•———

Knowing that the twins are safe is like being freed from a suicide bomber's vest that has been strapped on too tightly—Mooney finally feels like she can breathe again. She and Tyler set up a meeting with their supervisory agent and the operations officer, and what starts as a thirty-minute briefing ends up incorporating eight more agents of varying ranks and taking until almost noon. Neither of them have slept and by the time they finally get back outside, she feels like they're running on adrenaline alone. She would have preferred not to involve humans—sometimes they are so fragile—but she and Tyler can't handle these Cihuateteo alone. At least with the Border Patrol backing them up, there'll be firepower and equipment, a lot more of a presence to push these crazy creatures back into Mexico, where the Mexican government could figure out what to do with them.

Theoretically.

———•———

To say it doesn't go well is like saying you were involved in a fender bender when your Volkswagen Bug was hit by a commuter train.

Tyler, who is much more gadget savvy than Mooney, used the GPS in the truck to mark the location before they left, so there's no problem finding their way back to the previous night's location. The area is saturated with everything from Border Patrol agents to ICE human trafficking specialists to county sheriffs. They are armed as well as Arnold Schwarzenegger in the Terminator movies, and as jumpy as a man walking barefoot across a carpet loaded with mousetraps. Everything—the agents, dogs, vehicles, portable spotlights—is carefully moved into place after dark, and at three a.m., the time some overpaid government supervisor deems to be optimal to catch human movement, someone throws a switch and that whole section of desert is lit up like a night game at Kino Stadium in Tucson. The agents use the illumination and the dogs as they thoroughly search everything within a widening circle.

Nothing is overlooked. It takes a good three quarters of an hour, but a couple of Border Patrol agents and a dog finally find the entrance to a tunnel.

Five minutes later, just enough time for several dozen agents and supervisors to push into the opening, the operation disintegrates into a particularly grisly kind of Hell on earth.

———•———

Mooney and Tyler are in the middle of the flow of men and women when the walls come alive.

At first the tunnel, which slopes downward abruptly enough to make the descent precarious, doesn't seem like much more than a standard drug-moving setup. But when they get past the narrow first four or five feet of crude, earthen walls, the passageway suddenly widens into a chamber that has supporting poles from the floor to the ceiling, the far end of which can't be seen from where they enter. Agents move forward in silence—there's nothing to see here, no empty water bottles, discarded clothing, or backpacks, nothing that indicates anyone has been here recently. Even with the stronger spotlights, the leading agents are no more than flickering circles disappearing into the darkness when the first scream comes. Then there's another, and another.

Mooney crouches instinctively and swings her Remington 12-gauge up at the same time she aims her flashlight at the ceiling. It's clear, but her peripheral vision catches a glimpse of something moving; she drops the barrel forty-five degrees and realizes the walls have come alive.

"Look out!" she yells. "They're coming out of the walls!"

The screams are escalating and now gunfire—automatic and semi-automatic—adds to the cacophony. In such an enclosed space, the noise is beyond deafening, nearly unbearable. The spotlights at the front go out, then there's a surge of smaller lights headed back toward her and the exit behind her—whatever's up ahead is enough to make the agents decide to retreat to where there's more backup. She loses track of Tyler and has to hope that the training ICE gave him is enough to get him out of here, then barely dodges out of the way as something swipes at her from between the mass of bodies. She spins and catches it across the face with the butt of her shotgun, but it falls back for only a moment. An instant later a white-faced female Cihuateteo is swaying in front of her. One cheekbone is shattered and spilling blood down her jaw and onto her shoulder.

"We should have known you would never be true to your heritage," the vampire spits out. Her mouth is a tooth-filled horror and Mooney doesn't want to think about what will happen if the woman gets close enough to bite. "You've betrayed us!"

"I'm not one of you. I never agreed to a deal with your boss," Mooney says icily. "And I won't be blackmailed. By anyone."

The vampire throws her head back and lets out a soulless laugh that sounds more like the scream of a wounded cheetah than anything else. "You'll be sorry, you stupid girl. Do you not think Nicanor already knows what you've done?"

"I'm sure he does," Mooney says. Around her is still nothing short of chaos, but the submachine guns and full auto pistols are starting to pull the agents—the ones still alive—ahead in the game. She grimaces and glances over her shoulder as someone stumbles against her; the smell of blood and gunpowder is everywhere, soaked into the walls and ground and the clothing of the dead and wounded. "Where is he?"

The woman laughs again and Mooney almost cringes. "Where do you think?" Before Mooney can respond, the vampire opens her mouth wide and leaps for her. She is so fast there's nothing Mooney can do to protect herself except reflexively squeeze the trigger of the Remington. The slug catches her attacker in the throat, almost decapitating her, and the heavy smell of blood in the chamber seems to increase by ten as Mooney is pressed back by the weapon's recoil. The woman's body slams against the wall, and only after the creature hits the dirt does Mooney realize that the Cihuateteo was so fast she'd been able to rake her claws across the front of Mooney's bulletproof vest. There are long, jagged rips in the nylon all the way to the panels underneath, and one of the Velcro straps has been completely cut in half.

The shooting and screaming sounds like it goes on forever, but in reality it's only a couple of minutes before it's all over. The Cihuateteo, at least the ones who were down here, are all dead, and Mooney can see that the death toll for the Border Patrol and ICE agents is into the double digits. The limited air is full of smoke and there's blood splatter everywhere—the walls, the floors, the ceilings, most of all on the humans. Mooney didn't see any vampires with guns, but there are injured people, too, men and women who went down under friendly fire or the teeth and claws of the Cihuateteo. The wounds are vicious and she suspects the death toll will grow by the time the medics get here and everything is cleaned up.

"Mooney!"

She spins at the sound of Tyler's voice, but her relief fast forwards into concern when she picks him out of the bodies moving and staggering around her. "Are you—"

"I'm fine," he interrupts. He waves off the hand she extends toward him. He doesn't look fine. There is a wide, three-inch slash on the right side of his face that runs diagonally from this cheekbone to the side of his mouth. Everything below it is drenched in blood.

"Unless you can miraculously heal, you need to get that stitched up."

"Later," Tyler says. His gaze drops to her vest.

"No damage," she tells him, then scowls at the mess surrounding them. Static-filled radio calls add to the discord, then a supervisor pushes past her with his radio clutched in one hand.

"Come in? Come in, base!" When he receives no response, he yells to no one in particular, "I'm going outside to get a signal!"

Mooney watches him leave, then turns her attention back to the bodies on the floor. Border Patrol green mixed in with the street clothes and black of ICE vests mixed in with scarlet. Lots of scarlet. After a couple of seconds, she walks over to where one of the vampire bodies lies face down, then bends and pulls the head up by the back of the hair. The creature's ink-colored eyes have gone the color of spoiled milk above a thin nose and the nightmare mouth. She lets it drop. "It's not Nicanor." When Tyler gives her a questioning look, she says, "I need to know if he's here."

"I doubt it," Tyler says as he looks around. "We haven't figured out if they're running drugs or people, but I think this is too much a peon's place for him. Beneath him."

"But talking to me wasn't?"

"I think he saw you as kind of a… bonus. Someone he could get both protection and info from if the law was getting too close to his operation." Tyler nods toward the other end of the room. "As soon as we get this all cleaned up and get the injured and bodies out, we'll get reinforcements and move up the tunnel to see where it goes. Nicanor's underground expressway will go down, but we're going to find out what he's moving first."

Mooney scans the poorly lit chamber. She steps over outstretched limbs and finds another dead Cihuateteo, but it's not Nicanor. "Not good," she mutters to herself as she searches for another dead vampire.

"What's not good?" Tyler asks.

"The woman I killed," Mooney answers. "She said I betrayed them. That Nicanor already knew that."

Tyler frowns. "You're right—not good."

"Yeah."

Abruptly he takes her by the elbow and starts working through the new people pouring into the tunnel, back toward the entrance. "Looking for him here is a waste of time," Tyler says as he shoulders through agents and medical people.

"We need to get the hell back to Sells."

———•———

But they're too late.

Being what she is, a vampire, and using those skills in her job as a Border Patrol agent to… eliminate certain unwanted elements along the US-Mexico border, Mooney has seen a lot of carnage in the relatively short time since the virus triggered her DNA and turned her. But this, she thinks dully, is not carnage.

It's butchery.

Half of the day shift has already arrived, and their patrol cars and personal vehicles are parked haphazardly around the Sells police station. Somewhere above the fog she's temporarily frozen in, Mooney can hear sirens; this tells her the rest are on their way. People are yelling inside and outside the building, their words cut by the static from walkie talkies. There's so much blood—

Her paralysis snaps and she lunges forward, shoving people out of the way to get to the front of the building. Tyler is right behind her. When she gets to the door, someone yells something at her and foolishly tries to stop her. She gives the man a push that knocks him on his rear and strides past him, heading for the cells in the back.

When she gets there, when she sees, all she can do is open her mouth and wail, while Tyler wraps his arms around her and holds her upright.

———•———

By noon the bodies in the holding cells—what remains of them—have been removed, along with the corpses of nine Sells police officers and two Border Patrol agents. The attackers didn't just kill their victims; they were particularly brutal, decapitating some, ripping the limbs off others, and, in the case of the people in the holding cells, splitting them open from throat to belly after they'd bent back the iron bars to get to them and then tearing them apart; what's left behind is a jumble of parts, like the leftovers from some kind of mad scientist dissection. The death scene has been photographed a dozen times, the names have been recorded, families notified, the paperwork started. Clean-up has begun at the station by a crew of specialists who handle such things, and Chief Delgado watches over all of it, orchestrating what seems like an impossible task: restarting the Sells Police Department after a third of it has been wiped out.

Through it all, Mooney sits in the chief's office, staring at the floor. Tyler is with her, but wisely keeps his distance. At no other time since she turned has Mooney felt so much like the rattlesnake that seems to have been incorporated into her DNA; she is devastated, yes, but not so deep inside her is an anger like nothing she's ever experienced. It makes her want to strike out at anything and everything, not just to bite but to rip and split, to savage flesh in a do-unto-others flash of fury and retribution for the same deeds that were done to her children. Worse, she has no desire for the feeling to pass. She wants to revel in it, let it take her and be damned to the consequences.

Eventually, however, it does pass. When it goes, hours later, it leaves an emptiness within her heart and soul that can never be filled again.

———•———

"We don't know who did it," Delgado says. His dark brown eyes are sympathetic but unyielding.

"It was the Cihuateteo leader." Mooney's hands are on her hips in a don't-fuck-with-me stance. She is not finished mourning, but she is done with the tears. For now.

"You can't be sure—" Delgado begins, but Mooney doesn't allow him to finish.

"Yes, I am." Her eyes flash. "I mistakenly thought the twins would be safe here."

"I'm sorry," Delgado says softly. "So did I." He pauses. "A great many people lost loved ones last night."

"Then all those people should be wanting revenge as much as I do," Mooney replies.

There's a knock on his office door and they all look over as a young policewoman motions to Delgado. "Excuse me," he says, and goes over to her. They step outside, and even though she can, Mooney has no desire to eavesdrop. The chief's expression is enigmatic when he comes back a couple of minutes later. He clears his throat. "My people tell me there's a chance the children might have survived."

Mooney's head snaps up. "What!"

"Are you sure?" Tyler asks. "How?"

Delgado shakes his head. "No, we're not sure. But here's the thing: although there was a lot of blood and... pieces in the cell, when it was all sorted out, they didn't find the children. We figured they would be found elsewhere in the building, but it turns out we were wrong. All the dead have been identified." Reluctantly he met Mooney's gaze. "Your kids aren't in this building."

Mooney stared at him, sitting very still. She'd assumed Sitol and Judum were dead. It had been an all-out massacre and there had been bodies and pieces of bodies everywhere, half in and out of the cellblocks, in the offices, the restrooms—even the other prisoners had been killed, apparently for the sheer pleasure of it. Every corpse had been dismembered, disemboweled. They were also all decapitated, the bodies bitten, the bones broken, no exception. So when the bodies of her children hadn't immediately been found, Mooney had been too far into shock to assume they wouldn't be discovered when the carnage was finally sorted out. To think they might still be alive...

That was almost worse.

What are they going through right now?

The terror that had come with the realization that the Cihuateteo would attack the station reared again, viciously. Had her babies been taken? Why?

To make me suffer.

She stands. "I'm going back to the tunnel."

Delgado looks up at her. "Red Moon, I don't have any manpower to send with you. It's too dangerous. If you can wait—"

"You know I can't do that."

Delgado nods as Tyler moves to stand next to her, then the chief sighs. "Load up on ammunition before you go. Extra pistols, automatic weapons." He glances at the doorway, then lowers his voice. "It would probably be wrong of me to tell you that the grenades are in the cabinet next to the M14s, and that the cabinet lock was smashed during the attack last night."

A slight nod is the only inclination that Mooney hears him.

"Be careful out there," Delgado says. He looks truly unhappy. "We don't know what you're getting into, and judging by last night, you don't either."

363

This time it's full daylight when Mooney and Tyler get to the tunnel's entrance. The area is full of both ICE and Border Patrol agents, so a few more won't make much of an impact. They both know instinctively that the key is to look as though they already have an assignment to complete, so they stride past the personnel at the tunnel's entrance without so much as glancing at them. The interior has been strung with lights and they follow them as far as they lead; it takes awhile to get to the end—the tunnel doesn't go very deep, but it's long. It terminates at a fissured slab of gray-black rock. A handful of ICE agents mill around, clipboards in hand. Their faces are bland but it's obvious they're at a standstill.

One man, tall with graying hair and an air of authority about him, turns to look at them. He doesn't bother to introduce himself but the name tag on his shirt says Williams, and the insignia marks his rank as a Supervisory CPB Officer. "Who are you?" he asks. "All BP agents have been assigned outside."

"Agent Mooney Lopez," she says, then indicates Tyler. "Agent Tyler McKinzie. We're from Sells."

His eyes darken for a moment. "I was briefed about that this morning. I hope you didn't..." He sees Mooney's expression and doesn't finish. "What can I help you with?"

"We're here to help you," Mooney tells him. When he lifts one eyebrow, she says it straight out. "We're vampires."

The murmuring that had been going on around them stops as the other personnel turn to stare at them mistrustfully. Williams instinctively takes a step back.

"Don't worry," Tyler says. "We chose our side a long time ago."

There's a long moment of silence. Finally, Williams jerks his head toward the rock wall, "Not sure what you can do. We've done everything but blow this end of the tunnel, but we're stuck. Only a handful of the, uh, attackers got away last night. But there are no side tunnels that we can find, so we don't have a clue how they managed it."

Mooney eyes the rock, taking it in inch by inch, carefully going over everything. She's sure they've done the same thing, but they don't have her instinct for detail, for prey. After a couple of minutes, she steps forward and runs her fingers along one of the jagged lines in the rock wall; this one is slightly deeper than the others around it. She glances at Tyler and he comes over and inspects it, then he steps sideways a couple of feet and passes his palm carefully back and forth on the cool surface until he, too, finds a corresponding place in the rock.

"One," he says softly. "Two—"

"Three!" Mooney yells.

They throw everything they have into it and push.

The wall doesn't give, at least initially. But Mooney feels it—the slightest scrape, rock against rock, grinding. Neither she nor Tyler lets up, keeping their weight going forward and their muscles tight. There's another nudge, and another, and Mooney thinks of her twins, fierce for their age but helpless against the vicious Cihuateteo, trapped in a jail cell that she'd insisted they be put into for their own safety.

Their safety, for God's sake.

Her heart twists inside her chest and her brain feels like it's boiling. The growl starts in her belly and works itself into a scream of rage unlike anything that's ever come out of her mouth. She hears Tyler's answering scream as he joins with her pain, and together they fight against this barrier as if it's the last thing in the world they need to get past, to find—

A grinding sound fills the tunnel as a solid three-foot-square chunk falls away and into darkness.

Mooney ignores the shouts behind her and dives through the opening. She doesn't have time for orders or humans and their sense of military do-this, don't-do-that. The tunnel is devoid of light and even her nightsight doesn't help, so she flicks on her flashlight and scurries forward. Tyler follows her, and she hears the voice of a dozen others behind him.

Abruptly, finally, they fall silent, so she can listen to the empty space ahead to discern whether someone—something—waits in the blackness.

Mooney and Tyler put on speed, leaving the rest of the agents so far behind that the lights from their flashlights turn to pinpricks before they wink out entirely. The passageway feels like it goes on for miles, and it probably does. They are close to the border, right on the line, and any drug smuggler or human trafficker worth a damn knows the tunnel entrances must be well hidden on both ends. Somewhere ahead will be Mexico and the point of no jurisdiction, where her superiors will demand she and Tyler stop and wait while they contact the appropriate police authorities, while they negotiate stupid things like who gets credit, who takes over, and a host of other bullshit.

The radio at her waist crackles but she ignores it. She cannot follow orders she doesn't hear.

The tunnel bends and twists as it snakes around underground boulders. Mooney and Tyler slip forward almost soundlessly, their way marked only by the occasional pebble sliding beneath their feet. Suddenly Mooney feels it—the beginning of a gradual incline. Another two turns and they are climbing steadily, following a worn trail that has been used by who knows how many people and vampires before them.

Then... light.

It's dim but unmistakable. Not daylight but too soft to be candlelight, some sort of lighting placed at intervals along the passage. The ground has leveled out and it's finally illuminated enough to switch off the flashlights and hook them back to their belts. Mooney's heart is thudding in her chest, but she can't tell if it's due to anticipation, dread, or fury—or maybe it's all three. The tunnel widens into a small room much like the one back on the US side; there are a couple of tables with a battery-operated lantern on each, a few chairs. Besides that, not much: an ashtray overflowing with American and Mexican cigarette butts, a couple of half-empty tequila bottles.

A second glance around the room reveals an exit neatly camouflaged by two walls, the edges of which overlap and blend into each other in the dimness. Tyler follows Mooney as she eases around the mazelike passageway, where the tunnel continues for another twenty feet and ends in a heavy wooden door. She pushes against it; it rattles slightly but holds—a padlock. Tyler comes up beside her and gives the door a kick that shatters the wood where the hasp was fastened on the other side and they hear a heavy clunk as the lock drops to the ground.

Mooney shoves the busted door out of the way and moves forward without hesitating. She takes three steps then stops, looking around carefully. Tyler is right behind her.

"What is this?" he whispers.

"A stable," she answers quietly. "We're in a horse barn."

They can hear the horses now, the restless movements of hooves interspersed with nervous whinnies. Something's making the big animals unhappy, but Mooney isn't sure if it's their own sudden appearance or something else, something worse.

They're in one of the empty stables and she moves to the gate, leaning over to check both ways before unlatching it and stepping into the main corridor. The air smells of hay and earth and large animals, of manure and horse feed. And something else… something that doesn't belong.

She and Tyler crouch and study their surroundings. There's a double row of horse stalls, some occupied, most not. The ceiling is clear, at least as far as Mooney can see; the rafters are empty but there's a loft to their rear that looks like it's filled to its edge with square bales of hay.

"Let's go," Mooney says.

They head toward the open barn doors at the far end. They see sunlight outside, but even after the menacing darkness of the tunnel it seems hot and vicious, not at all a welcoming sight. They move silently from stall to stall, checking each. There are only a few horses, geldings and mares plus one glossy black stallion in a larger enclosure reinforced with metal fencing. Nothing but the beautiful animals on the edge, pacing and nickering because they sense that something isn't right.

Until the last stall on the right.

Mooney and Tyler stare over the gate. There's a heavy canvas tarp, thick with the red dust of the desert, covering the entire floor, but the top of it isn't smooth. It's…

Lumpy.

In a smooth, quick move, Tyler does what Mooney can't bring herself to: he pushes open the gate, then bends and yanks back the tarp.

Mooney gasps. "No." Her words deteriorate into a stutter. "Oh, p-please, no…"

She takes two steps forward and goes to her knees, not registering when Tyler crouches beside her and puts his arms around her. He rocks her while she sobs into his shoulder, holding her as tightly as he can.

"I'm sorry. Oh God, Mooney, I'm so, so sorry."

———◆———

By the time the rest of the agents and the supervisors arrive, Mooney has retreated into a stone caricature of herself, an emotionless clone who can deal with the kind of pain that no mother, especially a vampire mother, should have to endure. She stands and answers questions as best she can, watches while others catalog the dead and fill out reports and make the calls that are required in order to coordinate with the Mexican authorities. Outwardly she is calm and collected, totally professional. She can see that a few people even think she is cold-hearted and uncaring.

There is nothing further from the truth.

"How many are there?" she hears Williams ask.

There is a moment of silence before someone answers in a hoarse voice, "Eighteen."

"How the fuck can eighteen children go missing and no one says a word?" The last part of his sentence rises to a frustrated shout.

"Sixteen," Mooney says.

Williams whirls to face her. "What?"

"My children are in there," she says in a flat voice.

"Your—" His voice cuts out and he shudders. "Jesus, Agent Lopez. I'm sorry."

She doesn't answer, just turns and walks back to the stall where the bodies are. There are three neat rows of six corpses each, placed side by side. It's a mix of Americans and Mexicans, mostly toddlers, but none older than five years old. Although they aren't the oldest, Sitol and Judum are—were—the biggest and, presumably, the healthiest. Geneva is in there, too. She looks at all of them, the small faces, the babyish features that will never grow up, the fine hair that will now never lose the silkiness of youth. Predictably her gaze keeps coming back to her twins, and she can't help think that death wasn't the worst thing that happened to them. Were they sacrificed by Nicanor to Cihuacoatl? A memory rises in her mind, how the now-dead Josh and Rose had tried to get to the twins because they believed that the blood of children, especially vampire children, would give them superior strength.

Whether or not it was true—and God, she hoped it wasn't—doesn't matter.

Because even when she squeezes her eyes shut, Mooney's traitorous mind still shows her the deep puncture marks all over Sitol's and Judum's small bodies.

One Week Later

"Are you sure about this?"

It's a valid question but Mooney is gratified to hear no doubt in Tyler's voice, no second guessing. He wants to make sure that this path, this irreversible course, is the one that Mooney wants to take. She wouldn't have blamed him had he backed out; after all, war was not what he had traveled to Sells to find. He'd wanted peace, somewhere away from the hatred and violence and prejudice. Instead, he'd found her.

"Yes."

They are standing in the barn at the end of the tunnel, on the Mexican side. The entire tunnel is scheduled for demolition at dawn, in another two hours; Mooney knows, because she helped set the charges in the deepest parts. She and Tyler slipped past the guards in the middle of the night. Once it blows, there will be no going back.

She and Tyler are more heavily armed than they've ever been, weighed down by more weapons and ammunition than even the most physically fit human could have handled. The heat is like a living thing wrapping itself around her as she moves from stall to stall, opening the gates and chasing the horses out of the barn and into the scrub-filled, empty pasture beyond. Tyler herds them through an open gate and into another fenced pasture that puts distance between them and the structure, then ropes the gate closed. In another moment he stands beside her and scans the horizon. "Do you think they will come?"

"Maybe," she says. "Maybe not. It doesn't matter."

He nods, then leaves her to stand in the sun while he strides back into the barn. Three more minutes and she smells gasoline, then the first hint of smoke. By the time he returns the barn is an inferno, the fire rising up before them like some kind of incarnation, perhaps of the goddess Cihuacoatl herself. Mooney watches it dispassionately.

In the upper right pocket of her vest is a picture of Sitol and Judum, her beautiful children. Nicanor took them and she will never get them back. But she will give something to him, and to his Cihuateteo. A gift from the twins, their legacy.

She will bring him war.

RED EMPIRE PART 4

By Jonathan Maberry

The Rose Garden
The White House
Washington, D.C.
Day 18 of the Red Storm

There was a moment of utter silence, and Luther Swann believed that it was a silence felt around the world. The entire planet— anyone tuned into the president's speech, everyone who had heard his words and those of Senator Maria Giroux—were sitting in absolutely shocked silence.

And then the moment passed.

Every reporter began yelling, screaming, their questions colliding and crashing into one another, turning words into noise. The president and the senator stood there and endured it. They both looked scared, thought Swann. And they both looked relieved.

The world had just hit another of those moments when the gear slipped and then caught. The engine would rev higher, building momentum. Whether it would race on into a new future or smash into a wall of unyielding reality was yet to be seen.

Yuki Nitobe stood in the front row of the press corps and it was she who got the nod from the president to ask the first question. It was a gift from Luther Swann. A bit of stage management for all the right reasons.

"Mr. President," she asked, having to yell above the din, "does that mean the V-Wars are over?"

The president took a breath. "It means that people of good heart—humans and vampires, bloods and beats—will unite to fight a common enemy. The Red Empire is a terrorist organization that does not speak for the vampires of America or the people of America. The Red Empire is a terrorist organization that does not want to build anything or repair anything. They want to tear down everything of value and replace it with pain, with destruction, with subjugation. They are dedicated to genocide and we will oppose them and defeat them. Not 'we' the humans of America. I speak for 'we' the people of this great nation. Human and vampire. Together. United to preserve our country and our world."

Yuki yelled, "I have a follow-up question for Senator Giroux!"

The president ignored every other reporter and nodded to her. "Ask your question."

"Senator—you've outed yourself as a vampire, as the Crimson Queen. That's huge. What will that mean for the conflict between bloods and beats?"

It was the crucial question, suggested to her by Swann and approved by Church.

The senator nodded and as the president stepped to one side she stood behind the podium, tall and elegant, regal. Queenlike, even though she was not wearing her mask.

"I echo what the president has said. However, I know that a speech is not going to change the hearts and minds of everyone. There will be conflict on both sides of the blood line. However, I speak now to all of those who know and understand what I have tried to do with the Crimson Court. We never took sides but have worked with both sides to try and prevent needless violence. So I speak now—openly—to every vampire who respects and acknowledges what we have tried to do. I do not ask you to lay down your arms and walk away. No, it isn't the time for that. The Red Empire is rising. They are powerful and they are many. But we are many more. And we are powerful. I ask you to stand with us against extinction, against genocide. You know the nature of the V-gene.

Everyone carries it. Everyone. That means that beats and bloods are one people. One essential species. The Crimson Court, my people, live within and without the United States and within and without hundreds of other countries. There are millions of us. From this moment forward we have only one enemy and that is the Red Empire."

Her voice rose as she spoke and those last few words came out harsh and clear and hard as daggers. The president took her hand and raised it as flashbulbs popped and popped.

In a large room filled with banks of computers, more than fifty people stood or sat and watched as the president and the senator began trying to answer an impossible number of questions.

Captain Joe Ledger stood with a cup of coffee and nodded to the people on the screen.

"Give 'em hell," he said.

Around him the staff at the Hangar, the Brooklyn headquarters of the Department of Military Sciences, began to applaud and then they shot to their feet and cheered.

In the hollow cavern of a dry goods warehouse in Baltimore a hundred people, men and women, stood watching the faces on the big screen TV. The president and the senator. They watched them declare war.

Only one person sat while everyone else stood.

He was thin, pale, with dark hair and darker eyes.

The press asked their questions. The faces on the screen gave their answers. The hundred pairs of eyes watched and a hundred pairs of ears listened in an eerie silence.

Finally the seated man raised a remote control and turned the television off. He tossed the remote onto the floor, lit a cigarette, and smoked in silence for a full minute. No one spoke.

"If it's war they want," said Michael Fayne, "then let's give it to them."

And then every one of the Red Knights roared out with voices of thunder.

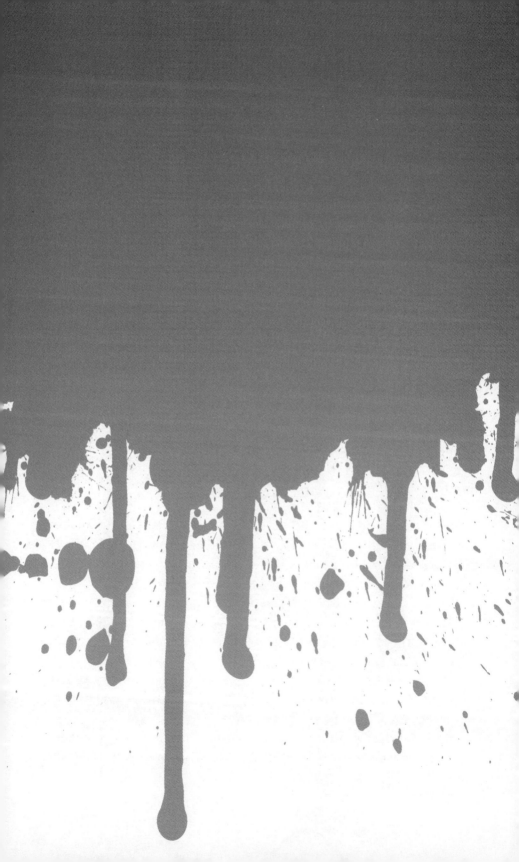

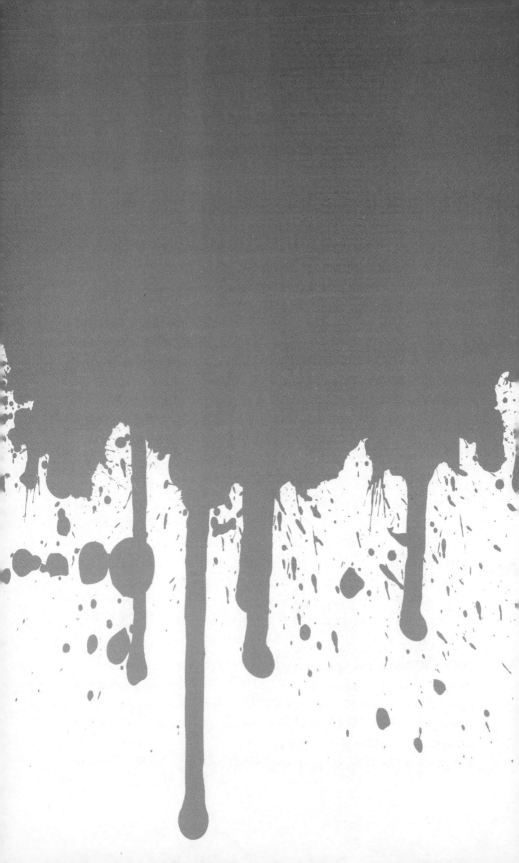

V-WARS CORRESPONDENTS

JONATHAN MABERRY is a *New York Times* best-selling author,
five-time Bram Stoker Award-winner, and comic book writer. He
writes in multiple genres including suspense, thriller, horror, science
fiction, fantasy, action, and steampunk, for adults and teens. His
works include the Joe Ledger thrillers, *Rot & Ruin*, *The Orphan Army*,
Patient Zero, *V-Wars*, *Captain America*, and many others. He writes
comics for Marvel, Dark Horse, and IDW. And he is the editor of
several high-profile anthologies including *The X-Files*, *Nights of the
Living Dead*, and *Scary Out There*. Several of his works are in development for movies and TV. He is a popular workshop leader, keynote
speaker and writing teacher. He lives in Del Mar, California. Find him
online at www.jonathanmaberry.com.

JOE MCKINNEY has worked in law enforcement for twenty years,
and has been writing professionally for the last ten years. Since
publishing his first novel, *Dead City*, in 2006, he has gone on to win
two Bram Stoker Awards and expanded his oeuvre to cover everything
from true crime and writings on police procedure to science fiction to
cooking and Texas history. The author of more than twenty books, he
is a frequent guest at horror and mystery conventions. Joe and his
wife Tina have two lovely daughters and make their home in a little
town just outside of San Antonio, where he indulges his passion for
cooking and makes what some consider to be the finest batch of chili
in Texas. You can keep up with all of Joe's latest releases by friending
him on Facebook.

DANA FREDSTI is an ex B-movie actress with a background in
theatrical combat (a skill she utilized in *Army of Darkness* as a sword-
fighting Deadite and fight captain). Through seven plus years of volun-
teering at EFBC/FCC, Dana's been kissed by tigers, and had her thumb
sucked by an ocelot with nursing issues. She's addicted to bad movies
and any book or film, good or bad, which include zombies. She's the

author of the Ashley Parker series, touted as Buffy meets the Walking Dead, and the zombie noir novella *A Man's Gotta Eat What a Man's Gotta Eat*. She's written numerous published articles, essays and shorts, including stories in *Cat Fantastic IV*, an anthology series edited by Andre Norton (Daw, 1997), *Danger City* (Contemporary Press, 2005), and *Mondo Zombie* (Cemetery Dance, 2006). Her essays can be seen in *Morbid Curiosity*, Issues 2-7. Additionally she's written several produced low-budget screenplays and currently has another script under option. Dana was also co-writer/associate producer on *Urban Rescuers*, a documentary on feral cats and TNR (Trap/Neuter/Return), which won Best Documentary at the 2003 Valley Film Festival in Los Angeles.

JADE SHAMES is a writer living in Brooklyn, New York. In 2014, he won the Fresh Voices screenplay competition grand prize. His work has appeared in the *LA Weekly, Thought Catalog, The Best American Poetry blog*, and the anthology *Scary Out There* (Simon & Schuster).

JAMES R. TUCK is the author of the Deacon Chalk series, co-author of the Robin Hood: Demon's Bane series (with Debbie Viguie), and (under the name Levi Black) the author of *Red Right Hand*. He also writes comic books, short stories like the one that appears here, and advice articles for other writers. His information can be found at www.jamesrtuck.com.

LUCAS MANGUM is an author living in Austin, Texas. He enjoys wrestling, cats, wrestling with cats, and drinking craft beer while crafting weird tales. His debut novel, *Flesh and Fire*, is out now as part of Journalstone's Double Down series with a new novel by *New York Times* best-seller Jonathan Maberry and Rachael Lavin. Follow him on Twitter @LMangumFiction and talk to him about books, pro wrestling, and horror movies.

Husband-and-wife team **JEFFREY J. MARIOTTE** and **MARSHEILA (MARCY) ROCKWELL** have written more than sixty novels between them, including their first collaborative novel, *7 SYKOS*. Other recent novels include *The Shard Axe* series and a trilogy based on *Neil Gaiman's Lady Justice* comic books (Rockwell) and *Empty Rooms* and *Season of the Wolf* (Mariotte). They've also written dozens of short stories, separately and together. Some of their solo stories are collected in *Nine Frights* (Mariotte) and *Bridges of Longing* (Rockwell). Their published or soon-to-be-published collaborations include *7 SYKOS* and short works "A Soul in the Hand," "John Barleycorn Must Die," "A Single Feather," "X-Files: Transmissions," and "The Lottons Show." Other miscellaneous projects include Rhysling Award-nominated poetry (Rockwell) and Bram Stoker Award-nominated comic books (Mariotte). You can find more complete bibliographies and news about upcoming projects, both collaborative and solo, at marsheilarockwell.com and jeffmariotte.com.

NANCY HOLDER is the *New York Times* best-selling author of over 90 novels and 200 short stories. Among her awards are five Bram Stokers from the Horror Writers Association. Her most recent novels include the young adult thriller *The Rules* and *Ghostbusters: The Official Movie Novelization*. She lives in San Diego.

JENNIFER BROZEK is a Hugo Award-nominated editor and a Bram Stoker-nominated author. She has worked in the publishing industry since 2004. With the number of different projects she juggles at one time, Jennifer is often considered a Renaissance woman, but prefers to be known as a wordslinger and optimist. Read more about her at her website www.jenniferbrozek.com or follow her on Twitter at @JenniferBrozek.

LOIS H. GRESH is the *New York Times* best-selling author (six times) and *USA Today* best-selling author (thrillers) of 30 books and 65+ short stories. Look for *Sherlock Holmes: The Adventure of the Deadly Dimensions* (Titan Books, April 2017), the first in a new trilogy of Sherlock Holmes thrillers. Lois's books have been published in twenty-two languages. Recent titles include *Cult of the Dead and Other Weird and Lovecraftian Tales* (Hippocampus, 2015) and *Innsmouth Nightmares* (editor, PS Publishing, 2015).

JOHN SKIPP is a Renaissance mutant: *New York Times* best-selling author and editor-turned-filmmaker. His latest book is *The Art of Horrible People*. His latest film as director is *Monsterland*. He's also the editor and curator of Fungasm Press, and is playing more music than he has in years.

When not flying suicide missions with the Skipper, **CODY GOODFELLOW** has written five novels and three collections; his latest are *Repo Shark* (Broken River Books) and *Rapture of the Deep* (Hippocampus Press), respectively. He wrote, co-produced, and scored the short Lovecraftian hygiene film *Stay at Home Dad*, which can be viewed on YouTube. He is also a director of the H.P. Lovecraft Film Festival–San Pedro, and cofounder of Perilous Press, an occasional micropublisher of modern cosmic horror. He "lives" in Burbank.

MIKE WATT is a journalist, author, and filmmaker, published in *Fangoria, Femmes Fatales, Cinefantastique, Film Threat*, and served as the editor of *Sirens of Cinema* from 2005-2010. He is the author of the non-fiction books *Fervid Filmmaking* and the Movie Outlaw series; the short-story collection *Phobophobia*; the novels *Suicide Machine* and *The Resurrection Game*; editor of the upcoming 40th Anniversary Special Edition of Paul Schrader's *Taxi Driver* screenplay. With Amy Lynn Best, he runs the company Happy Cloud Pictures and wrote and/or directed and/or produced *The*

Resurrection Game, Splatter Movie: The Director's Cut, A Feast of Flesh, Demon Divas and the Lanes of Damnation, and *Razor Days.*

JOHN DIXON's *Phoenix Island* and *Devil's Pocket* won back-to-back Bram Stoker Awards and inspired the CBS TV series *Intelligence.* A former boxer, teacher, and stone mason, John lives in West Chester, Pennsylvania, with his wife, daughter, and freeloading pets.

WESTON OCHSE is a former intelligence officer and special operations soldier who has engaged enemy combatants, terrorists, narco smugglers, and human traffickers. His personal war stories include performing humanitarian operations over Bangladesh, being deployed to Afghanistan, and a near miss being cannibalized in Papua New Guinea. His fiction and non-fiction has been praised by *USA Today, The Atlantic, The New York Post, The Financial Times of London,* and *Publishers Weekly.* The American Library Association labeled him one of the Major Horror Authors of the 21st Century. His work has also won the Bram Stoker Award, been nominated for the Pushcart Prize, and won multiple New Mexico-Arizona Book Awards. A writer of more than twenty-six books in multiple genres, his military supernatural series SEAL Team 666 has been optioned to be a movie starring Dwayne Johnson. His military sci fi series, which starts with *Grunt Life,* has been praised for its PTSD-positive depiction of soldiers at peace and at war.

YVONNE NAVARRO lives in southern Arizona and is the author of twenty-two published novels and well over a hundred short stories. Her writing has won the HWA's Bram Stoker Award plus a number of other writing awards. She also draws and paints, and is married to author Weston Ochse. They dote on their three Great Danes, Ghoulie, The Grimmy Beast, and I Am Groot, and a talking, people-loving parakeet named BirdZilla. Visit her at www.yvonnenavarro.com or on Facebook.